CLUSTER

On the far future planet of Outworld, where primitive men and nubile women still battle giant dinosaurs, the barbaric genius Flint is summoned by the Earthborn to fulfill a mission of galactic magnitude—the experimental transfer of his Kirlian essence to an alien Sphere.

From the brutal world of Canopus, a place of masters and slaves, to the undersea lands of the Undulants, where sex is submerged and always done in threes, to Capella, a planet in the midst of an intrigue-filled Elizabethan Age—the magnificent Flint blazes a ribald trail to the distant reaches of the Andromeda Cluster, and his ultimate erotic adversary: the powerful and sensual Queen of Energy.

CLUSTER is Part One of a grand outer space opera which includes CHAINING THE LADY, KIRLIAN QUEST, THOUSANDSTAR, and VISCOUS CIRCLE.

Other Avon Books by
Piers Anthony

BIO OF A SPACE TYRANT
VOLUME 1: REFUGEE
VOLUME 2: MERCENARY
VOLUME 3: POLITICIAN
VOLUME 4: EXECUTIVE

BATTLE CIRCLE

THE CLUSTER SERIES
CLUSTER
CHAINING THE LADY
KIRLIAN QUEST
THOUSANDSTAR
VISCOUS CIRCLE

MACROSCOPE
MUTE
OMNIVORE
ORN
OX

PIERS
ANTHONY

CLUSTER

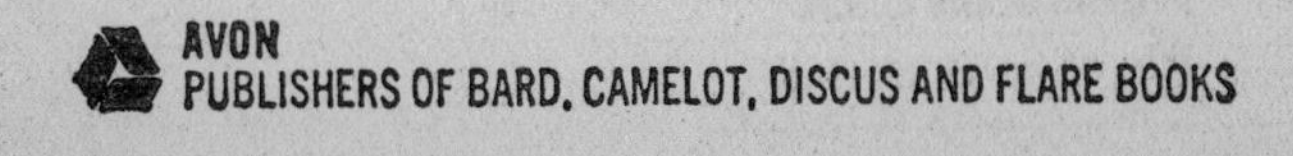
AVON
PUBLISHERS OF BARD, CAMELOT, DISCUS AND FLARE BOOKS

CLUSTER is an original publication of Avon Books. This work has never before appeared in book form. This work is a novel. Any similarity to actual persons or events is purely coincidental.

AVON BOOKS
A division of
The Hearst Corporation
1790 Broadway
New York, New York 10019

Published by arrangement with the author
Library of Congress Catalog Card Number: 77-84308
ISBN: 0-380-01755-5

First Avon Printing, October 1977

Printed in the U.S.A

K-R 15 14 13 12 11 10

Contents

Prologue

"We have ascertained that this person is an alien creature occupying a human body," the Minister of Alien Spheres said formally. "His Kirlian field is extremely intense, on the order of eighty times human normal, and its pattern is unlike anything we have on record. We believe he is what he claims to be: an envoy from a non-Sol Sphere."

The Ministers of the Imperial Earth Council contemplated the subject. There was little to distinguish the alien. He was male, of normal height, about thirty years old, in good health. There were no telltale emanations from his eyes, extraordinary nuances of expression, or any visible aura. He was just an ordinary man—with a bright tattoo on his right wrist.

That tattoo was the mark of a recipient body: mindless, empty, without personality. Even without the Kirlian verification, the intelligent animation of this body was highly significant. Only a freak accident could have done it—or alien possession. For there was no known way to forge a Kirlian imprint, and Sphere Sol lacked the technology to transfer identity from one body to another.

The Regent of Earth Planet spoke next, formally addressing the possessed body. "Sir, we accept you as such an envoy, and accord you the courtesies of that office. Welcome to Sphere Sol. Please acquaint us with your mission."

Now there was an almost tangible tension in the hall. Such visitations had been known only half a dozen times before in all human history, and each had had cataclysmic impact. One had confirmed the existence of intelligent alien life elsewhere in the galaxy, and revealed the presence of transfer technology. Another had defined the limits of direct human colonization—120 light-years' radius from Sol—so that there would be no question of conflict with neighboring Spheres: Polaris, Nath, Canopus, Spica or giant Sador. Another, from neighbor Sphere Antares, had effected one fundamentally important exchange of technology: Sol had yielded the secret of controlled hydrogen fusion in return for Antares' secret of matter transmission. That had revolutionized the human stellar empire, making rapid communication possible—and had presumably done something similar for Antares, starved for safe local power.

This could well be the moment of the century.

"I am Pnotl of Sphere Knyfh," the alien said. "We are about five thousand of your light-years in toward the center of the galaxy. Our two Spheres have not before had direct contact."

The Council Ministers nodded. They had only vague knowledge of the interior Spheres, most of whose stars of origin were not visible from Earth. But it was certain that many of them were highly advanced. In fact, Sol was a very new, very minor Sphere, a galactic backwater only now opening relations with its civilized contemporaries. Some Spheres had endured for thousands of years, and achieved radii of many hundreds of light-years, while Sol had achieved its full size only a century before.

"We place your locale," the Regent said. "Please continue, Envoy of Knyfh."

"I am embodied here to enlist the cooperation of Sphere Sol in a mutual crisis of galactic proportion. I ask you, at this moment, to ascertain which individuals of your sapient species are suitable for identity-pattern transfer."

"That is not necessary," the Minister of Alien Spheres said. "We maintain continuous survey. After the difficulty the first envoy had in making contact with our government, five hundred years ago—"

"That was not the first," Pnotl said dryly.

"The first we recognized," the Regent said, flushing. Historical research had revealed the probability of several prior attempts at transfer contact. All had failed because earlier cultures had preferred not to believe in the possibility of intelligent alien visitation or possession. What chances had been squandered by that ignorance!

"We felt we could not afford to risk any further such embarrassment," the Minister of Alien Spheres continued. "So we maintain a number of potential transfer host bodies—such as the one you now occupy—and we have every

Kirlian field on record." He paused. "Unfortunately the technique of transfer itself has eluded us. We cannot transfer the mind of an individual of our species into another body." He made a small gesture of apology, as though this were a minor matter. "We just don't have the know-how."

Pnotl turned on him a polite yet uncanny glance. "We grant it you," the alien said.

It was as though a stun-bomb had detonated in their midst. There was now no pretense of unconcern. "The secret of the galaxy!" the Minister of Alien Spheres exclaimed.

The Regent held up one hand. "We cannot conceal our interest," he said. "But such information is extremely valuable. We must know what you require in return, before we make any commitment."

"What price?" the Minister of Technology rasped, almost drooling in his eagerness and apprehension.

That sobered the others. All eyes returned to the envoy. Surely the secret of the galaxy would exact the ransom of the millennium.

"No price," Pnotl said evenly. "We wish you to have this capability."

Now there was open suspicion. "Why?" the Regent asked.

"Our entire galaxy is in imminent danger. Unless we unify the Spheres and utilize our maximum capabilities, all of us may be destroyed. We have no other way to form a galactic coalition."

"Forgive us for our cynicism," the Regent said grimly. "We have a fable about Greeks bearing gifts. This means that we do not trust seemingly unmotivated largesse. And we are not likely to react to nebulous, undocumented threats."

"And why *us*?" the Minister of Alien Spheres demanded. "Sphere Sador has a radius of almost five hundred light-years—a volume of controlled space a hundred and twenty-five times as great as ours. They are the obvious candidate for your coalition."

"Such cynicism is a survival trait," Pnotl replied. "We are pleased to find it in you." But something in his tone suggested that he was not delighted. "I shall satisfy you on three scores: the practical, the technological, and the intellectual.

"First, why not Sador, or Mintaka, or any of the other larger Spheres of this galactic segment? Because though well established, these Spheres are decadent. Their controlling species no longer possess the initiative to tackle a problem of galactic scope. And your other neighbors have not had the foresight to arrange for transfer hosts, as you have. We have therefore contacted the most capable Sphere in this region, Sol."

The Council Ministers nodded, pleased at the unsubtle flattery.

"Technologically, I shall simply confer with your scientists immediately following this meeting, and will convey to them the details of the transfer mechanism. After all"—Pnotl paused to smile gravely—"if you do not achieve this capability in short order, I shall lose my own identity. I shall be the first transfer you make, since I cannot otherwise return to my Sphere."

"Fair enough," the Regent said, relieved that they would not have to undertake the enormous expense of mattermitting the envoy home. "If you trust the process enough to be the first subject, it would certainly seem to be authentic. But we can promise nothing until we know what the requirements are for membership in the galactic coalition." He was still suspicious, and let the alien know it.

"To understand the need for cooperation, you must understand the nature of transfer itself," Pnotl said. "Transfer is a modification of matter transmission, but such an unlikely aspect that only one species in a thousand discovers it independently." The Minister of Technology nodded, remembering how devious the method of matter transmission had proved to be. A whole new system of logic had had to be mastered before the necessary computations could be made. But that logic had avoided the paradox of relativistic limitations, and allowed a particular type of signal to transmit across light-years without lapse of time. If identity transfer were worse than this, they would not master it soon, even with a full blueprint. The finest minds of the Empire had been trying for decades.

"Transfer operates at a thousand times the distance, at a thousandth the cost in energy," Pnotl continued. "This is because so much less actually has to be transmitted. Only the Kirlian ambiance moves; the body is left behind. It is my Kirlian force alone that animates this body—and it will quickly fade if I do not return to my own body, which is quite alien in comparison. Thus transfer is by no means a substitute for matter transmission, or even for physical travel through space. It is merely our most economical means of communication over galactic distances. And though it is a million times as efficient as matter transmission, it can still be costly in energy."

The Minister of Technology nodded. That was the great liability of mattermission: its cost. A million dollars' worth of energy had to be expended to transmit a hundred pounds one light-year, approximately. In fact, that had become the practical definition of the modern dollar. The expense cubed as the distance squared, so that it cost a billion dollars to transmit that same mass ten light-years and a trillion dollars to move it a hundred light-years. Consequently very little freight was shipped that way; most mattermissions consisted of microscopic coded message capsules. It was still an essential means of maintaining Imperial communications.

Transfer, at a millionth the effective cost, would still have to be used sparingly, if it were not to deplete the Imperial exchequer. But it would lay open the entire galaxy to human contact, and the benefits could be enormous. For if there was one thing more valuable than energy, it was knowledge.

"The threat is linked to this," Pnotl said. "The civilization of another galaxy proposes to solve its own energy problem by draining off the fundamental energies of the Milky Way Galaxy. I speak of the atomic interactions themselves, and the force of gravity. I think you will appreciate what would happen to us all if these forces were weakened."

"Disaster!" the Minister of Technology said immediately. "Our whole framework would disintegrate."

"But how—?" the Regent inquired, always practical.

"Apparently they have rediscovered some of the science of the Ancients," Pnotl said. "They are using the bodies of local galactic species to build and operate enormous power-transfer stations."

"Transfer of energy?" the Minister of Technology asked, amazed. "I didn't know that was possible."

"We did not know either," Pnotl admitted. "It seems there are ramifications of transfer technique we have yet to master. It may be that some forms of energy possess Kirlian fields. As I pointed out, the threat is fundamentally connected to transfer."

"We must make a special search for more Ancient artifacts!" the Minister of Technology exclaimed.

"In short," Pnotl concluded, "we are about to be ravaged

by Galaxy Andromeda. If we do not act immediately, we all shall perish."

"Exactly what sort of assistance do you expect from us?" the Regent inquired, shaken despite his cynicism.

"Merely to use your power of transfer to contact your neighbors and bring them into the coalition. You will freely relay the transfer technology to them. They will then patrol their own regions, destroying any Andromedan stations and agents discovered. Galactic vigilance is the price we all must pay for survival."

"We have to do the dirty work you balk at," the Regent said. "That is your real price."

Pnotl nodded. "Unkindly put, but accurate enough. We must concentrate our own major effort in our own region of space. If you can reach ten or twenty Spheres within a radius of two thousand light-years of Sol, it will suffice. Our own sweep will complement yours tangentially, for Sphere Knyfh is covering a radius of three thousand light-years. All over the galaxy the other major Spheres are performing similarly." The alien made a bow of dismissal. "If you will now convey me to your technicians, I shall begin working with them immediately. It may take some time to clarify the specifics and construct the apparatus, and my time is limited."

The alien smiled, and several Ministers smiled with him. He was speaking the literal truth; he had at most eighty days before his identity became submerged within the ambiance of the human host. It would have to be a terrific effort, on his part and theirs.

"But we haven't even agreed!" the Regent protested.

Pnotl's glance hinted that he thought the Council to be a bunch of unlettered idiots, but his tone was controlled. "'Since your survival, like ours, depends on the early unification of our galaxy, so that we may muster our entire resources to combat this menace, I believe your agreement is assured. But I shall give you the information regardless—just as you will have to give it to other Spheres, however negative they may prove to be."

The Regent gestured, and the Minister of Technology conducted the alien out of the audience chamber.

"We seem to have been committed," the Regent remarked sourly. "But if he really delivers transfer. . . ."

The Minister of Population produced a printout. "Assuming that we have a use for it, I have here the list of our top prospects for transfer. As you know, the strength of the Kirlian field is the overriding factor—"

"We *know*!" the Regent interrupted. "Summon the top five prospects. I want them here within twenty-four hours."

"That will be awkward. Our leading name is on the Fringe."

The Regent bashed one fist into the opposite hand. "I don't care if it's as far as Outworld! Fetch it here!"

The Minister permitted himself a fleeting smile. "It *is* on Outworld. Star Etamin, one hundred and eight light-years distant. Our farthest viable colony."

"The Stone Age planet!" the Minister of Culture exclaimed. "Disaster!"

"We'll have to use the second choice, that's all," the Minister of Alien Spheres said. "Where's that one?"

"Sirius." Again a small smile.

"That's close—and civilized! Saves us ninety-nine light-years' postage. Much better."

The Minister of Population shook his head. "It's a woman."

There was a general, discreet groan. The cultural prejudices of the Ministers were emerging in the absence of the alien envoy. "Worse yet!" the Minister of Culture said.

"Stop this bickering!" the Regent cried. "Bring them *both*—and the next three. I'll decide when the time comes."

"But the *expense*!" the Minister of Finance cried, appalled.

The others ignored him; expense was irrelevant when the Regent gave an order. If he overreached himself, he would have to answer to the Emperor, whereupon there just might be a new Regent. This particular Regent was unusually competent, and therefore it was likely that his tenure in the office would be brief.

"What's the top name?" the Minister of Alien Spheres asked. The arrival of the envoy from Sphere Knyfh had enhanced his prestige of the hour considerably, and he spoke with a new timbre of authority.

"Flint. Flint of Outworld. Age two-thirds—"

"What?" the Minister of Culture squawked.

"Sorry. Their year is thirty years long; I forgot to interpolate. Age about twenty-one. Male. Single. Heterosexually inclined. Intelligence about one point five."

"*About?*" the Minister of Culture demanded. "Can't you measure it accurately?" His tone reeked of contempt.

"No. He's a primitive—like some here. Can't even read.

Runs about naked. Has green skin. But he's smart—very smart."

"Lovely!" the Minister of Culture said sarcastically. "A smart naked ignoramus!"

The Minister of Population shook his head. "This savage has a Kirlian intensity of just over two hundred—the highest we have ever measured."

"Two hundred!" the Minister of Culture gasped. "Two hundred times human normal?"

"That's right," the Minister of Population said smugly. "The next prospect, apart from the liability of being female, is only ninety-eight on the Kirlian scale. The barbarian is something special."

"We're stuck with the Jolly Green Giant," the Minister of Culture muttered.

"Disaster," the Minister of Population agreed.

"On the contrary," the Regent said briskly. The alien envoy had evidently viewed these men with a certain condescension; the alien had been a sharp judge of character! "Ideal. This innocent will hardly realize what he is getting into. What better choice for our first experimental transfer of a human being to an alien Sphere? We can have no notion of the risks this entails! If the advanced entities of the Inner Galaxy won't even *try* the Spheres of our region. . . ."

The Ministers exchanged glances. A smile passed among them.

1

Flint of Outworld

The old man and the young man lay in the cool of pre-dawn, looking up at the stars. The old man wore a ragged tunic; under it his skin was an off-shade of white. The young man was naked, and was a delicate green all over. He was large and muscular, even for Outworld.

"Can you see Arcturus, boy?" the old man asked.

"Yes, Shaman," Flint said with good-natured respect. He was no longer a boy, but he made allowances for the old Shaman's failing vision. If there was one thing the wise Shaman had taught him—and indeed there were *many* things—it was not to take offense irresponsibly. "Shining as always, about third magnitude."

"And Vega?"

"Yes, fourth magnitude." Each distinction of magnitude meant a star was about two and a half times as bright—or dim. It seemed to help the Shaman to be reminded that Vega was dimmer than Arcturus, so Flint always repeated the information. On cloudy nights these magnitudes changed, if the stars were visible at all. He could have called them out from memory, but the Shaman had also taught him never to lie unnecessarily.

A pause. Then: "Sirius?"

"Fainter. Fifth magnitude."

"And—and Sol?" The old man's voice quavered.

"No. Too faint."

"Use the glass, boy," the Shaman said.

Flint raised the small old telescope, a relic of the first colony ship that had brought his ancestors, over a century ago. He oriented on faint Sirius, then slid toward the nearby region where Sol was to be found. The instrument magnified ten times, which meant that stars of up to eight and a half magnitude should be visible. But magnification was not enough: the scope did not fetch in sufficient light to provide proper clarity at night. So Sol, magnitude seven and a half, was a difficult identification, even for Flint's sharp eye. For the half-blind Shaman, it was impossible.

Now Flint was tempted to lie, knowing how important it was to the old man to spot Sol, even secondhand, this night and every night of the season it was in the night sky. But the Shaman had an uncanny knack for spotting that sort of thing.

Then, faintly, he saw it. "Twin stars! Sol and Toliman!" he cried exuberantly.

"Sol and Toliman!" the Shaman echoed. The words were like a prayer of thanksgiving.

Flint set down the telescope. The ritual had been honored. They had seen Sol tonight.

There was still an hour until dawn, and the Shaman made no move to rise for the walk down the mountain. Flint had work to do, but he had learned not to hustle the old man. The Shaman had never quite acclimatized to the fifteen-hour days of Outworld. He would sleep one full night, seven and a half hours, then stay up a day and a night, fifteen hours straight, then nap in the daytime. He had, he said, been born to a twenty-four-hour cycle, eight hours asleep and sixteen awake, and this was as close as he could make it on Outworld. Flint had once tried to duplicate that odd rhythm, but it had made him irritable and muddle-minded. No one could adopt Shaman ways except the Shaman.

Sometimes the Shaman liked to talk a bit, as he neared the end of his day-night vigil. Flint pretended to the other tribesmen that he merely humored the old fogey, but the truth was that the Shaman's words were almost always fraught with meaning and unexpected revelations. He had taught Flint amazing things—and some of the best had been almost by accident.

"Shaman, if I may ask—"

"Ask, boy!" the man replied immediately, and Flint knew that this was, indeed, a talking night. Perhaps it would make his early awakening worthwhile, apart from the necessity of helping the old man up the steep hill.

"What was it like—on Sol?"

"Not Sol, Flint. *Earth.* Sol is the star, Earth the planet, just as Etamin is the star here, and Outworld the planet. A small star, Sol, and a small planet, 'tis true, but the home of all men and still lord of all Sol Sphere."

Flint knew. Etamin was a hundred times as brilliant as Sol, and Outworld twice Earth's mass. That was why Outworld, though ten times as far from its star as Earth was from Sol, had a similar climate. Lower density, heavier atmosphere, and faster rotation brought the surface gravity down to within 10 percent of Earth's, effectively, so man had been able to colonize and survive here. Of course Outworld's year was thirty times as long, but what the Shaman called a severe precessional wobble provided seasons similar to Earth's. All this was but a fraction of the knowledge the Shaman had dispensed in the course of prior conversations. The tribesmen hardly cared, as long as hunting was good—but Flint was fascinated, and always wanted to comprehend more.

"Earth, of course," Flint said. "But the planet—was it like this? With rains and vines and dinosaurs?"

The Shaman laughed, but had to stop when it triggered off his cough. "Yes and no," he gasped after a bit. "Rains, yes—every few days in some sections. But no vines—not such as you mean. None you could really climb on. Dinosaurs—not today, only long ago, a hundred million years ago! Only birds and mammals and fish and a few small reptiles and not many wild animals, with the human species overrunning the last wilderness areas. Earth is crowded, boy—more crowded than you can imagine. Hundreds, thousands of people per square mile. Even more!"

Flint had heard this before, too, but he allowed for exaggeration. It would be impossible for the land to support more than ten or fifteen people per square mile; the game would all be destroyed by overhunting. He had had experience hunting; he knew the limits. "Why is there such a difference, Shaman? Why isn't Outworld just like Earth, since it was colonized directly from Earth?"

"An excellent question! The experts have wrestled with that one for decades, Flint. The answer is, we don't really know. But we have some educated guesses."

"There must be a reason," Flint said complacently. "There's a reason for everything—as you have told me."

"Reason, yes. Understanding, no. But the prevailing theory—or it was when I left Earth—is called the Principle of Temporal Regression, and it applies to all Spheres, not just ours. Earth is civilized, but since our fastest ships can achieve only half light-speed, it takes many years to reach the farther colonies. Vega is twenty-six and a half light-years from Sol, so it takes over fifty years to travel between them, one way. Sirius is within nine light-years of Sol; that's about eighteen years. Even Toliman—it was called Alpha Centauri—was just over four—"

Flint cleared his throat, gently.

The Shaman chuckled ruefully. "I ramble, I know. The point is this: it takes *time* to communicate between the colonies—so they are always somewhat out of date."

"Not with mattermission," Flint objected.

"Matter transmission is prohibitively expensive. It would be ruinous to transport a single man that way, let alone a factory. So we lack the base for an advanced technology."

"But we should not be more than two hundred years out of date!" Flint protested. "Even without mattermission, Etamin is only a hundred and eight light-years from Sol—"

"*Only!* It's Earth's farthest colony! Oh, there are a few men scattered farther out, and quite a few in the Hyades cluster—but those are really alien Spheres."

"There are some aliens here," Flint reminded him. "Polaroids."

"Don't call them that. *Polarians*. Don't assume they don't know the difference; they're as smart as we are, even though they do have trouble with our mode of speaking." He paused, letting the rebuke sink in. Then: "But they are in *our* Sphere, subject to our regulations. Just as the few men in Sphere Polaris are subject to Polarian government, according to galactic convention. Such admixture is good; it promotes better understanding between sapient species. We are fortunate that they are so similar to us—"

"Similar!" Flint snorted. "Know what Chief Strongspear calls them? Dinosaur T—"

"Chief Strongspear is a bigoted lout whose time is getting short. There are qualities in Polarians—and in all sapient aliens—well worthy of your respect. Remember that."

Flint raised his hands in a gesture of surrender. "I'll be extra nice to the next Pole I meet." Then he caught himself before the Shaman could protest. "*Polarian,* I mean." Despite his bantering tone, he fully intended to keep his promise. He was curious about the alien residents anyway.

"To return to your question," the Shaman said. He never lost a thread, no matter how far the conversation might wander. "Why aren't we within two hundred years of Earth, in culture and technology? That is the crux of dissension. There seems to be a cumulative regression, a logarithmic ratio—"

Flint cleared his throat again.

"All right, all right," the Shaman said, more than a tinge of petulance in his tone. "In nontechnical language, it gets worse as you get farther out from the center, unless progressive subcenters develop. Somehow that two-hundred-year delay multiplies, until—well, Outworld is frankly Paleolithic. Old Stone Age, to you."

"And a good thing!" Flint said. "What would I do for a name if there were no stoneworking?"

The Shaman sighed. "What, indeed. Be glad you're not on Castor or Pollux or Capella, with their Victorian cultures and musket diplomacies!"

"Why did you come here, Shaman? You had so many worlds to choose from. . . ."

The old man gazed at the first faint light of dawn, as mighty Etamin gave herald of his rising. The Shaman's eyesight improved greatly by day. "I suppose it was because of the challenge. Certainly I didn't relish the odds for survival—only half the freeze-passengers ever make it, you know."

"What happens to the others?" This was new to Flint; he had assumed that all ships got where they were going without a hitch.

"Natural attrition. One ship in four is lost—either it is struck by a meteor, or goes astray to perish in uncharted space, or its internal systems fail and destroy it. And one body in three, aboard the intact ships, does not revive."

"That's more than half lost," Flint said.

The Shaman smiled. "That is exactly half."

"Uh-uh! You taught me fractions, remember? Find the common denominator, add them up. One in four is three in twelve ships lost; one in three is four in twelve bodies dead. That's seven of twelve dead—more than half."

The old man chuckled. "Bright boy! But you are mistaken, because you have not really found the common denominator. You can't add ships and bodies."

"All right. If one ship in four is lost, all the bodies *in* it are lost. So that's still one body in four."

"But you are now counting bodies twice. Those in the lost ships have to be excluded from the surviving-ship tally."

Flint wrestled with that, but the concept was nebulous.

"It will come to you in time," the Shaman said. "The obvious is not always the truth—in mathematics *or* in life."

"Maybe so," Flint said dubiously. "Either way, it's one hell of a risk."

"I was not really aware of those statistics at the time I volunteered," the Shaman admitted. "And there is nothing very personal about it. It is not like fighting a dinosaur. The journey is like an instant—that's why I was able to leave Earth at age thirty-five and arrive here at thirty-five." He sighed again. "Thirty years ago!"

"Another freezer is due soon, isn't it?" Flint asked.

"In a couple of years, yes. They are spaced out about three ships to the century, so that at any given moment half a dozen ships are on their way here. In this way there is a steady, if small, supply of educated Earth natives to guide us and see that Outworld progresses. The same is true for all Earth colonies, of course. Otherwise Sol would not be a true Sphere, but just a motley collection of settlements."

"Why didn't my ancestors travel by freezer?" Flint asked. "Then they would all have been Earthborn, and Outworld would have started off civilized."

"Well, the survival rate is better in the lifeships. And without the complex, heavy freezing and resuscitation apparatus, twice as many people can be shipped in each vessel. So about three times as many make it to the colony, at a fraction the expense. With a program the size of Earth's, that's a critical saving. In fact, Outworld would not have been colonized at all, without the lifeships. But there is that one disadvantage: In the course of the seven isolated generations the trip takes, much regression takes place, even though books and tapes are available. The spaceborn just don't have the inclination to maintain complex systems of knowledge and rigorous skills that aren't needed aboard the ship itself. And once they emerge on the planet—"

"Who can study dull books when he's fighting a dinosaur?" Flint asked.

"That's about it. So I think we have a complex of reasons for the retardation. It starts in the original colony lifeships, and is not corrected by the freezers, because the majority culture is already set. Perhaps the lowered density of population also has something to do with it. As you know, only so many people can survive on a square mile of land by hunting and gathering. Until rising population forces them to change, they take the easy way—and that's what you have here on Outworld. Enjoy it; it will not endure forever."

"You know what I said, when I learned I had been apprenticed to you?" Flint inquired mischievously. " 'What? That old fool?' "

The Shaman laughed with him. "Right you were!"

But Flint was abruptly serious. "No, *I* was the fool! You know so much, I can hardly comprehend it even when you tell it straight. But you're always right, when I finally figure it out. Compared to you, I know how stupid I am."

"Never that," the Shaman said. "Ignorant, yes; stupid, no. There's another fundamental distinction for you. I chose you because you were by far the brightest and most talented child in the tribe. You have a peculiar, special, intense vitality. I saw real leadership potential in you, Flint—and I see it yet, stronger with every question you ask. You must work, you must learn, you must not be content like the others, for one day this tribe will be yours."

"But I am no Chief's son!" Flint cried, flattered.

The Shaman seemed not to have heard. "You will have to lead your people out of the Paleolithic, and into the Mesolithic—even the Neolithic, the New Stone Age! Progress is much faster here than it was on Earth, *because now the knowledge exists.* I have been teaching you to read; the books are here, waiting to teach you more than I have ever known. You can accomplish in a generation what took millennia on Earth. Centuries from now, Outworld will be civilized. . . ."

Flint let him ramble. He looked through the telescope again, locating Sirius, fainter now with the coming dawn, and then, with special effort, the twin stars of Sol and Toliman. This was his last chance before Etamin blotted them out for the day. Strange to imagine that man had evolved on that far little planet circling that almost invisible star—

"Shaman!" he exclaimed. "Sol's gone!"

The Shaman started, then relaxed. "That would be an eclipse. One of our satellites. With nine moons, these things happen." He paused. "Let me see—that would be Joan. She's the only moon in the Sirius constellation at this hour. I had forgotten."

"You need a memory bank," Flint said, smiling. If there was one thing that grew even longer and clearer with time, it was the old man's memory.

"I need a *computer*—to figure out all the nine orbits, the patterns of occlusion, so unpredictable by the naked mind. On Earth the early cultures, not so far ahead of you, *had* a computer. A marvelous device. It was made of stone—huge stones, each weighing many tons, set in a monstrous circle. It was called Stonehenge by the later natives. With that, they could accurately track the phases of the sun—Sol sun, I mean—and predict the eclipses by Earth's moon, Luna. It was a monstrous moon."

"A moon covered up the sun?" Flint asked incredulously.

"It happened. Here, the moons are too small and distant. There, its disk appeared to be as large as that of Sol. The ancient astronomers went to extraordinary trouble to chart its cycles—"

"Civilized Ancients!"

"Not the way you mean! It is true that there appears to have been a pattern of early artifacts on Earth, prehistoric yet vast. So vast that the evidences of that primal civilization went virtually unnoticed for millennia, and only recently have they been appreciated for what they are. They—"

"That *is* the way I mean!" Flint said, growing excited. "Here on Outworld there are artifacts of Ancients, things we can't understand. Why not the same on Earth?"

"The Earth Ancients dated from four or five thousand years ago," the Shaman said indulgently. "The Alien Ancients may date from four or five *million* years ago. There is no comparison! It's like the common error of putting cavemen and dinosaurs together, because both are prehistoric, when actually—"

Flint burst out laughing. The Shaman seldom made jokes, but when he did, they were beauties! "Cavemen and dinosaurs! It's an error to put them together, all right!"

The Shaman sighed. "I keep forgetting. . . ." Then he sat up, startled. "Sol? Are you sure? Sol has been obscured?"

"Sol. I see Toliman—"

"An omen! An omen! Clear as the star itself!"

Flint put down the telescope. "Do you really believe in such?"

"On Earth, thirty years ago—I mean, two hundred and thirty years ago—no. I wasn't superstitious. But here on

Outworld, in the Old Stone Age, the people expect it from me. After a while it becomes easier to accept. And I must admit, for those who follow omens, this is as clear as they come. Sol is going to change your life—significantly. And soon. Take it from an old scientist who converted to a medicine doctor to survive among savages: you have been warned by the stars."

"No!" Flint said. "Sol is nothing to me, and I don't believe that rubbish." But he felt a premonitory chill, for despite his denials, he *did* believe.

"Flint! Flint!" the child cried. "The hunt—you must come!"

Flint stopped in the path, letting the lad come to him. It was a messenger runner. "I'm not involved in hunting anymore; you know that. I'm the stonemason." He did not need to add that he was also apprenticed to the crazy Shaman.

"Three are dead, five gored, two trampled. We need help!"

"Three dead! That was supposed to be a routine morning hunt! What did they flush?"

"Old Snort," the boy cried despairingly.

"No wonder! That dinosaur is best left alone. Anyone fool enough to tangle with him—"

"Chief Strongspear—"

"That explains it!" But Flint was on nervous ground, for if word of his insolence reached the Chief there could be unpleasant repercussions.

"Chief Strongspear's son is dying. Old Snort won't let them recover the dead. You must come."

"I told you—I no longer hunt!" But he wondered. The Shaman had spoken of leadership, and now the Chief's son was dying. The heir was stupid, like the father—but who would fill that office if the muscular Chiefson died? In a year the Chief would be retired. And Sol had been eclipsed. Since Flint had seen it happen, he was the one directly affected by the omen.

"Chief Strongspear says if you don't come now, he'll put a pus-spell on Honeybloom."

The Chief was fighting dirty! The very thought of such disfiguration on the prettiest girl in the tribe turned Flint's stomach. "I'll come. Show the way."

The boy showed the way, running swiftly ahead. These runners were agile and long-winded; they could keep the pace better than any man. Flint followed, pausing only to don his harness and secure his best handax. They left the fruitpalms of the oasis behind, hopped from hummock to hummock through the thornreed swamp—the village's chief bulwark against predatory dinosaurs—and climbed nimbly up the trailing tentacle of a vine. At first it was only a few inches in diameter, requiring careful balancing, but as they approached the vine's center web it swelled to more than a yard across.

Out along the opposite tentacle they went, dropping to the firm ground beyond the swamp. They passed a bed of fragrant honeyblooms, the big green-and-red flowers as pretty as they smelled, reminding him poignantly of their namesake: his woman. He and Honeybloom would be wed in midsummer. He would go to her tonight. . . .

The boy slowed. An alien was squatting in the path. A Polarian.

They drew up before the strange creature. It was a teardrop-shaped thing with a massive spherical wheel on the bottom and a limber tentacle or trunk at the top. When that tentacle reached straight up, it would be as high as Flint, and the body's mass was similar to his. But the Polarian had no eyes, ears, nose, or other appendages.

The Shaman claimed they were similar to human beings because they liked similar gravity, breathed the same air—though they had no lungs—and had a similar body chemistry. Their brains were as massive and versatile as man's, and they were normally inoffensive. But they *looked* quite different, and such details as how they ate, reproduced, and eliminated were mysteries.

But Flint had promised himself to treat the next alien he met with special courtesy. He and the boy halted politely. "Greetings, explorer," Flint said.

The creature's body glowed with simulated pleasure. It put its stalk down to the ground. In this position it looked more than ever like a dinosaur dropping. Flint stifled a laugh.

A little ball in the tip of the trunk spun rapidly. "Greetings, native," the ground said.

Flint was not surprised. He had been familiar with the mechanism from infancy. The little ball vibrated against the ground—or any available surface—to produce intelligible sounds. As the Polarian had no mouth, it could not talk as humans did.

"I am Flint, Solarian male." What was obvious to a

human was not necessarily evident to a Polarian—and vice versa. Protocol did not require such an introduction; he could have gone on after the first exchange. The runner boy was already fidgeting at this delay. But Flint had a resolution to fulfill: appreciate an alien.

"Tsopi, Polarian female."

"Peace, Topsy."

"Peace, Plint."

Was this creature laughing back at him? What did the human form resemble, to the alien perception? A bundle of vine splinters? Flint became intrigued. "I go to a dinosaur hunt. Would you like to accompany me?" In one sense, this too was protocol; Polarians liked to be included in activities. But they were appropriately wary of dinosaurs.

"I would be gratified," the teardrop said.

Now he had done it! He had never suspected the creature would accept! Well, it couldn't be helped. "It is an emergency. We shall be hurrying."

"I shall not impede you," the Polarian replied.

Fat chance! But Flint smiled graciously. He gestured to the boy. "Show the way."

The runner was off, sensing a race. This was firm, level ground, excellent for making time. Flint followed, stretching his legs.

But Tsopi followed right along, rolling smoothly on her ball-wheel. She was at no disadvantage. Polarians could move rapidly and effortlessly when the terrain was right; their wheel was efficient. Flint had not before appreciated *how* efficient. On occasion he had wondered how the aliens kept themselves upright. The Shaman had remarked that a man on a unicycle performed the same feat. But there were no unicycles on Outworld.

Then they came to a ravine. One vine crossed it. The boy leaped up, caught a trailing sprout, and hauled himself topside. Flint started to follow, then paused. The Polarian could never make that leap.

"Permit me," Flint said, extending his linked hands. He had heard of this kind of cooperation, and was curious to see if it worked.

The Polarian looped her trunk around the hands. It was warm; the body temperature was similar to man's. Flint braced himself and heaved up, hauling the entire weight of almost two hundred pounds into the air. Then he swung—and the torso of the creature bumped against the underside of the vine.

Instantly the trunk disengaged from his hands and whipped about the vine. The bottom wheel spun against the bark, shoving the torso up. The entire body elongated momentarily; the aliens had no bones. In a moment, by a splendid feat of acrobatics, the Polarian stood upright atop the vine, ready to move on.

Flint hauled himself up, and they proceeded, running single file across the chasm. Purple mud bubbled far below; trash was disposed of here, for what dropped into that mud never reappeared.

The vine trailed near the ground on the far side, so the Polarian needed no help. Actually, Flint realized, she could have used a small ramp to hurl herself a few feet into the air at speed, high enough to catch the vine with her upraised tentacle. His assistance had merely facilitated things.

A mile farther along Flint heard the noises of an enraged dinosaur. "Trouble, all right!" he gasped, and tried to run faster. But he was winded.

Tsopi rolled up beside him, effortlessly. The tentacle touched the ground. "Permit me," she said. Then the trunk reached over, circled around Flint's waist, and tightened elastically. In a moment he was lifted into the air, head forward.

Then Tsopi accelerated. Faster than any man, she zoomed across the plain, carrying Flint like an elevated javelin. Thirty miles an hour, thirty-five, forty—the wind whistled past his ears and forced his eyes and mouth closed. No wonder the Polarians had no such organs; they were unusable at this velocity. He held himself perfectly rigid, knowing that any upset in the alien's balance would be disastrous.

In moments they were at the scene of action. Tsopi slowed and set him down. The runner was far behind.

"Thanks, Topsy," Flint muttered, not entirely pleased at this demonstration of the alien's superior ability. But he realized that the Polarian might have felt similarly about the climb to the vine. It was a lesson, and a good one, vindicating the comment of the Shaman—yet it galled him that he should have had to learn it this way.

"Welcome, Plint," the Polarian responded, making a momentary glow of amusement.

Flint turned his attention to the situation. It was a disaster, all right. Two bodies lay in the trampled dirt, and Old Snort paced angrily around them. He had already worn a brown track in the turf. He didn't want to eat the bodies, for he was herbivorous, but he was intent on killing any other men who approached. Some ancient instinct told him that eventually they were sure to approach their dead.

The dinosaur was old, but neither small nor feeble. He measured thirty feet from snout to tail, and weighed about fifteen tons. His long-range eyesight was poor, but his nose and ears more than made up for this deficiency, and his muscles were huge. He had been wounded by several spear thrusts, but the cuts were superficial and only increased his rage. This hunt had been botched, all right!

"Where is the Chief?" Flint demanded of the nearest warrior, who was cowering behind the stump of a withered vine.

"Wounded," the man cried. "He watches over his son, who is dying. He calls for you."

Flint hesitated, remembering the eclipse of Sol. The omen could signify the direct intervention of Sol in his affairs, but an alternate interpretation was that he could face a crisis of leadership. Sol was literally the center of the human empire, but figuratively the symbol of power, anywhere. If he bailed out Chief Strongspear, in the absence of the Chief's natural son, Flint would become the odds-on favorite for adoptive replacement. The Chief was too old to sire a new son, and too near retirement to raise a young lad to the office. But he had to have an heir, and soon. The custom of the tribe required it.

Flint wasn't certain he *wanted* leadership. There were many strictures on the Chief. He had to officiate at all sacrifices, marry all widows, lead all major hunts, and settle all tribal disputes. Any of these could be sticky matters. It was a dangerous, unpopular office, with little occasion for romance or star-gazing. Worst of all, the Chief had to practice magic, to ensure good hunts and fertile tribeswomen, and to compel discipline. Just as Strongspear had compelled Flint's own attendance by the threat of the pus-spell.

Flint did not believe in magic—at least, not for himself. Others could cast spells that worked beautifully, but Flint had never been able to succeed. The Shaman had told him it was a matter of confidence and suggestion, that the spells worked because the ignorant tribesmen really believed in them. And the Shaman had demonstrated this by casting a mass sleep-spell on the entire tribe in the middle of the day. All had either succumbed or pretended to. Flint himself had gone under. The Shaman, figure of ridicule that he might be, knew human nature well, and was the ultimate magician. But Flint's own efforts didn't compel sufficient belief, and so failed. Already the others well knew his liability; men Flint could back off in a physical encounter could back *him* off in magical competition. It didn't help to have the Shaman explain that their very strength came from their ignorance; the plain fact was their magic worked.

Even Honeybloom had once given him a stiff finger, mischievously. He had been forced to gather three five-leaved thornblooms, at terrible expense to his hide, before she relented and put them in her red hair. "Intelligent people are highly suggestible," the Shaman had observed, unperturbed.

And there was one crowning drawback to the Chiefship: retirement. At the end of his term, the Chief was ritually slaughtered and offered up for sacrifice to the Nature Spirits of Outworld. The Shaman, knowledgeable in everything, had explained that though in one sense this represented an unfortunate primitivism, in another it was practical. No Chief had any incentive to store private wealth, and so he was generally honest. "And the hunting *does* seem to improve the year after such a sacrifice," the Shaman had admitted.

Naturally, Flint thought. Because the hunters had the fear of extinction goosing them, after witnessing human murder.

No, Flint did not want to be Chief! But as he came into the presence of Strongspear, he realized that he would probably have little choice. The old man's eyes glittered with grief under his ornate headdress of rank. Blood dripped from a shoulder wound. He was in no mood to be balked. Any trouble from Flint, and there would be much worse than pus-spells as punishment.

Yet the very seriousness of the situation provoked an antisurvival mirth. Here were cavemen and dinosaurs together! Flint bit his tongue to stop the smile, but it burst out anyway.

"What the hell you laughing at, boy?" Strongspear demanded.

"Not a laugh—a grimace," Flint said quickly. He bared his teeth to amplify his horror—and his horror was real, in its fashion. What a place for a foolish smile!

"What's that Pole doing here?" the Chief rapped.

Flint had forgotten the Polarian, who had unobtrusively followed him. "This is Topsy of Polaris," he said hastily. "Topsy, this is Chief Strongspear." He faced the Chief again. "Topsy is merely observing."

"Well, let him spin his wheel out of here!" Strongspear snapped. "We don't need any damned aliens—"

"The Chief means it might be dangerous for you," Flint told the Polarian. "No offense intended." It did not seem to be the time to advise Strongspear that he had mistaken the sex of the alien.

The tentacle touched the trunk of a vine. "I quite understand, and appreciate the consideration. But the dinosaur poses no threat to me. Perhaps I can be of help."

"Perhaps," Flint agreed politely. He wished Tsopi would get well clear, but she was slow at taking such hints. Already he was regretting his vow to the Shaman to be nice to the aliens. If Tsopi died in the midst of a human dinosaur hunt, there could be Spherical repercussions.

"The Polarians control a Sphere twice the diameter of ours," the Shaman had explained. "They've been in space longer, and they have better organization. And no doubt they're more advanced technologically in their origin-world than we are at Earth. Out here at the Fringe they're primitives, just as we are—just as every species is at the edge of its Sphere. But don't let that fool you. Someday we may need their help. Always remember that."

This was one of a great many fundamental lessons the Shaman had taught Flint: the respect of alien culture. There were few Polarians on Outworld—but there were billions within their own Sphere. In many respects, Outworld was closer to Polaris than to Sol.

Suddenly Flint had an idea. If the Polarian could be made to seem instrumental in relieving this crisis, there would be little credit due Flint himself, and thus no question of becoming heir to the Chief. Strongspear would never confer honor on an alien!

"Your offer of assistance is much appreciated," Flint said to Tsopi. "I noticed you move very swiftly. Do you think you could lead Old Snort toward our deadfall, without running the risk of getting trampled or gored?"

"This would be simple," Tsopi said, glowing with pleasure. Flint wondered whether her constant illumination was a Polarian trait or a female one.

"Get that dino turd out of here!" Strongspear yelled,

furious that the alien should witness the human predicament.

"We shall clean up Snort's refuse as soon as we get him in the trap," Flint said, hoping that the Polarian would misinterpret Strongspear's reference. If only it weren't so apt!

They moved out. Flint showed Tsopi where the deadfall was, then they rounded up the scattered tribesmen and approached the dinosaur.

"The idea is to lure him away from our dead," Flint explained. "But since he has killed men, he must be killed, not just removed. So we have to lead or drive him over the deadfall. The only problem is—"

"He can outrun us!" a tribesman finished.

"Yes," Flint agreed grimly. "Therefore the Polarian has kindly agreed to take the lead. Old Snort can't outrun a Polarian on level ground."

The men looked dubious, but acceded to Flint's evident authority. If he muffed it, *he* would be in trouble, not they. They formed a half-circle around the dinosaur, a wide arc, for they were not eager to provoke him into another devastating charge. The monster would tend to shy away from a large group of men at a distance, unable to see or smell them well enough to attack them with confidence. But this was still chancy.

Flint and Tsopi came near. Old Snort snorted as he became aware of them. He stomped the ground, making it shudder. From up close, he was huge—twice the height of a man. The bones of his head opened out into a massive shield about the neck, and he had three great horns on his nose. "A triceratops," the Shaman had said. "Not a true reptile, here on Outworld, but close enough for practical purposes. The planet permits larger development. Convergent evolution. . . ." Flint hadn't cared about the technicalities; all he knew was that Old Snort was about as formidable an opponent as the planet offered. True, there were also predator dinosaurs, but they seldom bothered to go after anything as small as men, and men stayed well clear of them, so there was little contact. There were many of these hornbeasts, in contrast, and their young made good hunting. The sheer stupidity of flushing this one, instead of smaller prey . . .

Flint shook his head. Old Snort, the most ferocious of the lot, terror of the plain for over a century!

The huge head swung around, attracted by Flint's

motion. The triple horns pointed at man and Polarian. Any notion that the dinosaur was dull or slow was dissipated by that alert reaction; Old Snort was stupid, but fully competent within his province. The opposite of the Shaman, who was intelligent but often incompetent about routine things, like gutting roachpigs for cooking. He tended to shy away from the squirting green juices. . . .

The dinosaur snorted again, the air misting out around his nasal horn with a half-melodious honk, and stamped one mighty hoof warningly. He did not like intruders.

Flint hadn't brought his own spear, and had no immediate use for his stone handax. The tool was good enough, but not against a standing dinosaur. His only advantage was his brain—and as the creature loomed larger, he was none too sure of that. But the job had to be done, and his perverse pride forced him to see it through, even at the risk of becoming the Chief's heir.

"Hee-ya, Snorthorn!" he cried loudly, waving his arms.

One moment the dinosaur was standing; the next, he was charging at a good twenty miles an hour. Or so it seemed.

There was only one response to such a charge: to get out of the way. He ran, straining his utmost, hearing the *thud thud thud* of Old Snort's tremendous hooves hammering the ground close behind. *Too* close behind; the animal could catch a man in full flight, and knew it.

Then Tsopi shot past, her tentacle looped down to touch her own body. From the small bearing came a piercing keening noise, as of an animal in terror.

Flint dodged to the side, caught his foot in a vine root, and sprawled headlong. The feet of the dinosaur smashed down—and missed him by a good yard. The turf sank several inches. Old Snort had seen him fall, but was unable to change course on such short notice—and Tsopi was buzzing along immediately ahead, commanding attention.

Flint got up, unhurt. He should have watched his feet better; now all the tribesmen would know of his clumsiness. But perhaps it was just as well, for he was obviously not the hero of this adventure. The Polarian was. He watched the chase with interest.

Tsopi approached the deadfall, dinosaur in galloping pursuit. The trap was a huge pit, ten feet deep and forty in diameter, covered by a network of crisscrossing vine stems. It was not concealed; dinosaurs' eyes were not so sharp, and their brains not so good as to decipher its menace before putting a foot in it. Natural hazards were one thing; natural selection had bred care. But artificial hazards were only a century old, and the dinosaurs had not had time to learn yet. All that had been necessary was to build it several weeks before the hunt, to give the man-smell time to wear thin. Old Snort would crash through the vine segments and fall in—and though his shoulder was two feet taller than the drop, his mass and musculature were such that he would not be able to climb out. Forward propulsion was not the same as upward movement, as the Polarian's problem with climbing showed.

Suddenly Tsopi veered away from the deadfall—followed of course by Old Snort. Both skirted the edge, and the dinosaur did not fall in.

"The alien fool!" the man next to Flint exclaimed. "Why didn't he go *over* it, the way we planned?"

Why not, indeed? Had the Polarian deliberately sabotaged the hunt?

Now they were looping back—toward the men. Tsopi accelerated right at Flint. If old Snort continued on his course—well, they could scatter, but one or two more men would be trampled.

"Plint!" Tsopi cried, her tentacle touching the ground. "I cannot cross the trap at speed!"

Then Flint realized his mistake. A man would have bounded from one vine to the other automatically, safely, but the Polarian could not jump. Not that way. The criss-crossing vines were an impassable menace.

"Move toward it—then dodge aside!" Flint cried. "Old Snort can't turn as fast as you can."

"Right!" The Polarian looped about again, and such was the concentration of the dinosaur that he charged right by Flint without seeing him. One-track body, one-track mind.

But Old Snort was slowing; he could not maintain charge speed for long. That would complicate the trap; he might lose interest in the uncatchable alien and turn to the slower men. "Let him follow close!" Flint called. And wondered how it was that the earless Polarian could hear him.

Tsopi eased off, letting the dinosaur catch up. They headed back toward the deadfall, the small form almost merging with the large one.

"Now she's playing it *too* close!" Flint muttered nervously, seeing Old Snort's horn almost snag the alien.

Tsopi dodged aside, right at the brink of the deadfall.

Old Snort tried to twist, and he was now going slowly enough so that his body did lurch over. But his front feet were on the vines, and under his weight they snapped like twigs and let him down. He plowed horns-first into the pit.

Vine logs flew up in a momentary splay. A foot-thick piece came down on Tsopi, knocking her into the pit.

"Oh, no!" Flint cried. Suddenly the peace of Spheres was imperiled. He sprinted toward the deadfall.

"Stay clear!" someone called. "There's no getting out of that hole!"

But Flint ran to the edge. The dinosaur seemed stunned; he was on his knees and not moving. The Polarian was wobbling crazily, but she was alive.

Old Snort shuddered. His head turned, and he struggled to rise from his knees. As he had half-slid over the edge, the dirt had been scraped into a pile at the botom. That, and the cushioning effect of the vines, had spared the dinosaur from immediate harm. Still, a drop of ten feet was a considerable jolt for fifteen tons, and in other circumstances could have been fatal.

Now the Polarian was in trouble. She could not climb out, even where the edge was broken down, and her gyrations were attracting the notice of the dinosaur. The massive head swung about, the three horns orienting. Half stunned and stupid the monster might be, but in the confines of the pit he would soon smash Tsopi flat.

Flint slid down the broken wall, landing solidly but safely at the bottom. He drew his handax from its harness and rapped Old Snort's longest nose horn smartly. It clanged like a dry hollow vine. "Hi-ya, stupid!" he yelled.

The dinosaur lunged to his feet, snorting. He had been well named; the blast was deafening. But his little eye was fixed on Tsopi; he had not yet realized that there were now two creatures in the pit with him. The beast bucked his horns forward.

"Permit me!" Flint screamed over the ringing in his ears from the snort. He threw his arms about Tsopi's torso and heaved the alien into the air. The torso squeezed together like a bag of water. The horns rammed into the wall of the pit, immediately below the Polarian's hanging wheel.

Old Snort wrenched his head up. Dirt and sand sprayed, and another section of wall collapsed. Flint leaped aside, carrying the alien. The surface of Tsopi's torso was oddly slick, though dry, as though it had been polished. The large wheel spun slowly.

Flint brushed by the flaring shield of bone that guarded Old Snort's neck; it was taller than he was, and monstrous muscles were attached to it.

The dinosaur whipped his shield about, trying to smash the two tiny figures. This was one maneuver he was good at! Flint put out one foot. The edge of the shield caught. As it swung through, Flint walked right up over the saddle-shape.

Old Snort bucked his head up and back, and the two were thrown off. They skidded down the corrugated back. They were now above the level of the ground—but there was no way to step across to it.

Flint half-slid, half-stepped on down to the ground beside the dinosaur's tail. He set Tsopi down. "I think we're in trouble, friend," he remarked. "Sorry if I squeezed you too tight."

"I am better now," the Polarian said. "I shall return the favor." And she scooted forward.

Old Snort was just turning, unable to maneuver freely because his flanks kept banging into the walls of the pit. They were in danger of being crushed between the hulking body and the hard sand of the wall. Flint made a mental note: if he got out of this, and if he ever had charge of a pit-construction crew, he would dig several man-sized holes in the base. Probably no man would ever again be caught in such a place with a live dinosaur, but . . .

Tsopi shot past the broad shield and around the blunt beak, making a keening noise. Even to Flint, that sound had an annoying quality. No doubt that was the intent.

The three horns snapped about, going after Tsopi with amazing accuracy. The Polarian squished aside and the horns missed—barely—and plowed into the wall again. More dirt tumbled down. Old Snort wrenched the horns up—apparently this was an automatic goring reflex, an excellent maneuver against a twenty-foot-tall carnosaur—and ripped out a larger section. What had taken the tribe weeks to excavate, this dinosaur was taking only moments to demolish.

But even as that awful armored nose cleared, Tsopi was wheeling back over the loose dirt, leaving cross-hatched treadmarks in the soft surface, taunting the dinosaur with that keening sound. For an instant the tentacle even touched one of the great horns, and the keening became momentarily louder as the hollow horn amplified it. It was like spitting in the face of the monster!

Suddenly Flint realized what the alien was doing. She was making the dinosaur dig their way out of the hole. Every pass meant another gap in the wall, another mound of dirt in the bottom. Already there was a yard of it piled, and a six-foot section of wall had been demolished.

Of course Flint himself could have made it out, if Old Snort gave him time. He could jump and catch the edge of the pit and lift himself out, if the turf didn't crumble. But he couldn't carry the Polarian out, and the alien was too heavy to throw that far up.

But Flint, glad as he was to see a viable exit developing, foresaw one problem: When it leveled out enough to make a passable ramp for Solarian and Polarian, the dinosaur would also be able to climb out. They'd be back where they had started: with an enraged colossus charging about the plain.

No, not quite at the start. There had been time to remove the dead and wounded from the field, now. That much had been gained, at least.

Soon the job was done, for the animal was a powerful worker. Maybe someday man would learn to tame dinosaurs, and gain tremendous leverage against the environment. When a fair ramp was made, Tsopi led Old Snort into a half-turn, away from the gap. Then Flint ran around, put out an arm to assist Tsopi, and scrambled up the steep incline. For a moment dirt flew out under the alien's wheel, making a hole; Flint lifted, and they were over the brink and out.

But now, what of the dinosaur? Flint stood at the brink, uncertain. But Old Snort did not follow them. He just kept turning, looking for the annoyance he had been chasing. He paid no attention to the ramp.

"Friend Plint, we must move!" Tsopi said urgently.

"In a moment," Flint said. Something was nagging him, and he was unwilling to run before he figured it out.

Then Snort's eye came up almost level with Flint's own eye, the powerful neck muscles elevating the head surprisingly. What control the animal had! For a moment they stared at each other. The dinosaur's muscles bunched—

"Plint!"

Old Snort turned away.

He hadn't even recognized Flint as the quarry—because Flint was not in the pit.

In fact, the dinosaur was trapped. He *could* climb out, by gouging a wider passage to accommodate his huge body, then tramping up the ramp. But he *wouldn't*.

Because he was too dull to look that far ahead.

It suddenly hit Flint: *Stupidity was the greatest trap of all!* There was no confine worse than a slow brain. "May I never look my enemy in the eye and not know him," Flint whispered to himself. "May I never miss the easy way because of slow wit." There, truly, was the difference between man and dinosaur!

"No offense, Plint," the Polarian said.

Flint was about to explain that he knew there was no present danger, but realized that this was not the question. "No offense," he agreed. The alien had something of import to convey, perhaps controversial, and now was the time to say it.

"I am not familiar with all your customs. Among my kind, when one entity preserves the life of another, there is a debt."

"Among mine too," Flint agreed warily. This pit experience had complicated his perspective of the alien; Polarians did indeed have worthwhile qualities.

"You saved my life, at risk to your own—"

To avoid Spherical complications—but it would be indiscreet to say that. "And you saved mine."

"We have exchanged debts," the Polarian said.

"We have." What was coming next?

"Farewell, debt brother," Tsopi said.

That was all? "Farewell, debt sister," Flint echoed.

The Polarian departed, zooming across the ground at the incredible velocity of its kind. Flint watched, shaking his head. What a day!

Now the other tribesmen came close. "You did it!" one exclaimed. "You trapped Old Snort!"

"Topsy the Polarian did it," Flint said. "She led the dinosaur into the trap, and helped me get out of it. The credit belongs to her, and to her alone. Tell Chief Strongspear."

They looked dubious, but one set off in the direction of the Chief. Flint knew that his statement, plus the evidence of the witnesses, would scotch any question of chiefly adoption. The only thing Chief Strongspear hated worse than an alien was an alien-lover.

Meanwhile, the hunters would be able to finish off Old Snort at leisure, if need be by starving him to death. The tribe would feast royally for many days to come. There would be good leather for sandals, good sinew for tying bundles, and excellent bones for spears. The blood would make puddings and dinosaur-malt; the vertebrae would make clubs. The fat would make tallow for candles and grease for cooking. Almost every part of Old Snort would be used, eventually. Not because the tribesmen were unduly conservation-minded, but because it was easier to use what they had than to go out after another dinosaur one day sooner than necessary. Today's dead would be long remembered!

Yet it disturbed him, this slaughter. They could never have overcome Snort in his prime. The dinosaur was well over a century old, and generations of men had changed course in deference to this monster's stamping grounds. His demise was the end of an era, and this was sad.

There were other dinosaurs, of course, and some were larger and more vicious than Old Snort. Snort hadn't been a bad neighbor, really. He had let the tribe alone just as long as it had left him alone. Soon some other monster would move in to fill the vacuum, for this was prime grazing territory, and then the tribe might discover how well off it had been.

Flint knew that this was merely the standard post-hunt letdown—but still he was depressed. So he did the sensible thing.

He went to see Honeybloom.

She was picking juiceberries beyond the West Thicket. Her red hair was radiantly lovely. Her green breasts were as lush as melonberries, and her skin as soft as a freshly peeled vine.

"Flint!" she cried with mock chagrin. "You're filthy!"

"I fell in a hole," he said. He looked at her appreciatively. "I'd like to fall in another."

She threw a juiceberry at him. The eyeball-sized globe splattered on his chest and dribbled blue juices down his belly. "Let me wash you," she said, instantly contrite.

She took him to the river pool and washed him thoroughly, in that special way she had. Her hands were marvelously gentle. He thought of the threatened pus-spell, and was supremely relieved that it hadn't come to pass. After a while he pulled her down with him, dunking her with a pretense of savagery as though he were a real caveman subduing a real cavewoman. Actually few of the tribe lived in caves; it was easier to make lean-tos under vines, and there were no resident predators to oust. But the myths of caveman violence were always good for laughs —and when Honeybloom laughed, it was something to see.

Her breasts floated enticingly, looking even larger than they were. Flint looked forward with a certain wistful regret to the time when he would have to give them up to his baby. That was the problem with marriage. . . .

Eventually, feeling much better, he made his way to his shop in the village. It was now noon; Etamin shone down hotly. He had lost half a day. But it had been worth it, in its fashion; he had learned enough to last him a week.

He brought out a large block of flint. Flint was a unique stone. Other material fractured unreliably, making large chunks, small chunks, pebbles, and dust—all irregular. Flint could be fractured in controlled fashion, to make flakes with sharp edges—knives. A flint knife was sturdy; it could kill a small animal effortlessly. It was durable; it never lost its edge, and it was exceedingly hard. All in all, it was a stone of near-miraculous properties.

But it had to be handled correctly. Strike a block of flint the wrong way, and useless chunks would flake off. Strike it the right way, and anything could be produced: a thin-bladed knife, a pointed speartip, a solid handax, or a scraper. All it required was the proper touch.

It was an inborn talent. Flint was one of the few who had the touch; in fact, he was the finest flint craftsman in the region. His blades were sharper, better-formed than anyone else's. But most important, he could turn them out rapidly and with very little waste stone. Flint stone was not found naturally in this region; the tribe had to trade for it, so it was precious. Fortunately Flint's talent had made this trade profitable for the first time in a generation. They could import as much of the stone as they needed in return for half the finished blades. That was why Flint was no longer obliged to hunt or to perform other onerous tasks like burying the tribe's dung. He was more valuable to the group as a craftsman. Until this morning, when the hunt had flushed Old Snort.

He oriented his master-block carefully, laid a bone buffer against it, and struck the core glancingly with a specially designed club. A long, narrow blade flaked off. He struck again—and another perfect blade appeared.

Flint made no secret of his technique; the skill was in his hands, not his tools. The strike had to be not too hard, not too soft, not too far from the edge, nor too close.

Others had tried to copy his motions, but they muffed it because they lacked his coordination and feel for the stone. The material was in his being; when he hefted a piece he could tell at a glance where the key cleavage lay, and he could strike that spot accurately. No one had trained him in this; no one had needed to.

On a good day, he could turn out several hundred assorted blades. A year ago, upon achieving his maturity, he had given a public demonstration. Thus he had earned his name and become the flintsmith. As long as there was flint to be had, and his hands remained uninjured, his position was secure.

That was another reason to marry Honeybloom. She was a sweet girl, and beautiful, always amenable, but not unduly bright. The Shaman had tried to argue him out of making the commitment to her, on the grounds that she would become poor company the moment her figure went to fat. But she had a fair talent for magic, and specialized in hands. Even as she had given him the stiff finger—retribution, she had claimed, for what he had done with it one time when he had caught her sleeping—she could ensure that his hands remained strong and supple. That was insurance he had to have.

Crack! Another blade. Crack! Yet another. It always took him a while to get the rhythm of it, the feel, but he was warming up beautifully now. With luck, he would turn out his full day's quota despite the loss of the morning.

"Flint." The voice startled him, destroying his concentration, and he muffed a shot. A foully misshapen fragment of stone skittered across the ground. Damn!

He looked up, his upper lip lifting in a silent snarl. But he didn't speak, for this was no ordinary intruder, no naked tribe child. It was a man wearing the uniform of the Imperial Guard. His skin was so pale as to be virtually white, slug-white, like the Shaman's, which meant he was Earthborn. From the spaceport, obviously; one of their idle personnel. But the Imperial Guard was not to be ignored.

Flint, like most natives, didn't care for clothing. It interfered with necessary activity. Only in winter would he don protective gear.

"I am Flint," he said.

"Come with me."

Once every five years the Imperials rounded up all the children of the tribe and ran them through a battery of tests. It was a meaningless procedure, but the kids got a kick out of it and it seemed to satisfy the Earthborns. But this was not the year or the time, and Flint was no longer a child. Earth had no present call on him. "Like hell I will!" he snapped. "I've got work to do."

The Guardsman reached for his weapon—a regulation blaster.

Flint was on his feet instantly, poised, a flint blade held expertly between his fingers. "Want to try it, Imp?" he whispered.

Now a crowd of children had gathered, gawking at the scene. The Imperial reconsidered. If he blasted Flint, he would be deemed a murderer, attacking a naked and effectively unarmed primitive. If Flint killed him with that blade, he would be dead. Either way, he would have failed in his mission. "You have to come, Flint," he said. "It's by order of the Regent of Earth. The capsule just arrived."

"What does the Regent want with me?" Flint demanded, not relaxing.

"He wants to send you to Sol. That's all I know."

"Sol!" the children cried, amazed.

Flint laughed. "Me to Sol! No one goes to Sol. They *come* from there!"

But then he remembered the omen. Could this be its meaning?

In that moment of Flint's hesitation, the Imperial Guard drew his blaster. "Nothing personal," he said. "But orders are orders. You're being mattermitted to Earth—today."

But the resistance was gone from Flint. He could have handled the guard, and hidden from the Earthborns—but how could he fight the omen? His magic was weak, and this sign had reached across 108 light-years to touch him. Against that, there was no defense.

2

Mission of Ire

notice target galaxy development

—notice taken report—

transfer logged 80 intensity motion 1500 parsecs from sphere knyfh to underdeveloped region

—potential interest evidently knyfh is searching for assistance unable to monitor outer galaxy alone futile no advanced cultures in that segment—

addendum number of technologically incipient cultures in vicinity cluster of spheres

—itemize—

canopus spica polaris antares sador nath bellatrix mirzam mintaka

—cluster of nonentities canopus is slave culture spica waterbound sador regressive to core mintaka interested only in music antares possesses transfer but uses it only internally polaris represents potential threat owing to efficient circularity this is where knyfh transferred?—

correction transferred to sphere sol

—sol! barely technological small sphere—

advanced rapidly in recent period after awkward breakthrough

—concurrence detail on sol—

abortive mattermission expansion depleted source planet almost to point of nonreturn followed by disciplined starship colonization 400 source planet cycles or years major colonies sirius and procyon atomic level altair formalhaut vega machine technology arich mufrid pollux arcturus denebola castor capella all pre-industrial commerce sheriton deneb-kaitos aldebaran alioth corserpentis sabik all medieval remaining colonies further regressed to subcivilized

—enough! with nucleus of only three atomic-level settlements including origin sphere represents very limited actuality and questionable potential no action required at this time continue monitoring to ascertain purpose of knyfh transfer if other than desperation quest—

POWER

—CIVILIZATION—

Flint looked about, still angry despite the omen. He was in a huge room, much like the main chamber of the Imp station on Outworld, but larger. Vents set high in the walls let in slits of light—no, it was artificial light after all, that was one of the things the Imps had—and there was a growling as of hidden machines running. The overall effect was awful.

"Flint of Etamin?" a woman inquired. She had no sex appeal; she was flat-breasted, cloud-white, and spoke with a strong Imp accent. Flint presumed this really was Imperial Earth, and he didn't like it.

"Etamin—double star on the Fringe," she said. Her voice was low but not soft.

This elicited a spark of interest. "You mean Sol *isn't* double?" he inquired. He was not being facetious; it had not occurred to him that Sol should differ from his home sun in this significant respect. No wonder Sol was so faint in the sky. But of course there was no reason a single star should not support life; it was the *planet* that counted.

"Please don this tunic," she said, holding out a bolt of red cloth.

"You want me to put on a red dress?" he asked incredulously.

"It is not a dress. It is an Imperial tunic. All citizens wear them, males and females. You will note that *I* wear one."

Flint looked again. This Imp was not merely flat-breasted, but *non*-breasted. "You're *male!*" he said, surprised. The dress and the smooth, unbearded face had deceived him, but the voice and chest should have given him the hint. He was being dangerously unobservant.

The man rolled his pale eyes briefly skyward in a feminine gesture. "What color tunic would you prefer? Anything except black."

"Why not black?"

"That signifies officialdom."

Flint disliked officialdom. "I'm happy the way I am."

Now an evanescent smile. "That simply won't do. You're no Tarot figure."

"Tarow people are naked?"

"That's Tarot, with an unpronounced terminal T. Merely illustrations on occult cards used by the cult of Tarotism. Its prime tenet is that *all* concepts of God are valid."

"*Aren't* they?"

Again the rolling of eyes. "You're to meet the Council of Ministers in fifteen minutes. You must be dressed."

Flint realized that argument would only delay his return home. "Give me a green one, then. I'm a green man."

"Very good," the white man said distastefully. He produced a green tunic that came reasonably close to matching Flint's skin, and Flint put it on over his head. He balked at using the silk undergarment the man tried to make him wear under it, however. A dress was bad enough, but no warrior or craftsman wore panties! Suppose he needed to urinate in a hurry?

A woman—a real one this time, with breasts and hips and hair, though dressed just like the man—came and slicked down his proudly unruly hair, washed his hands and feet, and trimmed off the better part of his strong finger- and toenails. She was, despite her pale skin, an attractive female with a musky odor and a deft touch; otherwise he would not have submitted to these indignities. He hoped he would not have to fight soon; his hands were now as embarrassingly dainty as Honeybloom's.

He was ushered into a capsule that closed about him and abruptly plunged through the wall. He had a confused glimpse of buildings like straight vertical cliffs, and crowds of robed people. Up above the sky was *blue*, not green, and the light of the sun was sickeningly yellowish. This was Imp Earth, all right! Then the capsule penetrated another wall like a spearpoint through hide, and stopped inside.

A bit dizzy, Flint got out.

A man stepped up to grasp his hand. Flint was tempted to grab that flabby hand and throw the bastard over his shoulder, but restrained himself. It was better to ascertain the facts before acting, as the Shaman always reminded him. *Then* he could throw a few Imps about.

"Welcome, Flint of Outworld. I am the Minister of Population. It was our excellent aura-intensity files that located you. The Council is ready for you now."

"Ugh," Flint grunted noncommittally. He followed the man through bare halls like the base of an overgrown vine forest. He felt confined, his vision, hearing, and smell restricted to the point of uselessness; surely this was one of the fabled Earth prisons. He kept a nervous eye out for predators, though he knew that the larger dinosaurs had died out on Earth.

The Council of Ministers was a group of undistinguished men in identical black tunics. Their faces and hands were bone-white, except for one brown man. They introduced themselves in rapid order, though they hardly seemed sufficiently distinct from each other to warrant names. Flint made disinterested note in case there were ever any future relevance. He had a perfect memory for such details; it came of practice in hunting and scouting. The Shaman called it "eidetic."

"I'll come straight to the point," the brown man said. He was the Regent, and seemed to have more character than the others. "You have a high Kirlian aura—er, do you know what that is?"

"No." This was something the Shaman had not mentioned, unless it was the Imp name for intelligence. *Keer-lee-an* aura?

"Very well," the man said, with a grimace that showed it was *not* very well. "I'll explain. It is a kind of a field of force associated with living things, like a magnetic field—do you know what *that* is?"

"No." Actually the Shaman had mentioned magnetism, but Flint was not in a good mood.

"Complete savage," one of the Ministers murmured in a comment he evidently thought Flint could not overhear. The man did not realize that a complete savage would have acute hearing for wilderness survival. Flint was proud of his primitive heritage, though he realized the Minister had intended the remark disparagingly. Well, toss one more Imp—in due course.

"Hm, yes," the Regent said. "Well, some four or five hundred years ago, when Earth was just emerging into the space age, the twentieth century, you know, scientists discovered that there were phenomena that could not be explained by conventional means. ESP, PSI, dowsing, precognition—fascinating concepts in their time—"

One of the Ministers cleared his throat, and Flint realized why they liked to be so similar: it was difficult to tell which one had interrupted the discussion.

The Regent frowned and continued. "At any rate, it was obvious that force fields of an unknown nature existed. In 1939 a Soviet electrician—uh, the Soviets were a nation, somewhat like a stellar system except they were right here on Earth—called Semyon Davidovich Kirlian photographed the patterns of bioluminescence—that is, a glow from living things—that appeared in certain high-frequency electrical fields. This effect resembled a fireworks display, with multicolored flares, sparks, twinkles, glows, and lines. In fact, a Kirlian photograph of a living human hand resembled the image of our galaxy with all its stars and clusters and swirls of dust and gas. And so this discovery—"

"Really, our guest isn't interested in this detail," the Minister of Population interjected.

The truth was, Flint *was* interested. A human hand that had fields of energy like the galaxy? But if he revealed how much he understood, he would spoil his image of barbaric ignorance, so he kept silent.

"My point," the Regent continued, "is that this was the start of what was to become the major science of bioluminescence. It has had profound effects on medicine, agriculture, criminology, archaeology, and other sciences, because every living thing has its Kirlian aura, whose pattern is unique to it and varies with its health and mood and experience. Some even call this aura the astral body or the soul. There are religious implications—"

Again the anonymous clearing of a throat.

"Well, the Kirlian aura is now subject to precise measurement. It varies in intensity and detail with different individuals. Some have weak fields, some strong fields. Most are average. You happen to have a very strong field. This means you would be a good subject for transfer of identity to another body, for where your Kirlian aura goes, *you* go—because your aura is your essence."

Suddenly Flint caught the man's drift. "Like mattermission—to someone else's body!"

"To someone else's body *and* brain—but you retain your own personality and memories, because they are inherent in your aura. As *you* change, *it* changes, reflecting your growth. Your aura *is* you. In this case, it goes to some-

thing else's body. You are about to have the magnificent adventure of traveling to the stars."

The notion had its appeal. Flint was intrigued by the stars, and all the stories connected with them. But he remained angry. "I just traveled from a star—and I want to go back."

"But this is a signal honor. No human being has done this before. You will be an extraordinary envoy to alien Spheres—"

"The old goat almost makes *me* want to transfer," one of the Ministers whispered to another.

Not only did Flint overhear this, he knew the Regent heard it too, for the man's lips twitched into the merest suggestion of a snarl. This Council was like a nest of piranha-beetles when the meat ran out, snapping at anything that moved, including each other. Flint's own ire was simple: he wanted to go home. The Ministers' ire was complex, but not his business, unless he could find some way to turn it to his own advantage. Maybe one of them would help him escape, just to spite the others?

For he had no intention of having his aura transferred. "Go to the stars—in some creature's body?" Flint thought of being a wheeled Polarian, and was revolted.

"Precisely. And you will bring to those Spheres the secret of transfer itself, and enlist them in the galactic coalition—"

But Flint had heard more than enough. He turned and ran out of the chamber so quickly that the assembled Ministers were left staring. "Stop him!" the Regent cried.

Imperial guards appeared, barring Flint's passage. But they were civilized and soft, while he was a tough Stone Age warrior. He dodged the first, ducked under the reaching arm of the second, and nudged the third into the fourth. He really felt crippled, without either spear or fingernails! He left them behind in a tangle.

He came to the capsule area and jumped into one. The transparent cover closed over him and the thing launched through the wall. This time Flint watched closely: The wall irised open as the blunt snout of the craft shoved in, so that it formed an aperture just the right size. He emerged outside, and looked back to see the wall closing behind like the anus of a grazing dinosaur. And what did that make the capsule and its occupant, ejected like this from the bowel of the building? Flint smiled briefly, thinking of what men called Polarians. Now Flint himself was the dinosaur dropping.

The capsule was on some sort of vine or wire that extended before and after, a bead on a string. That was why it didn't fall into the chasm between buildings. Flint felt nervous, peering down into the void; if that string broke—but of course it wouldn't. The Imps were very careful about things like that, being extremely dependent on their machines.

Now he had only a moment to make plans. The Imps would be waiting for him at the next stop. He had to outmaneuver them. But it would be foolish to go out into this awesome city; he would give himself away in an instant even if he found a way to cover up his green skin. He had to act in a manner they did not expect. And he had to get home.

The capsule punched into the next building. Evidently it was a shuttle, going back and forth between the matter-mission center and the Ministry. Yet that was limited, and outside there had been a network of lines like the spreading limbs of a large vine tree. Surely the string continued to other places.

There was a little panel of buttons before him, and a sign. He could not read it, but could guess: This was a manual control system, like reins on the horses that more civilized worlds than Outworld used. He punched buttons randomly as the capsule slowed to a halt. He could see the Imp guards clustered at the landing.

Abruptly the capsule took off again. It shot past the surprised faces of the guards and on through the opposite wall. Now he was back in suspension, seeing the connecting lines spreading every which way. Each one represented potential escape, if only he could figure out the system in time. Flint punched more buttons, and the capsule slowed, as if confused by the multiple directions.

By quick experimentation and use of his excellent memory, Flint got a notion of how to operate the thing. Each button represented a preset destination, like telling a child runner "Go to Chief Strongspear." The question was, where did he want to go—and illiterate as he was, how could he choose that particular button?

Once he got home, he would ask the Shaman to teach him how to read. It had become a survival skill.

Well, maybe he could use his own ignorance to advantage. Every time he punched a button, the capsule shifted its route to head for that location. By punching new buttons, he kept shifting his destination, so that the Imps could not tell where he was going. Evidently they could not intercept him here in the capsule en route, so he was safe for the moment. He had a chance to think.

First, he had to delve into his own motives. The Shaman had always disciplined him in this: "Know thyself." Sometimes the obvious became spurious, and new truths manifested from the hidden mind.

Why was he fleeing? After a flurry of superfluous reasons, he penetrated to the basic one: He could not face the notion of being placed in the prison of an alien body. He had always been allergic to weakness, abnormality, or illness. Honeybloom's stiff-finger hex had been more than a nuisance; it had forced a recognition of physical incapacity on Flint, to his emotional discomfort. Chief Strongspear's threat of a pus-spell had been devastating, for the thought of making love to a sick woman completely unmanned Flint. He had always been supremely healthy himself. Good clean combat wounds were all right, but anything festering—ugh!

The idea of becoming a monstrous bug or stupid dinosaur or slimy jelly-thing—no, Flint could not face this. He knew himself to be brave in the conventional sense, but an abject coward in this. His essence, his spark of individuality, was his strength, and any weakening of that was like suffocation. He had to remain in his own good body. Even if this meant dying in it.

He spied a different kind of area, cleared of the huge buildings. What could this be, here in the perpetual metropolis of the Imperial Planet? A bit of forest?

He brought his capsule closer to it by punching buttons, coordinating them like the fracture lines of imperfect flint rocks. He had, after all, the touch of an expert. A little *here,* a little *there,* and the capsule jerked closer to a destination that was not programmed for any of its buttons. Finally the clearing expanded, and he spied a spaceship.

Flint had seen similar craft at the little spaceport on Outworld. It was an orbiter shuttle, a jet-propelled ship that carried things up to the orbiting interstellar ships. A starship would break apart if it ever tried to land on a full-sized planet, but there was no need for it to come down when the shuttle relayed everything.

This was Imperial Earth, origin planet of man. Spaceships still set out from here for all parts of Sphere Sol. If he could locate one going to Outworld and get aboard it. . . .

But of course it would be two hundred years before he got home. Even if he were frozen—a notion he didn't like—so that he didn't age, he would still be way too late for Honeybloom. But at least he would be going in the right direction.

Who the hell was he fooling? Half the people on Freezers died in transit. Of every twelve shipfuls, three were lost in space and three more were lost in failed revivals. For some reason, he had once thought that was more than half gone, but the Shaman had corrected him. In any event, why should he risk throwing away his young life like that? The Shaman's case had been different: He had been old, thirty-five, when he embarked on his freezer-voyage to Outworld.

Yet he couldn't stand being cooped up in a metal lifeship for the rest of his life, either. He'd be stir-crazy, as the Shaman put it, before two months were out. There was no way home but mattermission: instant transport.

But he knew there was no chance of getting mattermitted back. Not on his own. Starships were not closely guarded; who in his right mind would stow away aboard a vessel that wouldn't dock for fifty or a hundred years? But mattermission was such a special thing that everything to be sent had to be triple-checked, though it were no bigger than a grain of sand. Which was just about the size of the message capsules that zipped back and forth between the major planets. No sloppy procedures there!

Which made it all the more amazing that he should have been mattermitted all the way to Earth. It must have cost a couple of trillion Solar dollars in postage—more than any person was permitted to earn in a lifetime. In fact, more than the annual budget of most systems in the Sphere. Not that the tribesmen of Outworld bothered with money; what use was it, after all? Oh, some of the villagers used it in trade for larger shares of food or help on their lean-tos, and there were Imp trinkets the girls liked that could be obtained only with money. But it really wasn't part of Paleolithic existence. Flint knew about it only because of the Shaman's education.

What was so two-trillion-dollars' special about him? Surely there were others who could transfer to bug-eyed monster bodies. Others who would be more amenable, with a lot more education than Flint had. Maybe some ugly or ill ones, who would be glad to get out of their poor human bodies, gambling on a better alien body. Why take a barbarian flintsmith from the farthest colony planet?

Surely there was good reason. Either the job was so dangerous or horrible that only the most ignorant person would go, or he had some qualification that made him so much better than others that it was worth the expense of mattermitting him here. Since an ignorant person would not *stay* ignorant long, the latter seemed more likely. The Regent had said that Flint had a very strong Kirlian aura. Apparently not many people had that—and only the ones *with* it could transfer.

How badly did they want him? If they had dozens like him, they would not bother to chase him very far, and wouldn't care if he died on an outbound starship. But if he were *the* choice, they would keep a very close eye on him. And the planet-ransom they had already expended in fetching him here suggested the answer. He could put that to the test—and might be able to use it to bargain with. If they really thought he was prepared to die rather than submit to transfer, they just might treat him kindly in an effort to bring him around. And the greatest kindness they could do him would be to mattermit him home to think it over.

His decision was made. He would gamble his life and sanity on the assumption that he was really important. That two-trillion-dollar investment suggested better odds than the fifty-fifty of freeze-traveling.

The capsule would not go all the way to the spaceport. Like his thoughts, it sheered off from the target unless really pressed. Was the spaceport off limits?

All right. Flint pushed buttons until the capsule, confused by conflicting directives, stalled in place. Like a dinosaur, it wasn't very smart. Then he forced open the lid, exerting pressure he knew was beyond the capacity of most civilized men. He climbed out and dropped to the wire. It was guyed at regular intervals—how the capsules got past these connections he wasn't sure—and poles went to the ground. He was at a dizzying height, but was confident of his ability. He took hold and swung to the nearest supporting pole, then let himself down to the ground. It wasn't as handy as a vine tree, but it wasn't difficult either. The gravity of this planet was slightly less than at Outworld, giving extra buoyancy.

Solarian pedestrians stared as he came down. It was not his green skin that impressed them, for the natives of Earth were of several colors themselves; it was rather his agility that claimed their attention. They were advanced culturally, but regressed physically. He could fathom their weakness just by looking at them, and it disgusted him. So he ignored them and made his way at a lope toward the spaceport. Naturally his whereabouts would soon be reported, if they didn't have a spy-beam on him already. However, that was the idea. He was acting exactly as they would expect him to. If they really wanted this savage, they would close the net quickly and thus provide him his leverage.

Starships were always in need of strong men for hull repairs en route and things like that, the Shaman had said. The dust of space constantly pitted surfaces, and sometimes larger debris gouged out little craters that had to be patched. Maybe that was why so many freezers were lost; no one to patch up the damage. It was not the big meteors that took out ships, but the steady accumulation of microscopic abrasion that could finally hole the hull if not watched. They'd take him aboard, no questions asked.

To one side of the spaceport, there was an incredible expanse of water. Flint had never seen water in greater amount than a temporary flood lake before. This was monstrous, stretching from the spaceport all the way to the horizon. And it had waves: large traveling ripples that moved to the shoreline and dissolved in thinning froth. It was hypnotic, and he quickly tore his eyes away lest he fall into a trance. So much water!

Then he saw something just inside the fence. It was a moving pebble—no, it was alive! A blob of flesh dragging along a housing of something like bone. In fact—his memory trotted out one of the myriad incidentals the Shaman had mentioned—this must be a snail.

Earth certainly had its wonders. But there was no time to gawk now. He had business to attend to. " 'Bye snail," he said, for the moment childlike in his discovery.

He navigated the fence easily, avoiding its electric shock by leaping, straightened out his ludicrous tunic, and walked boldly into the little office. "I'm looking for work," he said, imitating the heavy Earth accent as well as he could.

The man at the desk didn't even look up. "Next ship's for Vega. Computer parts. Fifty-year haul. Standard enlistment bonus. No stops. Sterile girls. Burial in space if you don't make it."

So they gave money for signing up, and provided playgirls for the fifty-year trip. The Shaman hadn't mentioned such details. Even so, it must be deadly dull, and unless the girl were Honeybloom, Flint wouldn't care for it. Which meant he'd better be guessing right.

Vega. Flint visualized his sphere map. Vega was roughly in line with Etamin, about a quarter of the way out. It was exactly the planetary system an ignorant savage would head for. "I'll take it."

"Where's your ID?"

Oh-oh. Outworld didn't use such things. A man was known by his face and skills, a woman by her face and body.

"No bonus without turning over your ID. Too many take the money and skip."

Oh. "I'll go now. I don't need money." Maybe the average enlistee blew his bonus in a night's binge, his last fling on Earth, but Flint was trying to make a point, not money. It really was time for the Imps to show up, if they were going to. If he stalled too long, they would know he didn't mean it.

"You're pretty eager. Got a record?"

A record? Flint didn't know what that was, so he bypassed it. "My business is private." The Imps said that a lot on Outworld, as if anything there were private. It was one of the things that made them unpopular. Sometimes an Imp would approach a native girl, and she would mock him by saying, "My privates is business."

A figure appeared in the doorway. Flint whirled, certain the Ministers had caught up with him. He moved quickly, but not as quickly as he could when really threatened, putting up his left forearm as though to shove the intruder aside, making his show. He might get stunned by a paralyzing beam, but he was pretty sure they would not hurt him. *Nobody* simply wiped out a two-trillion-dollar investment!

But this was no minister. It was a stranger in white. And with the light touch of arm against arm, something happened. There was a strange, almost electric aura about the man that affected Flint profoundly. Suddenly he didn't want to fight or flee, even in pretend; he just wanted to know about this stranger.

"I am Pnotl of Sphere Knyfh," the man said, and the words assumed a transcendant importance. "I am an alien sapient in human guise. I have come to ask you to help save our galaxy from destruction."

The words were simple, but the aura was compelling. Only one other person had ever affected Flint so strongly, though in a different way. That was the Shaman. This Pnotl, who claimed to be an alien creature, was far from being repulsive; he was magnetic, almost godlike.

"I don't know what it is about you—"

"It is my Kirlian aura," Pnotl said, and Flint had a vision of a hand radiating like a galaxy: yes, there was something of that in this creature's touch. "It is eighty times as intense as the sentient norm. I feel it in you, too, most strongly."

"I don't know what you jokers are up to," the man at the desk snapped. "But either sign up for Vega or get out of my office."

Vega suddenly seemed to be so close as to be negligible, compared to the reaches of far-distant Spheres. Flint glanced at the deskman curiously. "He doesn't feel it."

"Only those who possess it feel it, as a rule," Pnotl explained, guiding him outside onto the plain of the spaceport. A small hovercraft rested there. "You have not before been aware of your gift."

"The Ministers—"

"Unaware."

"But they told me—"

"Their machines give them readings, their computers give them readouts. They think by their analysis of holographic photographs of the Kirlian aura they understand what is important. They reduce it to statistics. But in themselves, they are unaware, as is an entity who has never experienced love."

"They're blind," Flint said, amazed.

"Blind, deaf, senseless. Yet they do what they must."

"Why don't you revolt me? I am an alienophobe, and I can't stand illness—"

"The intense Kirlian aura does not reflect sickness, but health. It is a function of extreme vitality. It transcends the individual, even the species. Some call it the soul."

"And I, myself, have—"

"Self does not exist. There is no true individual consciousness. We are all vessels of a larger force, all aspects of the flame of life. Only the ramifications of our separate environments and experience provide the illusion of distinction. The Kirlian aura is all, and it meticulously reflects the influence of the physical and mental vessels we occupy. Through it we share the universe. We *are* the universe."

Flint was awed. The Regent had said much the same thing, but from Pnotl it had the force of conviction. "My mind does not understand, but I have to believe. You are—my kind."

"I am your kind. We two are Kirlian entities. But your aura is more than twice the intensity of mine. You may be the most potent aura in the galaxy. You must go out into that galaxy, not merely to preserve it from external threat, but to seek your own level. You will not find your like among your physical kind."

"You're telling me I have to transfer," Flint said.

"It is the only way. For you and your Sphere and our galaxy."

Once more Flint visualized the hand like the galaxy. The two were really the same, aspects of the Kirlian cosmos. "Exactly what is my mission?"

"You must bring the secret of Kirlian transfer to the other Spheres of this cluster, this galactic segment. You are best equipped to do this, for though the Kirlian aura is the essence of the communal Self, it associates with its original vessel and fades relentlessly when removed from that vessel. Every day that passes in transfer reduces the intensity of the aura by approximately one sentient norm, so that ordinary entities cannot retain their original identities in transfer. Those with more intense auras can, their limits defined by the potency of those auras. I can remain in transfer up to eighty Earth-days. You can do it for up to two hundred days. That is what makes you crucial to our effort. You can accomplish more, with a far greater margin of safety."

"Yes." It was obvious, now. "What's this about the galaxy being destroyed?"

"Come with me and I shall explain."

And Flint went with the alien, committed.

3

Keel of the Ship

alarm priority development

—summon council available entities linked thought transfer immediate—

COUNCIL INITIATED PARTICIPATING*—: :

—only one additional entity? why do we bother! proceed—

new transfer entity object galaxy potent

—specific data?—

scale approximately 200 intensity motion 60 parsecs mid-rim segment

: : 200 intensity! surely misreading? : :

—review prior manifestations for entity : :—

recent transfer 80 intensity motion 1500 parsecs from known sphere knyfh to object region formerly undeveloped

: : call 200 undeveloped?! : :

—indication emissary from established transfer culture successful promoting subsidiary transfer activity recruited extraordinary potency now extreme threat priority target initiate action promptly—

: : indication noted call for concurrence : :

CONCURRENCE

: : nature of proposed action summon agent highest expertise matching alien entity scale dispatch earliest opportunity destination transfer recipient station target galaxy mission destroy 200 intensity threat entity : :

contraindication no available agent scale 200

: : solution preempt top agent from lesser mission we *do* have a 200 intensity agent? : :

one

—::CONCURRENCE::—

—stipulation concealment of agent mandatory—

:: modification of concurrence mission destroy 200 intensity threat only in manner concealing motive and origin ::

— *CONCURRENCE*—

:: signoff ::

—*POWER CIVILIZATION CONCURRENCE*—

The transfer was instant and painless. One moment Flint was standing in the lab; the next he was hanging from chains in the blistering sun, looking out over a field of ripening burl berries.

He also had a complete new mindful of information; too much to assimilate all at once. His life experiences had suddenly been doubled, but only his Kirlian identity fell into place readily. He was still Flint of Outworld, pressed into Sol Sphere service; he was also—who? With concentration, it came: Øro of N*kr, Slave laborer in the local burl plantation. Not much to choose between these two identities!

It took time to work out further details, but he had time. He hung alone, untended. The steady dull pain was distracting, but the need to ascertain his situation overrode it. Øro *had been* a laborer—until he committed the infraction of balking at performing illicit overtime during the Slave holiday. An apologetic petition would have brought nominal punishment and probably redress, for the schedule had been an oversight. But an overt balk was quite another matter. So the holiday labor had been confirmed, to the grief of all the Slaves, and Øro had been chained and tortured until his mind snapped. No, not his mind; his soul.

Flint felt dizzy and nauseous, and not entirely because of this just-relived history. He was from a frontier himself; pain and death did not appall him unduly. It was the alien perspective that sickened him. He had come here, at least in part, in quest of high-Kirlian entities like himself—and here he was in an *un*-Kirlian body in the throes of torture. Øro's entire life was available for his inspection; all he had to do was work for it. But the effort filled him with disgust. He had to ease off, to get his bearings slowly, to become acclimatized not only to Øro's situation but to the fact that strong, free Flint was weak and chained. It had to be done a little at a time, or his own mind would crack, his own soul fade.

Ølro's mind had died only recently, his personality at last giving up the ghost (literally), for the memories carried through the increasing distress until this very morning. This was a fresh body and brain—probably the freshest on the planet, attracting Flint's aura the way a high point attracted a bolt of lightning.

The best host-body on the planet: a chained Slave!

A foreman approached. Flint/Ølro recognized him: Ølliw of V⁰ps, a Slave of status, harsh but fair.

"Last day, Ølro," Ølliw said, raising the punishment-box. "Think you'll make it?" He spoke in the native language, of course, but Ølro's brain rendered the meaning as though it were Flint's own.

Silence would mean a stiff jolt of pain; a plea of contrition would reduce it. Ølro had maintained stony silence through the first two days of the three-day ordeal. But Flint, knowing Ølro's cause was just if stubborn, ignored these alternatives. "Go soak your beak in acid, Ølliw."

It was a triple insult, culled from the depths of Ølro's admirably rebellious nature. Only the birdlike carrion-eaters had beaks; acid was the slang term for liquid offal brewed to high potency; and the intonation of the double bar //, or baton sinister, meant "Slave of a Slave." In human heraldry it could suggest illegitimacy, but since Slaves had no legitimacy and no marriage, that was irrelevant here.

"Unrepentant," Ølliw remarked blandly. "That elevates the scale." He turned the dial on the punishment-box, moving the indicator up a notch. "And foul-mouthed." He turned the dial again.

And paused. The dial stuck; it would not complete the second notch. Ølliw looked at it, startled, then turned the dial all the way down to neutral, counting clicks. "Great One!" he swore, taking the title of a Master in vain, the strongest possible expletive. "The dial's out of adjustment! It was set on eleven!"

Flint's new memory made this clear after a moment of effort. Actually, this seemed to be the best mode of operation: to allow events to call forth the necessary background in their own fashion. As long as he did not try to grasp too much at once, he suffered no further nausea. The punishment-box had twelve settings, with one being minimal and twelve maximal. Ølro was supposed to get a jolt of six each hour of the day and night until his scheduled ordeal was over. Contrition would reduce it to five; his insult should have raised it two notches to eight. But Øro had actually been receiving, by accident, near-fatal jolts of eleven. No wonder his soul had succumbed!

Ǫiw spoke into his Master-band. "Problem in the field, sir. Defective punishment-box."

A melodious voice responded immediately, sounding bored. "Noted. Exchange for another."

"Complication, sir. Convict Øro jolted eleven, not six."

"Convict damaged?"

Ǫiw looked at Flint. "No apparent damage, sir."

"Administer scheduled punishment. Check other boxes. Report."

"With dispatch, sir." Ǫiw lowered the box, studying Flint. "Slave, you know the difference between six and eleven! Why didn't you speak?"

But Flint, wiser now, did not answer.

Ǫiw went to the control center and exchanged boxes, giving the convict temporary respite. Why, Flint wondered, *hadn't* Øro spoken? Why had he tolerated an appalling intensity of pain for so long, when it could have been reduced at any time? And why hadn't Øro made the properly subservient petition for redress at the outset.

It was because he was unrealistically stubborn, and not very bright. Øro would die before allowing himself to appear craven, to beg for mercy. In fact, he *had* died, for the pain had killed his essence. The death of a valuable, powerful Slave—for Øro was physically strong as if in compensation for his intellectual weakness—would have gotten Foreman Ǫiw in trouble—except that no one outside of Øro's body knew of it. Now Flint was here, taking the place of the Slave.

All he had to do, he realized suddenly, was *tell* them—and he would be on his way.

Ǫiw returned with the new punishment-box. "Shall we try it again?" he inquired as he carefully calibrated it to Øro's frequency.

"I'm not Øro," Flint said. "Øro died this morning. I am an alien from Sphere Sol."

"Unrepentant, one notch," Ǫiw said. "Sarcastic, another notch. Right back on eight."

"Wait!" Flint cried. "I'm telling you—"

Terrible pain overwhelmed him. His body strained against the chains as the soul-shattering agony tore through every cell of his being. He tried to scream, but the muscles of his lungs were knotted, unable to respond.

It lasted an eternity: a few seconds stretched out interminably by the sheer volume of pain. For it was not mere surface sensation, such as that produced by the quick slash of a knife; it was complete tissue involvement, as of fire projected inside to cook the muscle and bone simultaneously. When it finally stopped, he collapsed, supported by the chains.

By the time his head cleared, Q̸iw was gone.

At dusk a young female Slave brought him his rations: dried burl and water.

Flint accepted the offering eagerly, for he was famished. The effort of pain dissipated much bodily energy, and part of Øro's punishment was to endure half-rations these three days. This was rough on an able-bodied giant. Fortunately the ordeal would be over in the morning.

As his chains prevented him from feeding himself she had to put the food in his mouth, as though he were an infant or an idiot. That, too, was part of it. Pain, hunger, and shame. The three-day sentence was a thorough humiliation and discomfort, guaranteeing that 90 percent of offenders would not soon repeat the offense.

Flint searched Øro's memory, but could not identify this girl Slave. She was extraordinarily pretty, and evidently new to this plantation. "Who are you?" he asked in the direct Slave way.

She flushed in humanoid fashion—for they were humanoid—and he realized that he had spoken too soon. His memory informed him that one did not inquire the identity of a female except as a prelude to more serious business. If she were not interested, she would decline to answer.

"I am Ȼle of Ath," she replied.

His Øro memory clicked over. Flint didn't want to make any more mistakes! A[th] was a distant Slave planet, small but well regarded among Slaves. There had been three major rebellions there in the past century. Now the Masters were spreading A[th] all across Sphere Canopus, preventing that nest of ire from achieving critical mass.

The Masters and Slaves, his memory instructed him, had evolved on neighboring planets within the Canopus system. Both had achieved sapience at about the same time, but the presence of readily refinable metals on the crust of the Masters' planet had given them an impetus toward technology that the Slaves lacked. Thus the Masters achieved space travel first, and came to their neighbors as conquerors. They had a tremendous need for cheap manual labor, and were quick to exploit what they found. They took care to see that the Slaves never had opportunity to learn even the most rudimentary technology, and so never gained even the semblance of equality. Thus it had been for a thousand years—and those years were longer than the years of Earth, though considerably short of the years of Flint's home planet, Outworld. As the Masters, buoyed by this cheap labor, expanded to full Sphere status, their Slaves expanded with them, while doing all the uglier chores. Most accepted this without objection—but some resisted.

"You A[th]s have real spirit," Flint said.

"So do you N*krs," she said, pleased.

Flint realized that there were possibilities here. He was not about to identify himself to the foreman again—but perhaps some of the lower slaves would believe him. If he were circumspect. This was as good a place to start as any.

"I am released tomorrow," he said. "Will you work beside me?"

"I would," she said dubiously.

More memories of Slave protocol. There were no permanent liaisons, by order of the Masters, for the family structure provoked loyalties to other than the Masters. But there were many temporary connections. A girl as lovely as this would always have a man. Flint's interest was in making connections with independent-minded Slaves, so that he could explain his situation and use their belief as a lever to compel the attention of the Masters. His heart was loyal to Honeybloom, back on Outworld, of course. But how could ¢le know that?

In fact, it would look suspicious if he failed to take note of her attractiveness. Better to play the game, until his mission was achieved.

That meant he would have to deal with her boyfriend. "Who?" The very intonation of his query implied contempt for that about-to-be-divulged name.

"&mg of Y^jr."

Once again, Øro's memory obligingly culled the essence: Y^jr was a rough tribe! To a man, those natives were warriors. And Øro's body had been decimated by the torture. Well, it had to be done. "I will meet him."

¢le put the last morsel in his mouth with a flourish, obviously pleased. It must have been a chore to get such a commitment, and that explained her readiness to approach a convict. How else could she rid herself of an unwanted boyfriend—one who could probably pulverize anyone else she might fancy?

As the darkness closed in, the stars came out. At last Flint could orient himself. He knew he was in Sphere Canopus, because that was where he had been sent, but as it was similar to Sphere Sol in size, with a diameter of over two hundred light-years, he could be anywhere within it. Probably fairly near Canopus itself, within a few parsecs.

The stellar configuration was vastly different from anything he had seen within his own Sphere's skies, of course, but still there were identifiers. There was a bright-red star that was surely huge Betelgeuse, and a bluish one that had to be Rigel, one of the brightest stars anywhere in this segment of the galaxy. That meant that between them should be—yes, there it was, just below Rigel: the triple lights of Orion's Belt. Those three second-magnitude blue-white stars in a line, Alnitac, Alnilam, and Mintaka. Each fifteen hundred to sixteen hundred light-years from Sol, and about the same from Canopus. His shift in viewpoint had removed them from between Betelgeuse and Rigel, but the constellation was certain. He knew where he was.

He contemplated the new configurations, doing a kind of mental triangulation from the Belt, and gradually the finer details fell into place. He was on a planet circling a star on the far side of Canopus. Canopus itself was extraordinarily bright—triple the apparent magnitude of Sirius from Earth (that was not the proper way to express it, but he hardly cared at this moment)—and Sirius was Earth's brightest star. It demonstrated the need for galactic orientation points, for in any area there would be a number of small stars that were very bright because of their proximity. Bless the galaxy for providing Betelgeuse, Rigel, and Orion's Belt!

Sol itself, of course, could not be seen. Even if he had been able to view that section of the galactic sky, Sol would not be visible without a telescope. Over two hundred light-years distant, Sol would be down to ninth magnitude, and bright Sirius down to five and one-half magnitude—just visible.

For a moment he visualized Canopus as seen from Earth. Canopus was in the constellation Argo, the Boat. In fact it was on the keel of the ship—the ship of the Argonauts. The mythological hero Jason had sailed in this ship with his fifty Argonauts, seeking the famous Golden Fleece and having other glorious adventures. He had vanquished a dragon and sown dragon's teeth that sprouted from the ground as warriors. He married a king's daughter, the enchantress Medea—a woman of splendidly mixed qualities. This keel-star had an adventurous and violent history, in the lore of Earth, and was a fitting Sphere for mortal individual combat.

Flint slept between his periodic doses of punishment pain, accepting them as necessary for now, and allowed his wastes to drop on the turf at his feet as they had to. Soon it would be over. He did not try again to inform Qiw of his true status—but neither did he plead contrition. And at dawn he was released—to work all day in the fields.

$mg of Y⩚jr was every bit as imposing as anticipated. He was gross and ugly, with the scars of many past encounters on his torso, and his eyes were fierce. Flint was glad that Øro had a big, powerful body; he would need it. He had spent the day beside Ȼle, wrestling the burls from their tough vines, recovering the strength sapped by punishment. He was still weak, but not critically so.

Memory told him how Øro had handled such occasions in the past. He had bulled ahead with such determination and heedlessness of pain that even stronger opponents had stepped back. Had he been smarter, Øro could have been a good Slave leader, perhaps a foreman. But he had never been able to hold women long, because he lacked the wit to keep them entertained and lacked the will to hold them against their inclinations. Thus he was not regarded as much of a threat; it was easier to let Øro have a woman as he was sure to lose her.

This time, however, he was up against a Y⩚jr. Pride would compel the other to try to prevail, and the innate sadism of that tribe would cause him to hurt Øro as much as he could get away with.

The meet was supervised by Foreman Ꝗiw. This was to ensure that neither worker was damaged unduly. The

Masters permitted these encounters, but always acted to preserve their property. Pain was allowed, even encouraged, but not mutilation.

On the occasions Flint had fought on Outworld, he had always won. This was due partly to his strength, speed, and extraordinary coordination, and partly the advice in martial art the Shaman had provided. But his fighting was effective mainly because of his brain. He was capable of rapidly analyzing his opponent's pattern and capitalizing on its flaws.

$mg came at him like a wrestler. Flint stepped aside and caught the Y⩓jr with a backhand chop to the skull. It was a hard blow, and his hand went numb; he had intended to go for the neck. But that was his human experience, suffering in the translation. For Øro's arm was jointed differently, and the fingers did not form a true fist. And $mg's head was not solid bone in back; it rose into a cartilage crest. Somehow these differences were more apparent to the sense of touch than to the sense of sight. As a result, Flint had actually hurt himself worse than he had hurt $mg.

But there was a hum of amazement through the audience, for Øro was not behaving the way Slaves usually did in combat. In fact, this strike at the hard head with the soft hand resembled a gesture of supreme contempt.

Flint saw Φiw watching him closely. Well, let the foreman be surprised; Flint had *tried* to tell him the truth!

Stung by the fancied taunt, $mg came at him like a boxer. Flint dodged his first swing, spun about, trapped his moving hand and twisted the arm into an armlock. This should be a submission hold, good for some satisfying pain.

$mg tried to jerk away. Flint bore down, throwing himself to the ground and carrying the trapped arm with him. Suddenly there was a crack, and $mg screamed. Flint had broken his arm.

He hadn't intended to. A human arm would not have broken. But again, he had misjudged the alien structure. The elbows bent the opposite way from those of human beings.

Φiw stepped forward, eyeing the damage. He spoke into his Slave-band. "Property damage report, sir."

The Master responded at once in his musical tones. "Details."

"Routine meet, sir. For favor of female. Upper appendage broken."

"Salvageable?"

"Joint. Uneconomic convalescence."

"Intentional?"

Q̸iw peered at Flint, obviously unable to figure out how someone as stupid as this had fought like that. "Accident."

"Dispatch damaged property. Five days discipline for instigator."

Five days discipline! Flint needed no survey of his memory to comprehend what that meant. For Øro it would be extremely unpleasant—but for Flint it could mean disaster. Every day he stayed here in this alien body meant a further diminution of his Kirlian aura. Eventually he would lose his identity, and become Øro in fact as well as form. The Earth authorities thought he was good for several months—but they weren't *sure*. Not until he completed his mission and returned, could they measure the actual depletion of aura. Meanwhile, all they could be sure of was that he had better not waste any time when out of his natural body. Five days of starvation and punishment pain, on top of the three his body had just undergone—that could be very bad trouble, and was not worth the risk.

Q̸iw was setting the punishment-box on $mg's frequency. Every Slave had a code imprinted on his torso, and any box could be tuned to that code, so that it sent its current through that specific body and no other. Q̸iw set the dial to twelve.

"No!" $mg screamed, scrambling toward him, the broken arm dangling. "I'll recover! I'll recover fast!"

But Q̸iw activated the box. $mg of Y^jr stiffened in utter agony, crashing helplessly into the dust. For five seconds the torture continued, ten, fifteen, without letup—until the Slave relaxed.

$mg of Y^jr was dead. The unremitting maximum-intensity pain, continued beyond the toleration point of life, had wiped out his mind, and with it his body. It was a terrible way to die.

The way Øro had died, vacating his body for Flint.

Q̸iw turned. "Now, Øro of N*kr," he said, beginning to retune the box.

Flint kicked the box right out of his hands. There was a moan of shock from the surrounding Slaves. Flint dived for the box, knowing that he could never escape as long as it was in working order and within range of him. He picked it up and smashed it down against a rock.

"The band!" someone cried. It was ¢le. "Don't let him call!"

But ȹiw was already calling. "Emergency!" he said. "Slave out of control."

Flint whirled about and charged him.

"Identity," the pleasant Master voice replied, unruffled.

Flint caught the band with one hand and shoved ȹiw back with the other. The communicator ripped off the foreman's wrist. "ȹro of N*kr!" Flint yelled into the speaker. "ȹro!" This time he omitted the Slave-intonation, no mere breach of etiquette, but a crime. "Shove it up your blowpipe!"

That would have been a vaguely obscene insult to a human being. It was not vague at all when addressed to a Master of Canopus, for this species really did have pipes through which digestive refuse was expelled under pressure, or "blown," in crude vernacular.

Then Flint smashed the band and whirled to face the stunned Slaves. "Who joins me in freedom?" he challenged them.

"*I* do!" ¢le cried.

But she was the only one.

"Let's get out of here!" Flint said to her, disgusted. They can't *all* be vegetables on this planet."

"The hills," she said. "There are FreeSlaves there—wildmen. If we can make it before the Masters come—"

The Slaves all seemed stunned, afraid to either hinder or help the rebels.

Except for Foreman ȹiw. Stripped of his punishment-box and his Master communicator, he charged Flint barehanded.

Flint sidestepped the clumsy lunge and tripped him. ȹiw fell to the ground, bashed his head, and lay still.

And Flint realized: *It was too easy.* ȹiw had not gotten to be foreman by being clumsy or stupid. Why hadn't he simply ordered the loyal Slaves to tackle ȹro in a group and overpower him?

Because he wanted ȹro and ¢le to escape? Naturally he could not permit this openly; his own position and perhaps his life would be forfeit. So he had made a show of obstruction, blundering into the fray exactly as $mg had, and taken his dive. Everyone present had seen him try. So he had fouled it up; what else could be expected of a mere Slave?

Would the Masters see through the act? If so, Ꝗiw's own punishment would not be token. "You play a dangerous game, Foreman," Flint muttered.

They fled across the fields of burl." You know the odds are against us," Flint said as they ran.

"Maybe not," she said, breathing hard. "The Masters don't realize Slaves can think. They'll underestimate us—and maybe Ꝗiw will stall them long enough."

So she had noted the foreman's act too! Ꝗiw—why would he allow a dangerous Slave to escape, if he had not understood what Flint had tried to tell him? And if he *had* understood, why hadn't he taken Øro directly to the Masters for more careful interrogation?

The question elicited its own answer: *Because Ꝗiw didn't want Flint to make contact with the Masters*. The Foreman was ultimately loyal to his own kind; he wanted Flint either silenced or with the FreeSlaves. So he had waited on events, cautiously, not risking his own position—and had acted when he had to.

Waited on events? Surely the Foreman had selected Ȼle of Ath to feed Øro, knowing she was a rebel at heart, untamed, and that she was looking for a new man, a strong one. Very cunning!

Ȼle made a half-choked little scream. Flint looked back.

A Master's saucer was skimming over the field toward them.

There was no way to outrun it, and there was no concealment here in the field. Their trail through the burl was obvious, and the saucer could crack the speed of sound when under full power in the open.

Øro's memory was no help; it merely informed him that the saucers were equipped with pain beams that could strike right through foliage, rocks, or any other cover to incapacitate the fugitives instantly—without damage. These beams were all-purpose; they did not need to be tuned like the boxes. The Masters had had centuries of experience at this sort of thing!

The Masters were the very authorities Flint was sent to talk to—but at this point they would dismiss anything he said as the ravings of a rebellious Slave. Probably Ꝗiw had made a report that suggested Øro was mad, because of the overdose of punishment pain. A neat maneuver by the Foreman.

And Flint was increasingly uncertain he *wanted* to contact the Masters officially. Maybe it would be better to give the Slaves a break. Sphere Sol had abolished slavery as uncivilized centuries ago, and if it aligned with *these* slaves—

"Are we going to fight, Øro?" ₵le inquired breathlessly.

"Yes!" he snapped, though at the moment he couldn't see how.

She smiled, though she was obviously terrified. "On A[th], they threw rocks."

"*Rocks?* Against a supersonic saucer?"

"The Masters thought maybe they were bombs, so they put the shield up, and then they couldn't use the beams."

Flint saw it. "Beautiful, ₵le!" he cried.

"I know it," she said, patting her fur in place. Slave females were vain about their fur, even as human girls—no, humans had hair. "Only one problem."

Now the saucer was upon them: a bowl-shaped flier large enough to hold two or three Masters. Flint dropped to the ground, scrambling for stones. "What problem?" he demanded, searching desperately underneath the burl vines.

"No rocks here," she explained.

This was a cultivated field. Naturally there were no rocks!

Still, Flint had had occasion before to consider combatting Space Age technology with Stone Age technology. He had come to the conclusion that a smart Paleolith could prevail against a stupid spaceman. *Could,* not *would.* It depended a lot on the individual circumstance. This particular situation was not what he would have chosen for the test.

Yet ₵le had given him the hint. The Masters could be deceived. They tended to underestimate the Slaves, then to overreact when surprised. This could be exploited—maybe.

A beam stabbed out from the saucer. ₵le screamed: pain this time, not fear. The beam had crossed her foot. She fell among the vines, rolling, and the beam lost her.

Flint grabbed a burl berry and ripped it from its plant. It was a green fruit, unripe and hard and solid, and his savage jerk uprooted the parent plant. He hurled it at the saucer, his arm moving in a kind of backhand swing that would have been impossible for a human.

The berry struck the underside of the craft and bounced off harmlessly.

Now the beam found him. It touched his arm as he tried to throw again. It was twelve-pain; paralyzing, intolerable! It was as if the bone were splitting open, the flesh burning to ash, the blood boiling and vaporizing right within its conduits. The berry fell from his hand and his arm knotted in utter agony, every one of his six fingers twisting spasmodically. He, too, fell among the vines.

But these were random beam-tags. It was difficult to keep the beam on target when both saucer and target were moving. And when it left, his arm recovered quickly, undamaged. Now he was glad of the Masters' design: pain without injury.

By this time he had more berries, and so did ¢le. He aimed higher.

The saucer was not an armored flyer. It was more like a concave dish, open on top, so that the Master could look out over the fields conveniently in any direction. But this also meant it was vulnerable from any direction, as long as its protective shield was down. And if that shield was raised, it would not be able to attack.

Flint could see the occupant now. It was a lone Master; evidently that was deemed sufficient for the occasion.

The berries struck the saucer on both underside and upperside. But they did not do any real damage, and only annoyed the occupant. The Master did not raise the shield. Instead the saucer circled low, the pain-beam sweeping about, orienting on Øro. No hysterical reaction here! This Master had full confidence that the fugitives had no bombs; the only concern was to maneuver the craft so as to allow maximum effect of the beam.

Flint dodged, but the beam caught him again: a swipe across the chest. Instant agony collapsed his lungs, and he began to lose consciousness. As he started to fall, the pain receded. With an effort he recovered his balance. He couldn't take too many more of those!

The saucer was now down almost to his eye level, hovering. The Master was looking over the rim at him: a slender dark shape, hooded against the sun, seemingly featureless. Flint discovered he didn't know what a Master looked like; Øro had never seen one close up, and had averted his eyes whenever a Master was visible.

The muzzle of the beam projector swung around to lock on Flint. This time the pain would not be transitory; the Master had taken time to be sure of his quarry.

Flint threw Øro's body to the ground. The beam grazed his back like a searing knife. He scrambled toward the saucer, getting under its edge, using it as a shield against the beam.

But the Master was no slouch at maneuvering. The saucer dodged aside, dropping ever lower. Once more the dread beam searched for him.

¢le rose up on the opposite side and threw a handful of dirt over the saucer. The Master whirled to cover her with the beam. The aim was excellent; she stiffened and fell, her mouth frozen in a soundless scream.

Flint leaped for the saucer. His fingers caught the rim. The weight of his body jerked it down.

The Master compensated beautifully. The saucer shot straight up, righting itself—with Flint still hanging.

In a moment, he knew, he would feel the pain-beam on his fingers. The saucer was now high in the air; the fall would be fatal.

Flint swung crazily, using Øro's muscles in a way Øro never had. The saucer rocked; the ground far below seemed to tilt. He flexed his torso, thrusting a foot up.

The pain caught his hands, but now he had a leg hooked inside the center depression. He twisted and rolled, cursing the backward joints that made this activity much more difficult than it would have been in a human body, but he made it up into the bowl of the saucer.

The beam played over him, a flexing python of agony, but inertia kept him rolling. He crashed into the Master.

Øro's memory carried only a dire warning: it was death for any Slave to touch a Master. The very act was unthinkable. But Flint, raised on the free, unruly, primitive Outworld of Sphere Sol, had no such restriction. The beam was off, the projector knocked out of the Master's grasp and lost over the rim of the saucer. Flint reached around the cowled figure and hauled it out of the control well in the center. The creature came up easily; it was paper-light, like a winged insect.

The saucer veered, angled, and skated down, out of control. Flint held the Master helpless. "How are you at dying?" he inquired.

The creature's face turned to him. The eyes were faceted, and the mouth parts had mandibles. "You are no Slave!" it said, no trace of fear in the melodious voice.

Flint plumped it back down into the well. Immediately the craft pulled out of its dive, as the segmented feet resumed operating the controls. The Master seemed completely unshaken.

Now was Flint's chance to tell the Master of his identity and mission. Yet he balked. Why deal with these parasites, further entrenching them in their power, when the Slaves were the humanoids? The natural affinity of human beings was with the downtrodden Slaves, not the insectoid Masters!

"I'm no Slave *now,*" Flint said. "Now tell me how to manage this craft, or I'll see that we both crash."

Still the insectoid was unruffled. Did it have nerves of steel, or did it lack real emotion? "I am taking you in for interrogation. You evince none of the mannerisms of a Slave, despite your history. An extreme oddity."

Flint had to admire the thing's courage. The Master was trying to bluff! And it proposed to do exactly what Flint had wanted—up until an hour ago. "I'm taking *you* to the FreeSlaves!" Flint shot back. "Unless you'd rather die right now."

"Die we may," the Master said calmly as the saucer looped smoothly about. "But *I* control the vehicle."

It simply would not be shaken. "Then I must take over the ship," Flint said. He hauled the Master up again.

Pain lanced into his arms. Numbed, he let go.

"I have activated my personal shield," the Master said. "You have the option of coming—or going." It nodded toward the edge of the saucer. Flint saw there could be no bargaining. A Master simply did not give way to a Slave—or any other creature.

Flint swung his half-closed hand at the creature's head, hard. The contact felt as though he had smashed every bone in that hand, but mere pain could not abate the force of his blow. The Master's head caved in like a structure of woven grass.

The saucer veered again. Flint grabbed the corpse, receiving no pain input this time; the creature's death had deactivated the shield, fortunately. He jerked it up and out of the well and threw it overboard. Then he lowered his own feet into the hole. They barely fit, for his torso was larger than that of the Master, and constructed differently.

There were knobs and pedals down there, inconveniently placed. Flint had no idea how they worked, but he experimented rapidly. Suddenly the saucer flipped over, redoubling its acceleration toward the ground. This was no Earth-type shuttle-capsule strung on a safe wire; this was a free ship, and any hesitation or mistake could quickly smash him flat. Flint clung to his perch and wiggled his toes, searching for the right combination of controls.

The saucer braked, looped, and headed down again, almost hurling him out. But Flint was catching on. There were a dozen foot controls, each with a wide range of positions. One was for the orientation of the craft, another was for velocity, a third for elevation. Just as he was about to intercept the ground at half-mach, he slowed the vehicle and brought it to a wobbly hover. Then he lifted it and started it back toward the spot where ¢le should be.

He spotted her easily, running through the field toward the distant hills. Sensible girl! He came down as low as he dared—for he was a long way from achieving precise orientation—and bobbed along behind her. "Hey, ¢le of Ath!" he called.

Startled, she glanced behind. "Φro!" she cried, amazed. "How did you resist capture?"

"Never mind," he called. "Get up here! We're going to the hills in style!"

The FreeSlaves were astounded. "You killed a Master?" they kept asking, refusing to quite believe it.

"Once again, lightly," Flint repeated. "I am an envoy from Sphere Sol, neighbor to Sphere Canopus, transferred to this body. I killed the Master and took over the saucer so as to make contact with you. ¢le of Ath helped me. If you organize, revolt, take over this planet, spread the revolution throughout this Sphere, throw out the Masters, you shall have the secret of transfer."

"Yes!" ¢le breathed. "That's what A[th] lacked. "Transfer!"

But the FreeSlaves only stood about uncertainly. They were a motley crew, ill clothed and ill fed. The Slaves of the plantation not only looked healthier, they seemed happier.

Flint saw it wouldn't work. These were not human beings; centuries of ruthless selection had bred out the backbone of this species. They could no more revolt successfully than the domestic animals of Sphere Sol could. Some might run amuck when prodded too far, but that was a far cry from organized, disciplined revolution. No wonder they were called FreeSlaves; they were just that. Slaves without Masters.

₵le was as disappointed as he was. "I wish you'd come to A[th] a century ago," she said to him.

The FreeSlave leader appeared. He had evidently held back, lost in the crowd, listening to Flint's story before committing himself. The attitude of the FreeSlaves changed, becoming more disciplined. Perhaps there was hope after all!

"I am T%x of D)(d," the leader said, omitting the Slave intonation. Yes, a man of power! "You tell an interesting story, and you bring an excellent piece of equipment. But it proves only that you are *here*—not that you are with us. I do not believe you could not have captured this vehicle by yourselves; the Masters gave it to you, and sent you here as spies to subvert our group."

"That's a lie!" Flint snapped. But he saw that the FreeSlaves didn't believe him. T%x had provided a believable rationale, and it gave them confidence.

"We shall make you tell the truth before we kill you," T%x said. He produced a punishment-box, no doubt stolen from the Masters.

"That won't work," ₵le said. "ɸro was put under eleven-pain for three days and didn't crack. And he *is* telling the truth; I believe him. No Slave could do the things he did!"

"No genuine Slave," T%x replied. "But a spy dealing with cooperative Masters and faked pain—"

"ɸffal!" she spat derisively, employing the baton sinister.

T%x grabbed her by the shoulder. "You're a pretty one!" he exclaimed. "I'll take you for my harem!"

She kicked him in the groin, which was fully humanoid. The blow was glancing, but it infuriated him. Flint took a step toward them, but was barred by the spears of a score of FreeSlaves.

"We'll torture her first!" T%x cried. "What's her number?"

Two men grabbed ₵le and read the number off her

shoulder. T%x laboriously set the box. Then he turned the dial.

₵le stiffened. The box was operative, all right.

"Now," T%x said grimly. "Talk, spy. Why are you working for the Masters?"

"I'm not working for the—" she cried, but was choked off by six-level pain.

"Stop it!" Flint said. "I can prove my origin. I can tell you all about—"

"We'll get to you soon enough," T%x said. "Now, girl spy, who are your other accomplices?"

"I have none! I'm a loyal A[th]—"

This time the pain was nine, held too long. ₵le writhed on the ground, her face grotesque in agony, her well-shaped legs spreading far apart, their muscles quivering. Someone chuckled evilly.

Flint grabbed a spear from the nearest FreeSlave and used it to knock the man down. This was a weapon he was expert with, in any body! He charged T%x. But the others piled on him in a mass and crushed him down, holding him helpless.

"One more time, spy," T%x said to ₵le. It was evident that the sight of her agony had excited him. He was a sadist, sexually stimulated by the infliction of pain. Which meant there would be no mercy in him. "What is the Masters' plan?"

₵le caught her breath and wiped the mud her spittle had formed from her face. "I don't know anything about—" she said. And leaped for T%x.

But the pain caught her in midair. Twelve.

Red froth bubbled from her mouth as she fell. Flint had never seen such an expression of total agony. Her entire body jerked and shook, her wide-open eyes scraped through the dirt unblinking, and she soiled herself involuntarily. The watching FreeSlaves burst into laughter.

"Turn it off!" Flint bawled. "I'll tell you anything you want!"

But T%x did not turn it off. He watched, fascinated, while the thing that had been ₵le shuddered and twisted.

Abruptly she stopped. Her features relaxed, as though she were sleeping, just as the broken-armed $mg of Y⇑jr had relaxed. "T%x," one of the FreeSlaves said nervously, "I think she's—"

"Dead," T%x said, turning off the box. "Serves the spy right." He was breathing hard.

But ¢le wasn't dead. Her body still breathed.

T%x turned the dial up again, experimentally, seeing whether he could get another kick out of the victim. There was no response. "Strange . . ." he muttered.

"Mindless!" the FreeSlave said, awed. "You killed her mind!"

T%x considered, startled. "All right," he said. "That's even better. Put her in my cave. I can still use her, and she won't be any trouble now." He turned to Flint. "Give me his number."

Flint realized that this depraved creature would torture and kill for the pleasure of it; the information he sought was merely an excuse. The Master in the saucer had been a better creature, an enemy but no sadist, and not stupid.

Saucers appeared in the sky—eight or nine of them. The FreeSlaves started to run in terror. Pain-beams cut them down, herding them back to the center. Cattle!

Flint made a break for his saucer. He scrambled over the rim and jammed his feet into the well, striking the lift pedal.

Nothing happened.

"Your carrier has been deactivated," a pleasant Master's voice said from a speaker in the saucer. "Remain where you are."

Flint hauled himself out and dived for the edge—and into an invisible pain-field. He crumpled. There was no way to resist that flesh-permeating agony; his muscles stiffened involuntarily and prevented controlled action.

The pain diminished. "Remain where you are," the voice repeated gently.

Now Flint could fight it, for the level was only one or two. But the moment he moved, it shot up to eight or ten. He got the message. He was captive.

"I am B:::1," the Master interrogator said. "According to your statement to the runaways, you are an agent of Sphere Sol, our galactic neighbor. Were you sent to foment rebellion among the Slave population?"

"Eat your own eggs," Flint said.

"I presume that is intended to be derogatory," B:::1 said mildly. "We do not react to the remarks of Slaves—but if you are from another Sphere, you are a special case, not subject to our customs. Since you took the life of one of our number, the latter status would be advantageous for you."

Flint did not answer.

"We have drugs," the Master said. "They are effective in making any Slave tell all he knows. But if you are *not* a Slave it would be bad form to use them on you. We do not want trouble with our neighbors, and we do not seek a quarrel with Sphere Sol. We ask only to be left alone."

Flint had expected to be tortured. This approach perplexed him. What was his proper course?

"Perhaps you have been influenced by the fact that the Slaves are humanoid, as we understand are the masters of Sphere Sol," B:::1 continued reasonably. "But you have now observed that the Slaves are not *civilized*. Before we assumed control, their history was wastefully violent. They were breeding themselves into planetary famine, and rapidly exhausting their irreplaceable resources, such as fossil fuels. Pollution disease was taking hideous toll of their health. They did not precede us into space because they were too busy warring with each other while despoiling their environment with seemingly suicidal determination. We brought lasting peace and health to the Slave populace by providing the sensible control and moderation they lacked. Otherwise they might well be extinct by now, or reduced to truly barbaric levels. Your true affinity as a member of a Spherical sapient species is with *us*, the civilized, regardless of the accident of physical form."

The problem was, it was true. The FreeSlaves were ignorant brutes, and not merely because of recent breeding. The Masters, in contrast, had treated Flint with a certain diffident courtesy despite his insults to them. They were—adult.

"Why did you not inform the Slaves of your mission at the outset?" B:::1 asked. "I refer to those of the plantation."

"I *tried*. They wouldn't listen." Then Flint jumped. "You bastard! You tricked me into admitting it!"

"It is obvious that you are not a Slave. Your entire manner betrays it. Since we know that through an error Øro of N*kr was subjected to unconscionable punishment, the sensible explanation is that his mind was destroyed and his body taken over by an alien. We know such things are possible; it has happened in the past."

"You're pretty smart," Flint said grudgingly. He decided not to mention Qiw of V⁰ps, the Slave foreman.

Why place a good man in jeopardy? "The Slaves simply would not believe me—any of them."

"That is because they are ignorant," B:::1 said, his mandibles making a little click of understanding. "To them, transfer is superstition, possession by demonic influence. But you could have reached us immediately."

"I could?" Flint asked, surprised. He had abandoned any pretense; he *did* have to deal with these Masters. This was what he had been sent here for.

"Verify it with your body's memory."

Flint checked . . . and discovered what had been there all the time: any Slave could petition for an interview with any Master, anytime. Such a petition was invariably granted, and the circumstance of the complaint promptly and thoroughly investigated. Justice was rigorous—within the framework of the system. The Slaves *did* have rights, zealously protected by the Masters themselves.

He could have made his petition, even on the punishment rack, and had the complete and personal attention of a responsible Master within an hour. His mission would have been completed had he really wanted to accomplish it that way. But he had preferred to fight, and to seek the humanoid Slaves.

What did he want—the elevation of brutes like T%x? That would hardly save the galaxy! He had been a fool, allowing superficial appearances and subjective feelings to interfere with his mission. He would not make that mistake again!

"I am Flint of Outworld," he said formally. "Sphere Sol, as you surmised. I have come to give you the secret of transfer."

"We do not desire transfer," B:::1 said without even a pause.

This set Flint back. "We are not demanding payment. We want you to have it. I'll explain why."

B:::1 made a little flutter of his wing-cloak, signifying comprehension and negation. "Transfer would disrupt our system. A Slave economy functions best when identity is irrevocably fixed in its original body. If it became possible for Masters and Slaves to exchange bodies, even briefly, it would evoke disastrous unrest."

Flint pondered. He did not understand the intricacies of politics or economics, but was sure this Master did.

"More than your system is at stake," Flint said. "The entire galaxy is in peril."

"That well may be. But the moment we begin to interfere with our neighbor Spheres, we become subject to interference from *them*. Since we do not desire this, we choose to minimize this possibility by keeping to ourselves."

"Even if you are all destroyed—Masters and Slaves together?"

"We must exist according to our dictates—even at such a risk."

Flint shook his head in an un-Slavelike gesture. He didn't know what to say, not having anticipated such a response. Yet he *should* have foreseen this, for now he recognized the same pattern shown by the Master of the saucer, who had died rather than yield even a fraction of his self-determination. "Well, I certainly can't force you. I'd better go home."

"Excellent. We shall construct a transfer unit to send you back, then destroy it. I think your government will understand."

Flint remembered the Council of Ministers of Imperial Earth. Yes, they were just the kind of fatheads to understand an attitude such as this!

Three Master technicians discussed the matter with him. They were intelligent, and quickly grasped the principles of what he was saying better than he himself did. He spouted incomprehensible formulas, the gift of his eidetic memory, and they shuddered with delight, admiring the sheer beauty of the logic. First he covered the Kirlian aura, and they modified their equipment to pick this up.

"As you can see," Flint said, "most entities have auras of a certain standard intensity. Some have stronger fields . . . and here is mine." He stepped into the sensing chamber. Their dial registered to one hundred, but the indicator jammed at the top. They were suitably impressed.

"Now you have to modify one of your matter transmitters to fix only on this aura—which is tricky, because it completely permeates the body," Flint said. "Here are the formulas. . . ."

But it was not so easy after all. The Masters used a different kind of transmitter—one that could ship larger amounts more economically, but was quite limited in range. Ten light-years was the maximum; five was the average. They traversed their Sphere by a series of hops from system to system, and had the routes so well organized that their Sphere suffered much less Fringe-regression than the human Sphere did. But the technology of their mattermitters was quite different from Sol's.

Since transfer was a refinement of mattermission, Flint's information was not applicable. A mattermission expert who understood the formulas of transfer adaptation could have adapted to the situation, but Flint was a Stone Age primitive with only rote information—set for the wrong equipment. It would take the Masters months or even years to iron out the wrinkles.

So Flint could not, after all, provide them with the secret of transfer. And he could not go home—not by mattermission.

"We shall take care of you," B:::1 said with insectoid cheer. "Perhaps within a decade or two some other Sphere will contact us, and you will be able to depart."

Small comfort, and the Masters obviously neither expected nor wanted such contact. "In a few months—maybe less—it will be immaterial," Flint explained. "My Kirlian aura is fading, day by day. In a few months I will be no more than a—a Slave!"

"There will always be a place in the burl plantations for you," the Master said consolingly.

"Thanks." Nothing like near-mindless drudgery, enforced by the punishment-box! And not even a pretty Cle to share it with.

That reminded him. "₵le—₵le of Ath—what happened to her?"

"Do not concern yourself about her," B:::1 said.

"But I *am* concerned. She helped me, she resisted torture. They thought she was one of your spies—"

"So she was."

Flint stared, but could not read the alien countenance. Yet why should the Master bother to lie?

"We hoped she would find her way to more formidable FreeSlave resistance," B:::1 explained. "There is a constant pilfering, minor disruption, firing of the crops. But all we got was T%x of D)(d and his ragged band. If she learned anything more, it is lost. Her mind was set to self-destruct before she betrayed her mission."

So she had not had the chance to betray ₵iw. Flint had, realistically, changed sides—but he was disinclined to turn in the Slave who had been sincere, clever, and courageous. "I'd like to see her," he said.

The Master made a negligent gesture with one thin black appendage. "She is in the Slave infirmary. You have freedom of this complex; we know you now. I suggest that you do not go outside."

"I am a prisoner?"

"No. It is merely that those outside would mistake you for a Slave."

Clear enough! "Maybe someone could escort me. To the infirmary—and back."

B:::1 made a little twitch of assent. "Go to the Slave service station."

It was evident that the Masters regarded him as akin to Slaves, despite their overt courtesy. Well, nothing he could do about it; he had failed his mission through no fault of the Masters. He went.

Slaves were not permitted to enter the Masters' domicile, but were summoned to the Slave station next to it. It was understood that no Master would deign to escort a creature resembling a Slave to a Slave function. A responsible Slave would be assigned the task.

The responsible Slave was there. "Φiw!" Flint exclaimed. "Φiw of V°ps!"

The foreman was as surprised to see him. "Φro of N*kr! You are free?"

"It's a long story. I am not what I seem."

They walked slowly toward the infirmary. "You seemed like a rebel," Φiw said. "Or an alien. I did my best to prevent your escape."

"The girl was an agent of the Masters. I am now working with them."

Φiw was well disciplined, but he was unable to conceal his agitation. "Then they know—"

"The Masters know you did your best to prevent our escape. The girl might have had another opinion, but she perished before making her report. Since I killed a mounted Master, it was evident that you, a mere Slave, could not have restrained me." Even if he had tried. . . .

Φiw was silent. Flint had reassured him, obliquely, but it was obvious that the Masters had hardly been fooled. Why else had they summoned this particular Slave from the field to perform this particular chore?

Φle was lying on a bunk in an isolated cell. Flint felt a terrible pity for her. Double agent or not, she had been nice to know, and she had died cruelly. "May I go in?"

"She has no mind," ȹiw reminded him. "She cannot be revived."

"I know. Still. . . ." Flint could not express what he really wanted, as he did not himself know. He felt the way he did at the death service of a friend: awed, useless, feeling a great loss yet unable to do anything to alleviate it. Grief. Yet a kind of perverse relief that he himself had not died—this time.

ȹiw, indifferent, touched the lock in an intricate pattern, and the gate slid open. Flint entered. ȹiw remained outside, perhaps in deference to the dead, and the gate closed between them. It occurred to Flint that he was a prisoner now, locked in—but the matter was academic. No prison was more confining than nontransfer.

He looked down at the breathing form, trying to tell whether she was awake or sleeping. But the mindless state made it irrelevant; she would never wake again. Maybe she was better off than he. . . .

He felt compelled to touch her. It was to a large extent his fault that this had happened to her. She was extraordinarily pretty, and had deserved better. Even though a spy, she had showed a lot of spirit.

"₵le . . ." he murmured as his hand met her flesh.

And he felt the intimate shock of her potent Kirlian aura.

₵le sat up suddenly. Her arms whipped around his neck, curling tight. She was hugging him!

No—she was *choking* him! Bemused at this seeming vengeance from the grave, and fazed by the remarkable interaction of their auras—for hers was as strong as his! —Flint nevertheless responded automatically. He took her two small wrists in his hands and ripped them away. Her weaker feminine muscles could not compete with his.

He held her before him. "If this is mindlessness, I'd hate to see you whole!" he said.

"What are you doing?" ȹiw demanded. "Put her down! It is profane to maul the dead!" He thought Flint had initiated the action.

₵le's foot came up to strike his groin, but Flint had indulged in hand-to-hand combat before, with male and female. Her muscle tension warned him; he twisted aside and threw her back on the bunk.

Pain caught him. He stiffened against the gate. ȹiw

had set the punishment-box for his number and activated it. "The dead are sacred," Øiw said grimly.

"She's *un*dead!" Flint gasped. The pain was set at about three—enough to be effective, but not so as to incapacitate him completely. Øiw had good judgment. "Look at her!"

Indeed she was undead. ¢le had already bounced off the bunk to come at him again. He was paralyzed with pain. She took hold of him and threw him to the floor in what he recognized as an expert combat technique. Then she applied a blood strangle to his neck, her fingers digging for the major artery. But she didn't quite have it.

Flint's pain cut off. The gate slid open and Øiw bounded in. He hauled ¢le off and applied a nerve grip of his own. In a moment she was unconscious. This verified Flint's prior suspicion: Øiw knew how to fight very well. He had been clumsy by design.

Flint sat up, rubbing his neck. "You know, you might have been better off if you had let her kill me—then killed her yourself. Unfortunate accident of timing."

Øiw met his gaze. "You aliens think all Slaves are stupid—and worse, that the Masters are. The Masters know what I did; they do not punish me because it would accomplish nothing. They know I will never again attempt disloyalty. They are just, and I have learned. Were they to accuse me openly, they would have to punish me, and that would cost me status among Slaves and decrease my effectiveness."

Flint nodded. "I have learned, too." Master and Slave—they understood each other. He had been foolish to try to interfere.

They carried ¢le to the border of the Master's domicile. B:::1 appeared. "This is strange," he remarked after hearing of ¢le's violence.

"It seems you were mistaken about her mindlessness," Flint said.

"We were not mistaken. Bring her to the examination room."

Øiw held back. "Sir, I may not enter—"

B:::1 turned his faceted gaze upon the Slave. "You may do what I tell you to do." Flint recognized this as a forceful rebuke. The Master's word was law!

Øiw bowed his head, acknowledging. He had, at any

rate, erred in the right direction. Then he picked Ȼle up and carried her into the building.

Flint followed thoughtfully. So the Masters were not hidebound about their own rules.

At the examination room the technician tested the girl's Kirlian aura. The indicator rose to the top of the scale.

"Another transferee," B:::1 said. "You are fortunate."

"But she tried to kill me!" Flint protested. "If Ꝗiw hadn't acted—"

"This is what is strange," the Master agreed.

Ȼle stirred. Her eyes opened.

"Alien, there is a pain inducer attuned to your body," B:::1 said to her. "Do not attempt any aggression." He turned to Flint. "Question her."

Yes indeed! "Who are you?" Flint demanded.

"I came—to seek you," Ȼle said.

"You're from Sphere Sol?"

"From Sol, yes."

Flint shook his head. "I didn't know they were transferring another envoy!"

"It is a common enough procedure," B:::1 assured him. "A backup agent sent without the knowledge of the first. The first cannot betray what he does not know, yet the second is available to help in case of adversity. We employ similar safeguards."

Flint realized he had been naive. He didn't like it. "Then why did she attack me? I was true to my mission."

"I did not know you," Ȼle explained. "I found myself imprisoned, and you touched my body. I—mistook your intent."

After that magic contact of Kirlian auras? Some misunderstanding!

"An understandable error," B:::1 said. "But the question of her intent can be removed by her performance in transfer technology."

Smart, smart! "You *are* primed with transfer information—that differs from mine?" Flint asked her.

She hesitated. "Yes."

"Go with the technicians," B:::1 said.

One of the Masters handed the punishment-box to Ꝗiw; such tasks were normally delegated to Slaves. But B:::1 made an unobtrusive gesture, and the other Master took the box back and departed with the girl. Ꝗiw, left with no specific task, stood awkwardly where he was. He was obviously extremely uncomfortable, here in the Masters' sanctum.

B:::1 turned to Flint. "Analysis of the female's pattern reveals substantial differences from your own," he said, reading a printout one of the technicians had given him. "Almost as though she were not only a different individual, but of a different species. We do not question your own motive—but we are less certain of hers."

Sharp! The Masters had not put any dummy in charge of alien operations! It had not even occurred to Flint to have the specific Kirlian pattern analyzed. "Maybe she *is* an alien," Flint said. "I thought there was no Kirlian aura above ninety-eight in Sphere Sol—but we are in contact with the Polarians and others informally. If one of those Spheres helped. . . ."

"Perhaps so. Ninety-eight is within the margin of error for our equipment. I did not mean to cause you undue concern."

"The major error in your equipment is in not being able to measure higher than a hundred," Flint said. "I am able to judge relative strengths of Kirlian auras, crudely—and this one seems parallel to my own. Close to two hundred. So I doubt she's human."

"We merely look out for your welfare so that there will be no reason for any future contact between our Spheres—or between ours and any of your allied Spheres."

"I appreciate that," Flint said dryly.

B:::1 turned to Øiw. "Your comment."

"Master, I trust him, not her," Øiw said. "She attacked him without sufficient provocation. Keep her within range of the box."

"Would your opinion be influenced by the fact that the female, Ȼle of Ath, was one our agents, possessing information deleterious to your own welfare? There can be no carryover of personality; however, the present entity would have complete access to Ȼle's memories and talents."

Øiw considered the loaded question. "Perhaps that influenced me. I know little of these matters, sir."

"Yet, compensating for that aspect, you would not see fit to trust her as you trust this man of Sol? Both are transferees."

"That is correct, sir." Øiw's discomfort was not abating. "Øro acted in an ethical manner; the female attempted to kill him. Perhaps she was confused—but she did not *seem* confused at the time."

B:::1 turned to Flint. "In this matter we are as Slaves, glimpsing portents whose wider significance we do not comprehend. Hence the opinion of a Slave has relevance. It is possible that the possessed ₵le cooperates only because of the punishment-box, and will turn against you when given opportunity. It is also possible that she is indeed of Sol or allied to Sol, and suspects that we have tortured you to gain your compliance with our own designs. We leave the decision of her disposition in your hands; we do not wish to become involved in Spherical intrigues."

"Ship her back to Sol with me," Flint said. "If her original body is human, that is the only place she can go." Then he reconsidered. "No—ship her one day later. I will have a thorough investigation made. If she is false, we will be ready for her when she arrives."

"If she is not of your Sphere, where will she arrive?" the Master inquired.

Flint shrugged. "If she has no host-body available in our Sphere, she probably won't transmit at all. There has to be somewhere to go, or the process doesn't work. So if she does not transfer when you attempt to send her, you'll know she's no friend of ours."

"Your Sphere would not then object if we interrogated her?"

Flint knew it would be an extremely thorough interrogation. "We would not object."

B:::1 faced Øiw. "We have acquainted you with private matters of galactic scope. Return to your position, suffering no further stricture than this: If ever you overhear anything relating to this subject, make immediate report to me."

"Master," Øiw said, relieved.

Flint nodded thoughtfully. This was Øiw's true penance. He was now in effect a spy for the Masters. Yet the assignment had been couched in such manner as to make it seem that the Slave had been promoted to the level of political counselor. No torture, not even any overt reprimand—yet a thorough job had been done. This was supreme skill in management.

After the Slave departed, B:::1 said: "In view of this development, and our uncertainty of decision, we feel we can no longer maintain our prior policy of disengagement. We shall participate in your coalition."

Flint's jaw dropped in a purely human reaction. "Because Sol sent another transfer agent, you've changed your minds?"

"One such visit is an anomaly. Two suggest a pattern. Were we certain that both emanate from Sphere Sol, we would not be concerned. But we cannot ignore the possibility that a third, possibly inimical Sphere has chosen to participate, perhaps competitively. There may well be others, in an expanding effort. We therefore choose to control to some extent the manner of our interaction with other Spheres by officially committing ourselves to this effort. We shall make a thorough search of our region of space in quest of aliens. Thus it will not be necessary for any other Spheres to seek us out to urge participation."

Just like that, success! Flint did not delude himself that any special competence on his part had been responsible. The Masters of Canopus had seen the way to cut their losses and maintain much of their isolation, so they had acted. Flint had blundered his way into it.

He did not belong in this business; if he ever transferred from Sphere Sol again, the odds were against his success or even survival. What a comedy of accident! At least he had discovered his inadequacy in a nonfatal fashion.

The end was routine. ₵le's knowledge sufficed; the technicians were able to convert the Canopian matter-mitter for transfer, invoking fairly minor but critical modifications of detail. The settings were arranged for the center of Sphere Sol. ₵le was held under guard with the punishment-box, scheduled for later transfer.

Flint stepped into the transfer chamber.

4

Lake of Dreams

notice initial mission destroy 200 intensity threat entity failed

—detail?—

own agent 200 intensity dispatched contact made owing to suspicions of natives of canopus unable to eliminate sol transferee necessary to provide transfer information to sphere canopus in order to

—WHAT?!—

to protect identity of agent origin and allay suspicion per directive judgment call on part of operative we intercepted agent at time of retransfer from canopus

—judgment call? more likely operative stunned by allure of equivalent aura and lost imperative for mission what sex agent?—

female

—precisely and target entity male route her through spot reorientation to ensure next time duty before pleasure and reassign for next available intercept unfortunate we have to work through these high-kirlian types never can be quite certain of their loyalties—

POWER

—CIVILIZATION—

Flint hopped rapidly over the surface of Luna, Planet Earth's huge moon, putting the mining station at Posidonius Crater behind him. The hopper's single plunger smacked into the bleak surface of the crater floor, compressing like a pogo stick, then thrusting him upward in a broad arc. He was only a fraction of his normal weight because of the reduced gravity, but the old-fashioned heavy-duty mining suit was twice his mass. The net result was a jumping weight of about two-thirds his nude-body normal. He needed the powered hopper to make real progress.

He bore west, searching out the gap in the crater wall. The station was inside a subcrater within Posidonius, capped over and pressurized. Nature had excavated the pit; now men used it as convenient access to the high concentrations of aluminum, titanium, magnesium, silicon, and iron there. It had cost a lot, a century or three ago, to emplace the first Lunar mines; they had paid their way many times over. Posidonius Mine was about worked out, as were most of the digs of this quadrant, and in fact the moon itself, but as long as the diminishing ores were worth more than the cost of operation, the mines continued to function. Today the planet Mercury of Sol and the larger moons of the outer Solar System—Ganymede, Titan, and Triton—were more important resources. Luna was largely forgotten.

Security was slack, which was why Flint had been able to pose as an itinerant miner and steal a suit and hopper to make a much better chase of it. By the time Imperial Earth traced him this far, he would be impossible to trace further. The Lunar surface was so pocked with the marks of other hoppers—and each mark was permanent the instant made, since there was no weather, no air to erase it—that his trail was not discernible. Once he got beyond the crater, beyond direct visual range, he would be lost. Bless that jagged rim!

He made it. The crater itself was fifty to seventy-five miles in diameter, depending on which way it was measured, and the mine was off-center, so he had about twenty miles to go. The hopper enabled him to do it in just about an hour without getting winded. Time enough; his next on-shift would not be for another two hours.

The crater rim, so fragile-looking from telescopic distance, was actually a phenomenal mountain ring several miles thick, though not tall. It had been formed millions or even billions of years ago by the impact of a large meteor, the material of the crater center scooped out and dumped in that circle. Not volcanic; there was very little volcanic activity on the moon. Here at the western pass the wall was broken, and he navigated the rubble without difficulty. It was against Sphere law to deface the visible landscape of Luna, but anonymous miners had blasted out an ascending channel at the narrowest part to facilitate passage from the central depression. It was too small to show up on most photographs taken from Earth, so no investigation had been made. Anyway, that had been in the heyday of the mine, when metals worth millions of Sphere dollars had been extracted every few hours. Miners were tough, ornery men and women; even the Imperium tended to let them alone, as long as they produced. The profession of mining, freed from the cave-ins and black-lung threats of ancient times, had become the stuff of adolescent fancy. Miners were heroes, prized and well paid and bold, and planet lubbers sought them avidly.

Now he emerged onto the broad *Mare Serenitatis,* the Sea of Serenity, an expanse of almost-level rock some four hundred miles across. The early Solarians, staring at their great moon from the vantage of misty Earth, had pictured these lava plains (here in the *mare* there had been volcanism!) as oceans and seas and bays, and named them accordingly. The illusion had been banished when Luna was physically explored, and perhaps even before then, but the intriguing names had remained. "Hope I don't get my feet wet," Flint muttered. His suit radio was turned off, of course; he would be a fool to let them trace him through his broadcast emissions.

His feet did not get wet, though the hopper made little splashes in the dust that disappeared almost instantly. With no air to hold the substance up, it collapsed without billowing. On the apex of each glide he could see over the Serpentine Wrinkle Ridge, an arm of which approached quite close to the rim of Posidonius. Had he been able to bound high enough, he might have been able to see all the way across the western edge of the Sea of Serenity to where its vast crater wall parted to give access to the even vaster *Mare Imbrium,* the Sea of Rains. His line of sight would give him a glimpse of one of that sea's craters, probably Archimedes. Flint had studied, and therefore had an exact visual memory of, the map of the adjacent geography of Luna—but this would be a narrow line-of-sight view between the encroaching mountain ranges of the Caucasus to the north and the Apennines to the south. Mountains on Earth were named after these—or maybe it was the other way around. There were three craters in that vicinity, so he couldn't be quite certain which one he would see from five hundred miles away. It really didn't matter, since the tight curvature of the moon put the whole area out of sight and he was not going there anyway.

He veered north, changing direction by shifting his weight to make the hopper lean. He skirted Posidonius, now shielded from observation by its rim. Ahead of him was *Lacus Somniorum,* the Lake of Dreams. Primitive that he was, he loved that imagery. *Flint* had dreams—of escape, of freedom, of eventual return to Outworld and his green darling Honeybloom. Pnotl of Sphere Knyfh, that alien transferee from the inner galaxy, had dazzled him into undertaking the mission, but in Sphere Canopus reality had caught up with fancy. He had encountered no high-Kirlian natives there, and had suffered torture and the constant threat of death. The one high-Kirlian entity he had met had turned out to be another transferee. He was unfit for this type of work; the edge was off. He hadn't even been able to complete his mission; the girl transferee had had to bail him out. Let *her* initiate the next mission! The Imps would not search for him long; they would know his suit-air could last no more than a day, so could assume he had perished. There was nothing like dying to avoid being pestered.

But he was not the suicidal type. He had a destination in mind, barely three hundred miles to the north. Burg Crater—where an abandoned mine shaft still had leftover stores of oxygen, water, and food. It was one of a number of craters within reach. By the time they checked them all—if they ever did—he would be gone again. They had little chance to catch up with him.

It was a fair distance. Even with the hopper it would take him about fifteen hours. He had picked a site near the limit of his range—but not *too* near it—so as to make it that more difficult for them to locate him quickly. But the marvels of the Lunar landscape soon palled. He was traversing a dull, seemingly endless plain, in the confined silence of his suit.

He remembered more of the bits of information the Shaman had given him. Flint had supposed they were mere stories, intended for entertainment or for dealing with immediate needs, such as the hunting of dinosaurs, but now he understood their true relevance.

Before mattermission, Earth had been in desperate need of new sources of supply and living room for its horrendously teeming population. Lifeship colonization had been inadequate and too expensive. So they had tried desperate measures, such as colonization of near space. The first settlers went to Luna, drawing most of the construction substance from its crust. Then space itself was claimed, drawing on what was there: the particles of rock and ice in orbit, the planetoids. It was much easier to collect materials from there than to bring them up out of Earth's gravitational well, and a number of the orbiting rocks were big enough to become homes themselves.

Gardens were planted, within shells of air, rotating slowly so that the light of the sun struck them half of every day, Earth-time. That same rotation provided gravity via centrifugal force. Flint had never really understood that concept when the Shaman explained it, but his recent experience on the space shuttle from Earth to Luna had brought it into sharp focus, along with a spot of "spin sickness." The rotation provided weight in a small craft, but the head was nearer to the center than the feet, and so became slightly lighter. The body reacted to this imbalance by becoming uncomfortably ill. Flint had never been ill before in his life, and it was a horrendous experience. So he had learned about practical centrifugal gravity the hard way. *Knowing* and *comprehending* were different things! Flint had known much, understood little. But he was mastering his background knowledge now, right down into his gut.

The Ministers of Imperial Earth had relied too much on his presumed naiveté, falling into the trap of supposing that ignorance equated with stupidity, though they knew better. (No one was immune from the know-comprehend dichotomy!) They had given him cram courses in the most advanced technology of the galaxy—that of mattermission and transfer—by relying heavily on his eidetic memory. He could now repeat paragraphs of complex formulas whose meaning he would never understand. He could now read—just enough to get by. In conversation he sounded like a highly educated ignoramus, which he was. But they had also trained him in multiple combat and escape techniques . . . and never supposed he might employ these more practical skills against them. It had been child's play to escape the Ministry of Alien Spheres, buy a black-market tourist's pass, switch places with a disgruntled miner on furlough, and land at Posidonius Mine.

One transfer experience sufficed; he was going back home to Honeybloom. The only mountains and depressions he cared to explore hereafter were hers. All he had to do was figure out a way to get mattermitted back.

That might take some figuring. It would cost about two trillion dollars postage to jump from Earth to Outworld. But he would have time to mull over that challenge, here on the moon. There had to be *some* way available to a bright primitive. . . .

The barren landscape continued. It was dusk here, with his long sharp shadow extending to the east, leaping far away as he went high, zooming back to meet him as he landed. The shadow was always barely in time for the bounce. Would it ever miscalculate, play it too close, and miss the connection? Flint smiled, half-believing it could happen. Nothing was perfect!

He was well north of Posidonius Crater now, in the Lake of Dreams. Two hundred miles to the east the curve of Luna's surface shrouded the craters in darkness. He had progressed north of small Crater Daniell, coming up parallel to Crater Grove. He could see these only when he was high; the horizon was so much closer than that of Outworld, Earth, or the Canopian slave planet, because Luna was so much smaller. On the other hand there was no atmosphere to cloud vision. But he "saw" as much by means of the picture in his mind as with his eyes. His photographic mental image merged with the reality, greatly extending his perception. As, perhaps, his Kirlian aura extended his perception of life.

He kept going, hour after hour. As a Paleolithic hunter he had developed endurance—but never before had he *hopped* the whole distance. The machine provided the thrust, but the little balancing mechanisms of his body were becoming fatigued. Now he was approaching the ill-defined depressions of Plana and Mason—old, worn craters, perhaps, though what was there to wear them down? On the map they lay together with their center nipples like the breasts of a woman, but there was no such resemblance now. He was through the Lake of Dreams, traversing rougher surface. His imagination had ceased to conjure fun-visions of Outworld and Honeybloom, and not even these twin circles could bring them back with any force. Fatigue diminished the enthusiasm of dreams.

His hopper gave a despairing half-thrust, and failed. It was out of power.

Flint came to rest in the crater of Plana, aware that he was in trouble. The hoppers were supposed to be kept fully charged between uses, but they were old machines, not as efficient as when new. This one had taken him about 260 miles, which might have been enough had he been able to proceed directly north from the station. But his jog to the west to get out of Posidonius, and necessary deviations around roughness in the terrain, had left him with still around fifty miles to go.

Well, he would walk it. He had to; there was no other way, and no closer respite, now. It would enable him to use different muscles, anyway.

Flint progressed vigorously, achieving a kind of running, jumping stride that carried him bounding forward at a speed of six to eight miles per hour. He was light, even with the suit, and strong, but the arms and legs of this thing were not adequately flexible for this, and they chafed.

He continued for an hour, crossing out of Plana and into the great doughnut-shaped plain of *Lacus Mortis*, the Lake of Death. Burg was in the center of it, a small crater compared to its neighbors Hercules and Atlas to the east, and Aristoteles and Eudoxus to the west. Oh, he had his mental map right before him, brilliantly clear as if illuminated by the slowly setting sun. Farther to the north was the large, long *Mare Frigoris*, the Sea of Cold. All he had to do was proceed from this point on that map to that point. So easy to *know*, so hard to *do*.

He plowed on, his speed slowing as he tired. His elbows and knees were raw from constant abrasion against the rigid joints of the suit. His air tasted bad, though he should still have several hours' margin—unless it, like the hopper, no longer performed at the original specs. Suit failure—that was all he needed now!

Strange yet fitting, how he had started in such nicely named terrain: the Sea of Serenity, the Lake of Dreams. Now that he was in trouble, the dream was turning to nightmare, the Lake of Death. What would have happened had he gone east toward the Sea of Crises, or west to the Ocean of Storms? Better south to the Sea of Tranquillity and Sea of Nectar!

But repeating the sweet names could not extract him from the grim reality. There was no longer any doubt: his air was turning foul, and he had not covered half the distance to the station since the hopper failed. He could not even see Burg Crater yet. His presumed demise was about to become an actuality.

And was that so bad? Better to die than be a slave!

Someone in Sphere Sol's past had said that. Maybe his hope of escape had been as illusory as the lovely moonscape names. Reality was this darkening airless void.

He fell. His faceplate nudged into moondust, the support straps about his head holding his face clear of the lens. It was not an uncomfortable position. He was prone now, resting—yet panting. The air could no longer sustain him. He had no strength to get up; his vital energy was being drained, as the energy of the galaxy was being drained by the Andromedans. At some point the loss of force from the strong interaction of the local atomic nuclei would diminish their cohesion, and matter as this galaxy knew it would cease to exist.

Those Ministers of Imperial Earth were not such bad sorts. They were only trying to do their job. They didn't like working with a Stone Age man, but they did it graciously. And the Masters of Canopus, slavedrivers yet sensible, reversing their eons-long policy of Spherical isolation, to help save the common galaxy. They had set their dream of privacy aside.

That female who had followed him to Canopus—who was she? The Minister of Alien Spheres had claimed to have sent no other agent there, and had affected great surprise at this part of Flint's report. But Flint knew they had a woman with a Kirlian aura intensity near a hundred, and they were surely using her somewhere. So they had to be concealing something from him, and he didn't like that. Too bad he'd never get to meet her, to find out the truth. Could she have transferred on her own, somehow, sensing his need? But she had tried to kill him at first! So she must be from some unknown enemy Sphere. Yet she had an aura very like his own; she was *his kind*. . . .

And his kind would soon be minus one, for here he was, perishing in weakness like one diseased. Not spinsick, but moonstruck.

"Oh, hell!" he muttered. "I'm not cut out to die like this! Not in gasping foulness. I've got to fight, to make it swift and clean, like an honest spearthrust. Those damned Andromedans . . ."

He turned on his suit radio. "Okay—vacation's over—come and get me," he said clearly just before he passed out.

5

Ear of Wheat

notice   kirlian transfer sphere sol to sphere spica 200 intensity

—that's what we've been waiting for   redispatch agent—

POWER

—CIVILIZATION—

As before, the transition was instant and painless. Flint found himself inhaling water—but not choking. He was in a sea, flushing the liquid out through gills in his shoulder region, though he lacked shoulders.

All right. His transfer identity always seemed basically human. Always these two times, at least. A man in a scuba-diving outfit would have as much to get used to as this. He was sure of that; knowing that the Sphere Spica Imperial Planet was waterbound, the Ministers had had him trained in scuba, just in case. For a man who had never seen an ocean prior to his first Earth visit, it had been quite an experience.

He flexed his arms and legs and found they were flippers. Excellent for swimming, not as good for manipulating objects. But they did have terminal digits. Man in deep-sea swimming gear: yes, the image would do.

"Bopek recovers!" a voice said, very close and clear in the liquid medium. Water was just great for transmitting sound.

"Swim, Bopek!" other voices urged. "Restore your system."

Flint swam. His powerful flipper arms and legs threshed the water and propelled him forward handsomely. Fresh water passed through his system, revitalizing it. It was a nice body, in a nice environment. There was some pain, however, and he turned his eyes on the affected part to investigate. It was easy to see—his eyes were on extensible stalks, highly flexible, able to look anywhere quickly.

His body was bulbous, balloonlike, and somewhat nebulous. He seemed to have no skin, no well-defined outer boundary; instead he thinned into a frothy fadeout. His breath was more than respiration, and his gills less than solid. He took in water through his mouth, then pumped it through his entire system and finally out in fine bubbles. This carried oxygen and nourishment into his system and carried wastes out. It seemed a reasonably simple, efficient, comfortable arrangement—as long as the water was fresh. A man in scuba gear, like one in a spacesuit on the moon, could die in an unfresh medium. . . .

But of course the human on Earth used air in a similar fashion. All people breathed from a common pool, and passed many of their wastes back into it. Plants and bacteria renewed it constantly—as they did for the water environment here. So this was a perfectly comprehensible system, not like a confined suit at all.

But part of him had been crushed. The normal froth-pattern was abnormally irregular and discolored, and much of the mass had suffered where the nutrient flow had been too long interrupted. The seawater was like blood; when it stopped passing through, the tissues perished. Too gross an interruption, and regeneration became impossible.

The body had been injured severely enough to cause the loss of its Kirlian aura: spiritual extinction. But Flint's far more intense aura had animated it, restoring it to life. What was fatal to an aura of intensity one was survivable to an aura of intensity two hundred.

Now he had a body and an identity. But after his experience as a transferee in the slave Sphere, he was cautious about advertising it. First he would ascertain the nature of this society, and of his place in it. Then he would make his contact—directly, properly, without dangerous missteps.

He explored his new mind. Its content was not immediately clear to him, but he wasn't worried. It was bound to be a serviceable mind, because of the nature of transfer.

Though Flint had the symbology of transfer memorized, his comprehension of its actual mechanism was vague. It was instantaneous, like mattermission. A subject could be "beamed" to a specific locale, generally a planet in a Sphere. But there was no receiving station; instead there had to be a host with which the arriving Kirlian aura could associate. There was no problem about getting lost or landing in an unsuitable body; if there were no appropriate mind in the target region, the aura bounced, reanimating its original body. There were other qualifications, having to do with the aura's notion of what was suitable; the potential host had to be sapient and of the same sex. Why this was so was not clear; there was a great deal the Solarian technologists did not yet know. But transfer worked; that was what counted.

So Flint knew he had a sapient, male body he could make function. But as before, he had to work at physical coordination, and to concentrate in order to isolate specific memories, while the language process was largely automatic. He swam some more, while he pieced it together. Swimming enhanced his alertness by providing greater flow of water through his system.

He was Bopek, an Impact. He was a courier. There were three groups of sapient Spicans, all waterdwellers: the Impacts, the Undulants, and the Sibilants. This was an Impact zone. As courier he had to convey Undulants from the Undulant zone through the Neutral Corridor to the Undulant enclave.

Did that make sense? Flint visualized it as a world of swimming dogs, cats, and mice, three of the animals who had helped man colonize Outworld. He was a dog conducting a cat past the mice warren to the cat enclave. Not exact, but helpful for orienting. It was important—and here a confusing complex of alarms sprouted from his host's memories and experience—to keep the three types separate except on special occasions. Any *two* could associate freely, in any numbers, but never all three types. Apparently cats did not eat mice except in the presence of dogs, and dogs did not chase cats unless mice were watching.

Right now there was a big construction project in the Impact (dog) zone, that required the cooperation of Sibilants (mice). So the Sibilants had been granted temporary access. But one portion of the project had to be done in cooperation with Undulants (cats). Since they could not enter the mixed zone, a special courier channel excluding all the others had been defined. But as only a native Impact was familiar with the home zone, all visitors had to be guided lest they stray.

Yes, it was coming clear, though this was about as much of the Spican system as he cared to assimilate at the moment. His host had been escorting an Undulant, avoiding contact with Sibilants. But he had made an error, or been misguided, and taken her through a destruct area. A portion of the demolition structure had collapsed, crushing them both. Such a collapse was slower in water than in air, and swimming entities could move quickly when they had to, so they had been able to avoid complete annihilation. But the shock and violence had been too much. The Kirlian auras had dissipated, leaving functioning but soulless bodies. Flint's projected Kirlian aura had animated the empty Impact, while the Undulant—

What had happened to her? She had been an exceptionally well-formed specimen of her type, a veritable queen of felines, a tigress.

He swam back to inquire.

His companion Impacts had broadened the Neutral Corridor into a temporary Undulant enclave. Llyana the Undulant remained unconscious, inanimate; they could not revive her, though her body lived.

No question about it. She, like his host, had been deprived of her Kirlian soul. But no alien had been waiting to animate her vacant body. She was effectively dead.

Too bad. It was an unfortunate waste of an excellent specimen. Looking at her, Flint/Bopek reviewed the ideal criteria for the Undulant species, and found that Llyana was to Undulants as Honeybloom was to women. She had the same eyestalks and nebulous body he did, but lacked his stout flippers. Her mass was similar, but proportioned differently: she was long and sinuous, propelling herself by means of fishlike or snakelike ripples of her entire torso. In addition, while he and the other Impacts were basically horizontal, somewhat like the swimming turtles of Earth's seas, Llyana was vertical, being flattened on the sides like most fish. Some Undulants were too long and thin, others too stout; Llyana was just right.

Flint realized with an internal chuckle of self-directed

humor that not so long ago he would have been appalled at the mere contemplation of such a creature, and would have considered the notion of a beautiful Undulant as sick humor. It was amazing how a mere change of body and brain altered esthetic perception.

Llyana, too, had damaged tissues. The other Impacts were forcing a flow of water through her mouth, setting up a suitable current with their flippers, keeping her technical life processes functioning. They assumed, reasonably enough for them, that if he had recovered, she would also. But of course Bopek had *not* recovered; he had been reanimated by an alien spirit: Flint.

The medic team arrived. "Conduct her down the Neutral Corridor to the Undulant enclave," the ranking Impact directed. He spoke, as did all sapients here, by vibrating an internal fin against a ribbed surface; the sound emerged from his mouth, but had nothing to do with his respiration.

"You to the Impact infirmary," the leader said to Flint. "You are motile, but have sustained similar physical injury. We must be sure you are fit for service."

One did not argue with a ranking member of one's kind. Flint stroked for the region his memory said was the infirmary. It turned out to be a building; a semifloating structure anchored to the depths by a stout braid. The braid was symbolic of the three elements of sapience: Impact, Undulant, and Sibilant. He paddled into the emergency bay and let the medics apply foam-salve. It was a marvelous relief; he had not realized how much he had been hurting.

"Now take it easy," the medic warned. "This stuff is excellent, but it has a certain intoxicating effect in some individuals. You'll need to rest for a cycle or two."

"Thanks." Flint paddled off.

He not only felt better, he felt good. He swooped through the pleasantly cool water, turned over and glided, eyestalks down. He had not noticed the scenery before, but now he could relax and enjoy it.

There were many sources of light in the water. Much was from the plankton, tiny creatures who grubbed nutriment from materials in the water and were in turn digested by larger creatures, including the sapients. The colors of the plankton varied with individual species, and an entity lacking a particular element of nutrition became increasingly attuned to the color of the plankton possessing that element. Thus feeding was a continual and ever-varied experience, satisfying the eye as well as the body. At the moment, all colors looked delicious to Flint, a warning of his condition he did not heed.

He dove down. Most fish on Earth possessed gas-filled sacs or bladders that provided buoyancy but inhibited rapid changes of depth. His present body was more sophisticated; he was able to compress or expand it considerably, so that he could dive without effort or discomfort, and rise again as easily. As he approached the nether margin of the sea, he spied the turrets of the anchored animals. They floated in the currents, their long thin tails descending to the ocean floor. They had intricate combs and networks of tubes through which they strained the water, and they too were of many colors. Flowers of the floor. Some made pleasant noises to attract the sea insects that pollinated them. But these were primitive forms; the advanced life was invariably triple-sexed.

Flint drifted upward, savoring the experience. He had never imagined sea living could be so blissful. He saw the hanging discoloration signifying the fringe of the Impact zone. Lower creatures could pass through it freely, but he knew he should turn back. But he felt like exploring! He was a courier; he had a right to tour out of bounds, didn't he?

On through the Sibilant boundary. What fun! The thrill of seeing unfamiliar territory added to his satisfaction. He could cruise indefinitely!

Then he spied something special ahead. It was a pair of entities, an Undulant and a Sibilant. Of course—the Undulants were working in the Sibilant zone this period, just as the Sibilants were working in the Impact zone. So long as the three types never came together in the same place at the same time, no problem.

So why did he experience this heightening, secret, almost obscene excitement?

The Sibilant had the same nebulous torso and eyestalks as the others, but it lacked both flippers and vertical flattening. It propelled itself forward by jetting water from its main body tube. This action was accompanied by a gentle susurration that gave the entity its name. It was capable of considerable speed through the water, and especially rapid starts.

But that was of no immediate concern to Flint. The

moment he spied the pair of creatures, something changed in him. He felt a guilty but powerful attraction. He shot forward on a collision course. If only they didn't see him too soon!

He was successful; by the time the others became aware of him, it was too late. He collided.

There was only a slight impact. His body did not shove theirs over; it merely overlapped theirs. Part of his flesh intersected that of the Sibilant, and part of it interacted with that of the Undulant. Their substance was so diffuse that it merged with his to make a solid-seeming cross-section.

This state of partial merging was tremendously exciting and compulsive. He now had a firm hold on each of the other entities, not with his flippers but with the actual flesh of his body. Diagrammatically, it looked like this, with Flint the center entity.

He gathered his strength and heaved. As his body flexed at the edges it thinned at the center, drawing them in closer to each other. Then he flexed outward, taking in more of their substance, extending his overlap, experiencing a phenomenal satisfaction in the process.

By a series of pulses he brought the Sibilant and the Undulant into contact with each other—within his own flesh. Now their efforts joined his, so that the pulses became more powerful. The effort became transcendentally important. Flint gathered his resources, tightened his grip on each of the others, and threw his entire strength into a convulsive contraction that hauled both entities all the way into his flesh and into each others' flesh. The process was both painful and fantastically rewarding. In fact it was orgasmic.

Orgasm. . . .

Flint's first transfer had set a pattern. He knew he was in an alien body, but it was much like knowing he was a man; it was *right.* He still thought of himself as human. His alien sensation translated so readily into the human equivalents that he was hardly conscious of it after the first moments. Intellectually, he kept noticing details and comparing them with his other embodiments, but that was much the way a man compared one world to another. While everything was changed, he was still fundamentally a man. Here in the Spican locale he had had a more stringent adaptation, to a swimming form—but he was still basically a swimming *man*. And the Undulant he had escorted was a swimming woman. Or he could think of it as a dog, cat, mouse system. Different, yet still basically comprehensible.

Now he was caught up in something beyond his prior experience. It could not be translated into human or animal terms.

It was sex—with three sexes.

His body, prompted by instinct, continued its heroic efforts, forcing a complete melding of masses. No, not complete; each individual had a private portion that did not overlap, and two segments of overlap with the others, and a minority segment of double overlap:

The individual portion was liquid, almost gaseous in its diffusion; the single overlaps were viscous; and the double overlap was virtually solid.

The three entities were penetrating each other—but not as a man penetrated a woman. Not even as a two-man/one-woman trio. They were *inter*penetrating.

Flint could not rationalize this into any human act. It was genuinely alien. Not perverted so much as inconceivable.

The concept sundered his rationale. He could no longer think of himself as a visiting human; he was immersed in an alien scheme.

Flint lost his sanity. He saw himself as two irreconcilable entities: one human, the other monster. A man's mind could not exist in the carcass of a jellyfish. This was a prison worse than the most gruesome sickness. He had to get out!

But he was trapped. Transfer of personality, once completed, could not be revoked. He could go home only by being retransferred, and that meant first completing his mission.

The host body went on with its repulsive act, generating its obscene pleasure. The animated pornography engulfed him within its horror. He reacted violently, with utter revulsion. With his whole force of being, he drove off the intolerable connection.

The globular mass exploded apart. Flint experienced a tearing sensation that was at once painful and climactically fulfilling. The two other creatures shot out from him, like a double arrow loosed from a bow, still linked with each other. But the moment they cleared his flesh, they underwent a subexplosion so violent that the overlapping portions of them were not parted but were torn loose as a separate mass.

Flint, feeling only relief at being free, paddled rapidly away from the carnage. He didn't care what happened to the others; he had to shield himself from the disgust of the experience.

Yet he couldn't. The act had been fundamentally shocking—but after the fact came comprehension, and that was even worse. Suddenly he understood the plight of a girl on Outworld who had been hurt and terrified by being raped—but then came to realize that she carried her attacker's baby, and would have to bear it and raise it, forever after a reminder of the experience. Illegitimacy was a cardinal social offense on Outworld. Flint, like other men, had shrugged and said "Too bad," and not given the girl's plight much further thought, and of course had been careful neither to help her nor support her in any way. The rapist had been from another tribe, and had later been killed by a dinosaur, so that ended the matter. Then the girl had killed herself, to Flint's amazement. He had volunteered for the burial detail—really, the Shaman had made him do it—carrying her body out to the place of exposure and leaving it there for the vulture-dactyls and other predators who would do the job of cleaning the flesh from the bones. He had gazed at her nude body, still quite pretty, since she was young and the pregnancy was not far advanced, and marveled that she should have been so foolish as to sacrifice her life when fate had already revenged her. Several days later he had come to collect the bones for burial under her sleeping place, so that her spirit would be at rest. Even her bones had been shapely, and very nice in their pure whiteness, except for a couple that had been cracked open by some larger predator for their marrow. He had tied those together so that her ghost would not be crippled, and he had interred the whole in a curled-up position under her lean-to. Everything had been done according to form—yet she had not rested. For months thereafter her lean-to had been haunted by her restless spirit, and finally the village had had to relocate. It had been a nuisance. Flint had shaken his head at the foolishness of girls. The Shaman had declined to explain it, though he had seemed sad. But now, faced with the growing realization of what he had just participated in, Flint understood why the tribesgirl had acted as she did.

Actually, the star Spica (a double star, as befitted Flint's notion of fitness, his home star, Etamin, being similar) was part of the constellation Virgo, as seen from Earth. There were many legends about this maiden, said by some to be the original harvest goddess; but since Flint's tribe had not advanced to the level of agriculture, being Paleolithic rather than Neolithic, he identified more with the constellation's identity as Erigone the Early Born. Erigone's father was Icarius, and when he died she hanged herself in grief—another curious feminine reaction that Flint suddenly appreciated. Tribesmen seldom lived to the age of forty on Outworld; if they lived long enough to see their children safely married, there was little cause for grief when they died. Their job, after all, was done. Flint's own parents had died before he was ten Solarian years, and that had been unfortunate, but the Shaman had taken him over and given him a better life than he had had before. Certainly no cause for suicide. But now he saw that for those who felt really strongly about another person or thing, the loss of such a value could evoke a reaction as strong as to require death. The maiden Erigone, patroness of the wheat field, had gone to heaven with an ear of wheat in her hand, and that ear of wheat was the star Spica. Perhaps the story of the death of her father was a euphemism; actually she might have been raped, and here was the evidence in the form of a planet of rape.

But how much worse for a man! A pretty girl was made to be impregnated by one means or another, but any such suggestion for a man was an abomination. He tried to put the horrendous concept out of his mind; he did not *want* to comprehend it. He tried to shove this debased body away from him, as he would the gore of a slain animal's ruptured intestine, knowing it was impossible, yet still making the effort, just as the pregnant girl must have tried to shove out her hateful baby.

orientation effected

What? A strange voice was talking in his brain. Not his *head,* for he had no head—that was part of the problem!—but his brain, integrated with his lateral line system, his pressure perceptors, balance organs, density control, and mergence response syndrome. Somewhere, in this mélange of suddenly realized synapses and feedbacks was an alien communication.

He tried to focus on the alien. Here was possible escape! What he was able to grasp was a picture of three spheres. Two were tangent, touching each other; the third was a little apart. The first was labeled SIRE, the second PARENT, and the separate one CATALYST. What did it mean?

—dispatch agent this time she'd better perform!—

There was that alien voice again. It spoke in an unfamiliar language or series of meaning-symbols that somehow he could understand. The picture, too, was becoming clear: each circle represented a Spican entity. Three entities, three functions—but which was which? Each time he concentrated, it seemed there was a different alignment. Impact, Undulant, Sibilant . . . sire, parent, catalyst . . . dog, cat, mouse. At times an Impact was a dog and at other times a cat or even a mouse. Dog mating with cat and giving birth to mouse? No, that wasn't it.

Yet he had *done* it! Why couldn't he *understand* it?

Because, as with human reproduction, it functioned best when there was no understanding, just instinct. Understanding brought complications such as birth control, and nature didn't like that.

Abruptly he realized that the spheres or circles were from his host's memory of a long-ago orientation session that had had a profound, even unnerving effect. It had been a sex-education class, pornographic in its implications yet necessary. What was pornography anyway, but the portrayal of the necessary with too much enthusiasm? "Why are the three sexes kept always apart?" immature Bopek had asked persistently, so they had told him. And shocked him. As Flint had been shocked, the first time he saw a grown tribesman put it to a girl. She had cried and kicked her legs, and Flint had thought he was killing her. But she had only been wounded, and not seriously; there was only a bit of blood between her legs. And she had been presented thereafter as a woman, her initiation complete, though her breasts were hardly developed. Within a Sol-year she had been married, happily; it was evident that she had not been harmed. That had been Flint's own sex-education class, in the direct Stone Age manner. It had been alarming at first, but reassuring when time showed there were no bad consequences. Next year he had laughed when younger children flinched at the annual demonstration, and the following year he had come of age by making the demonstration himself. But when he took up with Honeybloom he had preferred privacy. Demonstration classes were one thing; love was another. So he understood Bopek's horror and gradual acceptance. That was the way of it.

He summoned another picture. In this one the three spheres had come together, each touching at the fringe, like the borders of stellar empires. Perhaps this was an analogy; when Sphere Sol had exchanged technology with Sphere Antares (though Sol had been only a system then, for it was the mattermission secret it obtained from Antares that enabled it to form its interstellar colonization program)—had it been a form of mating? Cultural intercourse. It was not an objectionable parallel. Yet young Bopek had thrilled to a guilty excitement. Three sexes touching! His very flesh had pulsed.

And so did Flint's, remembering that pornography:

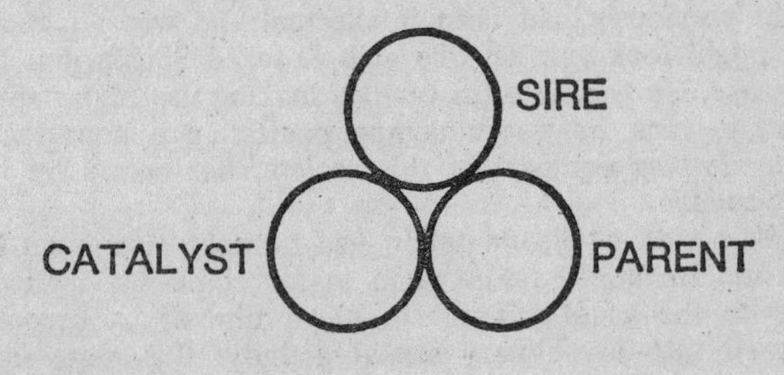

POWER

—CIVILIZATION—

"Get out of my mind!" he yelled at the meaning-bursts. Now, where was he? Cat—sire—dog . . . no, not cat, but catalyst. Forget the Earth animals, concentrate on the lesson material.

Nowhere else were the three entities depicted together, actually touching. Now Flint applied his own memories, and merged them with Bopek's—and it started to become clear. The human equivalent—there was no precise parallel, but as close as he could make it, and he *had* to find some kind of parallel, in order to regain his orientation—was a fragrant soft bed of flowerferns in a private glade, bearing a naked, spreadeagled voluptuous girl being kissed by a naked, tumescent man. The curve-sided triangle between the three tangent circles matched the pubic triangles of hair—the two triangles about to be superimposed. And now they drew together, overlapping, forming the single mass he had visualized before. Raw sex, without question. Secret, lewdly exciting, sniggers, repression, desire, unspeakable urges, interpenetrating—

: : CONCURRENCE : :

"Fush!" Flint cried aloud, expressing in that one distorted syllable the exact superimposition of lust and condemnation and fascination and outrage he felt, balked by the interfering meaning transmission. No better syllable existed, since his present body was unable to render the human word.

In moments he was back in the security of the Impact zone. Now, as the excitement of revulsion and discovery abated, his identification with his host-body returned. Once again he was Flint—in alien circumstances, and with a matured awareness and acceptance and cynicism, but indubitably himself. Now he grasped emotionally what previously had been intellectual: he was an alien. He might look and act like a three-sexed Spican, but he was *not*. He was an alien essence making use of a native host; in fact, he was a demon possessing a poor local boy. He was not part of this society, not bound by its conventions.

His period of disorientation had brought him much to ponder. He hoped never again to forget his basic alienness to the host, and not to allow himself to become trapped into involuntary sexual activity. But more important: his Kirlian aura, temporarily extended from the host in its vain effort to separate, had somehow ranged out and intercepted some kind of message in the transfer medium. At first that had been confusing—but Flint, however naive he might be about Spican sex life, was no fool. One of the tools at his command was an efficient mode of integrating information. His disorientation now separated into three elements that could be analyzed: his repudiation of the act of his host body, the reproductive lesson material from the host memory, and this alien transmission. His revulsion was out of line: He was not Spican, the Spican was not human, and there could be no transfer of morality either way. It was important that he understand, accept, and perhaps even use this distinction. For his job was not to preserve himself or spread Sol Sphere culture, but to enlist other Spheres in the cause of saving the galaxy.

Yet evidently there was a Sphere that opposed this cause. They had traced his transfer to Canopus and sent an agent there, not to help him but to kill him. She had failed, and had had to turn about and help him, ironically, in order to protect the secret of her identity. The alien voices in his brain had indicated she was to be sent to the Ear of Wheat.

And he had a fair idea whose host-body she would occupy.

He had to act quickly, for the agent was deadly. She knew transfer technology, so could return to her Sphere after dispatching him. She probably didn't even have to educate the Spicans; her knowledge was so sophisticated that she just might be able to make do on her own. Or maybe her government was able to recall her without a transfer unit at this end. He should not gamble with it. He had to nullify her first, and return to Sphere Sol with the news. Maybe the Minister of Alien Spheres would know which Sphere it was, from the hints Flint had picked up; or maybe Flint could transfer to Knyfh Sphere and consult with their experts. One thing was certain: The galactic allies had to locate that enemy Sphere and neutralize it, or the whole effort would be sabotaged before it ever touched Andromeda.

Could he somehow trap and interrogate the alien agent? Flint rejected that immediately. He lacked the expertise, and it was too risky here. Better to nullify the agent, return to Imperial Earth, and let them send a party to deal with the agent. Or have her shipped to Sol Sphere with him—no, he had tried that before, and she had somehow slipped the net. He could not trust her to transfer again. Play it safe; give her no chance to foul him up.

Yet he retained an image of Cle of Ath of Sphere Canopus, a pretty little thing in humanoid terms. The host-body was not the transfer mind, of course, and he could not judge the nature of the entity that had possessed her, yet it was hard to disengage the two entirely. Body *did* make a difference; he had to admit to himself that he would not have loved Honeybloom had she been ugly. And that powerful Kirlian aura of the other Sphere entity, as strong as his own; alluring. He had begun traveling to other Spheres partly to find his own level of aura, after all. Enemy she might be, but he did not want to kill her. Not yet.

Two Impacts spied him and swam up. "Bopek—a charge of rape has been lodged against you," one said. "You will accompany us to the hearing."

"Rape?" Flint was stunned. "I never—"

"Did you not depart the Impact zone without authorization and enter the Sibilant zone?"

Oh-oh. Violation of the zones was a serious matter, as he would have known had he bothered to check his host's memory. He had been careless. Better to admit the truth. "I was under the influence of the healing salve—"

"And there you encroached on a Sibilant/Undulant pair and assumed the role of catalyst, forcing on them involuntary mergence?"

"I did not realize—"

"And as a result of that union, a Sibilant offspring was created, forcing unanticipated parentage on the original Sibilant?"

Flint realized that he was in trouble. Ignorant of the mating system of this species, and intoxicated by the salve, he had not taken time to explore the cultural restrictions stored within his brain. The whole matter had seemed complex and irrelevant to his mission. Now it was clear: Mating was a three-entity affair, impossible with two, compulsive the moment a third appeared. The third served as a catalyst, forcing the other two to mate immediately. Like the game of scissors-paper-stone, which he had played as a child on Outworld though no real scissors or paper existed there, the order of the matchings determined the outcome. Scissors cut paper, paper wrapped stone, and stone crushed scissors. So the sex of the catalyst determined the sex of the offspring—but the offspring did not match the catalyst. Hence the intricate zone system, in which visitors of only one sex were permitted at a time. The game could not be played unless all three were present.

Since major construction required the talents of all three types, some subzones had been instituted, and couriers brought otherwise unauthorized Undulants through the Impact zone to that subzone without encountering any Sibilants. When Bopek had danced into the Sibilant zone, he had trespassed in much the way a strange male trespasses when he enters a harem. He had thus encountered a Sibilant with an Undulant visitor, and had become the catalyst, forcing involuntary mergence. That, by this culture's definition, was rape.

He was guilty.

But he could not linger for the trial and penalty. The foreign Sphere agent might already be here, and he had to nullify her before she got oriented and nullified *him*. His mission came before the niceties of Spican etiquette.

"Fellows, I apologize," he said.

Whereupon he invoked the most disgusting crime of which a Spican sapient was capable. He "fushed" them. He visualized them as a Sibilant and an Undulant, himself as a catalyst, and puffed out his bodily perimeter to intersect theirs. He overlapped them both, then contracted, hauling them together inside his flesh.

The act was appalling. Only in the filthiest of jokes was it even conceivable. A wave of intense revulsion almost overwhelmed the mind of his host. This was despicable homosexual rape! But Flint, desperate and rendered cynical by his recent experience, forced the two to intersect each other. Then he expelled them violently, firing them through the water, linked to each other.

Both Impacts were unconscious, overcome by sheer shock and horror. And Flint was now guilty of a capital offense. His Impact brain urged immediate penance in the form of suicide. But he had already suffered his readjustment, his impairment of sanity. The sense of separation he had achieved during his prior sexual encounter shielded him. He hated himself, but he swam on.

Now he was near his original awakening spot, guided by Bopek's unerring directional/distance sense. And the injured Undulant was still there, in the temporary subzone, swimming uncertainly. He was in time—probably because her sudden awakening must have canceled their plans to remove her from the area.

This would be tricky, but he had to risk it. He swam up boldly. "I see my client has revived. Good work! I must now convey the Undulant to the assigned construction site."

The others had not yet received news of his crime spree. Relieved of responsibility, they turned the Undulant over to him.

The Undulant accompanied him without protest, as he had been sure she would. The mind of the recent transferee was still orienting, still trying to assimilate the complexities of this Spican scheme. He had to keep that mind distracted until he could nullify her.

But first he had to make quite sure that she was his enemy agent, and not the real Undulant. So he touched her.

There was the powerful aura, equivalent to his own. "So you know me already," she said. "You are aware of my mission."

"You tried to kill me, there in the Keel of the Ship," he replied. "If need be, I shall counter you with love, here in the Ear of Wheat."

"Ear of Wheat?" she inquired, perplexed. "Love?" She was confused but also playing for time, until she could ascertain the best way to kill him. But he had the advantage of prior experience in this realm.

"I'll explain about the wheat," he said as they swam. With one part of his mind he noted how smoothly she moved, despite her injury. Did the Kirlian aura of a lovely creature seek out a lovely host, or did the animation enhance the host? Twice she had been beautiful; it could be coincidence. "My species began to be civilized when it mastered wheat. Wheat is a grain, the seed of a grass, a type of plant. You have plants on your home planet?"

"Yes," she said. "But not wheat."

"This grain is nutritious and it keeps well. It enabled my ancestors, who were more civilized than I am, to store food over the barren winter months. They ground it up between stones and cooked it into masses of substance called bread. This reliable supply of good food greatly increased their survival capacity. In fact, we call it the Neolithic Revolution, the great progress of the New Stone Age. They had to learn to weave baskets to store the grain, and had to make records to dispense it fairly, and this led to many other skills. Eventually it resulted in complete modern civilization." How glibly he reiterated the Shaman's discourse on the subject! The Paleolithic Flint himself had little affinity for such concepts. But it was one of the bits of knowledge that was becoming clear as he perceived the astonishing manifestations of advanced civilization. "Wheat was so important that man even placed it in the sky. The system of Spica is called the Ear of Wheat, held in the hand of the Virgin. It covers her bare bottom, for she is evidently modest. But the relevance of wheat to Spica is even more pertinent."

"Its pertinence eludes me," she said. She was willing to talk, for she too was stalling for time, thinking him a fool. Last time they had met, she had tried to kill him violently; this time she was being more cautious, but her objective was the same.

"Consider the mode of reproduction of wheat," Flint continued blithely. If his plan worked, he could nullify her harmlessly. He didn't *want* to kill the entity possessing such an aura! "There are male and female elements, the pistils and the stamens. But they do not reproduce directly. There must be the intercession of a third element, to bring the pollen to its proper place. This is the wind. It carries the pollen from one plant to another. Without it, the wheat would not reproduce. Some other plants use insects as the third agent. The wind or the bee may be considered a catalyst, enabling the act to occur. It promotes reproduction, though of itself it may be sexless." Now they were approaching the Impact zone boundary. Beyond it was the Sibilant zone: forbidden territory. But thanks to his distractive discourse, Llyana did not yet realize this.

"Now the Spicans actually have three sexes," Flint continued, guiding her on through the veil. "They are interchangeable, after their fashion. The third sex is always the catalyst, initiating the act without being affected by it, like the wind or the bee. The other two sexes become the sire and the parent, depending on the order in which they meet. This is complicated to explain. Perhaps it is simplest to identify the pattern by means of the catalyst. If the catalyst is an Impact, the offspring will be a Sibilant. If the catalyst is an Undulant, the offspring will be an Impact. And if the catalyst is a Sibilant—"

And now, of course, they encountered a Sibilant, for

this was the Sibilant zone. It saw them and tried to take evasive action, but Flint zeroed in on it, bringing Llyana along, forcing an encroachment within the critical range. Like a man suddenly confronted with an act of human copulation in progress, the Sibilant had a reaction. But in this case voyeurism was not sufficient; it had to participate. Because this was the nature of this species; proximity was courtship and consummation.

The Sibilant turned about and closed on them. Llyana did not yet realize the danger; Flint's explanation, despite its accuracy, had prevented her from exploring the practical aspect of her host's knowledge. He had not told her the whole truth, just as some humans fail to tell their children the whole truth.

For the Sibilant was the third entity, the separate one, the catalyst. Position, not sex, determined the roles of the three participants in any sexual encounter. Since the approaching mergence was involuntary—at least on Llyana's part—this was technical rape. But the investigation would show that the Impact and the Undulant were intruders in the Sibilant zone, exonerating the Sibilant. Flint, as Bopek the courier, had to have known this. Therefore *he* was the true rapist—again.

Now the compulsion of propinquity was upon the Sibilant. Like a buck winding a doe in heat, it jetted right into contact, extending its substance to interact with that of Flint and Llyana. *Now* she realized something was happening. "You are overlapping!" she exclaimed, exactly like a woman goosed in a crowd, indignant but not wanting to call too much attention to her complaint. She tried to move away—but could not.

The throes of mergence were upon them. Stimulated by the envelopment of the catalyst—as if it were a cup of fermented honey, or a soft bed of fragrant foliage, or a lovely nubile nude girl—Flint proceeded to what was natural.

Llyana was a beautiful creature, literally. Her torso was as sleek yet rounded as any he had experienced, and her perimeter was delightfully permeable. She was formed to be permeated, penetrated, suffused, and as the ineffable environment of the catalyst brought them together he did all these things with her. Her potent aura enhanced the effect. He thought of Honeybloom as his flesh sank deeply through hers, and the whole of his being expanded with instant love. This was not after all so different from human mating; in fact it was better, for the presence of the catalyzing entity guaranteed a perfect union. There would be no last-minute hitches, no frustrating feminine changes of mind, no awkwardnesses of mechanical copulation. And the volume of interaction was so much greater; the whole body was involved, not merely one small organ. Like a perfect program, it scored—every time.

Llyana was struggling. "This—this—I am being violated!" she protested. "Who *are* you? What are you doing?"

"I am Sissix the Sibilant," the catalyst replied. "Let the inquest show that I did not seek this union. Nevertheless, I do not protest it; you are both handsome specimens." Actually, the catalyst had little reason to protest; catalysm was as close to completely free pleasure as this world provided. The parent was responsible for the offspring, and the sire gave up a healthy chunk of his flesh; the catalyst experienced the same triple orgasm, but without penalty. The Spican sentient's traditional view of heaven was a warm ocean filled with pairs of the other two sexes, so that the individual could travel from pair to pair in perpetual catalysis. Unremitting ecstasy!

"Your motions only enhance the interaction," Flint told Llyana, knowing this was like telling the victim of ongoing rape not to struggle.

"This—this is *mating*!" she screamed, shocked. Her message came through her body as much as her vocal apparatus, for they were now overlapping each other's nervous systems.

Flint had never before felt such extreme pleasure. In the human body, the joys and pains of various experiences were actually self-generated. No actual transfer of sensation occurred, merely external stimulus. But here there was the enveloping joy of literal mergence, of becoming one with one's species. Sissix and Llyana pooled their nervous impulses with Flint's to make a symphonic unity of amazing depth and intensity. Before, when Flint had been the inadvertent catalyst, he had been too revolted by the concept to appreciate the pleasure; now he relished it.

"And what a mating!" Sissix agreed. "No wonder you two sought a catalyst! I have never partaken of such a powerful union before. By pure chance, I am a participant in a greater experience than I ever could have initiated deliberately."

Still Llyana protested. "I am not your kind! This is an abomination!"

And there it was: her open confession of alien status. With that unguarded admission in the presence of a witness (actually so much more than a witness, for this verification occurred on the complete range of apperception, not just sight), Flint had the key. Overlapped as he was, he could read it directly from her own system and force further testimony. His defense against the charge of rape would hinge on his own identity as an envoy from Sphere Sol, and Llyana's identity as—who?

"You are . . . an agent of an inimical system, from far, far away, beyond Sphere Knyfh . . . no, in another direction," he repeated, picking it out despite the almost overwhelming urge to complete the procreative act. "Your home Sphere is—"

"No! No!" she screamed, every nerve jangling with a current that only increased his pleasure to the bursting point. "Three different species . . . miscegenation!"

What an experience humans missed, unable to draw directly from their lovers' systems. To experience their mates' orgasms; in fact, to mate the orgasms themselves, fashioning a pyramid of rapture impossible to any single entity.

"What an experience!" Sissix agreed, picking up part of that impulse. "I feel as though I'm careening through the vastness of an infinite ocean, seeing clusters of glowfish—"

"That is deep space," Flint informed it. "Those glows are stars. We are aliens from distant Spheres."

"Noooo!" Llyana reverberated. But she could no longer hide it; her own nervous system, so powerfully animated by her intense Kirlian aura, betrayed her. The two strong auras were the real source of the enhancement the Sibilant felt; because it was actually sharing their aura-imbued systems, it was for the moment an enhanced entity. Yes, it would definitely be able to testify as to the alien nature of its mergence companions.

Flint had experienced orgasm before. Now he knew that no mating of his with Honeybloom could approach the enchantment of one with this alien. Because Honeybloom had a Kirlian aura of about one, or average: a washout as far as interaction with his own aura went. Llyana/Cle's aura was about two hundred, matching his own. There was simply no way to beat that. Interpenetration of extremely intense auras, combined with the physical and emotional rapture of sexual mergence. . . .

Then Llyana got smart—and Flint was able to appreciate

how intelligent and disciplined she was, again because his nerves were hers. She concealed her origin and purpose by throwing herself into the mergence with full force.

And the climax was upon them. They drew together until the three were a tight, rock-hard ball, with only small portions remaining discrete, and there was appalling pressure. The urgency of completion was so great it seemed that their very substance would sunder.

And it did. Rapture became rupture. The ferocity of the explosion was soul-shattering. Impelled by the atomic nucleus of their triple overlay, they smashed out in three directions. There was an instant of exquisite pain as a gross chunk of flesh was ripped out of his body; then Flint was rushing through the water, incomplete yet completed.

He agreed with the Sibilant: what an experience!

Ordinarily the three participants of a union separated after climax, allowing their explosive impetus to carry them far from each other. Flint as the sire and Llyana as the parent had lost portions of their mass, and needed time to heal and regain full size. Both had already suffered from the accident that had made the hosts available, so recuperation was critical. Sissix, as catalyst, had escaped without loss, of course. If Flint chanced into another mergence as anything but catalyst, he would lose yet another portion of himself, and that could be disastrous. So he had to be careful, and to get out of the Sibilant zone as soon as possible. He understood now that these zones were not merely prudery, but necessary to the survival of the species. Uncontrolled matings could be fatal!

Nevertheless, he swam around to follow Llyana. It was a risk, but a necessary one. He had to be sure he had nullified her.

He found her, undulating along with an infant of her kind. The little creature was scarcely formed, and was technically a neuter, but recognizable by its lack of flippers or propulsion jet. Babies had to be sexless, or they would be inadvertently caught up into mergences and not survive into maturity. Like humans, they developed when they were ready.

"Well, happy motherhood," Flint said.

She spun on him, coiling like a snake. Undulants had more supple bodies than Impacts, and could bend more readily. In the absence of a catalyst she had no further specific sex appeal, but she remained an esthetic specimen. "Schlish!" she exclaimed.

He chuckled as well as the alien vocal apparatus permitted. "You can't swear in Spican. There is no equivalence here, and the phonetics cannot be literally rendered. I believe what you're trying to say is 'fush!' "

"Schlish! Fush!" she agreed vehemently.

"Please—not in front of the child," he cautioned her. "And you'd better let me show you out of the Sibilant zone, or we may encounter another roving catalyst. I don't think you'd want to mate again so soon."

She swelled up as if ready to explode. But his warnings did have effect. She swerved to follow him, and did not make any more intemperate remarks. Their infant swam docilely after her. Alien she might be—but her body was Spican, and the biological ties of motherhood were controlling, just as they were among humans, even when the child was the result of rape.

"Why did you do it?" she demanded more moderately.

"To force an admission of your origin from you," he said. "That was successful, though I admit I didn't quite pinpoint your Sphere. And I had to prevent you from trying to kill me or otherwise balk me from the performance of my mission. With a child to care for, you can't go chasing after me, can you? Not to other Spheres."

"Schl—" she started, then caught herself, glancing at the innocent infant. Flint was amazed at how readily he was able to accept this new reality: in just a few minutes by Sol time he had mated and become a father, and here was his child—by a completely alien mother. "There will be another time."

"I hope so," he said. "I'd really like to repeat this performance—in my own body, with you in human form. You're quite a female."

She was silent for a moment. "And you are quite a male," she agreed at last. "I have not before encountered an aura to match my own. I underestimated you, assuming you to be a primitive of your kind."

"I *am,*" Flint agreed. "I'm a Stone Age man. But that doesn't mean I'm stupid."

"That is true." Then she hardened. "But I shall not make that error again. Twice I have failed; that suffices."

And twice he had let her live, when perhaps he should have killed her. If only it weren't for the fascination of her aura, and his curiosity about her Sphere of origin. "Meanwhile, take good care of our baby," he said cheerfully. "I believe it takes about six months, my time, to raise a neuter to independence. If my interpretation of the nature of transfer is correct, you do possess the maternal instinct and will not permit your baby to suffer—because your Spican host would not have done so. You can't go home before it is old enough to be weaned, or it will die, and you can't take it with you because its Kirlian aura is native to this planet and would quickly fade in another host. I hope your own aura will last sufficiently long?"

"You know my aura is as strong as yours!" she flashed.

"Good. Then you will have a full month's clearance, and then you can go home and recuperate for a similar period, while *I* complete my missions at other Spheres. After that, there will be no point in your seeking me out to kill me. The job will have been done. Are you sure you don't want me to send a message to your home Sphere to let them know you're busy?"

"You have nullified me!" she cried angrily.

"This is music to my auditory perception," he said, realizing that he didn't have ears. His whole surface picked up the sound waves. "Well, I would have hated to kill so lovely a creature as you. Maybe after all this is over, we *can* get together again. It was a lot of fun this time."

This time even the presence of the child did not restrain her. *"Schlish!"*

But now Impacts were closing in, their fringes bubbling a bit in reaction to the foul language they had just picked up. Flint knew he could not escape arrest. And he realized there was a hole in his plan: he remained an outlaw. They might refuse to listen to him.

"Now I'll make you a deal," he said quickly. "You do not press charges against me for involuntary mergence, and I will not tell them of your alien origin."

"Fush!" she said. "I'll not cover for you! I can make them hold you here until your aura vanishes."

"All right—I'll tell them all about it," he said brightly, though he was worried. "And I'll call in the Sibilant as witness." He turned to the nearest Impact. "I am an alien sapience in possession of this Impact body," he announced. "Your cultural rules do not apply to me. This Undulant is—"

"I agree!" Llyana throbbed.

". . . is an involuntary victim of my ignorance of local custom. Please take me to the Council of Impacts for interrogation."

"That we shall," the Impact said a bit grimly. "Do you, the victim, prefer charges against this entity?"

"No," she said grudgingly. "It was an accident. I am pleased with my offspring. Only give me safe conduct to my zone."

"As you wish," the Impact said. "These things do happen."

And so she departed with the little one, and Flint was conducted to the ruling council of his sex. He knew from data within his host's memory that the council entities possessed the acumen to comprehend and verify his message, and the self-interest to cooperate. After all, this trisexed species could not have formed a stellar empire without knowledge of space and a high technology. Their achievement in doing it from a water base was phenomenal; it spoke well of their potential and drive. He would soon be back in his home sphere, mission accomplished.

He hoped the two Impacts he had fushed would not come forward to testify against him. But probably they would hide that embarrassing secret, as a human man might hide the fact of a homosexual attack on him. Justice was not worth the notoriety.

He rather hated to leave Llyana behind. He doubted he would ever again encounter a Kirlian aura that intense. And she had spirit and intelligence. She was in many respects his ideal mate.

But then he thought of Honeybloom, and remembered that he could never marry a nonhuman entity. How could they stay together any length of time, with fading auras? No, he belonged with his own kind.

6

Eye of the Charioteer

notice agent mired in sphere spica cannot remove for some time

—we *know*! what of the target kirlian?—

retransferred to sphere sol no subsequent transfer

—well check the mattermission indications, idiot!—

target kirlian mattermitted to system capella within own sphere

—detail on system—

renaissance culture despotic center of internal resistance to domination of earth planet some infiltration by agents of anti-coalition spheres dominated by scheming queen

—excellent that system may take care of our problem for us!—

POWER

—CIVILIZATION—

Capella was forty-five light-years from Sol, in the general direction of Sphere Nath but only a sixth as far. Its closest colonized neighbor was Castor, about as far away from it as Sirius was from Sol. What were eight or ten light-years between friends? Nothing like the hundred and some light-years to Etamin. Some day Flint meant to stop in at his home planet—but alas, Capella was not on that route.

He arrived in his own body in the afternoon, unannounced. Sol controlled the mattermitter, so that could be arranged. The station attendant, another pale-whitish specimen in an Imperial black tunic, introduced himself as Ambassador Jones of Earth. Flint identified himself. The man looked him up in the Orders of the Day and became more affable. "I've never met a genuine Outworlder before," he remarked. "I had understood that planet was—"

"Stone Age," Flint finished for him. "Right. And I

really *am* a jolly green giant. And I chipped stone for a living, until the Imps snatched me. I'm here to—" he hesitated.

"Do not be concerned; I am cleared for such information. It's in your dossier. You are our chief transfer agent, on temporary leave to recover your aura. I gather it fades somewhat during transfer."

"Yes. They did not trust me to visit my home world. Afraid I might skip back to the better life."

"Ha ha," the man laughed dutifully, though Flint had been serious. "Well, we shall take good care of you. Tonight is a very special occasion, locally. Good Queen Bess is having a birthday party. Capella is in the midrange of regression, culturally and technologically, you know. Post-medieval, early Renaissance, though of course that isn't exact. You'd think that in the three hundred years it's been settled they'd have advanced further, but there have been complicating factors. A number of the parallels to Earth history are contrived; the Queen is a student of history, and you can guess who her idol is."

"I'd have to," Flint remarked. "I'm more of a student of Paleolithic events myself. I'm not much on contemporary Earth."

But he did remember that the Shaman had called Capella "Victorian." Evidently it was further regressed than that. Maybe its population had been too thin to sustain the Victorian level.

The Ambassador chuckled again. "Well I have made arrangements for you to attend as the representative from System Etamin. Should make quite a splash. Do you have any idea what it costs to mattermit a man your size a hundred light-years?"

"Two trillion dollars," Flint said immediately.

The Ambassador looked startled; evidently he had expected ignorance. "Ah, yes. Queen Bess will be flattered to think that a system over thirty parsecs distant has sent a man to honor her. I would imagine you'll be feted. You should enjoy it. These are a lusty people, for all their mannerisms, much given to feasting and, er, wenching."

Flint thought of Honeybloom, back on Outworld. When would he see her again? At any rate, she was not the jealous type. His dallying elsewhere would not bother her, as long as she knew he preferred her. Men were men, after all. "Sounds great."

"Let's get you outfitted." The man brought out an armful of costume clothing. "This habiliment may seem outlandish, but believe me, it's what they wear. This is a suit appropriate to a high-ranking envoy."

"Wouldn't an authentic Outworld outfit be better?"

"Possibly. What is the established Outworld costume?"

"Nothing," Flint said. "We run naked."

The man forced yet another laugh. Flint got the message. When in the Capella system, dress Capella style.

He tugged his way into the skintight pants. "These are awful," he complained. "They're one size smaller than my skin."

"That's the style. Actually, you have very nice legs. The Queen has a fine eye for that sort of thing. Muscle in the right places, no fat. Now this."

Flint eyed the bright-red bag. "What's that?"

"The codpiece."

"A piece of fish? Looks more like a scrotum."

"Precisely. A crotch guard. This one's armored, just in case."

"It's uncomfortable as hell! Suppose I need to—?"

"Ha ha. It's removable. Wait till you try on the armor."

"Armor?"

The Ambassador brought out a pile of metal. "This is a parade vest, decorative yet functional. Note the articulation of the joints, the polish of the surface. They have fine metalsmiths here."

"I'm a flintsmith, myself," Flint observed, frowning. But he struggled into the thing, clank by clank. And suffered an unpleasant memory. "It's worse than an old Luna spacesuit!"

"Undoubtedly. But even more proof against punctures." The man got it on him efficiently, then dropped an elegant blue sash across his right shoulder, knotting it over his left hip. Then slippers with blue bows. And some kind of trinket.

"I'm no lady!"

"You misunderstand the role of jewelry historically. Many virile men have worn it. But this happens to be a watch. These are very important here. Queen Bess has her own palace watchmaker."

Flint looked at it: a round object about the heft of a good throwing stone, glassed on one side, with a decorated dial and two pointers. "What's it for?"

"For telling time. You wear it on a chain, tucked into a special pocket, here."

Flint balked again at the next object. "A snuffbox," the Ambassador explained. "It contains powdered tobacco—don't do that!"

But he was too late. Flint had opened the box and done what was natural: taken a good sniff to find out what it smelled like. His paroxysm of sneezing blew tobacco powder all over the room, setting the Ambassador off too.

When the spasms subsided, the dressing resumed. "I think we can safely dispense with the snuffbox," the Ambassador said. Flint agreed emphatically. "And we won't need the helmet and gauntlets, since this is a festive occasion. But the sword must be worn. It is a mark of honor."

"But it has no cutting edge!" Flint objected, running his thumb along it. Swords were not yet in use on Outworld, but the Shaman had told him of them, and he found them intrinsically fascinating.

"It is a rapier, not a machete," the Ambassador said. "Remember the level of culture here. Three musketeers—know what I mean?"

"Guns haven't yet been invented on my world. But I thought a musket was a firearm."

"Come to think if it, you're right. I wonder why they called them the three *musketeers*? They were French swordsmen of the seventeenth century. Furthermore, there were four of them, counting D'Artagnan. Though of course they did have muskets there—and have them here too—but they aren't used as weapons of honor. Except for pistols, in arranged duels." He shrugged. "Well, we've dressed you for the part, and if you watch your manners you won't have to use the sword. You can't get into any trouble wishing the Queen happy birthday. So long as you don't mention her age, ha ha."

So the Queen was an old bag. Well, he could wish her happy birthday, all right. Then get into the feasting and wenching.

The ritual of dressing had taken some time. It was night already. They went outside to wait for the transportation provided by the Queen. The stars were bright, but Flint hardly had time to look at them before the thud of hooves signaled the approach of his coach. He did identify his home star, Etamin, and that made him feel he had gotten his bearings, though the constellation it now occupied did not look much like Draco the Dragon. A shift of forty-five light-years to the side made a big difference in the apparent positions of the nearer stars. There was no Charioteer constellation, of course, because Capella was *in* it, as the eye of Auriga, mythological inventor of the chariot. The colonies were well aware of the places of their systems in human mythology, and Flint had no doubt the chariot was an important symbol here, just as the dragon was around Etamin. The visible constellations changed with each planet, but they lacked the human authenticity of the Earth-sky, and had not built up followings of their own. Even as a child in Etamin's system, Flint had learned the constellations of Sol's system. And some, like Orion's Belt, were the same anywhere in Sol Sphere, because those three stars were so far away.

Flint had a premonition about the probable nature of his steed. Sure enough: what hove into view was a dragon drawing a chariot. "They have several beasts of burden here," the Ambassador explained. "Since your world is considered to be a primitive warrior-system—"

"An accurate description," Flint agreed, pleased. Actually, from what he had seen and heard, more civilized cultures were far more combative than his own. There were no wars on Outworld, and few individual combats. But each man liked to think of himself as a warrior.

The man coughed. "Yes. So you will be expected to have a rather crude, forceful bearing. But remember: The Queen's courtiers are all expert swordsmen, and dead shots with pistols. No one not raised to the manner can match them. Whatever you do, don't get into a duel! Don't draw your weapon at all in the palace."

"Tantamount to a challenge, eh?" Flint inquired as servitors guided the dragon in, like little tugboats beside its mass. "But why would they bother an honorary delegate from another system who only comes to wish their Queen well?"

"They wouldn't, ordinarily. But there has been unrest recently. There's a lot of local intrigue; it's part of the manners of the period. The Queen had her last lover beheaded some time ago for treason—he was guilty, incidentally; she's very fair about such things—and that heightens it."

"Because they're afraid there'll be more beheadings?"

"No. Because all the young nobles are jockeying for her favor, hoping to become her next lover. The Queen's specific favor means a lot, as she is the source of all power here. So she has been in a bad mood, and the whole planet reflects it. Duels are frequent. But as I said, you aren't part of this, so you're safe enough so long as you don't go out of your way to antagonize anyone. Sol isn't sending a delegate, and I'm staying here in the embassy. Diplomatic immunity goes only so far. Rumors of transfer have gotten about, and these people have confused medieval notions about that. The mood is generally antiscientific. Do you know what I mean by the Inquisition?"

"No." But Flint made a mental note to find out, at his convenience; the Ambassador had spoken the word with a suggestive intonation that hinted at horrible things.

"Well, Queen Bess has suppressed the Inquisition anyway. But it typifies the alienophobic attitudes to which such cultures are prone. To them, Earth is alien. So Sol and Sirius are in bad repute; they make much of the fact that Capella is a hundred and fifty times as luminous as Sol. But Etamin is well regarded, perhaps because it is far away and primitive. So just be careful not to mention transfer, and you'll have a good time."

"A good time—in the midst of this caldron of animosities?"

"For a Stone Age man, you have quite a vocabulary! But perhaps I have exaggerated the situation. Those in favor are very well treated, and when the Queen throws a party, there's nothing like it in Sphere Sol. Their ladies are very provocative and, er, free. But I'd advise against —well—"

"Why not?" Flint asked, more curious than alarmed.

"Well, the Queen—" The Ambassador paused. "You really don't know much about this culture, do you? No reason you should, of course. I just hadn't thought it through. I think as a precaution you'd better take this."

He held out a flattish flesh-colored bit of plastic. "Stick it to the roof of your mouth."

"Why?"

"It's a communicator. Two-way radio. Picks up all sounds in your neighborhood, including your own speech, and transmits our messages through the bony structure to your ears, inaudible to anyone else. Essential for guiding you in local etiquette, just in case."

"Just in case *what*?"

"You're very direct."

"You're beating about the bush. If this is such a party, why all the precautions?"

The Ambassador sighed. "We don't expect any trouble, but this is a volatile situation and you are a very important individual. If you met with any misfortune my head would roll. Literally, I fear. Imperial Earth holds you in high regard."

"No accounting for tastes," Flint said.

"I may be overreacting, but now I question the advisability of sending you to this party. We can make an excuse—"

"No, I want to go," Flint said. He inserted the radio, pressing it into place with his tongue. It was small, and bothered him only momentarily. Since he valued his hide fully as much as the Ambassador did, this was useful insurance.

His transportation had been docked and was waiting with growing signs of impatience. Flint walked up to the chariot and stared at the dragon. "That's some animal!" he remarked appreciatively.

"Of course. The Queen employs the best. Don't worry—it should be perfectly tame, and it knows the route."

Flint eyed it. There was something about it, a kind of nobility, quite apart from its impressive size. The animal was like a dinosaur, with huge bone flanges ridged along its backbone. But it was no dinosaur, neither of the Earthly nor the Outworldly types, but a genuine dragon complete with fiery breath and bright wings. Its feet terminated in claws so massive they resembled hooves; one of those extremities could readily kill a man by puncture and squeeze. Yes, magnificent!

Under his cynosure, the thing turned its head, swinging it on a sinuous neck, and brought a steely eye to bear on Flint. No figure of speech; the surface of the eyeball shone like polished metal.

Tame? Flint was reminded of the time he had looked the trapped dinosaur, Old Snort, in the eye. This dragon-creature held him in contempt. Flint's gut level reaction was to view this as a challenge.

Flint stepped up close and extended one hand. "Don't touch it!" the Ambassador cried with the same alarmed tone of his warning about the snuffbox—again, too late. Flint placed his right hand on the massive snout, firmly.

The dragon swelled up visibly at this indignity. A kind of furnace-roaring emanated from its belly. Its nose became burning hot. A puff of steam jetted from its nostrils, heating Flint's slippered toes. But Flint stood firm, staring the beast down, and after a moment the dragon broke the contact.

The Ambassador gaped. "That was very chancy," he said, wiping perspiration—or perhaps it was condensed steam—from his brow. "They're tame—but not pets. They tolerate the harness because they like to run, but only a given dragon's master may touch it about the head. If the master dies, the dragon usually has to be destroyed, lest it run wild. You must have the eye of a charioteer. The locally fabled gaze of command. It's rare."

Flint shrugged. He knew it had not been his gaze but his touch that had daunted the dragon. He was familiar with this type of creature, so had respect without fear—but more than that, he had the Kirlian aura with special intensity. *And so did the dragon.* Animals, like men, possessed it, usually of indifferent intensity but highly variable. And a high-intensity creature responded to Flint's aura in much the way Flint himself had responded to the aura of Pnotl of Sphere Knyfh. There was now a mutual respect between man and dragon.

Flint mounted the chariot and took the reins. A tiny twitch put the dragon in motion. "Don't let it go too fast," a voice said.

Flint glanced about, but there was no one. "Where are you?" He believed in dragons, but not in ghosts.

"Here. It's the Ambassador. I'm using the radio."

The voice was in his own skull. "I'll keep it in mind. The dragon's not going to wreck himself."

The countryside was hardly visible at night, just a varied mat of vegetation, as on Outworld, the way a planet should be. Flint looked at the sky again, feeling nostalgic. He saw the tenuous cloud of the Milky Way, and the large faint patch of Galaxy Andromeda to the side, just as they were in the sky of Outworld. He pondered the notion that all his adventures stemmed from the malign influence of that distant cluster of stars.

He looked across to Etamin again, halfway around the sky. Home, so far away! What was Honeybloom doing now? Was the Shaman looking this way?

The dragon did know the way. It found its dragon-path and put on speed, spreading its vestigial wings for additional stability when banking around turns. The white steam jetting out from its nostrils puffed into the sky and drifted back, bathing Flint in its warm aroma.

He knew that steam was invisible; this was merely the condensation of water droplets as the breath cooled. Small matter; it was pleasant being a dragonmaster, and he urged the creature on. This was an attitude it appreciated, for it responded with a burst of speed that had the chariot wheels bouncing over the irregularities of the trail. Now it was a high-velocity ride, but Flint gave the animal free play. The chariot shook so hard it seemed ready to fly apart, and Flint reveled in the sensation. Was this what it was like to be a god, coursing through the sky?

Yet he wondered. Why had the Queen provided an unchaperoned dragon for the visitor? A soft, civilized man like the Ambassador could have been injured or even killed. Was she testing him? He grinned in the dark as the waves of vapor blew out his hair. If the Queen were curious about the mettle of Outworld, she would learn!

In due course they steamed into the palace demesne. There were a cluster of buildings and appurtenances, ornate affairs with columns and turrets and arches and flying buttresses—probably a mishmash of Earthly medieval architecture. What sort of buildings had resulted when the pleasantly primitive Goths become Gothic architects? This was the physical manifestation of cultural regression toward the fringe of the civilized Sphere. It was the same for all Spheres, whatever sapient species controlled them, for there was a built-in limitation—the lack of energy. With unlimited energy, all the Spheres could have been maintained at the highest level of civilization. Maybe it was really a blessing, for galactic conquest would become possible, and there were many creatures more advanced than humans. But as it was, many Spheres could flourish and their outer reaches had to fade. In no case was history reenacted; the technical approximation was echoed by culture. Where rapiers were the most advanced weapons, etiquette honored the proficient swordsman. The guidance of Earth history helped set the patterns, but this was a very general thing, with anomalies the rule. So there was no firm guide to the authenticity of the palace. The palace was what it was, and that was by local definition correct.

"Rogue dragon!" someone screamed as they slammed into the terminal. Men scurried about, spreading out a huge net with which to snare the rampant beast. But

Flint smiled, and drew in on the reins gently. The dragon screeched to a stop precisely on target, its giant claws chiseling furrows out of the packed dirt. Flint dismounted in a cloud of steam and dust, gave the dragon a comradely pat on the nose, and marched regally into the main gate.

A shaken flunky took his name and planet, and another led away the dragon, who gave Flint another brief but meaningful glance. The rapport of Kirlians operated independently of species or intellect. Right now Flint had other things to do, but he would come to see the dragon again. He preferred its company to that of ordinary human beings.

And where there was one high-Kirlian animal, there might be others. Were all dragons like this here, or just this one? Probably no animals had been measured for this quality; few natives understood the nature of the regular Imperial surveys. Flint had been ignorant as a child and young warrior. Now he understood the secret of much of his success as a hunter on Outworld, and perhaps as a flintsmith too. Some animals and even some objects possessed auras, and he had unconsciously related to these.

"Ooooh, there's a handsome one," a female voice remarked as he entered the gate.

Flint picked out the owner of that voice. It was a girl —like none he had seen before. Her face was pretty, and her breasts were astonishingly uplifted and full, seeming about to burst out of harness, but the rest of her was grotesque. Her arms were grossly bloated to the wrists, and her hips jutted out at right angles into a posterior like an overgrown swamp hummock, a massive mound dropping vertically to the floor. Two pegs protruded from that voluminous skirt, and Flint realized these were her slippered feet. And her face and hands and the alarming cleavage of her bosom were light blue.

"Haven't you seen a woman before?" she inquired.

"Don't stare," the voice in his skull said. It was the Ambassador, on the job. "I can't look through your eyes, but I'm assuming from the voice that you've just met one of the palace escorts, a handmaiden to the Queen. She—"

"Shut up," Flint mumbled, not pleased to have had this encounter intercepted.

The blue girl gave him an arch glance. "Well!"

"Not you," Flint said quickly. "I was addressing my beating heart. I have not before observed such beauty." The Shaman would not have approved of such a lie, but it seemed necessary.

"Wow! You'll do fine here," the Ambassador said. "That's the ticket." Flint wondered what a ticket was.

The girl flushed very prettily, her face, breasts, and hands turning so dark they were almost green. That made her look better. Flint realized that the flunkies outside had been blue too, but he hadn't noted it in the poor light. Just as his own people were green, and Sol's people were shades of white, brown, and black, these Capellans were blue. It all depended on the environment, especially the type of stellar radiation they received.

"You must be the envoy from Etamin. We know there are real men there."

"Yes," Flint agreed. "Will you guide me to the . . ."

"Throneroom," the Ambassador supplied.

"Throneroom?" Flint finished. "I am a stranger here."

"Gladly, sir," she agreed, putting one hand on his elbow, sliding her arm inside his. "I am Delle."

"I am Flint of Outworld," he said as she walked him down a long hall. "I am from a primitive world."

"Yes. The gossip is all over the palace, how you brought Old Scorch to heel. That must have been some—"

"The dragon?" But of course it was. Just as the most ornery dinosaur of his region of Outworld had been dubbed Old Snort, a term both respectful and descriptive, the most ornery dragon here would be Old Scorch. Evidently news traveled like lightning in the palace, unless the girls had been watching from a window. "He's a fine animal."

"He's burned eleven men in his day," she said. "That's approaching a record. Usually an animal is destroyed after three, but he's the Queen's pet. He never scorches *her*, you bet. He's not supposed to be used beyond the palace grounds, but there must have been a foulup."

"Very interesting," the voice in his skull remarked. "They were supposed to send a docile animal."

"As I said," Flint proceeded, "I am primitive. Please do not take offense—but I am unfamiliar with your apparel. Does it reflect your form?"

"My form?" She looked perplexed.

"On my world, women have thinner arms and—"

"Watch it!" the Ambassador snapped.

"—legs," Flint finished.

Delle laughed so heartily her breasts actually flopped in the rigid half-cups. "Here, I'll show you." She glanced back down the hall, then drew him into an alcove. When she was satisfied they had privacy she pulled the side of her neckline away from her shoulder, baring her upper arm and half of the rest of her breast. "See, these are padded sleeves. It's the fashion, also warm on cold nights. I'm really quite skinny underneath."

And all blue. "Oh." Flint was relieved. "Forgive the confusion of a barbarian."

"You really thought all that was *me*?"

"I could not be certain. The skirt—"

"What a fat ass you thought I had!" she exclaimed, delighted. "Well, catch a glimpse of *this*!" And she drew up a bulging hank of her skirt and petticoats to display as slender and symmetrical a pair of blue legs as Flint could have wished. "This is a farthingale, a kind of bustle under the skirt. I'm quite human underneath. I have all the things a woman needs. Here, put your hand—"

"Careful!" the voice in his skull cried.

"Why?" Flint asked both girl and voice.

"To feel my thigh," Delle said. "To prove it's real. And whatever else you may doubt. It really is all there."

"Because she'll seduce you if she can, quite without qualm," the Ambassador explained at the same time, like a conscience. "You are a handsome man from an enticingly primitive planet, and she would gain notoriety. Don't let it happen. Suppose the Queen wanted your service, and you just had exhausted yourself with a handmaiden, little better than a chambermaid? Very bad form."

Oho! Flint did not know the distinction between a handmaiden and a chambermaid, but he got the drift. First the dragon, then the flirt, testing him. The Queen was taking a greater interest in him than he had supposed.

Flint put his hand on her firm thigh. "Excellent," he remarked sincerely. He slid his fingers up to cup her supple buttock. "How I regret I cannot explore this matter further."

"Oh, but you *can*," Delle said warmly. "I know a room where no one goes, and it has a huge bed—"

"But my urgency to wish Queen Bess a happy birthday is so pressing that all else palls. I may not dally." And as he spoke the word "pressing" he gave her buttock a good hard pinch, so that she jumped involuntarily, and withdrew.

"Beautiful!" the Ambassador said. "You are a born diplomat!"

No, Flint thought. No diplomat. He merely liked to make his own decisions, to seduce rather than be seduced. The more someone pushed him, the more he went his own way. As the bastard speaking in his skull might find out in due course. The Ambassador was taking entirely too much interest.

The girl could make no serious objection. She was loyal to her Queen—perhaps a direct agent doing the Queen's specific bidding. Flint had learned on the slave world of Sphere Canopus not to confuse the relation between master and servant. People who failed the Queen could lose their heads. Probably nothing that went on in this palace was hidden from the monarch. This place was like a giant spider web (one of Sol system's more intriguing phenomena), and woe betide the visiting fly who misstepped.

They came sedately to the entrance of the main hall. "Now you must wait for the herald," Delle explained. "Then walk slowly up and make obeisance to the Queen."

"That's right," the Ambassador said. "I will guide you. After that formality, you should have no trouble. Once the liquor starts flowing, just about anything goes."

Flint clicked his teeth once in acknowledgment. Maybe then the Ambassador would kindly take a nap and leave Flint to his own devices. He needed no advice in handling liquor, food, and pretty girls.

"His Excellency Lord Pimpernel, Envoy Extraordinary of System Sheriton, realm of the Ram," the herald announced. A rather pudgy little man with spotty skin minced up and made a deep bow to the Queen, who was out of the line of Flint's vision.

"The Lord High Poopdoodle of Pollux, Most Gracious Tzar of the Twins, Gentleman of Gemini." And a tall, thin, old man marched out, almost stumbling over his hanging sword, while Flint stifled a laugh. Poopdoodle of Pollux? It sounded like dragon refuse.

But the next introduction was even worse. "The Regent of the Fabled Green Planet, Scion of Star Etamin, Conqueror of the Dragon, Flint of Outworld!" the herald bawled.

Flint stood still, stunned by the audacity of the fanciful credits he had been assigned. Outworld had no Regent, and he had no authority even in his local tribe, let alone his planet. Were they trying to mock him?

"Get in there!" the skull-voice cried. "*All* their titles are ludicrous. Popdod of Pollux is just an ambassador, same as me. *He* didn't balk!"

So Popdod had become Poopdoodle. The Ambassador was right: Flint had nothing to complain about.

He marched in. Now he saw the Queen, standing before her throne. She was short and blue, but impressive in padded sleeves and farthingale hoops that made her skirt even more like a barrel than that of Delle's. The material of her dress was thick and quilted, with golden thread and bright jewels at every interstice. She wore several necklaces of jewels that hung halfway down her body, reaching out to the edge of the vertical skirt. On either side of her neck were huge ruffs and wire frames extending the lines of her head out a foot or more. She wore an obvious wig pinned to her scalp, but still looked almost bald beneath it. Her crown perched at the top like the spire of a church. In her right hand she held the scepter of power.

"Bow," the voice said urgently. "Slow and deep."

Flint faced Queen Bess and bowed.

"Well, it has manners after all," the Queen said. Her voice was harsh and somewhat scratchy. She was a robust woman, not young but not yet old, with makeup caked on her face so that it looked like a fright mask. Flint suspected that her body under the elaborate dress did resemble the outer configuration: bloated into the shape of a hogshead of strong liquor. Maybe that was why she had set this style: to cover her defects, and make all others cover their assets.

"She's the spitting image of the original Elizabeth of England, you know," the Ambassador remarked. "She uses the caked makeup deliberately, because that's the way the original did it; underneath she's actually a somewhat younger woman. Like Elizabeth, Bess is tough and smart. No coincidence, of course; she's studied history. Don't forget that for one instant. Wish her happy birthday, but don't mention her age."

Small chance; Flint didn't *know* her age, and the Ambassador had warned him about this before. But she was obviously older than the average Outworld tribeswoman.

"Planet Outworld bids you an enjoyable birthday, gracious Queen."

"The whole planet!" she exclaimed, chuckling mannishly. "We welcome the emissary of the Dragon."

"Now back off," the Ambassador said. "There are others to be introduced, but you're home free. Queen Bess has accepted you."

Flint backed off. So far so good; if this were the worst of it, he would have an easy evening. The smell of the feast was already circulating through the room, and he saw barrels of liquor being set up in a corner. He was hungry and thirsty, and he might even get a chance to go out and look at the stars at greater leisure. That was one thing about having a party at night: the stars were out.

He bumped into someone. A young man was standing in his way, a man who hadn't been there a moment ago. He wore brown tights with a padded codpiece, a brilliant red cape, and a supercilious sneer. "I beg your pardon," the youth said loudly. "I was not aware of your optical infirmity. Stupid of me not to realize that anyone as green as you could not be in the best of health."

"He's baiting you," the Ambassador advised. "Ignore him. The court's full of young dandies on the prowl for trouble."

"Green is my natural color," Flint said mildly. "It has to do with the radiation of my star and the atmosphere of my planet, as most people know. My vision is satisfactory—but the eyes of my head were on the Queen, and I do not possess eyes elsewhere."

"Are you suggesting that I *do*?" the dandy demanded, his hand going to the hilt of his sword. He seemed more than willing to be insulted. "I, Lord Boromo of the Chariot?"

"Ignore him," the voice in the skull repeated. "I recognize the name. He's a notorious troublemaker, but an expert swordsman, as these things go. He's killed several innocent men, but if he draws in the presence of the Queen, he insults her, and his head will roll. And don't *you* draw!"

Flint turned away from the young man, though he would rather have bashed him. But Boromo would not let it drop. "Only a complete barbarian stumbles into his betters and lacks the wit to apologize."

"Agreed," Flint said, moving on. There was a ripple of

laughter through the hall. There had been more than casual interest in the encounter.

"Boromo must be jealous of you," the Ambassador said. "He was trying to provoke you into a duel, so he could kill you, or at least humiliate you, and win favor for himself. Politics is like that, here. You handled it well, reversing the insult—but I had not anticipated this. Perhaps you'd better excuse yourself and return to the embassy."

"When the party's just beginning?" Flint demanded. *And let the young punk have the satisfaction of putting me to flight?* he added mentally "I'm enjoying myself." And he drifted toward the liquor.

From behind a drape an orchestra starting playing. The fancy courtiers began to dance with the hoopskirted girls. The movements were measured and stately, stylized like the courtship ritual of certain animals. The barreled skirts began to sway, then swing like great bells, in time to the music, while hinting at enticingly shapely derrières beneath them. There was, Flint realized, some point in this complicated clothing; proper suggestion had a refined sex appeal that could build to a higher peak than mere exposure. Honeybloom, back on Outworld, was lovely in her nakedness—but she lacked the artful challenge of these boxed beauties.

Delle glided up. "Do you care to ask me to dance, handsome envoy of the Dragon?" she inquired pertly.

Flint had no notion how to do this dance, suspecting he would make a fool of himself if he tried it. But he thought it inexpedient to advertise this. "I prefer to watch," he said.

She made a moue. "Sir, you humiliate me."

Another dandy came up, as brightly and tastelessly clad as the first. "Do you have the audacity to insult a lady?" he demanded.

"That depends on the lady," Flint replied.

The dandy swelled up. "This insolence cannot be tolerated!"

"Why not?" Flint asked.

The first dandy, Boromo, approached. "The animal lacks the wit to take umbrage."

"A prick of the sword could be the cure of that," the other said. A glance of understanding passed between them.

Delle faced Flint angrily. "Are you going to let them talk about you like that?"

Flint affected surprise. "I thought they were addressing each other."

There was another ripple of laughter in the hall. Both dandies glowered, their hands going to the hilts of their swords in an obviously well-rehearsed gesture.

"Ho! What is this?" the Queen demanded, sailing forward majestically.

"Oh oh," the Ambassador said. "Bess is in on it too, and the maid. They must know what you are, Kirlian and all."

Flint agreed. It did look like trouble. There had been too many little episodes. Suppose these people, antiscience as they were, opposed the formation of the galactic coalition? They could strike a real blow for their dubious cause by eliminating him. But still they dared not do it openly, lest a twenty-fourth-century battleship be dispatched from the nearest Imperial space armory. One barrage from such a ship could put this planet back into the Dark Ages, literally. So they had to be at least somewhat subtle.

He had walked into a nest of vipers. Still he had certain assets. One was the putative battleship; another was the Ambassador in his skull; then there was his own ingenuity. A bit of bold initiative might work. It really wasn't worse than being a transferee in an alien Sphere!

"This oaf insults Your Majesty," Lord Boromo said.

Flint made a little bow to the Queen. "I fear there has been a misunderstanding, Queen Bess. I proffered no insult."

"And now he calls me a liar!" the dandy exclaimed theatrically. "I call these assembled to witness. . . ."

And the others would back the dandy up, of course, completing the frameup. They were only waiting to see which way the Queen wanted it.

"I'm sending an Imperial Guard to get you out of there!" the Ambassador said. "But it will take a few minutes. Stall them if you can. Whatever you do, *don't draw!* Then we'd have no case at all."

The Queen faced Flint, and he saw the calculating glint in her eyes. She had not quite decided what she could risk. "I had not supposed the Dragon would send a minion to disrupt our party," she said.

Flint had had enough of this mousetrapping. "Even the Dragon can at last become annoyed at the yapping of curs."

Queen Bess's mouth dropped open. Both dandies drew

their swords partway from their belts. *"Lese majesty!"* they cried together. "Give us permission—!"

The Queen nodded almost imperceptibly. The swords moved up to clear the belts—and Flint acted.

He backhanded Lord Boromo across the face, his knuckles making hard contact with the bone of the jaw. The man went down as if clubbed—as well he might have been, for the barbarian fist, augmented by Sphere Sol karate training, was like a club, capable of breaking bones. Then Flint caught hold of the emerging sword of the second dandy. Because the weapon had no edge, he suffered no cut on his fingers. He brought it up, twisted it easily from the man's grip, put both hands on the metal, and flexed his muscles in one violent spasm. The sword snapped in half. Flint then kneed the man in the bulging codpiece and let him fall. He threw away the two parts of the sword.

The action had taken only a moment. Flint was not even disheveled. He bowed again to the Queen. "The Dragon apologizes for allowing the curs to annoy the gracious Queen, and begs forgiveness."

"He didn't even draw!" someone murmured in the throng.

"The two best duelists in the realm!"

The Queen smiled as graciously as she could manage. She could not admit complicity in the plot to embarrass Imperial Earth, and did not care to subject herself to public embarrassment. Had Flint threatened her, she could have had her guards mob him; but Flint had put himself on her side, an ally, and that was distinctly awkward.

"The Dragon shows more mettle in apology than others in victory," she observed. "It is fitting that the Dragon determine the appropriate mode of disposition of these ruffians."

"They failed in their assassin's assignment," the voice in his skull explained. "Death is the penalty—not only for failure, but to ensure their silence. Don't protest it."

But Flint didn't like it. He could kill in the heat of battle, but not coldbloodedly. He realized Queen Bess was still testing him. A true friend of hers would not hesitate to do her bidding. "The Dragon does not deign to kill curs," he said. "Let them redeem themselves by serving loyally as attendants to the Queen's chariot dragon." A probable sentence of death, as Old Scorch would not take kindly to such types—especially if the Good Queen wanted them dead. But it shifted the responsibility back to her. "If they fail to perform well, their bodies shall be exposed to the scavengers of the wilderness, and when the bones are clean they shall be buried under the floors of their living quarters. In this manner their ghosts shall continue to serve their Queen."

There was silence. Flint had prescribed the honorable tribal burial of Outworld, but he was aware it would seem otherwise to these more civilized people. And he had dodged the actual sentence of death. How would the Queen react?

"My man is almost there," the Ambassador said.

"Get lost, Imp," Flint mumbled subvocally.

"Your sword, Dragon," the Queen said, holding out her blue hand.

Somehow he had miscalculated. Whom did she plan to dispatch—him or them?

Flint put his fingers on the upper blade and drew the sword out, placing his hilt in her hand. As it touched her, something like an electric current traveled along it to his hand. It was the channelized impulse of a strong Kirlian aura!

"Kneel," she said firmly.

Well, he had done his best. The penalty for failure might be death, but he was not going to beg for his life. If he had misjudged her, it was his own fault. He kneeled.

Queen Bess raised the sword, then brought it down. The tip tapped one of his shoulders, then the other. "I knight thee Lord of Valor," she intoned. "Rise, Sir Dragon."

Flint stood, amazed, as she handed back his sword.

The Queen winked. "I suspected you had a strong aura when you tamed Old Scorch," she murmured so that only he could hear. "He is a very special beast—my own pet. Tonight, after the party, you shall have opportunity again to prove your valor. Come to my chambers."

The last was said loudly enough for others to overhear. There was a murmur of surprise and awe.

"She means it," the Ambassador in his skull said, sounding awed himself. "She hasn't taken a lover in months. You'll have to go, unfortunately. We'll try to slip you an aphrodisiac so you can perform—"

Flint poked his tongue up under the radio unit, dislodging it from the roof of his mouth. He swallowed it. Now the voice was gone. "May the union of the Imperial

Empire be as strong as that we shall experience tonight," he said with a flourish.

"So you ditched the Imp radio," she murmured.

She had known! She probably had a constant monitor on it. The culture of this planet might be pre-Machine Age, but there would be ways to obtain samples of higher technology, and a smart ruler would see to it. There was no law against it, after all; Earth *wanted* the colonies to progress. No wonder she was right on top of the situation—and no wonder she had been provoked by him. He must have seemed like a very active spy, with his constant advice from the Sol embassy.

"The Imp insulted me—and you," he said. "I don't need civilized snooping. It takes a man to know a real woman—though she be a queen."

"You may be surprised at how young a queen can be when she washes off her makeup."

"Not beneath the age of consent, I trust," Flint said, raising an eyebrow.

"There is an age of consent in your culture?"

"Of course not."

She smiled, glancing down at the fallen dandies, and she looked younger already. He had supposed the makeup was intended to make her look younger than she was, but the opposite could be true. "So you *are* from Outworld," she said.

"Yes. But I do work for Earth, in what capacity you surely know."

She smiled. "I admit we have had our doubts about Imperial policy in the past. But I doubt very much there will be any difficulties in the future. The Empire sends impressive envoys." And she turned away and floated regally back to her throne area.

The music started, and the dance resumed. Delle smiled.

Flint knew it would be days or weeks before the Queen chose to dispense with his services. She *was* a real woman, with strength and intelligence and nerve—and a Kirlian aura that gave her more sex appeal than any of the palace beauties possessed.

These humans were in many ways odder than the alien creatures of other Spheres, but Flint fully expected to enjoy his stay here in System Capella.

7

Tail of the Small Bear

notice subject kirlian transfer to sphere polaris agent remains unavailable

—polaris is the most advanced sphere of that region! ready another agent necessary to eliminate subject immediately—

caution local factors make infiltration difficult for any but high-kirlian experienced agent

—*what* factors?—

polarian philosophy of circularity presence of cult of tarotism debt system excellent intelligence network

—won't those same factors inhibit mission of subject entity?—

true

—POWER—

what?

—signoff, idiot power, as in what we need for—

oh sorry CIVILIZATION

—(what a mess!)—

REPORT—SPHERICAL RECONNAISSANCE

TO: His Ultimate Circularity, Pole Prime:

O Biggest of Wheels, my little report: as thou didst direct, I placed myself in the way of he whom our Neighbor Sphere sought, he of the extraordinarily intense Kirlian aura, the Solarian Flintsmith. I intercepted him as he traveled to the hunting party of his Chief, he of the Powerful Stick. (Solarians, O Illustrious Spinner, do not employ the wheel at this fringe of their Sphere, and tend to think in terms of the stiff hinged rods by which they ambulate. Hence "Powerful Stick" or "Strong Spear" translate loosely into "Big Wheel," no offense to thee.) We held converse, and the alien Flintsmith, worker of stone, was obliged to invite me to accompany him on his round, and I accepted. In the course of our journey we exchanged minor favors and I had occasion to make physical contact with him, and so verified that he does indeed possess the strongest Kirlian ambiance I have ever touched: a hundred, perhaps two hundred times as dense as my own ordinary one. The report we intercepted from the Solarian government was accurate; it may well be the single finest Kirlian aura in our galaxy.

Having ascertained that, O Honored Cog, I could not conveniently disengage, for we were now amidst the Solarians' primitive hunt. There was danger to the Flintsmith, and because we maintain amicable relations with these stick figures, I felt constrained to protect him somewhat. Though his body is grotesque in the fashion of his kind, there may never be his Kirlian like again within our region of the Myriad-Mote Galaxy. In fact, taking no presumption to suggest to advise so massive a Revolver as Your Wheelship, I would be inclined to spin into the tightest cultural and economic affinity with the Solarian Sphere, in the interests of exploring this remarkable Kirlian manifestation. Perhaps when our breakthrough into the secret of transfer occurs—apology, my association with Solarians has affected my vocabulary: I mean when our revolution of transfer occurs—we can discover how to engender similar auras in our own kind, where at present our highest intensity is about fifty.

I was able to preserve the Flintsmith's life from extinction by the animal they hunted, "Ancient Nose-Blow." (Solarians of most species, sapient and sentient, possess separate respiratory apparatus capable of producing sounds, particularly in the presence of infection. Thus the creature frequently honked or snorted; hence its name, variously rendered as "Aged Honk" or "Old Snort.") But thereafter, the Flintsmith also preserved my own life from a similar threat. In this manner we inadvertently exchanged life-debts, and were obliged to make the Compact—the first, if I mistake not, between a Polarian and a

Solarian. (And there have not been many between Polarians and Nathians either. In fact, Exchanges between Spheres are quite rare.) (But of course Sphere Nath is our longest association.) I therefore terminate my report as of the moment our mutual vow was completed, and resign from this case. In no way shall I betray the interest of my Debt Brother, and should he ever manifest within our Sphere I claim Debt Priority with regard to him.

FROM: Small Bearing, Pole Agent Tsopi, Perimeter Detail.

APPENDED CIRCULAR by Big Wheel:

How brazenly the Small Bear twists her tail into Wheelish matters, presuming to inform us of elementary history and even proffering advice! Yet despite her frequent irrelevancies and truncated spin, there goes one of our best field agents. Note how subtly she imposed on the Solarian in the interest of her mission, and how loyally she protects his own interest now that she has wangled Debt Exchange. The little disk has rolled into love with an alien stick, overwhelmed by his Kirlian aura. Beauty and the Beast! She probably wanted to get into the Round of Records: first Debt Exchange between Pole and Sole. Now she even demands Consummation! Well, we can gyre through this vortex too; if the Solarian Flintsmith ever does manifest here (fat chance!), assign Tsopi as his guide. A cycle or two of forced association with the alien will cure her of such looping fancies; she'll have her notoriety, and soon her wheel will be spinning normally. (We'd never put up with this, if she weren't such an efficient operator, and cute as a whirlbug too.)

Flint started to fall, tried to put his foot forward, found he *had* no foot, grabbed with a hand, and had no hand.

A strong, supple tentacle caught him. "Gently, friend," a soft voice said against his glowing skin. "Use your wheel; you're a Polarian now. No rodlike appendages, no human reactions. Think circular."

He used his wheel, gaining a precarious balance. It was like logrolling in a river; he had to keep reversing to avoid getting dumped. Intellectually as well as physically. "You *know!*" he said—and discovered that he had spoken by spinning the little ball in the end of his trunk against his own illuminated hide.

"Our Spheres maintain diplomatic channels," the other replied. "We were advised of your coming by mattermission capsule, and I was summoned from the Fringe to escort you."

Now he contemplated his companion. He had no eyes, but his skin-surface was a radiation receptor that provided a less specific but quite adequate notion, somewhat like human peripheral vision extended into a full circle—or rather, a full sphere. He could literally see in all directions at once. He was in the presence of a female Polarian, shaped like a huge chocolate candy kiss and very nicely proportioned from little ball to great wheel. In fact, she was beautiful. "Then you know that I am Flint of Sphere Sol," he said. "May I know you?"

"I am Tsopi of Sphere Polaris," she replied.

Something clicked. "Topsy—of Outworld?"

She glowed good-naturedly. "The same, Plint."

"But you should be out at the Fringe, two hundred light-years from—"

"I claimed preemptive right. We are debt-siblings."

Oh, yes. She had attached some importance to that, he recalled. They had saved each other's lives from Old Snort. Still. . . . "And your government mattermitted you *two hundred light-years* to nursemaid me?"

"It is our way," she said. "I will see to all your needs."

Several trillion dollars' worth of energy expended to bring her here—because it was their way. Yet he found he liked that. It was not just that she was the prettiest entity in the limited memory of his host-body; it was also that he *knew* her from his human experience, and respected her. This was the first time he had seen a creature from both the human and the transfer views; it provided an added perspective.

But business first. "I must deliver the secret of transfer to your government."

"There will be occasion for that," she said. "We shall meet with the Big Wheel himself in a few days." Local days, his memory informed him, were somewhat longer than those of either Outworld or Earth, but the essence was similar.

His communication ball made a sound like a human fingernail rasping across slate. (He noted peripherally that the little talk-ball was termed a ball, while the ambulation-ball was called a wheel, though both were spherical. And the tentacle-appendage was a male trunk, or a female tail.) "A few days! Topsy, this is urgent!"

"There will be occasion," she repeated, like a nurse calming a distraught patient.

Flint let it drop for the moment. Tsopi knew him, and shared a bond with him that was evidently important to her. Was she trying to tell him something? After the mannered intrigues of System Capella, he was not surprised to find complications here in Sphere Polaris, but he was disappointed.

She showed him the way through the building. It reminded him strongly of its counterpart at Earth-Prime, with its broad halls, high ceilings, forced-circulation air and lack of growing things. What was there about civilization that made it so restrictive? Yet his host-mind informed him that this was natural to Polarians, even pleasant; individuals of this species, like native Earthians, *liked* to be massively enclosed by their architecture.

How did no-handed creatures manage to build such edifices? Again his memory provided the answer: Polarians were adept at circular manipulation of objects and concepts. They did not carry building blocks into place, they rolled building spheres into place. Where men laid bricks, Polarians rolled stones. Where men hammered nails, Polarians squeezed glue. The end result was rather similar, as though civilization shaped itself into certain configurations regardless of the sapient species invoking it. Here there were no square skyscrapers, but domed dunes serving the same purpose.

They passed down a smooth ramp, where on Earth there would have been stairs. Of course; ramps were better for wheels, stairs for legs. Ramps were everywhere, contributing to the fluidity of the architectural design.

They had to roll single file, for efficient progress through the throng. Tsopi's trail just ahead of him was sweet; she had a tantalizingly feminine taste.

Taste? Flint concentrated, and it came: Polarians laid down taste trails with their wheels, much as humans laid down scent. No, more than that: These were actual, conscious signatures of passage, like the trails of Earthly snails. He remembered the first snail he had seen, beside the huge water of the ocean inlet, under the odd blue sky of Earth. Today he didn't even notice the color of the sky of a given planet; sky was sky color, right for its world. But this taste; every Polarian was really a super-bloodhound, sniffing out every other, all the time. It was the natural way. In fact, it was already difficult to imagine how it could be otherwise.

"These are our power generators," Tsopi murmured against his hide, flinging back her tail in a very fetching way. This mode of communication was pleasantly intimate: touch and speech together. In fact, Polarians were a togetherness species, expecting and requiring closer camaraderie than the creatures of Sphere Sol. "Orbiting micro-satellites reflect half the sunlight passing near our planet into our generators, and that fuels our matter transport system. Our remaining energy needs are met by—"

"The center of power," Flint said, rolling his own ball on her surface. My, this was fun! "The highest Minister, Regent, ruler—"

"Big Wheel," she supplied. "He's really more of a coordinator, a converger of spirals. We don't have your sort of—"

"Whatever you call him: the one to whom I should report. He's in this vicinity?"

"Yes, the Wheel is here. But there is no—"

"I'm sorry if I affront your sensitivities," Flint said. "I like your company a lot, and do want to learn about your Sphere. But my mission is of galactic importance. Business before pleasure." And he broke away from her, dodging into the nearest crosshall.

"You do not understand," she buzzed against the floor, dodging after him. "With us, there is no separation between—first there must be—"

But Flint, in any body, was adept at pursuit and eluding. He accelerated, getting the feel of his wheel—and it was a good wheel, even though it was spherical. Tsopi could outspeed his human body on level ground, but his mind in a healthy Polarian body was too much for her. He zipped around another corner, shot across the ramp, and damped out his scent amidst a welter of tastes on a well-used trail. In moments he had lost her, as surely as he had lost his pursuers on Luna, back three worlds ago.

Yet he had not, in the end, been able to escape his fate, there on Earth's huge barren moon. He had carried his destiny within himself. Poor parallel, though; now he was not running *from*, but rolling *to* his mission.

He paused to reflect, working out his rationale after

the fact. Flint trusted his primitive instincts, but his mind refused to give them complete play without comprehending them. There were civilized aspects to his mind, like them or not, and he had to give them their turn. Why had he needed to free himself of so helpful and lovely a creature as Tsopi? Especially since he had known her back home on Planet Outworld and chased a dinosaur with her. Rather, had *been chased* with her; nobody chased Old Snort!

Because she was threatening to interfere with the performance of his mission, yes. Perhaps not intentionally. But it would be very easy to become romantically distracted by her, because she was not only sweet to the taste, she was genuinely nice. He did not want to sully his memory of Honeybloom by chasing after the first pretty tail he met. Yet he should have been able to persuade her of his mission's importance, had he really tried. So that was not the whole reason. He had to dig deeper.

And it came: *Tsopi knew too much about him.* That made her dangerous, however well-meaning she might be. Until he confronted the authorities of this Sphere, he was vulnerable; if anything happened to him, Polaris would be lost to the galactic coalition. Sol had now tried other agents, sending them to other Spheres such as huge Sador, and they had not returned. Remembering his misadventures in Canopus and Spica Spheres, Flint could understand why failure would be common. Only Flint himself had been able to negotiate the intricacies of transfer to alien bodies and cultures and return to Sol. He had succeeded twice, as much by luck as by skill, and this one promised to be his easiest mission yet—but he could take nothing for granted. He could not afford the risk of delay, however attractive it might seem at the moment.

Yet even this was not the whole problem. Every time he scraped to the bottom of his apprehension, he found a deeper level. Was Tsopi a well-meaning innocent—or was she in fact an active anticoalition agent, either native or possessed by alien transfer? She did not have a potent Kirlian aura—but he could not assume that the Polarian-body perceptions could pick this up, or that it was impossible to conceal such an aura. If she were possessed, could she really be Cle of Ath, or Llyana the Undulant of Spica—the persona that had animated them? Even the least-threatening situation could have its complications. Perhaps it was his slightly paranoid suspicions that had enabled him to survive while others perished. If Tsopi were actually a transferee, she was extremely dangerous. Of course the chance of her being possessed by that malignant yet intriguing alien-Sphere entity who had tried to kill him before seemed remote, as he had anchored that female to the host-body for some time to come, but much could have happened, such as the accidental death of the infant, freeing the mother. Or a similar entity could have taken over. They knew how to locate him; the question was, how badly did they want him?

Yet Tsopi had been here *before* him. Unless the spies had access to Sphere Sol information, that virtually eliminated possession. They could not trace his transfer *before* he transferred! Nevertheless it was a risk, for no one had told *him* he would be expected in Sphere Polaris. Of course it could be an administrative foulup; they happened often enough. It would be just like Earth's Council of Ministers to have forgotten to inform him, the most critical party, of their plans for him. Or maybe the Polarians had such a good intelligence network that they had tapped in on Sol's secret and acted on it. If it turned out Tsopi were innocent, he would apologize to her most handsomely—*after* the Big Wheel had the technology of transfer.

Meanwhile, he was lost and alone—as usual. It didn't bother him. He could best proceed on his own.

Exactly where would the Big Wheel be? Since Tsopi would undoubtedly raise the hue and cry for him—or whatever rolling equivalent Polarians had—he had to act fast. Somewhere in his host-memories would be the information he needed, but he had already expended too much time exploring his own motives and could not take time to sift tediously through the host-library now. What he really needed was time; his prior missions had taught him to avoid acting precipitously. At the same time he had to complete his mission immediately—a paradox.

He crossed a scent-trail that offered a safe temporary haven for troubled entities. It was a priestly taste, consciously laid down—perhaps a Polarian monk. Since Flint dared act neither slowly nor ignorantly, perhaps this would help. He wheeled to follow the trail.

With this guidance, it took only moments to thread the network of ramps and locate the sanctuary.

At its portal he paused, for suddenly the taste gave warning. It was the flavor of a foolish young creature, ambitious and intelligent but about to roll off a precipice. Associated with it were the burning of fire, the fluidity of water, the rarefaction of air, and the solidity of ground. The overall suggestion of the taste was not merely haven, but knowledge—more than the average intellect might crave.

But no danger per se. Flint did not fear knowledge; on the contrary, he craved it. He rolled across the threshold.

And the ramp collapsed. He dopped sickeningly into darkness—Polarians being every bit as vulnerable to a fall as Solarians—and flung out his trunk to catch any available support. But there was none.

Then his wheel touched something. It was a wall, or a steeply inclined plane. Too steep to travel on. But to prevent himself from scraping, he spun his wheel against it, letting it guide him down. This might not make much sense if he were about to crash, but it was a largely automatic reflex. Polarians preferred to die with their wheels turning.

The slant changed; the wall was angling into a surface he could almost grip. It was tasteless; no one could have passed this way recently. Now it was a steep channel, actually enabling him to slow his fall somewhat.

Gradually the channel leveled, though it remained uncomfortably barren of taste. He came to a smooth stop at the base. He had fallen a considerable distance, but was after all unharmed. Good enough; the threshold warning had been accurate. No one else was likely to follow precipitously—unless there were an alternate entrance. No—his host-memory, keyed by the dramatic fall, indicated that visitors always used this aperture. They left by another, equally single-directional, completing the circuit forcefully. It was common knowledge, available to him had he but known where in his mind to look. Which was why he did not want to act before exploring that mind. The next pitfall might not be as safe.

Sometime he'd have to find a way around that initial informational block. It was like learning all the rules of a complex new game at once, or trying to chew too big a nut so that his mouth wouldn't close or gain purchase. Though he now had no mouth. If there were a shorthand, an instant keying system—but *if* there were, Llyana the Undulant surely would have used it to avoid the romantic trap he had sprung on her. Maybe this problem had helped him more than it hindered him.

But now he had arrived—somewhere. His host-memory could not help him, for the host had never actually been *inside* a Tarotist temple. Not that it was any great secret; it was just one of those experiences, like dropping into a deep hole, or sleeping in a haunted cave, that hadn't seemed necessary.

Tarotism—there, inadvertently delivered, was the name. It was the cult, a system of beliefs he had heard mentioned in passing back on Earth. Its prime tenet was supposed to be that all concepts of divinity were legitimate. The concept translated into taste—yet unmistakable because of the symbol at the door. The first key of the pack, the Fool. He should have made the connection before, for that had been a *human* memory. What use to delve into the confused recesses of his host's brain, when he was neglecting his own?

And what in the galaxy was Tarotism doing *here?* A human religion among the Polarians? There had hardly been that much contact, not between the Sphere centers. Humans and Polarians merged amicably on Etamin's planet Outworld, Flint's home at the fringe of each of their Spheres—but Tarotism had not yet reached that world. So how—?

A dark Polarian stood before him. Flint had not been aware of the entity's approach. More likely he had been there from the start, and only now showed himself in the brightening light. That was a thing Flint missed: the acute, direct binocular vision of the human eyes, eyes difficult to fool. The Polarian light awareness was serviceable in most instances, but useless for fine definition in a crisis. This body was taste-oriented; sight, touch, and hearing were secondary.

"I am the Hierophant," the entity said. "What is your Significator?"

Flint applied his ball to his own skin. His host-memory was blank; no help there. "I do not understand."

"This is the Temple of Comprehension," the Hierophant replied. "Do you wish your nuclear identity to be open or hidden?"

"Hidden," Flint said. He was not about to betray his origin and mission to this priest.

"Then we shall ask the Arcana to select your Significator—that symbol of yourself. Actually it is you who make the selection, random though it seems; your Kirlian aura will not be comfortable with any but the appropriate representation."

Kirlian aura! How much did the Hierophant know?

"I know little; the sacred books know much," the Hierophant answered. "Do not be alarmed; we mean you no ill, and shall not detain or importune you. We seek only to provide the aid you came for."

"I came for solitude, a chance to explore my mind," Flint said. That much was safe enough to say.

"Precisely. Now if you will shuffle the Tarot symbols. . . ."

How did a no-handed creature shuffle anything? But now Flint's host-memory provided the answer, for this related to an everyday problem of manipulation. He used his trunk to work the control of the mechanical shuffler on a pedestal beside him. This was no random effort; by expert twitches of his ball he made the printed cards in the lighted chamber riff through each other again and again, until they were hopelessly mixed. Then he picked one randomly by touching another surface; the card flipped out of the pack to present itself for identification.

He ran his ball over it. It portrayed a lone Polarian whose trunk reached out to hold a lamp, whose source of light was a bright star. A simple figure, on the surface —yet as a parallel symbol there was a single swimming sperm cell.

Flint's mission was to bring secret information to foreign Spheres—news that would transform them, enabling them to expand their influence enormously, and to merge into a single galactic coalition. He was a tiny sperm cell coming to the huge egg of each Sphere to fertilize it in unique fashion. His knowledge was the illumination of a star—faint in the distance, yet of tremendous significance. How well the Tarot had chosen!

"You are the Hermit—the ninth key," the Hierophant said. "Alone, concealed, not what you seem, bringer of light. You say, 'Where I am, you may also be.' Though you walk in seeming isolation, your light shows the way for the multitude."

How much did this bastard know? (Though there was no concept of bastardy in the Polarian intellect; that was a purely human derogation.)

"Please do not insult the Temple by your suspicion," the Hierophant said. "We respect your privacy, and we are politically and socially neutral. The Temple of Tarot transcends matters of mundane import. If the key seems apt, it is because you have chosen it so, not we."

"Sorry," Flint said. "It *is* apt."

"Hermit, we shall now accede to your will," the Hierophant continued. "You may have a private cell for meditation, or a reading of the Arcana to facilitate your thought."

A private cell was what he had come for, but now Flint changed his mind. This Tarotism was strange, and it had some connection to Sphere Sol. It was possible that it could be of aid to him, if he could learn more about it. "I choose the reading."

"I deal the keys as you have arranged them," the Hierophant said. "Stand at the animation plate, and do not be afraid. No harm will come to you; it is only your own mind made manifest. No news of what the Tarot reveals will pass beyond these premises except as you make it known yourself."

"Thank you." Flint rolled to the circle that illuminated itself in a chamber before him. As he touched it, he became the Hermit, in a long gray robe, standing in the darkness atop a mountain, holding his stellar lamp aloft in his right hand, supporting himself by a staff in the left. Yellow light shone down where he looked, cutting through the literal chill of the still air. He was no Fool; he contemplated his next step as well as the far reaches. His feet were cold on the snow.

And Flint leaped out of the chamber. *It had been a human representation—not a Polarian one!* Hands, not a trunk; feet, not a wheel. Direct vision, not peripheral. Eyes.

"I perceived it," the Hierophant said. "You are of Sphere Sol, surely a transferee, though we were not aware your kind possessed that marvelous secret. Your animation was the most intense I have experienced, and it suggests a truly remarkable Kirlian aura. Are you the Founder, come to correct us?" And his skin glowed apprehensively as his body sank into a globular mass. When a Polarian was worried, his shape-control suffered.

"I am of Sphere Sol, but I am not your Founder," Flint said. "I come on a mission unrelated to Tarotism; my presence here is coincidental." Yet it was amazing that his intense aura should relate so directly to animation; certainly there was some kind of connection. Was animation a nonmechanical, nonsentient way to identify the

Kirlian aura? If so, he had been guided by fate into a highly significant insight.

The Hierophant regained his composure. "It is not that we have anything to fear from such a visitation; we have followed the principles of the Arcana faithfully. But the very presence of the Founder after these centuries would suggest some serious development."

"I understand," Flint said, considerably reassured himself. "I respect your privacy as you respect mine; no news of this shall leave these premises. Let us proceed with the reading." And he rolled back into the chamber. When he returned to Sol Sphere, he would do some research on Tarotism and its Founder.

The Hermit manifested again—this time as a Polarian. The card dictated the symbol, but his mind animated it. Or rather his Kirlian aura did. He could control the image to some extent. And in dealing he must have controlled the order of the cards—but if the supernatural had some hand in it, that was as valid. Flint trusted to superscience, but at his core he accepted magic also. He was still a Paleolithic man, and he had seen the effect of spells, and learned civilized behavior from the Shaman, the tribe's magic man, still the wisest person Flint had ever known. Was there really any difference between superscience and magic?

"This covers you," the Hierophant said, touching the machine to make it deal the first card. "This defines the influence upon you, the atmosphere in which you relate." And Flint found himself standing naked and sexually neuter within a circular wreath. Around him stood four figures: a flying animal, a Polarian, Old Snort the dinosaur, and a wheeled carnivorous beast. These in their diverse, devious fashions symbolized the four conditions of existence: gaseous, liquid, solid, and energy. More specifically, air, water, ground, and fire; as at the Temple entrance, the four elements.

"This is the Cosmos key," the Hierophant explained. "The Crown of the Magi. It signifies that your mission relates to the whole of our galaxy, affecting all creatures. It is also the key of great promise; what you do is good, reaching for perfection."

Flint didn't comment. He agreed with the card—but who *wouldn't?* It signified nothing but flattery. If this were the practical nature of a Tarot reading, it was a waste of his time.

"This crosses you," the Hierophant continued, dealing the next. "That is, what opposes you." And before Flint appeared a handsome queen on her throne, holding a staff in one hand and a flower in the other. A cat stood before her.

"Good Queen Bess," Flint murmured wryly, reminded of his experience at System Capella. But this was *not* Queen Bess, but a superficial figure whose ultimate nature he could not fathom. He concentrated, defining it, and the image became Polarian: a female rolling over an elevated ramp, beneath which flames leaped. A two-wheeled carnivore moved complacently beside her.

"Beware the Queen of Energy!" the Hierophant said. "Observe the destructive flame, her hallmark."

Queen of Energy. Flint's mission was concerned with the problem of civilization, which was the problem of energy. Transfer enabled the Spheres to elevate their level of civilization without increasing their consumption of energy—and a foreign galaxy was trying to steal the energy of the Milky Way galaxy, incidentally destroying its substance. In short, the card was right on target—and somewhat more specific than the first card. But chance would have both relevant and some irrelevant symbols.

"This crowns you," the Hierophant said, dealing another card for animation. "This is the ideal for which you strive, your best potential."

It was a massive fortress, not quite square in Sol fashion or round in Pole fashion, but a cross between them. It was girt by four sturdy towers of similar ambiguity: one flaming, one filled with water, one hollow, and one solidly packed. The four conditions, or elements, again. "The Four of Solid," the Hierophant said. "The symbol of power. But it is primarily a matter of maintaining what you have, and achieving equilibrium through negotiation. And," he added a bit slyly, "on the purely personal level, it means pleasant news from a lady."

That put Flint in mind of Tsopi, as pleasant a female as he had encountered. Could this Tarot tell him anything of her?

"This is beneath you," the Hierophant said, dealing again. "The foundation, the basis of your mission." And it was the crater of Luna, or rather the region known as the Lake of Death, inverted as it had looked to him in the hour of his capitulation, when he had made the decision to continue with the transfer mission, rather than to die alone. Then the image receded as if he were rising, and the surrounding landscape of Earth's moon came into view: the Lake of Dreams, the craters Burg, Posidonius, Hercules, and Atlas, the Sea of Serenity . . . and then the larger Sea of Rains, Sea of Cold, and Ocean of Storms. Finally the entire face of the moon was visible, and it *was* a face, the Man in the Moon, the Lake of Dreams forming its left eyebrow. It became small in the distance, and the horizon of a planetary landscape rose up, with two towers, and two carnivores sitting beside a river, howling at that lunar face.

"The moon," the Hierophant continued. "Adapted from that of your own Imperium. Few planets are blessed with such a close, magnificent companion. This is the symbol of secrecy, of hidden urges, horror, fear, dragging through poisoned darkness in the absence of air—"

"I *know!*" This card was so relevant it was stifling.

The Polarian went on quickly. "This is behind you, that which has just passed." And it was a charging chariot.

"Enough!" Flint cried against the floor, not caring to expose his experiences in the Eye of the Charioteer on System Capella. They had been good experiences, with a strong-Kirlian Dragon and a Kirlian queen who had, as promised, been very young in bed. These cards, seeming to orient on him with demonic perception, were striking entirely too close to the mark.

"This is before you," the Hierophant said, dealing the next immediately. "Perhaps it represents your next mission." It was a human heart, pierced by three swords. "Three of Gas, meaning sorrow." This time the dealer did not dally, but proceeded to the next four keys in succession—and the animation plate became subdivided so that all four were evident at once.

One was a Polarian suspended by its trunk so that its wheel could not touch the ground, rendering it helpless, yet it did not seem to be in distress: "This is yourself, unable to make an informed decision." Next a tower being blasted by lightning: "Yet your illusions will soon be destroyed to make way for new understanding." Then a pattern of six swords, their points touching within a cross: "The Six of Gas—your hopes and fears expressed within the concept of science. Your mission surely involves some modern technological concept." And the last: a dancing human skeleton wielding a scythe. "A strange animation—we Polarians have no bones—but it represents what is to be, the culmination of all these influences. And it is—"

"I see it!" Flint cried. "Death!"

"Not necessarily," the Hierophant hastened to clarify. "It is also called Transformation, a shifting from one plane to another. All of us die a little with every experience, and are reborn a little. Life itself may be considered as the process of dying."

"Maybe so," Flint agreed. "I'm not sure this is getting us anywhere, though. It's all drawn from my own mind, isn't it? That's why it seems so damned relevant. So it represents what I *think* will happen, nothing more. The reality could turn out entirely differently."

"What will happen is governed by what we are," the Hierophant explained. "And you are very special. The reading does not predict the future, it only tells what is in you. On its own terms it is valid. Your mission is important; you cannot give it up."

"I wasn't about to. But what I need are specifics. Such as who exactly is this Queen of Energy who is balking me? Can you name her?"

"No. I do not pretend to comprehend the full meaning of your reading. But *you* can identify her. Here, let me take this key as the Significator and further define it, using the keys as you have arranged them." The other images faded and the flaming Queen formed. "This covers her." And the next image showed: a huge, goatlegged, horned creature, laughing.

"The Devil!" Flint exclaimed. "And look—he has us chained to his post—" For there were two small human figures manacled to the Satanic perch, and they seemed familiar.

"Satan is God as seen by the ignorant," the Hierophant murmured. "You see the male and female figures as you and the Queen of Energy?"

"Yes I do—and now I know who she is!" Flint paused. "No, I don't know; I have never seen her in her natural form, *or* in human incarnation. But she tried to kill me twice, and may be after me a third time. How can I stop her?"

"We shall see. This crosses her." And it was four swords. "The Four of Gas. It means truce. You cannot destroy her, you can only neutralize her—declare a cessation of hostilities, if she agrees."

"Ha! I can deal with her if I can identify her. Can we verify her Polarian identity, or find out whether she's here at all?"

"We can try. Where do you see her influence?"

"In the key for the near future—Three of Gas. Sorrow. If she's here, she will cause me sorrow, all right. And the first thing I have to do is complete my mission."

"You have a good memory for the layout," the Hierophant remarked. It was actually Flint's eidetic memory in operation that seemed to accompany him regardless of the brain of his host. "As you wish: Three of Gas the Significator." The triply pierced heart returned. "This covers it." And it was overlaid by—"The Queen of Liquid."

"*Not* the Queen of Energy!" Flint said, surprised.

"Definitely a different female. Do you know one with the qualities of water? Soft, supple, beautiful, pliable, loving, with an affinity for flowing streams, not intelligent but wise in her timeless fashion, virtuous, the ideal spouse—"

"Honeybloom!" Flint cried with a pang, looking at the triply pierced heart within the Queen's bosom, struggling to continue its beating despite its transfixion. "I was to marry her, before this. But she would never hurt me!"

"Not intentionally, perhaps. This crosses her."

Flint cried out in horror. For ten terrible swords converged to pierce the Queen's body, destroying her.

"There certainly is much Gas in your reading," the Hierophant remarked. "And that is the suit of Trouble. This is the Ten—signifying ruin. Not of you—of *her*. Are you sure you have not—"

"I have to return to her!" Flint cried. "Poor, sweet Honeybloom, my green girl! She waits for me—"

"The Tarot—which I remind you is merely the animation of information you already possess—suggests it is already too late."

"I don't believe it! Right after this mission, I don't care *what* the Imps say—that's what I should be checking. My mission! Let's have a supplementary reading on that."

"We shall have to select a Significator for your mission—"

"It has to do with the Big Wheel. I must see him—now."

"The Big Wheel! That would be the Key Ten, the Wheel of Fortune, the most important one to Polarians."

It formed: a huge wheel surmounted by a sphinx. "Your Sphere Sol images are fascinating; I have never seen them animated so neatly. I refer to content as well as clarity of image. The Founder—"

"Get *on* with it."

"This covers him." Four staffs appeared, with a castle in the background. "Four of Energy. Completion, peace—"

"That's it. On."

"This crosses him." A woman, bound in front of a line of tall swords. "Eight of Gas. Interference, accidental yet—"

"I know who's been *trying* to interfere, maybe well intentioned. A Polarian female, young, pretty—"

"Has she borne issue?"

"Had children, you mean? I don't think so. She's really very sweet, in a down-to-ground sort of way, but not—"

"Page of Solid, then, for her Significator." The image formed. Tsopi.

"Yes—that's her! Check her out—I want to know if she's my enemy."

"This defines her." The image was of two overflowing cups. "Two of Liquid, signifying love, harmony. There is no enmity here."

"So she's innocent!"

"So you believe. I would be inclined to trust that judgment."

"What crosses her?"

"This crosses her. Two of Solid, signifying change. Not really a negative indication—"

Flint had had enough. "Thanks, but I have to be on my way. Can you direct me to the location of the Big Wheel?"

"I don't really advise—"

"I *know* you don't. But you have helped me—you really have!—and it's my decision."

The Hierophant glowed, resigning himself. "We do not impose advice beyond the Querent's desire. I shall show you a map."

The map was a pattern of tastes on a sphere, unlike anything Flint had used before but quite adequate to the present need.

He soon found himself at the entrance to the palace of the Big Wheel. "I have important information for His Rondure."

The guard was unimpressed. "Your identity?"

"Emissary from Sphere Sol, transferred."

The guard checked as though this were routine. "The Wheel regrets he cannot interview you at this time."

"He can't speak with a Spherical Emissary?" Flint demanded incredulously. "This is important!"

"There is an unexpiated debt."

"Well, I'll see him anyway." And Flint shoved by.

"Please desist," the guard replied. "I do not wish to incapacitate you."

But Flint continued on into the palace, certain that no attack would be made against an identified agent of a friendly Sphere.

The guard shot him on the wheel with a jet of frictive powder.

The effect was immediate and alarming. A patch of the surface of his ambulation ball became painfully rough, preventing him from controlling it properly. Uniformity of friction was vital to the control of the spherical wheel; the body was always making small adjustments of balance. When the compensation for a slippery surface was applied to a rough surface, that section grabbed and threw the body to the side. But adjustment for extra friction fouled up the minimum-friction surfaces too. The result was an increasingly erratic motion, ending in an ignominious crash.

Then Tsopi was there. No doubt the guard had notified her as soon as Flint identified himself. "Plint!" she cried on his prostrate hulk. "How did this happen?"

"The watch-cog bit me, Topsy," he explained wryly.

"He tried to see the Big Wheel," the guard explained. He did not react to Flint's pun, as there was no similarity in Polarian to the words for "dog" and "cog." Concepts could be translated; puns were lost. There were, however, dogs in this Sphere; they were twi-wheeled, fast-rolling carnivores, readily amenable to domestication.

Tsopi glowed with distress. "You cannot see him yet! I thought you understood that."

"I thought *you* understood that I *have* to see him. My mission—"

"It means that much to you?" she asked. "You risk injury—?"

"Cutespin, it means that much."

She glowed with vexation. "Then I shall not clog your roller. Come." She wrapped her supple tail about his torso and drew him upright. Her touch was delightful.

"Page of Solid," he murmured against her skin as he

tested his wheel. The friction was wearing off, being diluted and cleaned away by his body, and he was able to function—carefully. "I'm glad I can trust you."

"You have been to the Tarot Temple!" she murmured back. "I never thought to look there, Knight of Gas."

"No, I'm the Hermit," he said. But he remembered how often the Gas cards, indicated by the flashing swords (the symbolism being the way they sliced through air?), had shown up in his reading.

"Not any more. You're not giving me the slip again." She drew up before a large door. "You're sure you—?"

"Yes." Could it suddenly be this easy?

She pushed through the door. It rotated very like some he had seen on Planet Earth. Of course, even stick figures employed some circular devices, and Polarians used some back-and-forth mechanisms. Nothing was pure. He followed her.

Inside was the throne: a high, ornate ramp set above a lovely alien garden. On it was the Big Wheel; actually a rather faded old Polarian.

"Your Rondure, I bring you Plint of Outworld, Envoy of Sphere Sol," she announced.

The monarch glowed with interest. "Has your debt been abated so quickly?"

Tsopi hesitated.

"Well, speak up!" the Wheel snapped.

"I—yield it," Tsopi whispered against the floor behind her, very like a guilty cur.

"You *what*?" The Wheel rolled close, looming over them on the high ramp.

"I—"

"I heard you the first time! Female, do you seek to dishonor your Revolver as well as yourself? You yield nothing to me! The moment the individual gives way to society, our Sphere becomes frictive." That was an allusion Flint would not have understood prior to his experience with the powder. Friction meant disaster! "What would the Big Stick of Sphere Sol say if we treated his envoy so abrasively? Stop spinning around uselessly. *Abate that debt!* I want his mission done and you back in service soon, or I'll dewheel you myself! You've already wasted several hours twiddling your tail while he gossipped with the Hierophant—and the secret of transfer is of the highest rotation."

"Your Rondure," Flint said. "I only want to—"

"Oh, get this lamewheel out of here," the Big Wheel said impatiently.

Tsopi drew Flint out. "He's got a terrible, uncircular temper when he gets mad," she murmured almost inaudibly against his hide.

"You bet your little bare bearing he does!" the Wheel blasted behind them. He had put his ball against the Royal Ramp, and it acted as a sounding board to amplify the volume alarmingly. Royalty had its prerogatives.

They coasted out of the palace. "All right, you explain," Flint said. "I'll listen."

"Well, it's not easily explainable," she said. "Let's go somewhere private."

An unusual request, from a company-loving Polarian. "Somewhere private it is," he agreed. "But *then* you'll make it clear?"

"I'll certainly try," she said. "But there may be a cultural barrier."

"I've experienced cultures odder than this," he said, thinking of the triple-sexed Spicans.

"Your own is odd enough," she agreed with a flash of her normal humor. He thought of Earth and Capella, and had to agree.

They rolled up to an elevator. An aperture opened in the round chamber, then closed pneumatically when they were inside. There was an abrupt wrenching. Then the portal opened and they rolled out—into a wheelwhirling wilderness.

Flint skidded to a halt. "This is another planet!"

"Of course. No satisfactory wilderness remains on the Home Ball. This is a little resort world fifteen parsecs out, very posh. Don't you like it?"

"We mattermitted fifty light-years just like that?"

"Why not? What's the use of technology, except to bring nature closer?"

"The cost—it must be a trillion dollars to move the pair of us—"

"As I tried to explain before, our values differ from yours. We like company, not crowding—but a certain concentration is necessary for ideal efficiency. So we precess, we compromise. Better to expend energy than live in discomfort."

"That's irresponsible waste!"

"Not as we scent it. Letting a star's light proceed uselessly into space, unharnessed—*that's* waste. We save that stellar energy and turn it to our purposes. But transfer would be better, we agree. We have already noted how well it works for you."

"That's what I'm trying to *bring* to you! Why won't you *listen*?"

"That's part of the explanation. Come, let's enjoy it."

He followed her along the path into the forest. The trees were neither vine nor wood, but humps of spongy substance bearing large sunlight-collecting disks. They resembled the sentient Polarians in broad outline, just as the trees of Earth resembled men, with their leglike roots and armlike branches and stiffly erect bearing. Evidently this planet had been seeded with Polarian vegetation centuries ago. Yes it had; now that he worked it out for himself, his host-memory confirmed it. But already what he saw was merging with what he remembered: these were *trees*, perfectly natural.

"You called me Knight of Gas," he said. "How did you derive it?"

"Tarotism came here three centuries ago; it was really one of our first direct contacts with Sphere Sol culture," she said. "It has never been really popular as a cult, but it has a certain circularity. It has become established, and the cards do make a compelling entertainment for many who ascribe no philosophical value to them—as in your own Sphere. The animation effect is the main attractant, I think. Thus many of us have had readings, and some adopt the Tarotism precepts. So we pick up bits about the cards. Males and females who have reproduced are Kings and Queens; those who have not are Knights and Pages. We retain the original Solarian nomenclature, you see. The suits are determined by the qualities of character and situation. Thus I, as a basically planet-bound creature, am Solid or Ground, while you, as a highly mobile off-planet creature, your essence expressed wholly by your Kirlian aura, are Gas or Air. In the archaic Solarian terms, I'm a Coin and you're a Sword."

"You certainly are a coin," he agreed. "You roll and you're precious."

"Thank you," she said, vibrating her ball against his trunk in a most stimulating way.

"And I have seen some combat in my time, so I'm a Sword. In fact, I'm a flintsmith—I *make* weapons. Good ones, too."

"I am aware. I knew you then. Remember?"

"So you did." He paused. "You knew me as a human being. So to you I'm a stick figure, all angles and bones. Doesn't it bother you?"

"No. We believe in outside contacts, in exogamous cooperation. It's part of our nature. We have known of the nature of Solarians for many centuries. The Tarot itself has prepared the way, for we associate ourselves with the circular Coins and Solarians with the thrust of Swords. The message of the Tarot is that all systems are valid, no matter how strange some may seem at first. I know you are a fine person in alien guise. And we have a common debt. And now you are here in rotary form, visiting my Suit of Solid as it were, and it is good."

"Yet you will not let me—the Big Wheel will not let me complete my mission."

She drew up on a fine expanse of hard foliage overlooking a flowing stream. Paddlewheeled waterfowl disported on its surface, and two-wheeled animals moved away, alarmed by the intrusion of sapients. Originally all creatures of the Solarian home planet had been bicycled, but in time the sapients had lifted one wheel, becoming unicycled, freeing the other to become the communicatory ball. The pattern seemed familiar to Flint; human beings had progressed similarly, from quadruped to biped status.

"Try to understand," she said. "To us, the individual is paramount in the circuit. Government exists only to serve the needs of the citizens. Where the interests of a single entity conflict with that of society, the entity takes precedence."

"That's backwards! Government must always serve the good of the greatest number."

"In a thrust-culture, perhaps that is so. Here, no." She made a little gesture with her tail, much as a human used hands to augment a difficult point. "What is good for the individual is good for the society."

"But centralized society would collapse!" Flint was not used to debating economics or political science, yet his point seemed irrefutable.

"Well, it is true we lack the straight-thrust dynamism of your muscle-and-bone mode. But we have achieved the equilibrium of the turning wheel. We accomplish much by accommodation and mutual respect, rather than force."

"And your Sphere is twice the diameter of ours," Flint said. "I don't claim to comprehend it, but I admit I like it. But what happens when the interests of individuals conflict?"

"This is the heart of our system. It is a form of mutual debt. They must work it out together."

"Debt. *There* is the key I don't have. How do you—"

"Divergent interests must be reconciled. Factions must unify. The interest of one entity must merge with the other, so that no dichotomy exists. You might call it love."

"Love thine enemy?" Flint remembered another of the fragments of wisdom of the Shaman that had not come clear.

"There can *be* no enemy. Only debt to be expiated."

Flint pondered. "Let me see whether I have it straight," he said at last. "Or curved, as the case may be."

"Circular," she supplied. "At Sol, a straight line may be the solution to most problems; here it is a spiral."

"Yes. You and I saved each other's lives, and so we owed each other our lives. A mutual debt, very hard to repay. You can't take *back* a life, after all. Now in our thrust-culture, we'd call that self-canceling. Equal and opposite forces. But I suppose if you plotted it on a spiral, it could start quite a spin. Equal and opposite thrusts applied to the two sides of a wheel can make it roll twice as fast. So—" But he stopped, beginning to realize. "Pleasant news from a lady. . . ."

"I'm aware that different conventions obtain in your culture," she said. "You tend to be indrawn, perhaps as the natural consequence of your outward thrust."

"That's what I was saying! The Shaman explained it to me, back when I hardly understood and had to stretch my mind to take it in. To every action there is an equal and opposite reaction."

"Yes. So you are an expansive, extroverted species—but also strongly introverted, alienophobic. Your mating pattern reflects this. You seek a stranger for the purpose of procreation, then establish lifelong liaison with that stranger. To us that seems extreme. We prefer familiar matings—but we form no restrictive relation."

"You're saying you're polygamous?"

"No, that would be the wrong connotation. We mate for social or economic reasons, but our love is intense while it endures. At the end, there is a child—and all debts have been expiated by that act of creation, all differences reconciled in that child. The chapter is finished; we never mate again with the same partners."

"To us that would be frivolous," Flint said. "Mating is

tantamount to marriage—a permanent commitment. This is my relation to Honeybloom, the Queen of Liquid. Or Water, Cups, or Hearts, by the cards. When I return to Outworld, I'll marry her."

"I understand that, and I wish you well. It is your system," Tsopi said. "But at the moment you are part of the Polarian culture, and you cannot complete your technical mission until our debt is expiated. There is no conflict between me and Honeybloom"—she had used his term, for there were no parallel concepts in Polarian, no flowers, hence no blooms and no bees and no honey—"so love me now, and never again. You may regard this in the line of duty, since the Big Wheel is anxious to have our debt abated, and will meet with you immediately afterward."

So, circuitously, politics had become sex. "On Planet Earth, that would be called prostitution," he said.

"I do not understand the term."

Indeed, there had been no concept for this either; he had had to use the human word. "Allow me to be a bit finicky," he said. "I can indulge in sex on a purely casual basis, or as a necessity of my mission, or I can marry. You seem to be offering something in between. Short-term love. And I don't even know how it is done here. You have no—do you know how Solarians do it?"

"Yes," she said, glowing with distaste. "It is linear, again. The male pokes his little stick into the female's—

"All right. You have the idea. Now how do Polarians get the male seed together with the female egg?"

"I propose to show you," she said.

"I could learn faster if you *told* me first," he said with developing exasperation. This reluctance to speak directly to the point—but of course, that was Polarian nature.

"Why did you stop me from describing the Solarian act?" she inquired in return.

"Solarian act?" For a moment he was baffled.

"How the male makes his stick stiff and—"

"Oh. That sort of thing isn't discussed openly among humans. Not in mixed company." Then he did a double-take. "I see. Some things are better performed than described."

"Yes. Also, your human viewpoint might cause you as much distress as our own viewpoint causes us in contemplation of the Solarian act, which seems aggressive and unnatural to us. Why, if the male poked too hard, or missed the opening—"

"All *right*!" Flint made a fluid shrug. "Better done than said, as we agreed. I don't promise to be an effective partner, but—"

"Is it not true that no instruction needs to be given to your individuals for them to procreate?"

"It is true. One look at a girl like Honeybloom and the rest follows naturally, if she's willing." He decided not to go into the subject of rape; she would never understand it. "But we have better vision than you do; we are visually stimulated."

"We have better taste than you do," Tsopi said. "Follow me." And she began a slow circle.

He rolled after her—and picked up a most sensual taste. She was laying down amour, and his host-body was electrified. His own glands responded with the masculine equivalent, which he knew she would pick up as she completed the circuit and covered his trail. Here was the true meaning of circularity!

Around and around they went, like two unicycles on a circus track. Slowly they spiraled inward, the taste stimulation intensifying. To hell with duty, he thought; this was *fun*. Every taste she laid down was a tangible caress, intellectual as well as physical. Tsopi was a most attractive specimen of her kind to begin with, and this courtship of hers enhanced her allure considerably. Closer together they came, until they were revolving about a common center like twin planets, almost touching.

And Flint broke away. "No," he said, though his whole body pulsed with desire for the culmination. "Not this way."

She paused, disappointed. "You do not wish to expiate the debt?"

"Not as a business transaction. Love is love, and my mission is my mission. I don't care to mix them." Actually it was more subtle than that, for he *had* mixed them in Capella System. But while it was all right to enjoy an interaction initiated for political expedience, it was not right to make political expediency from an act of love. The act had to justify itself. He had come to like Tsopi too well to use her—and though she was quite willing to be so used, in fact almost insisted on it, he could not. His mission had become an albatross, destroying the validity of his personal interaction. Now he was enough of a

Polarian to place that personal matter first—but not enough to work it out this way. Let no one ever say or think he had cultivated Tsopi only as a means to the end of his mission!

"But this is the way it is done in our culture!"

"Not in ours—and I *am* a Solarian."

"The Big Wheel will not see you unless—"

"Unless I compromise my personal ideals. *I* won't see *him* on that basis."

It was as though he had struck her—and he *had,* figuratively. The Polarians had utmost respect for the rights of the individual, and he had told her his rights were being infringed, not facilitated, by her well-meaning action.

"In trying to abate my debt with you, I have complicated it," she said. "It was wrong of me to impose on you. I will tell the Big Wheel the debt has been expiated."

"There never *was* any debt!" he said. "We humans save the life of a friend as a matter of necessity. To fail to make that effort would be cowardice and perhaps murder. You helped me, I helped you; if there was any debt, it canceled out right there. That's the way it is, in my culture; I cannot claim otherwise."

"I should have understood you better," she said. There was a muffled quality to her voice; perhaps the wood of the tree was damping it.

They returned to the mattermitter but did not enter. "The Big Wheel must not see us," she explained. "He would immediately know that we have not—"

"He would?" But he took her word for it. "Then how do—?" But already his host-memory was supplying the answer. The Polarians had refined the technology of micromattermission so that they could ship individual message capsules the size of a living cell, and move them along in a steady stream so that virtually instantaneous communication resulted. These capsules could carry a complete sonic and visual image, but generally the visual part was dispensed with as not worth the effort. In this case, their demeanor would probably betray their lack of expiation.

Tsopi provided the palace identification code, and Flint spoke it into the message-coder. The Big Wheel responded immediately. "So you tweaked the tail of the Small Bear, eh?"

And Flint realized that the literal meaning of Tsopi's name in Polarian was "Small Bear," a bear being another carnivore similar in habit to the Earthian type, though dissimilar in appearance. And of course the star Polaris was in the constellation of Ursa Minor, the Small Bear, right in the tail. The mythology of the skies, like that of the Tarot cards, had uncanny relevance. Or was his life actually dominated by the stars and cards? It was difficult to come to a complacent conclusion.

"Uh, yes," Flint said, taken aback by this familiarity of the governor of a Sphere. "Now I'd like to give you the key to the mechanism of—"

"Take the mattermitter. I have precoded your destination."

So the Wheel was ready for personal audience now. "Thank you." Actually, the expression of thanks was not usual, here; a substantial favor constituted a debt, and an insubstantial one merely enhanced circularity and needed no additional expression. The exchange cut off.

He turned to Tsopi. "That did it. Let's go."

"I cannot go," she said. "The Wheel must not see me at this time."

"Oh, yes." How was she supposed to have changed? It was way too soon for her to manifest pregnancy, if Polarians had such a state. The information was surely buried in his host-brain, but there were layers of emotional repression that blocked it off. The host had perished because of a blighted romance, it seemed. The surest indication of the essence of a given species seemed to be in what it guarded most ardently: its mode of reproduction. But Flint's mission was too urgent to permit time-consuming introspection, and now that he had his appointment with the Wheel he didn't need to delve. "But where will you go, then?"

"I will seek my own repose. Now, do not keep His Rotation waiting."

"Right. 'Bye." He rolled into the mattermitter. With luck, it would not take long to acquaint the technicians with the transfer equations. Then he could return to square things with Tsopi—his way. Or round them off, in the local vernacular.

He rolled out at the spaceport of a medieval Polaris Sphere planet. He knew it by the architecture in the distance; his host-memory had no reticence about identifying it. Of course Polaris suffered Spherical regression the way *all* Spheres did. That was why transfer was so crucial. It was an instant, *cheap* mode of communication that could bring civilization right to the Fringe and keep it there. Or at least reduce the cultural lag. For even on Imperial Earth there were backward sections, so efficient communication was not the whole answer.

A port official coasted up. "Salutation, Flint of Sphere Sol," he buzzed. "I am Dligt, the Polarian Ringer of this region. It is most circular of you to assist us in this difficult contact."

"Hello, Delight. I understood I was to meet with the Big Wheel," Flint said uncertainly.

"Of course. Immediately following your dialogue with the aliens. I do not know how we should have managed without your kind presence."

What was the Wheel pulling? Obviously this misrouting was deliberate; Ringer Dligt had been advised of his coming, and there was a job in progress. "It is the least of spinoffs," Flint said politely. "But in order that there be no confusion, would you rehearse what is anticipated?"

"Gladly." The official pointed into the yellowish sky with his trunk. "In close orbit is a craft from Sphere Sol. One of your lifeships. We were uncertain how to approach them, as they have been traveling for three hundred of your years and know nothing of our Sphere. It seems the automatic mechanical devices of the ship have selected this as a suitable planet for colonization, and in due course a landing will be attempted. The shock of discovering it to be already inhabited by unfamiliar sapients may be uncomfortable. But with you here, a genuine Solarian, one of their kind—no offense—"

"But I've never seen a lifeship!" Flint protested. "My world was settled one hundred Earth-years ago—about three and a half Etamin-Outworld years. Our own lifeship is long gone."

"We understand. We have similar problems at our Fringe, and the voyage takes up to four hundred years on that scale. But this ship must have started its voyage the same time as your own ancestors did. You were contemporaries at the start, and also in space for two centuries. And you have suffered the same regressional displacement, even as we have here. And you are of their kind, a thrust-culturist. You are ideally suited to explain the situation to them."

"That they can not settle here?"

"Oh, no. Refusal would not be circular. We would welcome a colony of Solarians. They would be a real asset to this world, a continual source of cultural stimulation. But they must be made to understand that they will be guests in our Sphere, subject ultimately to our government. They must acknowledge the legitimacy of the Big Wheel and refrain from interspecies altercations."

"Yes, of course," Flint agreed, thankful for the education he had received at the Shaman's wheel. Shaman's *hands*, rather. Spherical codes required that the authority of the native Sphere species be acknowledged. That was why Polarians yielded to human authority on Planet Outworld. The rights of such minorities were carefully protected by the host-Sphere, and inter-Sphere complications were anathema. It would be prohibitively expensive to wage Spherical war, and the Fringe areas were hardly worth it. There was also, as Dligt had mentioned, considerable positive stimulation when divergent sapients shared a planet amicably. But of course a ship that had traveled in isolation for three centuries would not be aware of that. Sol's Spherical boundary had been established only in the past 150 years, filling in the region of space not yet taken by Spheres Polaris, Nath, Canopus, and Spica. "Mattermit me aboard and I'll talk with their captain."

"I must demur, implying no uncircularity," Dligt said against his own hide. "We have established a visual-auditory communication channel, though we have not as yet implemented contact. We can project your image into the ship, and it will appear substantial to them. We believe this would be the expedient mode."

"Why?"

"Regressives of any Sphere tend to be alienophobic, and yours more than most," the Polarian explained. "There could be personal danger."

"Um, yes. I *am* in alien guise—no offense."

"Offense? Oh—uncircularity." Flint had heard this concept as "offense" but that was not quite accurate. He would have to watch that, and make sure he understood what was intended, rather than what he expected. There were so many little cultural pitfalls. Most were minor, but some could mean real trouble. "Naturally not. This is why your help is so important. You understand such matters from the Solarian view. You wil be able to interview them without creating avoidable uncir—that is, affront."

So Dligt was also trying to accommodate himself to Flint's linguistic mannerisms! A diplomat, surely.

The Big Wheel was pretty smart, Flint realized. This matter had come up while a Solarian was in the vicinity, so the visitor was being drafted to help tide over what could be a difficult contact. If anything went wrong, Imperial Earth could have no complaint. Strictly speaking, an emissary was not under local Sphere authority, but it would be pointless to object. Definitely uncircular! And Flint was curious about the regressed humans; it would be like meeting his own ancestors as they arrived at Outworld. "Right. Make the connection."

The Ringer showed him into the communication booth. "Our operator will monitor the contact," he said. "Should there be any problem, he will spiral off transmission."

"What problem could there be? It's only an image."

"We are not certain. But we prefer to be careful."

They were apt to be so careful they ended up running around in circles, Flint thought. Better the straight-line thrust of the human mind, that could move into and through a situation efficiently.

Suddenly he was in the Solarian lifeship. Everything was metal—a flat, featureless floor, bare walls, and complicated ceiling. The automatic mechanism kept the ship largely sterile.

But where were the people? Could they have regressed to the point of extinction? The ship really didn't need them for its operation, but it was supposed to take care of them and see to it that they were equipped for colonization. But regression could lead to primitive violence, possibly wiping out the living complement. It wasn't supposed to happen, but it *might*. The ship could protect its cargo from almost every danger but human nature.

Flint tried rolling forward—and it worked. The floor of the communication booth was movable, like a mat on rollers, and so he could shove it about with his wheel without actually going anywhere. The projection translated those floor-movements into modifications of the image, so that he could travel about the ship exactly as if he were really on board. Very nice; he had not experienced anything like this on Planet Earth. The Shaman had been right, as always: there was much to respect about Sphere Polaris, technologically and socially. Overall, it seemed to be somewhat more advanced than Sphere Sol.

He moved about the chamber, noting the banks of buttons and dials. This was evidently the control room, perhaps sealed off to prevent meddling by the passengers.

He found a passage exiting from it; sure enough, it was blocked by a closed door, like an airlock.

Well, he was accomplishing nothing here. He rolled right at the bulkhead—and through it. "Now I know what a ghost feels like," he murmured, and was startled by the sound of his own voice. His image-ball could not have produced it. He spoke against the supporting wall of the communication booth, and it was broadcast here along with the rest.

He emerged into another hall, similar to the first. There were side passages branching off. He should have thought to study a map of the ship; he was in danger of getting lost.

Well, he didn't have all day. If he went straight ahead he was bound to get somewhere, as the size of the ship was finite. He passed through another sealed portal—and suddenly faced the residential portion of the ship.

It was breathtaking—though in this host he did not breathe, exactly. The whole cargo section had been left open, a monstrous cavelike chamber, with the housing of the colonists on the outer wall. The spin of the ship held them there at approximately Earth gravity; this was a lot simpler and cheaper and more reliable than artificial gravity, and simplicity was the keynote of a lifeship, for all its sophistication. The less complicated it was, the less could go wrong with it; that was a universal principle.

By the same token, the necessary recycling of organic substances was done by natural means. Assorted plants grew, in some sections amounting to a veritable jungle. He recognized berry bushes and fruit trees. This was very like that ancient Garden of Eden the Shaman had told him of.

Had man come to Earth originally in just such a vessel, and the legend of Eden was all that remained after regression had wiped out the memory? If so, where had man come *from?* Could there be genuine human beings elsewhere in the galaxy, never connected to Earth or Sphere Sol? He would have to meditate on that sometime.

He moved into the nearest field, skirting a small lake where fish swam. He rounded a tangle of hedge—and encountered his first sentient.

Flint wheeled back, appalled. The creature was grotesque. It stood on a split fundament, with bony joints at intervals. Two bent sticklike appendages projected from the sides, terminating in splays of miniature digits. The thing was all angular and rigid, yet with an irregular covering of flesh that made portions of it bulge outward like spilling candle wax, half-congealed. At the top was a head perforated by several holes, half-buried under a tumbling mane of hairs.

Flint's system revolted. He felt sick, which was a problem, because this body had no way to vomit. He had never liked illness or grotesqueries, and never before had he contemplated anything so inherently disgusting. For this was no primitive monster; it was conscious and sapient.

Then he realized: This was a human being. A naked female.

He forced himself to reorient, as he had in Spica when disorganized by the enormity of the triangular sexuality there. Gradually his human essence assumed command. By the definition of his kind, this was a nubile young woman, lithe and healthy and sexually desirable, like his fiancée Honeybloom. Monster indeed!

How thoroughly he had merged with his Polarian host! This was a plain warning: his Kirlian aura was fading dangerously, reducing his human identity. It was supposed to diminish at the rate of one intensity-norm per day, but evidently this was variable. He would have to wrap up this mission and return to his own body—he quelled a surge of distaste at the notion—for a prolonged recuperation of aura. Maybe he was fading faster as a result of the fatigue of repeated transfer missions.

But at the moment he had another mission: to explain things to these lifeship primitives, and to give the secret of transfer to the Polarians.

The girl, meanwhile, seemed as startled as he was. In a moment she would bolt in terror. "Do not flee," he said quickly. "I will not hurt you."

She screamed piercingly and ran, her torso and limbs flexing in a manner that would have intrigued Flint had he been in a human body. He could not afford to have her depart in confusion, so he wheeled after her, overtaking her easily. He reached his trunk around her, to stop her flight—and it passed through her without resistance. He had forgotten he was only an image.

So he paced her, keeping up easily because of his superior mode of travel. "Listen to me! I represent Polaris Sphere—" And stopped. Idiot that he was, *he had been speaking in Polarian.* No way for the girl to understand him.

In fact, he had gone at this all wrong. He should have had the technician arrange for a human image rather than this Polarian one; surely the equipment was capable of such a translation. As a strange human, he could have commanded the girl's attention, and spoken to her in her own language. Obvious—in retrospect.

Now the girl's screams had alerted her tribe. Naked men appeared, carrying homemade spears: crude weapons, preflint, he noted professionally. What a boon flintstone was to ancient man, with its supreme hardness and chipability. Yet here, amidst the advanced metal of a functioning spacecraft, they had lost even good stone. Probably there was no flint to be had. Without hesitation they threw these clumsy shafts at Flint—without effect, of course.

When they saw that, they all fled. Flint rolled to a halt. He had bungled the mission brilliantly. "Cancel the projection, before I do any more harm," he said.

And he was back in the booth.

"I'm sorry," he said. "I ruined it. A complete disaster. As a Paleolithic man myself, I should have known better."

"Do not be unwheeled," Dligt said. "You may have been too close to the problem, lacking the vantage of dissimilarity. We have failed many times in initial contacts; your involvement was an experiment in linearity that has taught us much."

"You're right; the straight-line approach can be completely wrong. I see that now. But I have spoiled it for your circular approach, too. I don't know how to make amends."

"Not at all. Being now satisfied that the linear system is not applicable to the present case, we shall return to circularity. We shall project a still figure of a Polarian, along with a tangible offering of trinkets to delight the primitive mind. In time they will discover that there is no harm in the projection, and will seek more trinkets, which we shall provide. This will lead inevitably to communication, because they will desire it. It will take time, and many circuits, but the end result is assured."

"Circularity . . ." Flint said. "Slow but sure. Yes, I understand now. And I suspect you understand the primitive mind better than I do."

"I do approach it from a more distant perspective," the Ringer agreed. "Also, civilization has an insidious effect, if you are not accustomed to it. It changes you subtly, until you are a different person—without knowing it. You are no longer Paleolithic."

"You are perceptive," Flint said.

"Merely trained in the field."

Flint thought of Tsopi, who had not tried to oppose his direct-line thinking. Had he appeared to her as the lifeship female had appeared to him? All angular and horrible? Then she, too, had overcome a formidable revulsion —only to run afoul of the human mode of thinking, as disastrous to social interaction as to initial contacts. "I am unused to the concept of circularity, but perceive it has merit. You have been most understanding. May I prevail on you to put a linear query in a separate matter?"

The official seemed surprised. "Linearity is your nature, yet you have done much to overcome it. I shall try to respond in that fashion."

"I appreciate it, Delight. If one of the parties declines to make a debt-settlement when the opportunity offers, what happens?"

"That is the subject of half our literature!" Dligt said. "The results are highly variable. Many debts cannot be settled."

"One that *can* be settled. If a male declined solely because he preferred to perform an unrelated mission—one that could wait a little longer, but—"

"To turn down a debt-settlement capriciously? Nothing is more important than debt. The entire culture suffers if any facet of individual prerogative is infringed. Are you familiar with the legend of Roller and the Bearing?"

Flint stifled a snort of laughter (not hard to stifle, since the Polarian ball did not snort well), realizing that this was serious. "I regret, no."

"Roller was a primitive yet attractive male who inadvertently incurred debt-exchange with an immature female, a bearing. Her age prevented immediate abatement. When she was of age she sought him out—but Roller did not recognize her, and so quite properly declined to mate. Maturation changes females, you understand—"

"I understand," Flint said, remembering the phenomenal change in Honeybloom, once a thin, shy child.

"Rather than off-balance the debt by informing him of his error, the Bearing sought her own repose."

Flint's memory jogged. Tsopi had used that phrase. "Does that mean what I begin to suspect it means?"

"She is now in the sky as one of our fainter stars. It is a beloved, sad story."

Flint's worst fear had just been realized. "She . . . died? Rather than tell him?"

"In linear terms, yes. Forgive me if I have become circular. I realize your query was theoretical, but it is a delicate subject, even so. The Polarian mind can conceive of virtually no circumstances that would justify such crude debt-abatement."

Dligt evidently had a pretty fair notion of Flint's problem, but was being most circumspect—as was the Polarian nature. "Such crudity is possible to a primitive alien mind, however," Flint said grimly, feeling a terrible rawness inside. "Please, I have made another uncircular mistake. Will you mattermit me directly to the palace on Polaris Prime?"

"Certainly." And without delay the official set the controls, and Flint rolled through the mattermitter into the palace a hundred and fifty light-years away.

The Big Wheel was right there. "So the emissary completes a circuit," he commented.

Suddenly Flint thought: What did Roller do, when he learned of the Bearing's fate? "In your constellations, where is the figure of Roller?"

"Odd you should inquire about that particular figure. Or were you already aware that it is otherwise known as Etamin, your Dragon star?"

"I am aware *now*," Flint said. And he knew what he had to do. Whether he was now more Solarian or more Polarian he could not be sure, but the Polarian way was what he had to seek. Every mistake he had made had been the result of linear thinking.

"I shall summon my technicians," the Big Wheel said.

"I regret I cannot meet with them," Flint said. "I regret that your Sphere must suffer, but at the moment its welfare conflicts with that of an individual. If you will do me the kindness of informing me of the place of Topsy's demise, I will join her there." As Roller had joined the Bearing in the sky.

The Big Wheel paused. "We do not seek to impose our conventions on the natives of other Spheres. We did not understand you properly, and now we make amends by facilitating your mission linearly."

"Please spare me the embarrassment of attempting to explain," Flint said. "It would not be circular."

"We seem to have crossed each other's boundaries."

"Yes."

"In cases like this, individuals have been known to visit the Temple of Tarot."

"Circularity." And Flint rolled rapidly out of the Palace.

Back on Earth, he knew, they would never understand. Perhaps there would be Spherical repercussions because of his demise. But all that had become secondary. He had to settle with Tsopi before he could undertake anything else. Now he understood Polarian nature, and had phased through far enough to be dominated by it—and it was not just a matter of fading Kirlian aura. His treatment of Tsopi had been as wrong as failing to avoid the thrust of a spear. The shock of seeing himself as other creatures saw him, there in the lifeship, had made a great deal clear, too late. Had he only paid proper attention earlier. . . .

He crossed the Temple portal and dropped inside. The Hierophant met him as he coasted up. "The Hermit returns."

"The Knight of Gas," Flint corrected him. Actually he had reproduced, making him the King of Gas, but that had been in a Spican host and probably didn't count. "I have come to join the Page of Solid. I must be one with the Small Bear." And what was a small bear, except a bearing?

"I am constrained to inquire whether you realize what this means, since you are not of our culture."

"It means the Three of Gas—and the Dancing Skeleton. Sorrow and Death, as the cards foretold. I did not appreciate their relevance before, but—"

"Neither do you appreciate them now," the Hierophant said. "You cannot substitute the Page of Earth for the Queen of Liquid and retain the relevance of the reading."

"At the moment, they are one," Flint said. "I balked on an abatement of debt, and I must repair that error in whatever way I can. Unite me with Topsy."

"Spoken like a true Polarian," the Hierophant remarked.

"Mock me if you will, for I deserve it. But deliver me to her."

"I would not mock so noble a gesture. It *is* the Polarian way, and you have shown creditable comprehension and decision. Stand in the animation chamber."

So it comes, Flint thought. Oddly, he was not afraid. On Luna, given the chance to die in his own fashion, he had declined, choosing instead to endure his problematical life. Now, rather than pursue a mission suddenly simplified, he chose the great transformation of death. It was not sensible, linearly, but it was right. He rolled across to the plate.

And as the light came, there was Tsopi, so real it seemed he could touch her, more beautiful than any creature he had ever seen before. "I come to expiate the debt between us," he said. "And—I love you, Small Bear."

For a moment she stood there, beautifully balanced on her wheel, like the tantalizing image she was. In that pause he realized that he had spoken only part of the truth when he said he loved her. He loved the other Small Bear too: the mode of Sphere Polaris.

Then she spoke, startling him—until he remembered the Polarian finesse with projections. Naturally they could animate her voice too. "And I love you, Alien Stone," she said, translating his name as he had hers. "It is like rising from the dead, finding you thus."

That hurt. What sadist was orchestrating this dialogue of his humiliation? "Wherever you may be, there I join you."

"I am in the Great Circle." Around them formed the huge bright sphere of the Polarian heaven, the Ultimate Circularity in which all of Sphere Sol was merely a faint constellation. There was the sound of perfect music and the taste of rapturous interaction and the sensation of harmony.

Flint reached toward her with his trunk, and she reached toward him with her tail—but he hesitated, not wishing to shatter the illusion by verifying her insubstantiality. Then she closed the gap—and there was physical contact.

Astonished, he drew her close. "You're alive!"

"Now I am," she said. "The Big Wheel bade me wait, so that he could remedy the matter."

So His Rondure had detoured Flint to an educational mission while he got the facts from Tsopi. "The Wheel is a meddling genius!" Flint exclaimed angrily. "He's downright linear in his fashion."

"That is how he retains his position," she agreed.

"Well, I meant everything I said, even if you *are* alive. I don't care *how* many Polarians laugh their balls off at my folly! I came to—"

"No one laughs," she demurred. "What you have done is beautiful, more circular than any native could have managed. You have reenacted the legend of your star."

He drew apart. "It is time," he said.

"Yes."

They circled each other, as before. Flint didn't care if the whole of Sphere Polaris was watching; he was going to abate the debt in style.

Tsopi laid down her provocative taste, and Flint augmented it with his own. The two trails fed on each other, building up the mood layer by layer as the two wheels spiraled inward toward the center.

At last they met. Flint's trunk and Tsopi's tail twined together, and their two balls touched each other in an electrifying spinning kiss.

Flint found that his body needed no instruction. As with Solarians and all other species both sapient and animal, nature sufficed. He knew it could not be worse than poking a stiffened stick into the body of the loved one.

Yet the steps of it astonished the human fragment of his mind. For at the height of his passion, Flint lay down and released his wheel. He had not realized that this was possible; he had supposed it was an inseparable part of his anatomy. Now it rolled slowly across the floor away from him, leaving him lame. Without that wheel, motion was virtually impossible; only in an extraordinary circumstance would any Polarian part with it.

The act of reproduction was one such occasion. Tsopi lay down opposite him and moved close—and Flint took the exposed portion of her wheel into his vacant wheel-chamber. The sensations were intensified excruciatingly, for they were direct; her secretions mixed with his without being diluted by an intervening surface. Trunk and tail reached around to twine together, drawing the connection tight.

Now the real action began. The rim of Flint's torso met the rim of Tsopi's, sealing all the way around their mutual sphere, so that none of it was exposed to the air. And the two of them spun it—rapidly. More rapidly than possible in any individual situation, for the wheel-controlling mechanisms of both parties were operating in tandem. Each had specialized adhesive muscles that touched the embedded surface of the wheel, moving it precisely and releasing it to other muscles. This was more than enough for ordinary locomotion—but now it was doubled.

The wheel spun so fast that it grew warm, then hot.

Both Flint and Tsopi secreted extra fluid to bathe that sphere in its sealed chamber and alleviate friction, but still the heat increased. It was like traveling through a boiling lake at super-Polarian velocity. Flint knew, now, that that heat was penetrating the globe, making it pervious to the special juices. The elixir was reaching inward, deeper, changing the cellular structure of the mass, activating unique enzymes.

At last something within the wheel reacted. There was an electrochemical shift, as of a fire flaring up. It was the climax, that first stirring of buried animation. There was an instant of almost unbearable rapture as the shock went through the mass, then exhaustion.

Flint and Tsopi fell apart. The wheel rolled free of both of them, steaming. And while they struggled to regain their strength—complicated by the absence of their wheels, through which they normally ate, respirated, and eliminated—the loose mass began to shake and flex as though something inside were trying to get out. But it did not break open like a hatching egg; it elongated and unfolded, stage by stage, until it emerged complete, sculptured by the hand of nature: a young Polarian.

The newcomer spent some time getting the feel of his wheel and ball and achieving proper balance. Then, abruptly, he departed.

"Children take care of themselves," Tsopi explained, her ball vibrating weakly against the floor.

"So I note. But what about us? We've been dewheeled."

For answer, she disengaged her tail, put it to her empty base, and popped the little communication ball in. Her base closed about it despite the disparity of size. With difficulty she got up, until she stood balanced precariously on that tiny ball. There was her new wheel!

Then she cast about with her empty tail until she found Flint's trunk. Her ball socket embraced the available portion of his ball, as he had embraced her embryo-wheel before. For a moment the little ball spun swiftly between them in a remarkably intimate, sweet kiss, a wheel-copulation in miniature; then she drew away, and took the ball with her. And with that pang of separation, Flint's remaining passion expired. He was sated.

Finally Tsopi wobbled over to his full-sized wheel, and nudged it forward with her body. Slowly it rolled until it touched him. He twisted about to seat it in its natural socket. The thing was cold and unpleasant at first, a slimy dead mass, but soon his torso warmed it and refreshed its surface lubricant, making it comfortable again. Now he was mobile. But he was unable to speak.

"Do not be concerned," Tsopi said, vibrating her new ball against him. Her voice was burred, as though she had not yet gotten the feel of the equipment; his ball was slightly larger than hers. The burr of abatement, it was called; a fond allusion to a common satisfaction. "You will soon grow another, even as I lay down new protein around your seed to expand my wheel to full size. In our species, the female suffers her confinement after parturition, and the male is mute." She paused. "We forgot about that, before; naturally the Big Wheel realized right away that the debt had not been abated."

Flint was already aware that the Wheel had done some uncircular scheming. But perhaps that had been necessary. How would the Big Stick—correction, the huge phallus—no, he was still fouled up in the symbolisms of translation, accurately as they might reflect the underlying thrust of Solarian culture—the regent or emperor of Sphere Sol have reacted to a Polarian emissary who refused to come to the point? He probably would have diverted the creature to some safe place, investigated privately to ascertain what the hell was the matter, then acted to correct the problem without much regard for the niceties of human convention.

So now at last the mystery of Polarian reproduction had been explained. The seed started with the male, becoming his communication ball, encased in just enough nutrient protein to keep it secure and serviceable, until he passed it along to his mate. Next time she mated it would become an individual entity. No, not necessarily; he realized now that this was an optional aspect of the exchange. Usually the female took the male's ball directly for her new wheel, in what humans would think of as a genital kiss. But if she had special regard for him, she saved his ball, substituting her own ball for the wheel, as on this occasion. In this manner she retained part of him for as long as she chose. After any mating she could transform that seed-bearing ball to wheel-status, thus setting up the union of their two genetic pools, or she could retain it indefinitely.

There was no parallel to this in human reproduction, but he liked it. The female had a very special control. Tsopi's next mating would be infertile, for her virginal wheel contained no male seed. Her first wheel, just manifested as offspring, was actually the legacy of her own male parent; in a sense she had mated with her father. But her first ball had been her own, therefore sterile, and it was now a sterile wheel. She could plan ahead, activating Flint's seed when she incurred a debt exchange with some other male she really respected, simply by having an interim non-debt affair to eliminate the sterile wheel. The debt system, in its subtler applications, was a very fine mechanism!

Actually, this was a variant of the three-sex system of Spica, for it required three individuals to produce one offspring. One male to provide the seed; the female to expand it to proper size; and a second male to trigger it into birth. That was why consecutive matings could not occur in a given couple; a male could not trigger his own seed. Hence romance was one-shot, and there was no permanent union. The notion of consecutive matings with one female now appalled Flint; it was akin to the incest taboo of his own culture. Repetition was *possible,* since Tsopi's new wheel in this case was not his ball, but only in an emergency such as near-elimination of the species, or unavoidable repetition of debt exchange, would that become permissible. Much as sibling or cousin mating was possible among humans, and theoretically practiced by the children of Adam and Eve and the children of Noah, but never otherwise tolerated. No doubt facets of the concept of "original sin" entered here; a man should neither kill his brother nor impregnate his sister.

Oh, there was much to meditate on here, and comprehension of the Polarian system led to penetrating insights into his own human system. It would take a Tarot deck to unravel them all!

"Farewell, Plint," Tsopi said. "The debt has been abated." And she minced unsteadily away on her tiny wheel.

Flint, though profoundly moved by the experience, no longer felt any desire to associate with her. All that interest, it seemed, had been concentrated in his ball—and now she had that. In fact, the male ball equated closely with the human testicle, in both practice and the vernacular of both species, and was the subject of dirty jokes—yet it was ultimately the same as the female wheel. There were very strict language conventions here. Just as the tentacle was always called the male's trunk and the female's tail, the communications sphere was always the ball, and the traveling sphere always the wheel. Scratch a seemingly pointless but absolutely firm distinction, and sex was bound to be at the root of it!

What of his male wheel, however? Could it also become a young Polarian? A wave of deep disgust at the notion assured him otherwise; it was merely a mass of protein, a kind of storage of resources. Males could survive for extended periods by feeding on their wheels. One terrible Polarian torture—oh yes, torture was known here!—consisted of isolating a male without sustenance for a prolonged period, so that his wheel gradually shrank, until it was as small as a ball. When he resembled a recently mated female, he would be released to suffer ridicule. Many preferred to seek their own repose, rather than endure that humiliation. Another punishment was to remove and destroy the wheel, letting the individual survive or die as he might.

Enough: He now knew more than he cared to of Polarian biology. Tsopi was now the Queen of Solid, a mature female; their mutual debt had been abated, and he was free to communicate the secret of transfer to the Big Wheel. But—

But how could he do that—with no communication ball?

He knew the answer, once he delved for it. He would have to take a little more time, growing in his new ball. There would be no problem; the replacement seed was already making its way to the end of his trunk, where it would form the nucleus of the new ball. He had merely to relax and enjoy his recuperation. He was sure, now, that his Kirlian aura was not depleted; he had suffered emotional, not Kirlian depression, and was good for months yet. Plenty of time to get back in physical shape. A valid excuse to get to know this delightful culture properly.

Flint rolled out of the animation area, heading toward the great, wonderful outside.

8

Letters of Blood

report: critical period notification of mired agent

—summon all available entities council—

COUNCIL INITIATED PARTICIPATING*—$^0_0$: :

—well, that's one more than last time proceed—

our 200 kirlian agent now available for retransfer provided low-kirlian replacement exchanged

$^0_0$ *low* Kirlian transfer? subject would rapidly be lost! explain rationale$^0_0$

200 kirlian agent is our best familiar with this mission low-kirlian would be expendable after exchange low-kirlian would lose identity but remain suitable for specialized mission

: : now *I'm* confused! how can . . . : :

specialized mission is foster-care of offspring engendered by enemy agent on ours

$^0_0$ our best agent mated with enemy agent? she was assigned to *eliminate* him! $^0_0$

—it is a long story, $^0_0$, as you would have been aware had you attended prior council—

$^0_0$ I was preoccupied with spherical matters $^0_0$

—this is a *galactic* matter, of overriding import—

$^0_0$ don't lecture *me*, —! you think you're so dashed superior where would this galaxy be, if we $^0_0$s hadn't $^0_0$

: : please, unity is the essence of power! : :

—maybe we should let them achieve their own galactic coalition then they would bicker themselves to death as we do—

$^0_0$ extreme humor noted $^0_0$

—accept our statement that this exchange is a necessary expedient—

:: but she *will* kill him next time? ::

—assuredly as victim of rape she is very angry no laser flasheth hotter than that of a female / wronged—

$^{0}_{0}$ spare us the aphorisms $^{0}_{0}$

concurrence?

:: signoff ::

—$^{0}_{0}$::POWER CIVILIZATION CONCURRENCE—$^{0}_{0}$::

It was strange being in a human host, with its angular perambulation and acute binocular vision and inadequate taste. Flint caught himself trying to roll, and tripping over his own feet. He had been Polarian a long time, and run his Kirlian aura low; it would have been easy to phase all the way into that sublime identity. He now regarded Sphere Polaris culture as generally superior to that of Sphere Sol . . . but that episode was over.

Return from transfer had been horrendous. He had suffered disorientation, pain, and convulsions. Apparently his human body had contracted some malady during his absence. That could have accounted for some of his orientation problems at Polaris; it was reasonable to assume that the connection between aura and body never broke entirely. The prolonged vacancy had weakened the physical vessel. But modern biotics and therapy would have the matter rectified in a few days, and then he could begin his long recuperation.

So they had had to bounce him out again in transfer while they gave his body special medical attention. He had insisted on a particular location although they had protested that there was no suitable host-body there. He had let them know that there might be no Kirlian transferee for future missions if they didn't *find* a host in a hurry.

Now, at last, he had returned home—in a fashion. For this was the system of Draco, the Dragon. Etamin, his home. How changed it seemed, after an Earth-year. The vines seemed larger, the terrain rougher. But of course the vines were larger than most Earth trees, and the landscape of Stone Age Outworld was violent—and he occupied a smaller, weaker body.

In fact it was the body of a child barely nine or ten years old. One foot had been mauled and one arm amputated at the elbow. Best available host on a primitive world!

He had only a short time, and he wanted to see Honeybloom, the Queen of Liquid. Back in Polaris Sphere he had converted Tsopi from Page to Queen of Solid, but that had been a temporary affair. His real love was his human girl. So he moved along as fast as his rather handicapped body was able.

A warrior challenged him at the entrance to his village. "I don't know you, boy—what's your business here?"

Flint recognized the man: Fatclub, because he preferred a broad, heavy log for his weapon. Not much of a fighter, really—which was why he was assigned to routine guard duty. "I am a runner for the Swampfighter Tribe," Flint said. That tribe was hundreds of miles distant, so none of its members were personally known here. "I bear a message for Honeybloom."

"You must've been a long time on the way," Fatclub said. "That bitch isn't here any more."

Flint reached for his sharp handax but caught himself. He could do nothing in this body, and did not want to betray his knowledge of the subject. But what an insult to the prettiest, sweetest girl in the tribe! "I move slowly," he agreed, indicating his mutilated foot with his single hand. "Where is she now?"

"Up on the hill with her bastard son." Fatclub made a contemptuous gesture indicating the direction.

With her bastard . . . Suddenly Flint realized what had happened. Honeybloom had borne his child—but she was unmarried, since Flint had been abruptly removed from the scene by the Imp government. Therefore she had been expelled from the tribe, and now was the object of ridicule. What a terrible fate for such a girl to suffer! If only he had known—

But he *had* known—for he had identified her as the Queen, not the Page, of Liquid, in that Tarot system he had learned in Sphere Polaris. The information had been there in his mind all the time. He knew how babies were made! He merely had not let himself think it all the way through, despite the hint the Tarot had provided.

He made his way up the mountain, amazed at the difficulty the route presented. The normal Flint-body would have hurdled the ravine, swung up to run along the vines, and shoved thornblossoms out of the way automatically. But this inadequate body had to negotiate the hazards tediously, always alert for lurking predators who would not have dared go after a grown man. This body was also wary of high places and insecure footing, and unable to swing from vine to vine. Wild Outworld seemed much less idyllic from this vantage!

At last he spied Honeybloom's solitary lean-to. An old woman was there, chewing on a reptile hide to make it workable for clothing. Tedious labor, hard on the teeth.

Old woman? No, she was too familiar. *This was Honeybloom!* Her hair had faded, the once-brilliant red becoming listless brown. Her glowing green skin had faded almost to Earthly white. Her upright virginal breasts had converted to the elongated dugs of the nursing mother. Her loveliness had been masked by the early wrinkles and sags of ill health and hard work and desolation. Her teeth were stained by the juices of the hides she had chewed. She was no beauty any more.

A pang as of the penetration of a knife stabbed Flint. Here was the realization of the Tarot's Three of Gas—terrible sorrow to his loved one. A heart pierced by three swords: the loss of her lover, the birthing of a bastard, and expulsion from the tribe. She might as well have died—except for her duty to the baby.

He had deliberately put Llyana the Undulant of Spica into a similar situation, never suspecting that its horrors were being concurrently visited on his own fiancée. The alien female had deserved it, and perhaps Flint himself also deserved this retribution of fate—but why had it been visited not on him but on poor gentle Honeybloom?

At least she had shown her mettle by carrying on, by surviving despite the callousness of her society. She would have made a good, durable wife, able to endure bad times as well as good. She had had more than mere beauty to recommend her; in this the Shaman had been wrong.

Of course he could right the matter now, by coming back to her in his own body. But now he knew that the authorities of Imperial Earth would never permit that. There was no one else in the Sphere whose Kirlian aura approached Flint's own; no one who could do the job he could do. And that job had to be done, lest the entire galaxy be destroyed by the Andromedans. Then there would be no life at all for Honeybloom—or anyone.

He could arrange to have her moved to a more civilized planet, where no stigma would attach to her. But she was a creature of Outworld; she could not be happy anywhere else. She had not even departed any farther than necessary from her tribe; how could she tolerate removal from her *world?*

The Tarot had spoken truly: there was nothing but sorrow here, and he was powerless to abate it. This misery had been set the moment Star Sol had projected its omen of eclipse to touch his life. He was the victim of fate. He—and those close to him.

But he could alleviate it somewhat. He moved on to the lean-to.

Honeybloom looked up listlessly. Her eyes seemed washed out, and there were cry-wrinkles around them.

"I bear a message . . . from Flint," Flint said.

"Flint!" she exclaimed, and for an instant animation brought her beauty back. But it dissipated quickly. "I am weary of this teasing. Flint will never come back."

There was only one way to end it. And it had to be ended. "He spoke to an official of Imperial Earth, just before he died—"

"Died!" she cried, horrified.

"—honorably, in the line of his duty to his Sphere. Hunting a monster." The monster of Galaxy Andromeda—but no use to attempt to explain that to her. "He said: 'Tell my dear wife Honeybloom of Outworld that I love her, and bequeath to my son my name and trade. Let him be a flintsmith.' "

"But Flint did not marry—"

That was one of her faults: she was honest. "I only repeat the message," Flint said. "You are listed in Imperial records as his common-law wife. Because he died as an officer of Imperial Earth, you are now entitled to his pension."

She stared, amazed. "But—"

"It will not be a great amount, but it will enable you to resume residence within the tribe. As his acknowledged widow, you have no stigma; you may marry again if you wish. In that event the pension will accrue directly to his son, until he comes of age."

"You mock me!" she cried, tears flowing. They were not pretty tears, but grief tears. How she had suffered!

She did not believe him—and why should she? "He also said, 'My finger is still stiff.' I don't know what that means."

But *she* knew what it meant. She flushed—and believed. For none but the two of them knew about the stiff-finger hex she had laid on him for the too-intimate poke he had given her lush posterior as she slept among the juiceberries. And of course more had stiffened than the finger. It was the kind of detail only the real Flint would remember or remark upon.

"All you have to do is apply at the Imperial office," Flint said. "The forms have been approved. That is the end of my message." He turned to go.

"Wait, stay!" she exclaimed, all aflutter with the abrupt change in her fortune. "I have juiceberries . . . you must be hungry. . . ."

"The bearer of bad news may not eat with the bereaved," he said, quoting a tribal maxim.

She paused. "It *is* bad news." Yet she did not seem mortified. The truth was, Flint's unexplained absence had been worse than his death, for by his death he had given her legitimacy. She was not glad for his death, and he knew she loved him—but by accepting his death she also accepted his love for her, expressed as part of that message of death.

How truly the Tarot had spoken when it signaled death in his future—but called it also a transformation. He had thought to die in Polaris Sphere, and had not; now he knew for what his death had been saved. This transformation would right things as no ordinary death could have done. Everyone in the tribe knew he had not married Honeybloom—but she would now be a comparatively wealthy woman, if no one objected—and to object would be to call the dead Flint a liar. No one wanted Flint's ghost to return for vengeance against that slight, so no one would say a word. Especially since the records of Imperial Earth would provide legitimacy. Flint had been a powerful man in life, quick and sure with his weapons; he would be a terror in death.

As his widow, Honeybloom would have to become the wife of the Chief, who took care of all widows in accordance with tribal custom. Since most widows were old—at least a year, equivalent to thirty Earth-years—she would receive more attention than the others. She would never be as lovely as she had been, but even her secondary bloom would be a marvelous thing, for she was full-bodied and gentle.

Now Flint's son would be legitimate, and perhaps grow up to be the leader of the tribe, for he would be stepson to the Chief and surely among the strongest and most skillful, as Flint had been. Yes, it was best this way.

But now, too, Flint could never return, even if he completed all his missions for the Sphere. This tribal life, and indeed Outworld itself, was forever behind him. That hurt.

He left Honeybloom, made his way to the grave of Old Snort the dinosaur for a sympathetic word, and finally sought out the old Shaman. It was night before he found the half-blind Earthman on the hill, squinting at the stars.

"Shaman, I grieve," Flint said, sitting down beside the white old man.

"All life is grief," the other agreed. Tribesmen often came to him for advice and magic; that was his job in this primitive society. "I perceive you have suffered grievously indeed—and I regret that no spell of mine can give you back your lost arm or do more than alleviate the pain in your foot."

"It is not for my arm I grieve, but for myself," Flint said. "For I am dead. I died today to spare my son the shame of bastardy. Did I do right?"

"You are but a child! How can you speak of dying?"

"I speak as messenger for one far removed. I am a ghost."

"A ghost." The dim old eyes tried to penètrate Flint's expression for a moment, then peered uselessly into the night sky. "We are the eye of Draco the Dragon, once the Pole Star as seen from Earth, now its farthest recognized colony. Yet there was another dragon, long ago. Draco the Greek legislator. In 621 B.C. he was given authority to codify the laws of the city of Athens, so as to alleviate the need for private individual revenge for wrongs. This he did—but his code was so severe that it was said to have been written in letters of blood."

"Letters of blood!" Flint echoed. "How well you understand!"

"In that code, debtors could be sold as slaves. You have abated your debt similarly—"

Abated his debt! "Not all cultures require so harsh a remedy," Flint said, thinking of Tsopi the Polarian and the debt he had shared with her. How much better that system was!

The Shaman turned to face Flint. "Honeybloom is a fine woman, better than I credited at first. You have done right."

Flint rolled to his knees and embraced the old man with his one arm. There were tears in his eyes. "You know me, Shaman!"

"It takes an old fool to know a young one. I note you have matured, and have mastered the art of transfer, only a rumor in my day. That was why they summoned you to Earth?"

"Yes. My Kirlian aura is very strong." Flint shrugged. "I will give them the word about Honeybloom's pension, and the Imps will do it." Because there was now enough credit in Flint's personal account to pay a hundred widows. As the most potent aura in the Sphere, he commanded an excellent rate of pay—for which he had had no use, until now. "But I wish to be sure that the money is used wisely, for the benefit of Honeybloom and my son. There might be those who would cheat her—"

"I will arrange for a trust," the Shaman said. He smiled. "Protected by magic, of course. There will be no abuse."

"I thank you," Flint said.

The Shaman looked at him again. "You have aged." That seemed incongruous, in view of Flint's present body, but it was true.

"I have had to age," Flint said. "I have become disgustingly civilized. I travel the galaxy, now—or at least our local cluster of Spheres."

"Cluster." The wrinkled, almost sightless eyes searched the sky again for the stars they could not see. "Will you tell me?"

Flint's mission was secret—but he knew he could trust the Shaman, his childhood mentor, the man who had given him the intellectual basis for survival in the amazing galaxy. "I will tell you everything."

And he did. It took several hours, but it was good in the telling, even the bad parts.

"Nothing could have given me more pleasure," the Shaman said at the end. "You have restored my sight; you have shown me the universe."

"No, only a few near Spheres," Flint said modestly.

"And a near galaxy. Do you not see the identity of the Queen of Energy?"

"No. It baffles me. It could be any Sphere, even a supposedly friendly one. I have looked upon my enemy many times and not known her."

"She is from Andromeda Galaxy—an enemy agent sent

to eliminate you, for you are the major threat to their project. You can go anywhere they can go, even to Andromeda itself, seeking out their secrets."

"Andromeda!" Flint exclaimed, suddenly seeing it. "That must be it!"

"And beware—for she obviously has a way to orient on your transfers. Wherever you go, she can go—and she will kill you, for she knows you while you do not know her, and you have humiliated her. Never forget she is a woman, though quite unlike Honeybloom. Whatever guise she wears, wherever she hails from, her motive is not yours. Hell hath no—"

"Hell is a straight line, in Polarian mythology," Flint said. "And a dry place without zones in Spica. Shaman, you have saved my life!"

"I hope so. Tomorrow I will see your widow about your death. That was a very nice gesture on your part, Flint."

"I do seem to achieve my best effects in the modes of my deaths! It was circular. What else was there to do?"

"Nothing else—but it took a man to do it."

They stood up and shook hands, Imperial-style. "Farewell, friend," the Shaman said.

"Farewell—friend," Flint echoed, feeling the tears in his eyes that had not been there when he parted from Honeybloom. He had thought he had come to see her, but now he knew it had been for this conversation with the Shaman. He would never see either of them again.

9

Daughters of the Titan

notice: multiple mattermissions to hyades open star cluster, including 200 kirlian enemy entity

—hyades! that means they've found it! send agent immediately—

she is only just freed from spica her kirlian is down

—I know mattermit her there—

*to *another galaxy?* the energy expense*

—call for concurrence, all available entities—

$^{0}{}_{0}$::CONCURRENCE

—that satisfy you? this is an emergency! mattermit her NOW!—

(sigh) POWER

—CIVILIZATION—

"We have another mission for you," the Minister of Alien Spheres said as Flint animated his own, restored body.

"Not today, Imp," Flint said. "My Kirlian's so low I'm ready to phase into the next host I animate. I must have been six months on the road."

"Three months. Your aura intensity is down to fifty percent, still the highest we have. You're not in trouble yet. But in this case you'll use your own body, because there are no hosts where you're going. In fact, no life there at all."

"What kind of a Sphere has no life on it?" Flint demanded, intrigued.

"An Ancient Sphere."

The Minister paused to let that sink in. Flint knew

about the Ancients, of course. Some of their earthworks were on Outworld, and others were scattered across the galaxy. The Ancients had had the hugest interstellar empire ever known, perhaps three million years ago; they had possessed secrets of technology that modern Spheres could only glimpse. "You have my attention," Flint said.

"We have located a well-preserved Ancient colony in the Hyades, a hundred and thirty light-years from Sol," the Minister said. "Do you know what that means?"

"Taurus Constellation. The Horns of the Bull." If there was one geography Flint knew well, it was that of the near stars.

"The horns of a *dilemma.* The Hyades are at the approximate intersection of four Spheres: Sol, Polaris, Canopus, and Nath. All have colonies there, but these have their own primitive mores and we prefer not to involve them. This is a matter for the Imperial Planets—but, none of these four exercise specific authority in that region."

"Because none *want* to. A hundred or so stars jammed into a cubic parsec of space. Hard to get a night's sleep with all that starlight."

"It's not that bad. It's an open cluster, not a closed one. The question is, which Sphere has jurisdiction now? This Ancient site may be the most important find in the galaxy. Who excavates it?"

"What makes you so sure there's any more there than there's been anywhere else? Three million years make a big difference."

"This one's on an airless planet—and it hasn't been touched."

"Airless!" Flint said. "No deterioration?"

"Almost none. It's the best-preserved Ancient site ever discovered, we believe. A peppering of meteorite pocks, but apparently its location in the cluster protected it pretty well even from space debris. Otherwise, it's intact."

"Which means there may be a functioning machine, an Ancient machine—"

"Or an Ancient library that would enable us to crack the language barrier and learn all their secrets," the Minister said, his pale face becoming animated. Flint had regarded the Ministers as basically devoid of individuality, but now a bit of character was beginning to show. This one really cared about his alien Spheres. "The

Ancients had no Spherical regression; they were able to maintain a galactic empire with uniform culture and technology, as far as we can ascertain. They solved the energy problem. If we had that secret—"

"Then I could retire," Flint said. But the notion no longer filled him with enthusiasm. He had had himself put in the records as officially dead, so that Honeybloom would have his pension. There was no longer any life to retire to. And this business of traveling to strange civilizations had slowly grown on him; this was his type of adventure.

"You could retire, having saved our galaxy," the Minister agreed, not aware of the irony. "We have elected to compromise. We have sent message capsules to all our neighbors with the news. The potential significance of this discovery transcends local Sphere boundaries. The other Spheres of this cluster have agreed to a cooperative mission, with all discoveries to be shared equally, for the good of the galaxy. They are notifying *their* neighbors, and we hope several of these will participate also. We have of course also advised Sphere Knyfh of the inner galaxy, but naturally they cannot afford to mattermit a representative five thousand light-years on speculation."

Flint nodded. "If all the Spheres mattermit their own physical representatives to the Hyades that will be some menagerie!"

"That's why we're sending you. You have had direct experience with some of these creatures. You will be able to recognize them and deal with them despite their strange or even repulsive aspects. Other humans would be at a severe disadvantage."

"That's true," Flint agreed, remembering the way human beings had seemed to him when he occupied a Polarian host. He had been shocked and nauseated, and so had blundered badly. Of course, he still suffered some from an aversion to illness or deformity—his recent excursion in the body of a one-armed boy had been a real exercise in control!—but alienophobia was a nearly universal phenomenon. This Hyades group would not be the most compatible assemblage!

Yet the prospect remained intriguing, and not merely because of the monstrous potential of the Ancient site. To deal physically, in his own body, with all the alien sapients he had known only in transfer. . . .

He arrived at Gondolph IV at night. Four bright stars

were visible in the sky, overwhelming the more distant field. They were Gondolph's neighbors, II, III, V and VI, all within half a light-year, but they had the aspect of stars, not suns. No perpetual day here after all; the cluster was not that tight. Maybe someday he would visit a closed or globular cluster; *then* he'd see something!

The cluster of civilizations was not that tight, either, he thought. Each Sphere functioned independently of its neighbors, with only minor interactions. Together the massed Spheres made up the disk-shaped cluster of the Milky Way galaxy, like so many cells forming a creature. The Milky Way had also operated largely independently of its neighbors in the cluster of galaxies. Until recently. . . .

Flint was in a spacesuit, and it was no more awkward than adapting to an alien host-body. This was not like the old Luna spacesuits, clumsy and suspect; the material of this suit fit him like a sheath of exterior muscles. It yielded wherever his motions required, but maintained comfortably normal atmospheric pressure. A porous layer next to his skin permitted the transfer of fluids and gases necessary to his health. His body would not suffocate from lack of oxygen or drown in its own sweat. It had discreet airlocks for intake and outgo, so that all natural functions could be accommodated readily and safely. The suit was tough—but it had limitations. If it were perforated and not immediately patched, he would quickly die of exposure and decompression. Therefore he carried no power weapon; it was too possible for it to be used against him. He was, however, armed—unobtrusively.

He looked about. The Hyades, mythologically, were the seven daughters of the Titan Atlas and the nymph Aethra, and they were half-sisters to the Pleiades. There were two ways to relate that to the present situation; the Titan was the Milky Way galaxy, and his daughters the Spheres, perhaps seven of which would be represented here. Or the Titan was the empire of the Ancients, and his daughters were the scientific and cultural artifacts left behind—each one of immense potential significance to the contemporary scene.

At a time like this, he longed for the ability to journey back into the time-frame of the Ancients. Not merely to penetrate their technological and cultural secrets, but just to get to know them as individuals. Surely they had been something very, very special!

But now to meet his companions—and commence the archaeological research. A Nathian lifeship had discovered the site and set down the first mattermitter. For reasons comprehensible only to the Nath mind, that device had sat on the planet unused for twenty Earth years. News of galactic peril brought by micromessage from Sphere Polaris, and the quick transmission of transfer information had brought this site back into awareness. The Nath government had recognized the possible relevance and finally revealed the existence of its device. After that, things had moved rapidly. More mattermission units had been sent through the first and attuned to their Spheres of origination. Thus all representatives could be shipped at a common time.

They were to meet at a designated staging area within the site. Flint wondered why the units hadn't been grouped together to begin with, but assumed it was to provide a certain initial privacy. The shock of coming face to face with alien monsters—yes, it was better to allow some spacing and nominal adjustment room. But the Nathian organizers might have had some quite different notion.

Flint's eye was attracted by a surprising but familiar form: the disk of a Canopian flying saucer. He had thought these craft were airborne, but evidently they used another mechanism. At least this one did, for it traversed the vacuum effortlessly. It spotted him, and coasted down to hover close above. "Conveyance, Sphere Sol?" its speaker inquired in the standard language of Imperial Earth.

"Sphere Canopus comes in style," Flint observed, grasping the flexible ladder that descended for his convenience. "You mattermitted the whole craft?" That would have cost tens of trillions of dollars worth of energy, unless they had worked out a really economical system.

His benefactor turned out to be a Master: facet-eyed, mandible-mouthed, with wings forming a cloak, and half a dozen spindly legs. It looked like a monstrous insect, and perhaps it was—but it was also highly intelligent and of inflexible nerve. In Sphere Canopus these were the Master species, while humanoids were Slaves—and Flint had learned the hard way not to interfere with that social scheme. In fact, he had developed a lot of respect for the Masters. "What we do, we do properly," it said in its melodious voice. "This does not imply any pleasure in the task."

Of course. The Canopian Masters wanted to be left alone to run their Sphere in their efficient fashion. Slavers generally did not appreciate the cynosure of dissimilar cultures. But the one in charge of Flint's case when he had visited there in transfer, B:::1, had yielded to the inevitable, and Canopus had joined the galactic coalition.

"I am Flint of Outworld. I visited your Sphere a few months ago."

The Masters seldom showed emotion, but something very like surprise made this one's mandibles twitch. "I regret I did not recognize your specific identity, in your natural host. I am H:::4, of Kirlian intensity forty-five."

"Your government risks a high-Kirlian entity on a mattermission mission?"

The Master extended one thin leg to touch Flint's shoulder. Even through the suit, Flint felt the power of the aura. It seemed higher than forty-five—unless his own reduced aura made the differential seem less. "The secret of the Ancients necessarily involves some aspect of Kirlian force. I suspect all representatives here will be Kirlian, even as you and I."

A good answer. Obviously the Council of Ministers had had more than Flint's experience in mind when they selected him.

"If we discover what we hope," Flint said, "the mutual threat will be considerably abated. With the science of the Ancients, whether Kirlian or otherwise, our galaxy should be invulnerable."

"Perhaps. Yet the Ancients perished."

"After maintaining their empire for a million years or so."

"Strange that they should fade so suddenly and completely, after such longevity," the Master observed.

"Yes. That is one of their fascinating mysteries."

"We regard it as ominous rather than intriguing."

The saucer dropped down, and Flint climbed out from the visitor's well. "Thank you for the lift," he said.

"It has been an honor to serve." The craft set off to locate a new entity.

Flint stood where he was for a moment, pondering. The exchange had been perfectly amicable, but the Master had shown him that it had come thoroughly prepared. An excellent ally—or an extremely dangerous enemy. The

Canopians evidently were convinced of the importance of this site!

Thanks to the ride, Flint was first at the rendezvous. He looked about, concentrating on the ground rather than the sky. Here, more than anywhere, he ran the danger of stepping over a material cliff while gazing at the ethereal heavens, like the Fool of the Tarot deck.

All around were the preserved ruins of an advanced civilization. Not the pottery shards and stone arrowheads of Earthly archaeological sites, but actual buildings of a former city, no more strange in design than similar constructions of modern Sol, Polaris, or Canopus. It seemed almost as if an Ancient sapient were about to walk out.

Flint had not expected much, knowing that most Ancient sites were evident only to the trained eye: an unnatural mound here, a pattern of depressions there, sometimes a vague depression overgrown by jungle. Or even a mountain slope, the site a victim of orogeny, mountain building, now tilted and perhaps buried or even inverted. Sometimes construction crews discovered deeply covered strata with the Ancient stigmata. But three million years was a long time; it was evident that the Ancients had been phenomenal ground-movers, but that offered little insight into their culture. Until this moment. . . .

There was motion, down near the ground beyond a collapsed building. Flint, suddenly nervous, unlimbered one of his special weapons, a telescoping spear. This required human hands and skill for proper application, and as a Stone Age man and flintsmith, he was expert in its use. It was unlikely that any other creature could turn this against him. He could attack or defend, and if he lost it, he was also adept at defense against it. He doubted that the other creatures would be mechanically equipped to balk it. Of course they would have their own weapons. He wanted no quarrel, for both personal and Spherical reasons, still, something strange was coming toward him, and he wanted to be ready.

The motion manifested as a traveling patch of brambles. Flint studied its approach, and realized that it had to be sentient and sapient; there was no native life on Godawful Four, as he called this planet. The only thing that could move were the mattermitted, spacesuited representatives of the Spheres. He was being unreasonably jumpy. He put away his spear, though his primitive inclination was to step on the thing, squishing it like a centipede.

It was legless and had thousands of projectile-spines, like the barbed quills of an Earth porcupine or the spurs of sandspur grass. These shot out on tiny threads to hook into anything, even the dust of the airless desert. These were then reeled in, winching the main mass forward. At any given moment, a number of tethers were in every stage of the process—retracted, shooting out, catching, drawing in. The overall effect was, once he adjusted to the notion, rather graceful; the creature traveled across the rock smoothly.

It had to be in a spacesuit, for no lifeform Flint knew of existed in a vacuum. But what a suit! Each tiny hook and tether must be enclosed and pressurized. This bespoke a fine technology. Probably those myriad little members had exquisite detail control.

"Hello, comrade," Flint said. There was no air to carry his voice, but he knew the sound would be transmitted through the ground. He also had a translator keyed into a radio transceiver in his suit.

He was answered by a staccato of faint taps, as of tiny anchors dropping. He turned on his unit, letting it orient on whichever language this was. In a moment it spoke. "Sphere Nath."

"Sphere Sol," Flint said. His unit did not translate his own words. For simplicity, each creature's unit would handle all incoming messages, rendering them into the native language. There had been no direct human-Nathian contact before, though the two Spheres were adjacent. The expense, risk, and delay of inter-Sphere contact had been too great, until this galactic crisis.

"Arrivals?" his unit inquired as the Nathian tapped again.

"Sphere Canopus," Flint said. "With a flying craft. No others I know of, yet."

"Message from Sphere Bellatrix. Cannot attend, but information relayed to Sphere Mirzam, who attends."

Flint visualized the map of the Vicinity Cluster of Spheres. Bellatrix was a small Sphere, about Sphere Sol's size, adjacent to Nath. It was about five hundred light-years from Sol. Mirzam was two hundred and fifty light-years out. Bellatrix had been invited to attend; Mirzam had not, as contact had not yet been made. Evidently the chain of contacts was still extending, and that was good. Soon this entire section of the galaxy would be alert to the Andromedan threat.

"We of Sphere Nath have held long discourse with Sphere Bellatrix," the creature continued. Flint knew the translation was approximate, as there had to be fundamental distinctions of concept. "Discourse" could mean war or slavery or cohabitation. But there were limits to what a hastily jury-rigged multiple translation system could do. "They are very shy of strangers, so could not attend. But they are affinitive to Mirzam, with whom their contact parallels ours, so they relayed transfer, and Mirzam attends."

Could be. On the map, Sphere Bellatrix overlapped both Nath and Mirzam, so that as with Sol and Polaris, they could have had centuries of interaction, cooperative Fringe colonies, trade, and so on. Their refusal to interact immediately with a group of unfamiliar entities was understandable. Flint had seen Solarians as others saw them, there in Sphere Polaris, and it was a lesson he hoped never to forget. He still had trouble adjusting to new forms—in fact was having trouble right now—and he was Sol's most experienced agent.

"We of Sphere Sol understand," he said. "We appreciate the message."

"Pull-hook," the Nathian said.

Oops, a mistranslation. Obviously, to hook and pull was an expression of affinity, of motion or success; acquiescence. But since there were literal meanings to the terms, the machine had oriented on them, taking the simplest route. Which was one reason inter-Sphere relations could not be trusted entirely to machines.

"Perhaps we should wait on the others," Flint said. "We want to coordinate the search."

"Meaning clarification: occupy what position in relation to others?"

Flint reviewed his phrasing. "Remain inactive until the representatives of other Spheres arrive," he said. Yes, he would have to watch his own language. These literalisms could be troublesome, even deadly. To wait *on* an alien creature might be to squash it, and his word might have been taken as a direct threat. His mass could do a lot of harm to a low-spread-out, thread-limbed creature like this. "We have translation problems; please verify all questionable remarks without taking offense."

"Pull-hook."

"Are you familiar with Sphere Mirzam?"

"I would recognize a Mirzam entity by sonar—they

are jumpers somewhat like yourself—but we have had very little direct contact. The expense of mattermission. . . ."

"Yes." That was a universal problem. By the map it was some five hundred light-years from Nath to Mirzam.

"Irritation to be avoided," the Nathian said.

Meaning "No offense?" Probably a personal question. "Comprehended, no irritation."

"How would you like to bash your head in?"

Hm. "Clarification," Flint said.

"Apparent danger of collapsing with damage, perched endwise."

Oh. "Solarian sapients have a sophisticated balancing mechanism. By being alert, we avoid falling and bashing in our heads. And we gain the advantage of perception from an elevation."

"Credit deserved, overcoming obvious handicap," it said.

"Pull-hook," Flint agreed.

The Nathian rippled its threads in seeming acknowledgment, shooting out burrs and snapping them back unanchored. A nice gesture—or maybe it was merely laughing. Flint saw no sign of eyes, and realized that elevation would have little bearing on hearing, so maybe his explanation had been gibberish to it.

"I understand—" Flint caught himself, realizing what a literal translation would sound like. "I have been informed that Sphere Nath discovered this Ancient site. Why didn't you explore it earlier?"

"There was no need for this technology," it explained. "Technology in advance of culture becomes detrimental. But when we were apprised of the Andromedan threat, we realized that a preemptive need now existed. So we offered this site in exchange for transfer."

Evidently Nathians saved information the way Solarians saved money! Well, why not? "It is a fair exchange."

The Canopian craft reappeared. This time it deposited a creature resembling the business end of an Earth-farm disk harrow. "Sphere Mintaka," H : : : 4 announced.

"Sphere Mintaka!" Flint exclaimed. "I didn't know *they* were in this party!"

"Their invitation was extended by Sphere Mirzam, which borders Mintaka," the Master explained, using both human sounds and Nathian staccato. "From this chain of contact they have learned the technology of transfer and the communicatory mode of Mirzam, Bellatrix, and Nath. The Mintakan utilizes flashes of light, and will code them in the Nath manner so that your translators can handle it."

Flint visualized the map again. Sphere Mintaka was just a huge, ill-defined arc in the direction of the galactic rim. Humans had no direct knowledge of it, only that it was big—a radius of some five hundred light-years, larger even than Sador—and far away. Star Mintaka was one of the three that formed the constellation of Orion's Belt, and it was fifteen hundred light-years distant from Sol. The Sphere might be decadent, like Sador, just the shrinking husk of former greatness, but how then had it been so alert about this expedition? The Sphere Knyfh envoy who had brought transfer to Sol had suggested as much: that it was fading. That might have been an error. Had Knyfh known this region well, it would not have needed to recruit Sol for the coalition mission.

The Nathian was silent, and Flint felt momentary camaraderie with it, knowing it had similar reservations about the Mintakan.

"I shall search out new arrivals," H:::4 said, and took off again.

That left the three of them. The Mintakan rolled forward on its circular blades, leaving deep parallel creases in the dust, and Flint noted how readily those edges could slice up a spacesuit or anything else. This was a combat-creature! Its lights flashed from lenses between the blades, blinking on and off so rapidly it was a mere flickering.

"Greetings, Sol and Nath," the translator said on the Nath band. "Much appreciation in this invitation, and in the secret of transfer, which transforms our society already."

With a five-hundred-light-year radius to that Sphere, or a thousand-light-year diameter, transfer would be a boon indeed! Regression must be ferocious, Flint thought. A hundred light-years in Sphere Sol carried man all the way back to the Old Stone Age; what would five hundred years do? Homo Erectus? Presapience? How could a Sphere even achieve such monstrous size *without* transfer? Surely it would soon fragment into smaller sub-spheres oriented on its most aggressive colonies, as the Earth British Empire had fragmented into America, Canada, India, and others.

That brought him back to this mission: How did the Ancients manage a Sphere that embraced a sizable segment of the galaxy? Well, maybe they were about to find out.

"We welcome any who care to join us in our effort," Flint answered politely. "Are you acquainted with our larger mission?"

"To save our galaxy from Andromeda—and to utilize whatever Ancient science we can recover toward this end. Sphere Mintaka, though no longer expansive, is quite concerned to protect its continuing well-being. So we participate."

"A fair response," the Nathian agreed. "Are there Ancient sites in your Sphere, too?"

"Many sites—but all corroded. We suspect the Ancients spread not only across our galaxy, but across other galaxies as well. Surely Andromeda obtained its expertise from some similar site as this. We marvel at the Ancients' boundless energy, and desire to know its source."

"We, too," Flint agreed. There certainly seemed to be a harmony of motive here, and that was good. "Whoever rediscovers Ancient technology might well achieve power over as great an expanse of the universe as they did."

"Hence we cooperate," the Nathian added, "so that no single Sphere may draw in unduly."

"As one of our luminaries said," the Mintakan flashed, "if we do not draw in together, we shall assuredly be drawn in separately."

"Interesting coincidence," Flint said. "One of our own early philosophers made a similar statement about hanging together."

"I doubt they knew each other," the Mintakan remarked, its lights flashing with evanescent humor.

"A universal truth," the Nathian said.

Now a new figure rolled up. Flint recognized it with gladness. "Polaris!"

"How circular to meet you, Sol and Nath," the Polarian replied politely. It was not, of course, Tsopi, the female Flint had known and loved; that would have been too much to ask. But it was like meeting an old friend anyway, and Flint was reassured at its recognition of the Nathian. It was through such intersections of Spheres that they could verify the identity of the members of this crew. If Polaris vouched for Nath, Flint trusted that.

The Canopian craft returned, this time depositing two

entities. "Sphere Antares," the Master announced, and left.

Flint had forgotten about Antares. Sol had dealt with that Sphere long ago, trading controlled hydrogen fusion for matter transmission. Antares had had transfer for centuries, but refused to divulge it to any other Sphere until very recent events had made that policy pointless. There had been no ill feeling about this, as *all* Spheres had protected their technological secrets until the Andromedan threat had forced better cooperation. Thus the forms of Solarian and Antarean were known to each other. Flint just hadn't seen one of these aliens in the flesh before. And flesh it was: Antareans were protoplasmic entities, moving by extension and consolidation. They were versatile, but lacked the speed and power of the skeletal and muscular creatures.

"Push-hook irritation to be avoided, Antares," the Nathian said.

"Anticipating your irritation, an explanation," one of the protoplasms said.

It communicated by erecting a pattern of small temporary extrusions along the topside of its body. As a result, Flint had to aim his translation optic lens directly at it to pick up the meaning. These creatures, too, had to be in spacesuits, though again these were not evident. But of course Flint would not know suit from skin until he had had more experience with particular entities.

"I am of Sphere Spica," the creature went on, "contacted recently by Sphere Sol and granted transfer. Since we are waterborne entities, we cannot go on land. Therefore we cooperate with our longtime associate Sphere Antares. I am a transferee to an Antarean host, mattermitted here. Trusting no objection by other parties."

"Glad to have you."

"Pull-hook."

"Circularity."

The Mintakan flashed amenably.

The Canopian saucer returned, but this time it was empty. "I suspect an unfortunate occurence," H: : :4 announced. "Please follow my craft."

"What is it?" Flint demanded.

"I prefer not to speculate." And the Master proceeded slowly back the way it had come.

They followed. Flint walked, the Nathian pulled, the Mintakan sliced, the Polarian rolled, and the two Antareans extruded. The last was especially interesting: They flung out globs of flesh in snakelike extensions, then humped the main mass of the body through the connecting tube into the forward extension. It was a bit like an inchworm, and a bit like siphoning water from one cup to another. Though it was slow, Flint realized that few barriers would stop such an entity long; it could pour itself through a tiny hole or fling a blob across a chasm without risk. Commitment was gradual.

The Polarian was the fastest traveler, then came Flint and the Mintakan. The others bunched to the rear. This was no race, but Flint made another mental note: Should he have to get somewhere ahead of any of these creatures, he knew his chances. He was glad the Polarian was the only entity faster than himself, for he had a basic trust and liking for Polarians. Of course the saucer-mounted Canopian was the speediest of all, but there would be places the saucer could not go. At any rate, rapid transit was not the only asset; it was likely that there would be different rankings for other tasks.

The saucer settled. Flint and the Polarian drew up at the spot indicated and saw the body of a creature. It appeared to be about the same size as the members of the group—there seemed to be a fair similarity of size, as though this represented the sapient optimum—but differed in detail. It was solid, with a tripod of extensions projecting from stout tubes.

"A prospective member of our party, defunct," the Polarian said, his ball touching the ground beside the corpse. Flint realized that the Polarian spacesuit had to be very cleverly designed to allow ball and wheel to function properly. But of course Earth had no monopoly on technical ingenuity. "Its suit has been punctured."

"But from which Sphere?" Flint asked. The defunct entity's suit did indeed appear to have been torn open. There must have been explosive decompression, too rapid to allow the creature to stop it before death occurred.

The Mintakan sliced up. "That's a Mirzamian!" it said. "What happened?"

H: : :4 looked around from his craft as the other entities arrived. "If I may make my supposition now: there would seem to have been an accident—or murder."

"Sapiencide!" the Antarean exclaimed.

The Nathian approached the body. "All that we understand about our sister Sphere indicates that Mirzamians are extraordinarily careful. They propel themselves by vigorous jumping, so pay extreme attention to their surroundings lest they be damaged on impact."

Impact. That reminded Flint of the three-sexed Spicans: the Undulants, the Sibilants, and the Impacts. He glanced at the Spican/Antarean, but noted no reaction. Of course he could not be sure there was any equivalence in that language. No sense in searching for clues where none existed.

"I observe no outcroppings of rock or other natural features that could account for such an accident," the Master said.

Flint remembered his experience with the power hopper on Luna. His mode of transportation there would have been rather similar to that used by the Mirzamian. There had been many rough natural features on Earth's huge moon, but he had not been in any immediate danger from them. This seemed to rule out accident.

"Yet if there has been slipshod anchorage—" the Nathian began.

"There must be a murderer among us," one of the Antareans finished. Flint observed it covertly, trying to distinguish it more certainly from the other. This was the larger, more translucent one, shot through with whitish strands Flint presumed were nerve fibers. The other, who claimed to be the Spican transferee, was milky throughout, and seemed more delicate: feminine. Not that that was applicable. How did the three-sexed Spicans react in transfer to a two-sexed form? Or *were* Antareans two-sexed? He should have checked that out.

The seven diverse creatures began to draw apart. "One of us"—the Mintakan flashed, paused, and resumed—"is a spy or traitor."

"Not surprising," Flint said. "News of this Ancient site has spread rapidly, and the Andromedans always have been aware of our activities. One of their agents tried to kill me in Sphere Canopus."

"Sphere Canopus resisted membership in the coalition," H:::4 said. "But we do not stoop to inter-Sphere sabotage, and are as cognizant as any of the mutual threat. Once we joined, we cooperated fully."

"I meant no criticism of Sphere Canopus," Flint said. "In fact, it was the intrusion of that Andromedan agent that brought Canopus into the coalition. My point is that we have since ascertained that it was an Andromedan agent, a female I have known as Cle of Ath or Llyana the Undulant, who animated those hosts, attacked me, and provided Canopus with specialized transfer information rather than betray her true identity."

"Pardon my misapprehension," the Master said.

"I trapped her for a time in Sphere Spica, but now I suspect she is one of our present number."

"You speak of a female," the Nathian tapped. "Our findings indicate that transfer cannot be made to a creature of a different sex from the original. This offers an avenue of investigation."

"But we are sexless," the Antarean objected.

"And our sexes are interchangeable," the Spican/Antarean added. "This is why this host is compatible: it is neuter. Transfer to a sexed species would be problematical."

"Neuter or interchangeable means no restriction, then," Flint said. "But Nath is correct: Where two sexes exist, sexual crossover is not possible in transfer. So a quick survey may succeed in eliminating some of us from suspicion. I, for example, am male."

"This is not circular," the Polarian said. "I too am male, but how am I to demonstrate this to those unfamiliar with my species? How can the rest of us be certain of the accuracy of statement by any one of us?"

"I am familiar with your species," Flint said. "I settled a debt as a transferee to your Sphere."

"Then you can name the defunct party of the debt-settlement," the Polarian said.

Flint snapped his spear into full length and raised it, orienting on the other. "You are in a Polarian body, but you could be an alien transferee. I believe I can puncture your spacesuit with this weapon before you can either attack me or escape—and if you attempt either, the others will know you are an impostor."

"Solarian, this is gross hook repulsion," the Nathian protested. "This entity has given no—"

"Debt-settlement is very special," Flint said, maintaining the poise of his spear. "There is no dead party."

The Polarian stood still. "That is my other point. Any or all of us could be transferees, and are therefore suspect. The Andromedans surely have male agents as well as female ones. Even if we verify sex, how may we know the true identity of each of us?"

"I assure you—" the Antarean began.

"You have not abated my suspicion," Flint said to the Polarian. "This is not based on sex, but on information. How do you settle debt?"

"This is not a matter we discuss lightly."

The Mintakan cut forward slowly. "The Solarian has challenged the Polarian. It seems likely that one or the other is false—but how should we know which one? I am familiar with neither entity, and do not know about debt settlement, so can not verify the validity of any given answer."

"I am familiar with the Polarian system," the Nathian said. "I begin to see the Solarian's point. It is a matter of—"

"Do not say it!" the Canopian Master interrupted. "You must serve to verify the answer given. It is true we have no direct way of knowing, on an individual basis, which of us is valid. But each Sphere overlaps at its fringe with one or more others. This is how we established initial contact with each other. We can employ that network to isolate the intruder . . . perhaps."

"I agree," Flint said. "Maybe this investigation should be handled by H:::4. We can put it to vote."

There was a general flurry of a confusion. Flint did not relax, but he realized belatedly that the Polarian's reference could have been a trap for *him*, unmasking him if he *agreed*. He really did not have much of a case, and should not have acted so rashly.

It was the Polarian who spoke. "Nath and Sol and Sador —unfortunately not present—intersect Polaris, and Nath and Sol also intersect Canopus. Exchange of interviews should verify the reality in circular manner."

"But Sol and Nath are suspect too!" the Spican protested. "And so am I, for I *am* a transferee."

"We have to decide on a course of action," Flint said, growing impatient. "We can vote—"

"What is a vote?" the Mintakan asked.

Oh—so *that* was the source of some of the confusion. The human concept of voting was as opaque as the Polarian concept of debt.

"It means each entity says yes or no, and all abide by the decision," Flint explained.

"Impossible," the Spican said. "There must always be three sides to any question, no majority. As the maxim goes, it takes three to mate."

"Push-hook," the Nathian agreed. "No entity can decide for another."

Flint saw that they were in danger of dissolving into chaotic debate and indecision. "Then I must act unilaterally. Polarian, I accuse you of being a transferee from Andromeda, murderer of this Mirzam entity and threat to this expedition. What refutation do you offer for me and Nath?"

"Your thrust is dismaying, but typical of your kind," the Polarian replied. "Permit me to round it off. I will satisfy your query—then query you myself."

"Fair exchange," Flint said, hoping the Polarian could vindicate himself. "Now stop stalling." The others were silent, waiting too.

"My prior statement was misleading," the Polarian said. "The Sol system of thrust abates debt by conflict. It would be natural for a Solarian to assume this was true in Sphere Polaris. Thus this Solarian's challenge to me verifies his stated Polarian experience."

"This does not pull," the Nathian said. "The push is to Polaris, not Sol."

"I abate it now. Please forgive my necessary indelicacy. Debt between male and female normally is abated by the mating of the two individuals concerned, and the transfer of the male's seed-ball to the female as her new wheel. This involves—"

"I am satisfied," Flint said with relief, lowering his spear. "I apologize for my suspicion."

"Now I pose my return query, completing the circle. How is debt abated between Polarians of similar sex?"

Flint's mouth dropped open. "I have no idea," he said. "I never thought of that!"

"Yet you actually abated debt as a transferee?"

"I don't expect you to believe this in the circumstance," Flint said, feeling the cynosure of the eyeless creatures around him. "I *was* in Sphere Polaris, but I never—"

"You, Nath?" the Polarian inquired.

"Two males with debt must seek two females with similar debt," the Nathian replied promptly. "One male then makes formal exchange of obligation with one female. He now abates her debt by mating with her debt sister. The other pair proceeds similarly. This is known as 'squaring' debt, one of the few examples of non-circularity in Polarian custom, the subject of ribaldry.

There are special conventions for debt between juveniles, or when one party to debt dies before abatement—"

"Obvious, now," Flint said. "I should have known—"

"Demurral," the Polarian said. "This verifies that even extended transfer cannot replace native knowledge or long-term acquaintance. A transferee cannot deceive one who is truly familiar with the culture."

"I stand ready to verify my own identity similarly," H:::4 said. "I am satisfied with this mode of—"

"*I* am not satisfied," Mintaka said. "Sol fouled up his own question, and Nath merely applied logic. Who would *I* exchange questions with? The representative of our neighbor Mirzam is dead."

"Impasse threatens," H:::4 said. "Let Sol challenge the others of us as he did Polaris. At least this accomplishes something. We cannot debate interminably, or we fail in our mutual mission through default."

"Now wait," Flint said. "This is a murder mystery, and I hardly know how to—"

"Agreement," the Polarian said. "Sol's forward thrust and linear thinking seem best here."

"Pull-hook. Sol gave us all transfer; Sol will not betray us."

"Solarian, you said you transferred also to Spica," the Spican quivered.

Flint sighed. It seemed he had been nominated, regardless. "Yes. But of course I know no more about Spican culture than about Polarian. So I can't—"

"We shall exchange questions. Please define the Spican mating system."

It always came down to sex, he thought. That was a fundamental drive in any species, and the most subject to social restrictions. So it was a good tool for verification. "That I can do. You have three sexes, the Impacts, the Sibilants, and the Undulants. The confluence of the three leads immediately to an explosive mergence. The third entity on the scene assumes the role of catalyst—"

"A moment," the Mintakan said. "Did you not say that the Andromedan also transferred to Spica?"

"Yes. In fact, the two of us became part of a mating trio."

The Canopian saucer wobbled momentarily as if suffering brief loss of control. "You met and knew the enemy—and *mated* with her?"

Flint spread his hands in a useless gesture. "Ridiculous as it sounds, I did. You see—"

"Then you informed the Spican authorities of her identity so they could kill her," the Nathian suggested.

"No. I—well, you see the situation—"

"My point," the Mintakan said, "is that she therefore knows as much about Spica as you do—perhaps more."

"That's right!" Flint agreed, surprised again by the obvious. "So this is no—"

"In fact, you could give an accurate answer to the question and still be the Andromedan spy."

"Not that particular one," Flint said with a smile. "The spy and I are of different sexes."

"I submit that the spy could be male," the Mintakan persisted. "Spica is irrelevant, but can Canopus assure us that the spy transferee there was the female?"

The saucer wobbled again. "We cannot," H:::4 admitted. "We dealt with two transferees, but knew them only by their auras, both extremely high, and their statements. Both claimed to be from Sphere Sol."

"So the female who provided the transfer information, after the male had failed, could in fact have been the real Sol envoy. She tried to kill the impostor, who in turn sought to discredit her."

"This is possible," the Master agreed.

"Yet this Solarian is true to his type," the Polarian argued.

"Unless the Andromedan is also of that type. Do you suppose Sol is the only thrust-culture in the universe? It would be natural for the Andromedan to transfer to the most similar species."

"Pull-hook," the Nathian agreed.

"Objection," the Spican quivered. "We have observed a circumstance, and postulated an explanation, but have omitted the third aspect. There may be no murderer among us; our comrade of Sphere Mirzam may have been dispatched by the Titan."

"The Titan!" Flint exclaimed. "Surely there is no living Ancient here!" but he looked about nervously.

"We do not know what their powers were, except that they were greater than ours," the Spican pointed out. "We believe they were land-borne creatures, yet even on our Spican planets, beneath deep and long-enduring oceans, we have found their stigmata. Indeed, these formidable evidences of past life and civilization provided the incentive that took us into space to search for new waters. The Ancients could have left an inanimate guardian, a machine—"

"A robot!" Flint said. "Or boobytraps, the way the pyramidal Egyptians did on our home planet, to stop intrusions."

"We remain at an impasse," the Antarean signaled. "I suggest we give up this futile search for a guilty entity within our number and form into pairs, each entity in charge of its partner. Anyone who fails to act in a manner conducive to the welfare of our own galaxy will be suspect—and we shall all gather here before any of us leave. Perhaps the Ancients will provide the solution for us."

"Good thinking!" Flint agreed. "The Andromedans obviously think there *is* something here, and they're afraid of it. When we discover it, they will have to act—or let us gain the secret."

"Which connections?" the Nathian asked. "Which entities pair?"

"Random is best," H:::4 said. "Let each entity pair with the one most nearly opposite it, here in this circle."

As it happened, Nath was opposite Mintaka, Flint opposite Spica, and Polaris opposite Antares. Canopus, suspended above the corpse in his craft, was isolated. "With your agreement," H:::4 said, "I will pair with the defunct Mirzam. Were I the one who killed it, I could do no further damage, and I will not be able to interfere with your search. If the spy makes its move elsewhere, the partner can summon me for help. I will hover here and remain in radio touch."

There was no demurral. Despite the murder, all parties were weary of the fruitless quest for the criminal. The three pairs set out in three directions, at last on the trail of the secret of the Ancients.

"I really don't know what we're looking for," Flint admitted. "This may be a wild goose chase."

"There is no native life here," the Spican in Antarean guise reminded him, the bumps on its back rippling as it oozed into its forward extrusion. It was able to make fair progress. Flint had to walk slowly, but this was not burdensome. "Thus there can be no flying fish, not even untame ones."

"Figure of speech," Flint said, smiling. "I mean there may be nothing we can use."

"Yet we must search."

"Yes." The others were already out of sight, except for the high Canopian craft.

Now the ruins of the site seemed to loom larger, almost threateningly, as though haunted. Flint dismissed it as nervousness resulting from the shock of discovering the murder. His companion might be an alien agent—no, that was unlikely, for the two Antareans had come together. And how would such a creature have punctured the suit of a jumping entity? There seemed to be no weapon. In fact, his spear was the most likely prospect.

His spear. Had the killer tried to frame him? That had failed—or *had* it? The Mintakan obviously suspected him. . . .

They came to a tall structure, an almost-intact dome rising out of the sand. There was just one hole in it, where air had evidently blasted out at the time of decompression. Yet if the loss of pressure had been that fast, killing every creature there instantly, why weren't there any bodies? No, no mystery there; an expedition would have come to pick them up. Recovery of the dead was common to sapience; it tied in with belief in the afterlife, laying ghosts to rest. Flint did not sneer, even privately; he believed in ghosts.

"This requires exploration," the Spican said. "Yet in my present body, I hesitate to traverse such territory."

"Which sex are you?" Flint inquired.

"Impact. It was thought this would be better for land traverse than Undulant or Sibilant, and perhaps this is so, but the mode is hardly comfortable. I must admit too that it is strange indeed to come close to so many types without mergence. I remain somewhat nervous."

"I can understand that. I was an Impact too, and know the correspondence of limbs is only very general. And of course you are not using limbs at all now." Flint was now reassured that his companion was legitimate—though the Mintakan's point about the Andromedan's knowledge of the Spican system was valid. He would have to trust his intuition—and keep alert. "Since I am in my own body, and it is an athletic one, I shall climb inside, and relay news to you."

"This is kind," the creature agreed.

Flint stepped gingerly over the jagged sill. His fragile-seeming suit was tough, but he didn't want it scraping against the diamond-hard fragments. He came to stand inside the dome.

It was bare but beautiful. The complete night sky was visible through its material. No . . . Flint's excellent visual recall told him that it was not the sky. It was an image, painted or imprinted holographically inside the dome so cleverly that it looked authentic. As he moved, it moved, as though he were traveling at some multiple of light speed, the near stars shifting relative to the far ones. The effect was awe-inspiring, technologically and esthetically—and intellectually, for it showed a configuration similar in general but completely different in detail from anything he had viewed before. Flint knew the stars as only a Stone Age man could know them; there were *no* correspondences here. Was it even any part of this galaxy? He would have to check it out when he got back to Sol, if need be querying Sphere Knyfh and any other major Spheres that were now in reach. This could be extremely important.

"The home sky of the Ancients," he breathed. "From this, we can determine their Sphere of origin. . . ."

He could have stared at the splendor of that strange sky interminably, but tore his eyes away. He looked around the floor of the chamber. It was bare—no machines, no furniture, no bodies. So he still had no clue to the physical aspect of the Ancients. But of course this was only one structure of hundreds. Possibly they had come here to gawk at the vision of the far-distant ancestral home, recharging their spiritual vitality. They must have had eyes, at least. It suggested something fundamentally good about the Ancients; they were, in their fashion, human. They had colonized much of the galaxy, yet they longed for home, and kept its memory fresh. Probably this had been a desolate outpost, a supply station, with forced tours of duty: a necessary function of empire.

Yet it had been wiped out, and suddenly. Perhaps some terrible beam from space had voided their pressure shield, releasing their bubble of atmosphere, killing them all. Maybe an enemy had landed, sacked the post, and removed all artifacts of potential value. In which case there would be nothing left for the archaeologists. Too bad.

"Sol. Spica," the Canopian Master's voice said from Flint's unit, interrupting his musings. "There has been a development. Please return immediately to the collection site."

"What happened?" Flint asked, certain he would not like the reply.

"The representative of Sphere Antares has been killed. I am holding its partner Polaris under guard pending group assembly."

"Oh, no," Flint groaned. "I thought we'd cleared Polaris." He ran for the opening, scrambled out, and landed beside the Spican. "You heard?"

"Dehydrated!" the creature replied in evident horror. To a water entity, dehydration would be a hellish concept on several levels, an obscenity. "Now we *know* there is a murderer among us."

"But neither you nor me," Flint said. "I was within the dome, with no other exit—and you could not have moved fast enough to do the job, even had you chosen to kill your friend."

"Agreed. We two are innocent—but four suspects remain."

"Polaris, Nath, Mintaka, and Canopus," Flint said. "We must hurry. Would it be permissible for me to carry you?"

"In the circumstance, permissible. But be careful."

"Yes." Flint put his two arms around the glob and heaved it up, feeling the associated Kirlian aura. H:::4 had been right: All entities on this mission were high-Kirlian types. Not just five or ten times normal intensity, but fifty or a hundred. The best their cultures had to offer. High Kirlians for high stakes!

The creature weighed about as much as Flint did, but it shaped itself to the upper contours of his body comfortably and was easy to carry. He ran as fast as he could toward the rendezvous.

The Polarian was there, the Canopian saucer hovering close overhead, as Flint tramped up with his burden. The Mintakan and Nathian had not yet arrived. "What happened?"

"I am under suspicion again," the Polarian said. "My partner of Sphere Antares is defunct."

"I challenged you before," Flint said, setting down the Spican carefully. "But you satisfied me that you were legitimate. I do not believe you would have done it."

"That is most circular of you. But unless you can identify a more immediate suspect—"

"I think we'd better all establish alibis," Flint said.

He had a suspect, but didn't care to name it at the moment.

"Alibis?" the Spican inquired.

"Each entity must explain where he was at the time of the murder," Flint explained. "If he were elsewhere, he cannot have been *there,* so would be innocent."

"Most ingenious," the Spican agreed. "You Solarians do have a marvelous directness. We must also ascertain the mode of demise."

Mintaka and Nath arrived. "This is very bad," the Nathian clicked.

Flint explained about alibis, giving his own and the Spican's.

"Demurral," Mintaka flashed. "We have not verified that there is no other exit to your dome. And if the Spican were the spy, the Antarean would be the first to know it, and would therefore be marked for death. And that death prevents us all from knowing how rapidly that type of entity can move. It could be the fastest among us all."

Devastating logic. Flint and the Spican were back under suspicion.

"However," the Mintakan continued, "the element of velocity is relevant. My companion of Sphere Nath certainly cannot move as rapidly as some of us, and furthermore must leave a typical trail in the dust. Even were I not able to testify that Nath went nowhere without me, the absence of the trail would vindicate him."

"And I assent that the Mintakan was always in my perception," the Nathian said.

"Perception," Flint murmured. "You don't have eyes. How can you be sure—"

"I possess acute auditory and vibratory perception," the Nathian replied a bit tersely. "This is equivalent or superior to your optics. When light fails, you are blind, whereas my sonar—"

"I accept your word," Flint said.

"Nath speaks accurately," the Polarian said. "Their perception of physical objects is excellent. We must accept that alibi."

"You know where that leaves you," Flint said.

"It would be uncircular to misdiagnose any suspect; we must ascertain the truth. We are all suspect, and none of us can alibi the Canopian."

"Correct," H:::4 said. "My craft could readily have

traversed the necessary distance and returned, and it is armed. I could certainly have done it, and I am thus a suspect. I suggest, however, that were I the Andromedan agent, I could kill you all now, and could have done so at the outset. I am well armed and have no need to act covertly."

This was exactly what had occurred to Flint. He had avoided a direct accusation because if he proved his point, one pellet or ray from the saucer could wipe him out. But why *would* the Master bother to kill in secrecy?

Perhaps because he could not safely leave his craft, and had to wait on the explorations of the others. If the secret of the Ancients were discovered here, it had to be salvaged or destroyed, according to the Andromedan view—and salvage would naturally be best. So it was simplest to eliminate any entity who caught on to the spy's identity. Or to keep cutting down the size of the expedition, until the one or two survivors could be controlled.

Flint believed the Polarian was innocent, and doubted that the Spican, handicapped as it was by an unfamiliar body, could have done it. Since the others had alibis, that left Canopus, with all his mobility and armament.

"May I remind you that there remains the possibility of some Ancient agency," H: : :4 said. "Perhaps it lacks the power to eliminate all of us, but seeks to sow dissent by selective killings."

There was that. "Let's get together to investigate the crime," Flint said. "Whoever or whatever is stalking us, it seems to strike only isolated entities. If there is safety in numbers, let's take advantage of it." And maybe there'd be a chance to get away from the Canopian craft.

They trekked along the route marked by the Polarian's wheel. The dust was undisturbed here, except for that. No way to conceal the trail. The absence of a trail could only implicate Canopus again.

They approached the mouth of a large tunnel angling underground. It seemed to be an avenue for vehicles. That suggested the Ancients did not fly or run rapidly; they preferred to ride.

"We discovered a sealed airlock below," the Polarian explained. "I notified Canopus, who asked me to emerge and show my location so that he could establish it specifically for the other members of the expedition. My companion, Antares, had investigated the lock and informed me that there was operative equipment within. Therefore we felt the discovery was significant."

"When I located Polaris visually, I followed him back to this tunnel, which I could not enter," the Master said. "He entered, then reported the demise of his companion. As you can see, there are no tracks besides those of Polaris and Antares. I therefore placed him under temporary detention and summoned the other members of the expedition."

Flint looked at the tracks. There was no question: There were three wheel-treads and one pattern of splotches formed by the motion of the Antarean. Polaris had come, gone, and come again, while Antares had come—and stayed. It looked bad for the Polarian: no other tracks, and the Canopian saucer too wide to enter the tunnel.

"It is my turn to remind you that we approached operative Ancient machinery," the Polarian said, applying his ball to his own suit. "That airlock could have opened in my absence. . . ."

"Does anyone on the ground have a power weapon?" Flint inquired. "If that portal should open again—"

There was no response. He knew why: Personal defense was now critical, and a hidden weapon could be more effective than one that was known. "Well," he continued, "be ready to fight or flee, all of you. I'll have my spear, but it has limits."

They entered the tunnel. The Spican began to glow, illuminating it; so did the Polarian. Flint walked first, spear poised, with the Spican close behind; Nath was third, Polaris fourth, and Mintaka brought up the rear.

The passage curved, and terminated at the lock. There was the body. The Antarean's spacesuit had been punctured, just like the suit of Mirzam, and the creature's gelatinous substance had burst out through that round aperture. Explosive decompression, quickly and horribly fatal.

"As you can perceive, I lack the capacity to make a wound of that nature," Polaris said.

"Your ball could vibrate rapidly, abrasively, against a given spot," Spica said. "It would take time to make a hole of that size, but if Antares were unconscious—"

"My spear might make a similar hole," Flint pointed out. "Or a laser beam. Or a conglomeration of sharp little hooks."

"Could Canopus have dismounted from his craft?" Spica asked. "While Polaris was absent?"

"Yes," Flint said. "And Canopus may be able to fly on his own. He is of insectoid derivation, with wings—"

"Not in vacuum," Mintaka pointed out.

That popped that bubble. Mintaka had a way of doing that; very sharp mind. Wings needed atmosphere in order to function. "But a jet pack?" Flint inquired.

"Then we all remain suspect," Nath said. "Any one of us could have hidden a flying device."

"Not so," Polaris said. "Such devices create turbulence, especially in confined spaces, and the prints are undisturbed."

"It becomes difficult to separate circularity from suicide," Nath remarked, since the Polarian seemed to have brought suspicion on himself again. "But I believe I can exonerate Polaris. I noted three wheel-tracks. Do your perceptions concur?"

"Yes," Flint said. "What's your point?"

"There should be four."

"That is correct," Polaris said. "I arrived with my companion, left to notify Canopus of the route, reentered to discover the murder, and reemerged. Four tracks."

"Prior to our present entry," Flint agreed. "You must have used one track twice."

"I did not. The taste of one's own trail quickly palls. That is a maxim among my kind, with philosophic undertones but nevertheless also literally true. My wheel is encased in its own suit, but it is not my habit to repeat a specific route exactly. I made four trails."

"Yet there are only three," Nath clicked. "Therefore one must have been erased."

"How could that happen in this dust?" Flint asked. "And why would anyone bother?"

"Perhaps it was the killer's own trail being erased, and the Polarian's trail was coincidental. Sonic application could do this."

Flint's eyes narrowed. "Could *you* do it?"

"Yes." And Nath demonstrated by clicking his hooks together in such a way as to cause the nearby dust to jump and resettle around it, wiping out its own trail.

"But Nath did *not*," Mintaka said. "He remained with me—and there are no gaps in his own trail."

"More than can be said for mine," Spica said. "My partner carried me partway."

"We now have a possible method," Flint said. "But it doesn't help much. Any of us, including Canopus, might have done it; it is evident that we hardly know enough about each other's capacities to be assured otherwise."

"Were I the guilty party," H:::4 said in their translators, "I could bomb the entrance to the tunnel and destroy you all. I admit the capability; I deny guilt or intent. Judge me unfairly, and you only strengthen the position of the actual spy."

"Maybe we'd better agree that there is an Ancient robot stalking us," Flint said, glancing nervously at the tunnel entrance. He had thought they would be safe from Canopus here, but obviously they weren't. There was no way out but forward—through the Ancient airlock. "It killed Mirzam, but could not catch the rest of us alone, until it found Antares. It is now outside, having erased its trail, waiting for us to separate again."

"This seems to be a satisfactory hypothesis," Mintaka flashed. "But it does not alleviate our peril. If it has laser armament, even Canopus is not safe."

"Why wait for it to strike again?" Flint asked. "Let's force open this lock and plumb its secrets. We have nothing to lose."

"Pull-hook."

"Concurrence," Mintaka said.

"Agreement," Spica finished.

"I, too, am amenable," H:::4 said. "I shall remain on guard. My apologies to Polaris; my suspicion was premature."

"Circularity."

Flint examined the lock. "This is a simple gear-and-pinion system," he said, glad of the dull training he had been given on Earth. "The Ancients must have had hands like mine." Could the Ancients have been humanoid? No, that was too much to expect of coincidence. He took hold of a half-wheel and turned.

To his surprise, it moved. Something clicked; then a blast of air shot out through a vent, almost knocking him over despite the baffle that inhibited its force. "Depressurization," he said. "For three million years it held its air—that's some mechanism." Truly a Titan, he added mentally.

"Evidence that the Ancients can retain operative mechanisms today," Mintaka said. "We are surely very close to significance."

Now the lock swung open to reveal a fair-sized inner chamber. "Canopus, we are entering the inner sanctum," Flint announced. "If our communications cut off, you had better return to your Sphere and issue a report." And if you are our spy, we are safe from you, he thought. And you won't get the secret of the Ancients. That's why none of us can afford to go home: We might miss the crucial discovery of the millennium.

"Understood. I will maintain contact if this is feasible. Under no circumstance will I dismount from my craft."

"Right." They crowded into the lock, and Flint pulled the door closed.

Immediately the locking mechanism clicked it tight. Air hissed in, pressurizing the chamber. "But let's keep our suits on," Flint said.

"It is helium gas, almost pure," Nath said. "Inert, but not suitable for normal life processes."

"I thought as much," Flint said. "Normal atmosphere on any world has corrosive properties."

"*Sentience* is corrosive," Mintaka remarked.

When pressure was up to about twenty pounds per square inch, making Flint feel as if he were in water, the hissing stopped. He worked the half-wheel on the inner door, and it opened.

It was a large chamber, illuminated by a gentle glow from the walls, with several passages radiating out from it. In the center was a circular platform enclosed by a pattern of wire mesh. There seemed to be an elevator or hoist within it, the cage suspended about twice Flint's height above the floor. That was all.

"Empty," Flint said, disappointed. "They must have cleaned it out before they closed up shop, after the wipe-out. Took all the bodies and equipment."

"Yet machinery below and around us is functional," Spica said.

"Oh? Where are the machines?" Flint asked. "I mean, specifically."

"Below me, here. Operative but not mechanical," Nath replied.

"Electrical in nature," Spica said. "I regret I am unable to utilize the full propensities of this body. The native Antarean could have read the flux precisely."

"You can perceive magnetic flow?" Nath asked.

"Yes. And the finer manifestations such as the Kirlian aura. Not merely as a presence, but as a specific pattern, typical of any given entity. This is a good body."

Something fell into place in Flint's mind. Sphere Antares had possessed the secret of natural transfer for centuries, so would be long familiar with related nuances. "Can you distinguish between a native entity and a transferee?"

"This is simple for Antares. Difficult for me, since—"

Flint kept his body relaxed, his voice casual, but he was ready to explode into action. "Are any of us transferees?"

"No. Only myself. My friend Antares verified this at the outset, and intended to inform you, being concerned that—"

"Including Canopus?"

"Canopus is native. This is assured."

So there were no transfer traitors among them after all. They were all the creatures they appeared to be. Had the Spican been the spy, it would have accused one of the others instead of exonerating them.

"Caution," Mintaka flashed. "Antares was within range of operative Ancient circuitry, detecting its function and pattern. The Ancient equipment should similarly be able to detect capacities in us. Antares was quickly killed. You, Spica, may now be in similar danger."

"We're *all* in danger," Flint said. "But I agree we'd better keep close watch on Spica."

"Triple appreciation," the Spican said. "I shall try to analyze this alien field further. I do not think it is capable of physical action, however."

Such as puncturing a spacesuit? That was certainly no magnetic phenomenon. Unless: "Electric engines are magnetic, and we have magnetic pistols in Sphere Sol. Could an Ancient circuit have—?"

"That was one of my considerations," Spica said. "As I orient on the fields of this site, I verify: The operative element is not capable of physical action. The currents are very fine, akin to those of living nervous circuits. No motors or heating units."

"Surely the Titan wasn't a pacifist!" Flint murmured dubiously. But he remembered those fascinating stars, obviously esthetic rather than practical, there in the dome. Had the Ancients' culture been as far beyond the contemporary scene as their technology?

"The system is"—Spica paused in evident surprise—"is Kirlian."

"Jackpot!" Flint exclaimed. "The Ancients *did* have advanced Kirlian technology—and now it is ours!"

"We should not tabulate our gains until hooked," Nath warned.

"Canopus, can you hear us?" Flint asked.

"I hear you, Sol," H:::4 replied immediately. "And I now confirm with the instruments aboard my craft that there is a diffuse Kirlian aura emanating from that region. It does not pulsate in the manner of a living aura; it appears to be inorganic. Inanimate."

"But the Kirlian aura is a function of life," Mintaka protested. "This is the distinction between life and death."

"Not any more," Flint said. "So now we know the Ancients had the secret of inorganic Kirlian aura generation. I'm not surprised. I'll bet this is what Andromeda is using against us. They are able to imbue matter and energy with a Kirlian field, then transfer that field to their home galaxy. Now we will be able to stop them. This is exactly what we have been looking for."

"Concurrence," Mintaka said. Something nagged at the fringe of Flint's awareness. It was the second time the creature had used that expression. But of course it was only a translation. None of these entities used human idiom or construction; its translator did that. "We must investigate this equipment thoroughly, and make report to our Spheres."

"This has the aspect of a Tarot temple," Nath remarked.

"Tarotism has spread to Sphere Nath?" Flint asked, surprised.

"And to Sphere Bellatrix," Nath said. "Perhaps further. I understand it originated in your Sphere."

"Yes, about five hundred years ago, in the time of Sol's 'Fool' colonization period. We almost bankrupted our origin planet, Earth, mattermitting the entire population to other worlds, as though that would solve the problems of increasing population and wastage of natural resources." He was merely parroting part of the indoctrination he had received after making his report on his experiences in Sphere Polaris. But it was amazing to discover how fast and far this cult had spread, more than humanity's own interstellar explosion. Would it survive mankind, as Christianity had survived the Roman Empire?

Flint continued: "One planet had a natural animation effect that a religious scholar, Brother Paul of the Holy Order of Vision, investigated and described. He had no intention of starting a pseudo-religious cult, but the notion of animation captured the popular fancy, and it went on from there."

"This Sibling Solarian of the Arrangement of Hallucination must have been a redoubtable figure," Nath said. "Tarotism has much pull in our Sphere, and we honor it without ridicule. And perhaps the Sibling is serving us well now, for animation is a function of the Kirlian aura. I suggest that we may profit most rapidly by drawing on the Ancients' equipment from this vantage."

"This might in fact be a communications station," Polaris agreed. "Perhaps we can animate the presence of an actual Ancient. This would be most circular."

"Amen," Flint agreed. "In fact, I would even call it 'most direct.' But we run the risk of evoking the killer who is stalking us—if it really is that Ancient ghost."

"At risk of antagonizing," Spica said, "I reiterate that the killer strikes by direct physical means, and this is not within the compass of the Ancient mechanism."

"Unless the Ancient mechanism generates a Kirlian field of sufficient power to override that of a living entity," Mintaka flashed. "It could then temporarily preempt or transform the individual consciousness, or otherwise influence it to implement physical action, even as your own transferred identity controls your Antarean host."

"This is most perceptive," Polaris said. "Sphere Mintaka, so new to transfer, has been remarkably quick to appreciate its intricacies." Flint had thought the same, and recognized this as a roundabout challenge.

"Merely ordinary intelligence that would have occurred to you in a moment," Mintaka flashed. "However, we have long been aware of transfer, and have maintained a cadre of potential hosts, hoping for the technological breakthrough. We are a large Sphere, and normal means of maintenance are cumbersome. Thus when the envoy of Mirzam came, we were very quick to implement the information provided. Though at present we know of no involuntary hosting, if this is indeed possible, it would seem to have been within the capability of the Ancients."

The Mintakan was very well coordinated, intellectually, Flint thought. But of course all the Spheres would have sent smart representatives, as well as Kirlians. This was a most select archaeological group, well versed in everything but archaeology.

"We become enmeshed in dialogue," Nath clicked a bit impatiently. "We are naturally hesitant to pull on the main problem—but pull we must. I suggest that two of us explore the Ancients' Kirlian arena while three maintain guard. Assuming that the aura is hostile, it still does not seem to strike openly. We may be able to ascertain what we wish without further loss if we act boldly and carefully."

"I agree," Flint said. "If the Ancient force can take over an individual life form and use it to kill, there are still certain limitations. Spica cannot readily make the kind of puncture we have noted, unless it carries a weapon we have not perceived, and I think similar attack would be difficult for Nath, and not easy for Polaris. That leaves Mintaka and me—"

"And me," Canopus said from the translator. "I am compelled to advise you that if I should be taken over, I possess enough weaponry in my craft, including pain-generating units and exposive devices, to eliminate all of you and destroy the site. I would not voluntarily employ it, but faced with this potential, I can only recommend that you treat me as a potential enemy of most serious nature."

Friendly advice—or a threat? "We are *all* potential enemies," Mintaka pointed out. "We may be forced to destroy the Ancient site in order to escape it. But first we must understand it, or our mission is pointless."

Flint was paying lip-service to the Ancient-malevolence theory, but he was skeptical. Why hadn't Canopus already been taken over, if that were possible? And why should the Ancients set such a boobytrap? All he really knew of them was their star-dome, but that indicated that they had been artistic, philosophical, peaceful entities, not warriors. Spica had said the equipment could not act violently, and Flint had the impression that included taking over the mind of another entity by force. It was safer to assume that one of the creatures here was an Andromedan spy. By elimination, he had a strong notion of who that was. Except that it had an alibi.

"Pursuing my prior line of reasoning," Flint said, "I suggest that those of us most able to kill in the fashion shown should be most suspect, and should therefore be treated with utmost caution. So Mintaka and I should enter the animation arena—if that is what it is—and try to make contact with the Ancients. The others should maintain close perception, and if only one of us emerges, that one should be immediately incapacitated, or killed if necessary." That put it on the line. If the Mintakan balked. . . .

"An excellent suggestion," Mintaka flashed. And rolled toward the great central plate below the suspended cage.

So much for that ploy! Flint suddenly realized that if Mintaka were the spy, it could try to kill him in the guise of self-defense, claiming that he, Flint, had attacked it, so Flint must have been the spy. Or that one of them had been taken over by the Ancient aura. Who would be able to prove otherwise? By a similar token, if Mintaka were the spy, and attacked him, and he killed it *he* would be suspect as the survivor. He had fashioned a trap for himself! But he was committed now, and hurried after. Together they entered what they presumed to be the animation arena.

Nothing happened. But why should it? It was necessary to imagine something. So he thought of Honeybloom, as he had known her: voluptuous, vibrant, lovely, her green body moving in that distracting way it had.

And she formed, ghostly at first, then more firmly, as if the mind's artist were strengthening the key lines—except that her eyes were like lenses, and they flashed laser beams. An imperfect rendition, but definitely animation. He even saw the emblem of her Tarot card, the Queen of Liquid, with a brimming cup—

"It strikes!" a voice cried in his translator.

Flint charged out of the arena. The girl-figure faded.

Polaris and Nath stood facing each other. Between them Spica lay puddled. Its suit had been holed, and though chamber pressure kept it from decompressing, the creature was obviously dead.

Flint hefted his spear. "Which of you did it?" he demanded. And realized that this approach was futile; each would accuse the other, preventing him from ascertaining the truth. Impasse, again. Unless he could bluff: "I'll spear you *both,* if I have to!"

"No, friend Sol," Polaris said. "I am innocent, and I know Nath would not do this thing."

"And I know Polaris would not," Nath clicked. "Our Spheres have known each other long. We trust each other."

"And we trust you," Polaris said. "A laser beam

emerged from the swirl of the arena. Neither of us perceive specific light well, so could not ascertain its precise orientation, but there was no question."

His vision of the flashing eye lenses! "It could not have been real!" Flint exclaimed. "An imaginary creature, a mere image, could not project a real—" Or *could* it? An image might clothe the shaping of existent forces. Had *he* inadvertently killed Spica?

Then he realized: "Mirzam was the only one who could directly identify a true Mintakan—and it was the first one killed. Antares and Spica could have detected any additional transfer activity, such as an Andromedan transfer message—and they died. Our Mintakan must be a fake."

"No," Polaris said. "The Mintakan is a genuine, physical representative of its species. But that species is not—" Suddenly he launched himself at Flint, his wheel screeching against the floor in the sheer velocity of takeoff.

Flint dodged aside, bringing his spear about, but he was not quick enough. Polaris struck him, bowling him over—and simultaneously there was a flash.

Flint flipped to his feet, raising his spear as the creature's wheel spun again. "Push-hook!" Nath clicked. "Polaris protects Sol!"

About to spear Polaris, Flint realized it was true. The creature had not been attacking him, but knocking him out of the way of the laser. He shifted his weight and hurled his spear at the creature just emerging from the arena.

They had all assumed that if a creature were a genuine Milky Way resident, it would be on their side. But if a creature were brainwashed or corrupted—

His shaft bounced harmlessly off the metallic disks. Another beam shot out, creasing the fingers of his left hand. The material of his suit melted, and his air leaked out.

Flint clenched his fist tightly, closing off the leak. In a vacuum this would have been a useless expedient, but the chamber was pressurized by helium. "Polaris! Nath!" he cried. "We know our enemy now. You investigate the Ancient equipment. Get yourselves out of laser range. I'll tackle the spy." And he leaped toward the Mintakan. He had been face to face with his enemy all the time, and not known him. But now the battle had been joined.

"What is the situation?" the voice of Canopus asked.

But a laser caught Nath. The creature convulsed, its

hooks firing out randomly, then lay flat. Apparently its central nervous complex had been burned out. Another down. Those beams were deadly.

And Mintaka was already rolling after Polaris, who fled across the room and through a far doorway. "*I* will distract, *you* search!" it cried to Flint.

Not much choice, now! Polaris could move faster than any human being could. Flint stepped onto the animation plate and made a wish for an Ancient. There was a swirl of mist, but no form developed.

"Mintaka is our Andromedan spy," Flint explained while he concentrated on the animation.

"But Mintaka had an alibi."

"So it seemed. But those lasers are devastating. I'd say he can beam any potency from conversational to killing. He must have stunned Nath before, gone and killed Antares, used some device—maybe a specialized laser—to erase his trail, and returned before Nath recovered. Nath only *thought* Mintaka was with him all the time; Nath had been unconscious or in a trance. This is another resourceful, unscrupulous agent, and we're in trouble."

"Sphere Mintaka cannot support Andromeda," Canopus protested. "Our entire galaxy will disintegrate! It must be a renegade, not representative of the government of Sphere Mintaka."

"A traitor to its species," Flint agreed. "Maybe a condemned criminal, with nothing to lose, desiring vengeance. If any of us survive this, the authorities of Sphere Mintaka will have to be informed. Now let me concentrate."

The Master was silent. Flint worked on the animation image, but it remained formless. The problem was, he had no idea what the Ancients had looked like, so could not re-create them.

But their *appearance* was irrelevant! He had a notion of their spirit, for they had loved the stars of their home region as he did. And it was the Ancient *science* he wanted—and he had a fair notion of that. It was similar to contemporary transfer science, only more advanced, and this field itself was an example. "Define yourself!" Flint whispered to that field.

"Explain, please."

Flint jumped. But it was not an Ancient voice answering him, but H:::4, who had overheard his remark.

"I'm talking to the Kirlian field, trying to get its secret," Flint explained."

"Try visualizing the equations."

"Good idea!" Flint animated the complex formulas he had memorized eidetically for spreading transfer technology. They took form in midair, the symbols of mathematical, engineering, and symbolic logic chains. He spread out the whole thing, then willed the complex calculus forward in thrust—beyond what he had in his mind.

Suddenly the equations spread. Perhaps through some kind of animation-enhanced telepathy he was drawing the answers from the Ancient equipment, reducing the field itself to its conceptual expression. Perhaps the equipment was geared to provide this sort of information. Maybe the Ancients had *wanted* this technology to spread! At any rate, here it was.

And Mintaka sliced into the room. Polaris was not in evidence; he had either been lost or killed. There was ichor on one of the disks: Polarian blood?

It took Mintaka only a moment to appraise what he was doing. Then the laser beam flashed.

Flint was a sitting duck. He threw himself to the floor, rolled, and flipped about to come at the disk-harrow feet first. It tried to move aside, but he caught the creature by surprise, and it was not made for sideways travel. His feet struck the disks, shoving them to the side. One of the end-tentacles wrapped around his left ankle and hauled his foot toward the nearest disk. The entire creature rolled, trying to pin his foot between the floor and the cutting edge.

If Mintaka were represented by a Tarot suit, Flint thought amidst his desperate effort, it should be Solid; otherwise known as Disks.

Flint had worked out a general plan of combat against this creature beforehand, in case of need. He had similar contingency plans for all of the group. It was the kind of thing he did automatically, as a Stone Age hunter who liked life. He jammed the reinforced heel of his right foot down between the first and second disks, forcing them apart in what had to be a painful hold. Then he grabbed the tentacle with his right hand and bent it at right angles. Like a pinched water hose it lost power, and he drew his left foot free.

But now the body twisted. From between the farthest two disks another laser flashed, similar to the communications signal, but more intense. The beam missed him—but the next one wouldn't.

Flint realized that the creature was too tough for him. Mintaka could finish him with a laser before he could knock him out. But at least he had bought time for his allies.

His allies? Only Canopus remained, and H: : :4 was not in immediate danger. Flint was fighting for his own life and information, nothing more.

Yet there *was* more, something highly significant. But he could not identify it in the throes of this battle.

He shoved violently with his feet, making the creature slide cross the floor. Before it could orient on him again, Flint leaped into the animation stage. And thought of himself.

Suddenly there was another Flint beside him, his duplicate. Then two more, and four more. In moments a score of Flints were running around the arena, capering like monkeys. The Mintakan's ray speared one, but had no effect. "You can't hurt me, nyaa, nyaa!" that image mouthed. "I'm only a *Doppelgänger.*"

The laser struck another image. Then a third. It seemed the spy had plenty of power, and was prepared to wipe out every image in order to nail him in the end. The law of chance dictated that this effort would succeed in time.

"Canopus!" Flint cried, and all his images mouthed it with him. Good thing the spy's translator couldn't orient specifically on the origin of the sound!

"Sol," H: : :4 replied. "How may I assist?"

"Use your armament. Demolish this entire site. Kill every creature in it."

"Do not do it!" Mintaka cried in translation. "Sol is the spy. He wants to prevent us from acquiring the Ancient's secrets."

Time and again, Flint realized, this creature had raised seemingly valid points that had led them astray. Even the agreements had been camouflage, making it seem to be a true Mintakan in spirit as well as in body. But it had given itself away by that "Concurrence," which Flint now recognized as an Andromedan transfer-message convention. "I commence action," the Master said. "I am recording our dialogue, since I will be obliged to defend myself from suspicion as the sole survivor. Can you provide the key formulations?"

"Yes," Flint said. He concentrated, and the equations appeared again, superimposed on the moving images of himself. "This is terrific! The Ancients had complete mastery of inorganic Kirlian aura: How to set up a field around energy that enables it to be transmitted any distance instantly, how to orient on any Kirlian transfer—"

"Begin with that one," H:::4 said. "I shall ensure its arrival at all our Spheres."

"Keep firing," Flint said. "If this spy survives me—and if *any* survive, it will be the Mintakan—it will ray you down. Destroy everything, and don't let anything you may see dissuade you. It will probably be an animation image calculated to deceive you."

"I understand, and commend your courage," the Master said. Already the shaking of his bombing could be felt. "I shall not fail. No living thing will emerge from this site."

"Orientation on transfer," Flint said. And he read off the array of symbols.

A laser struck him dead center, holing his suit. Flint moved with seeming casualness, so as not to attract attention to himself by reaching. His stomach burned ferociously, but it was not a mortal wound; either his flesh was too solid for the beam to penetrate far, or the spy was losing his power, after all that firing. There had to be *some* fatigue! Flint dared not even make all the images imitate his action, for then Mintaka would know the critical one had been hit. He put his left fist over the puncture and pressed it tight, inhibiting the leakage of vital gases.

It worked. The agent of Andromeda thought he was merely another image, and moved on to the next. And he continued reading off the equations without break, so that his voice would not give him away. He also made one of the images gesticulate and collapse when rayed, drawing several more beams: a decoy.

He completed the readoff for transfer orientation—so *that* was how the enemy had always located him before!—and started on the Kirlian-energy formulation. He could not rush this, for any mistake would make the whole effort a waste.

Meanwhile, the Canopian's bombing progressed. The chamber shook with increasing violence. The walls and ceiling cracked. H:::4 had not been bluffing about his armament!

Now Mintaka gave up with the laser, having struck every image, and entered the arena physically. The harrow charged through the images, slicing them with the disks.

Flint kept the figures moving around, but the spy would surely catch him soon. He was already handicapped by the two holes in his suit, and was in no position to renew physical conflict. All he could do was keep dodging and reading off formulas until the end. If he made it through a couple more concepts, he would have given his galaxy the key to victory.

The ceiling split open. But instead of falling in, it blew out, as the gas dissipated into the vacuum of the surface. *Then* it imploded. Debris funneled down, dropping through the images. His life-air hissed out around his pressing fist.

"You're right on target," Flint said, interrupting his reading. "Drop one right down the hole and finish it. The Mintakan is right here."

"But the formula is incomplete," the Master protested.

"What, are you wavering?" Flint demanded. "We can't let Andromeda escape with this stuff. I'll try to get out the last—"

And Mintaka caught up with him. The devastating blades sliced into his feet, cutting off his toes. His remaining air exploded out, jetting him up momentarily; then he fell across his enemy. He made a last effort to call in H:::4's final bomb to finish them both, but his mind suffered a short-circuit. All he could remember was the need to inform the authorities of Sphere Mintaka what had happened, to warn them—

Mintaka! he thought with all his being as he died.

10

Blinding the Giant

alarm! priority development

—out with it—

ancient mode transfer from hyades open cluster

—disaster! initiate council available entities—

too late milky way galaxy has mastered ancient technology our agent failed we are helpless

—recall all agents from that galaxy immediately we may be able to salvage something—

but that would mean surrendering our energy transfer stations

—that's right we'll have to gamble by leaving them in place and putting all our personnel on alert—

POWER

—oh, disconnect!—

His body was astonishing. Whenever he moved, he jangled, beeped, and boomed. His several feet were little clappers, supporting a triple web of taut wires like three harps. Fitted within the inner curves of these were tiers of drum-diaphragms. Strong tubular framing provided resonance for moving air, with emplaceable reeds. In short, he was an animate orchestra.

He had some kind of sonar/radar perception. He used it to orient on something more familiar: the night sky, perceivable through the image-porous ceiling. There were stars, not exactly bits of light but similar centers of emission. He concentrated, determined to find some point of orientation. This was not the sky of the Ancients, but it was within a galaxy, for there were the massed clouds and stars, the milky way to be seen within any galaxy.

He visualized (though this was not exactly what his new mind did) the night sky as seen from Sphere Sol, and from Etamin, Canopus, Polaris, and the Hyades, trying to superimpose some aspect of it on what he saw here. This was a challenging exercise, the more so because he was aware that some stars had different intensities of emission in the range he could now perceive. What appeared to be a small-illumination visible star might be a large-emission infrared star. But his mind was trained in this, and he made the necessary adjustments. It was rather like rotating a sphere of galactic space, taking cross-sectional slices, sliding them around, searching for any region of congruence.

A fringe of familiarity came. Here was a large red giant, like Betelgeuse, just about the same magnitude he knew. There was a cluster of—could it be the Pleiades? But they were over four hundred light-years away from Sol, whereas this cluster was twice that distance by the aspect of it, even after allowing for his changed perception, if it were of the same absolute brightness, and there was no Taurus constellation associated with it. Here was one like Rigel, but a bit brighter, therefore closer? And—yes it was! The Great Nebula of Orion, not in Orion at all, but brighter, in the correct position relative to Rigel and Betelgeuse.

Abruptly it clicked into place. This was Sphere Mintaka! Naturally the Great Nebula was not in this constellation now; *he* was in it, looking back five hundred light-years toward Sol, where the Nebula was. He was well beyond Rigel and Betelgeuse, on a planet in the Belt, fifteen hundred light-years from Sol.

So this had to be a Mintakan host. The Ancient animation arena had really been a transfer station whose destination was controlled by the thought of the transferee. He was thinking of Mintaka as he died—and here he was!

So his life had been returned to him—for a while. For his Kirlian aura was at reduced strength, and his human body had been blasted apart. No one at home would know what had really happened to him. He had, in his fashion, gone to heaven.

Well, he would communicate from the dead. He retained the remaining formulas, and this added revelation of the nature of the Ancient equipment would enable the Milky Way galaxy to overcome the Andromeda galaxy. He had perhaps sixty Earth days, maybe more, before his Kirlian aura faded below the threshold of human individuality. That should be time enough, considering that Sphere Mintaka had already been contacted by Sphere Mirzam and given transfer. Providing that was not a lie told by the renegade Mintakan.

Renegade Mintakan? How was that possible, when this

musical body was the true Mintakan form? The spy could *not* have been any form of Mintakan. Yet it had not been a transferee either. Paradox!

No—merely erroneous conclusion. The representative from Sphere Mirzam had been the first killed, for it would have known the spy was no Mintakan. Yet if neither Mintakan nor transferee, what could it have been, so fierce in the defense of the interests of Andromeda?

Who else but his nemesis, Cle of Ath or Llyana the Undulant, native of Andromeda? Now he remembered: The creature he had fought in the Hyades had had extremely high Kirlian force, parallel to his own. He had not been able to make the connection in the midst of the battle, but now it was obvious. The Queen of Energy!

She had been mattermitted in her own body all the way from Andromeda. The cost—beyond belief. Which was why he had *not* believed it. What value the enemy had put on that site!

Now she was dead, and it was doubly important that he get his information to his galaxy. Andromeda had set that value, and Andromeda was in a position to know. It was, literally, the ransom of a galaxy.

All right. Mintaka would have transfer technology *now*, because he would provide it. Then he would get in touch with Sphere Sol, making a complete report that would change the face of this section of the universe. This cluster of stars known as the Milky Way would survive. Then he could fade out, satisfied that he had done his job. His galaxy had been saved, and Honeybloom would live happily in her Stone Age idyll, and Tsopi the Polarian in her circular one.

A nurse approached. Her castanet feet made a pleasant clatter, and the lines of her tubing were esthetic. Flint always had acute perception for feminine allure, whatever form it happened to take, and this was a good specimen. "Welcome to Sphere Mintaka," she played.

And that was literal. Her strings and tubes played an intricate little melody counterpointed by the beat of her drums. The meaning was in the music itself. "From what Sphere do you sing?"

No need for concealment! "I am from Sphere Sol," Flint played in reply. The music came automatically, for it was inherent in this entity's nature; still it was a pretty melody. "I am pleased to discover Mintaka so well provided with hosts."

"We are pleased to possess at last the secret of transfer," she fluted. The music for the concept of transfer was a complex chord with undertones of technology and overtones of spirituality: a completely fitting definition. Already Flint liked this mode of communication better than any of the others he had experienced, including the human. Every entity an expert musician and orchestra combined! "And we owe it all to Sphere Sol, who released the information to the galaxy. We regret very much that we are not suited to vacuum maneuvers and could not participate in the Hyades exploration, but we are most interested. Please come with me."

Flint followed her, relieved that contact was so easy right when he needed it. It had been similar in Sphere Polaris, but he had messed that up with his own unwarranted suspicions. Now he was in the final Death/Transformation stage of his Tarot reading—how apt that was!—and had no cause for anxiety. His clapper-feet made a tapdance of satisfaction-syncopation. His paraphernalia, at first so strange, was becoming normal. Music was the most natural thing, so why not make it naturally?

They emerged into an open walkway. Here there were many similar creatures, varying in colors, size, and tonal quality, and a few Mintakan animals. The sapients kept their music sedate, exuding noncommittal harmonies, but the animals made constant sounds of low-grade meaning, akin to the barking of Earth dogs. There were plants spaced decoratively that were shaped like musical instruments but these could not make music.

His nurse-guide brought him to a vehicle. It had a low sill so that it was convenient for their little feet, and high sides to support their upper frames comfortably. It extruded myriad fine wires beneath and brushed along its channel. It was somewhat like a boat and somewhat like a car and somewhat like a magic rug. Flint explored his host-knowledge and ascertained that the wires vibrated under the guidance of special frequencies. As they moved in their almost imperceptible patterns, the vehicle was impelled forward. It was a sophisticated yet basically simple mode of transportation that reflected both the level and the type of civilization here. This was another Sphere in advance of Sol—as it had to be, to maintain so huge a volume of influence.

Soon they left the city. The large structures of the central metropolis shaped to reduce untoward acoustical vibrations gave way to simpler residential dwellings. Their shapes were quite different, being oriented on acoustic principles, but they resembled in their fashion the individual family houses on Earth, or lean-tos on Outworld. The plants became larger: tree-lyres, thicket-drums, flute-vines. Though they were not musical singly, they became so in concert; they did not *make* music but they *became* music.

At length the brushcar entered a region of massed bubbles. The two of them stepped out and approached one, their feet evoking melodic echoes. Flint tried to break his pattern of walking experimentally, to disrupt the adumbration, the foreshadowing of his own sounds by prior echoes, and found he could not comfortably do so. Music was ingrained; to be unmusical was anathema, fundamentally uncomfortable.

The nurse played a special tune Flint could not quite hear, and the portal opened. They entered, and the door fastened firmly behind them.

It was a well-appointed private apartment. There was a basket of wormlike wires Flint recognized through his host-memory as a Mintakan food delicacy, a vapor spray for thirst, an assortment of powders for detuned anatomy, and a disposal tube for wastes.

"I expected to meet your officials," Flint played with undertones of mild confusion. "What is this place?"

"A mating chamber," she hummed sweetly. Now that he had to explore the concept, he realized that Mintakans, like Antareans, were sexless. He thought of his companion as female because she had the aspect of a nurse, and he regarded that as a female occupation. He had encountered several nurses in the course of his initial Earth training. They were generally pretty, and remarkably agile when eluding the male grasp.

"I did not come to this Sphere to mate," he jangled, though he remembered the confusion caused by the Polarian mode of debt settlement. "However, if it is part of your necessary preliminaries to Spherical business—" How the hell did sexless creatures mate? His host-memory, typically, had that information hopelessly buried in suppressions.

"It is for the sake of complete privacy," she explained. "No one will disturb us here for any reason. No sound will escape. Therefore we can proceed to our business."

"But I have no business with you!" The something connected in his melodic mind. "Unless—"

"Concurrence," she played with an ironic trill.

He was in the presence of Andromeda, the Queen of Energy. She had been with him when the Ancient site collapsed; she had transferred with him. It was obvious, yet it hadn't occurred to him. He moved near enough to perceive the fringe of her Kirlian aura: yes, it was true.

"You still possess dangerous information," she played. "Therefore I must finish my task."

"How did you get away from Spica?"

"When I was emotionally able to part with my offspring, I arranged to have another Andromedan female, of low aura, exchange with me. Her aura faded into the host-identity almost immediately, but the child was not aware of the change, so I was free. This was a complex procedure, details of which I need not go into. You succeeded in isolating me for some time, and I compliment you on your cleverness. You will note a certain musical justice in this present reversal."

"Trapped in a mating chamber," Flint played. "Yes, I appreciate the irony, and compliment you in turn on its neatness of concept and execution. Perhaps I can escape it as neatly."

"Perhaps," she played with a drumbeat of smugly challenging doubt.

She must be pretty sure her trap is tight, he realized. "You knew what we would find at the Ancient site," Flint played with harmonies of accusation. This melodic mood-conveyance was extremely convenient!

"Of course. We excavated an Ancient site in Andromeda three centuries ago, though it was not as good as yours."

"The Ancients colonized Galaxy Andromeda too?" Flint was amazed at this confirmation. He had supposed, comfortably, that the Ancients had been a local phenomenon—local within a few thousand light-years of Sol, at any rate.

"They colonized the entire galactic cluster. Everywhere we go, they have been there first. They were a remarkable civilization."

"You've been to other galaxies?" Flint realized she was only playing freely because she expected to kill him here; but this was most interesting information.

"Via transfer, of course. Looking for new sources of energy. But there are none, only the strong atomic interaction of matter, whose exploitation destroys that matter. So we had to concentrate on taking what was most convenient, with the greatest margin of safety."

"And destroy our galaxy!" Flint sang with a triple harmony and discordance of outrage.

"It was a hard decision, but it had to be made. There have always had to be sacrifices for higher civilization. Would it be better to have two fragmented, semicivilized galaxies—or one fully civilized one? We judged that, considered in terms of the universe, consolidation warranted the sacrifice. Our coalition of Spheres could not embrace all of Andromeda unless we had virtually unlimited energy to abate the Spherical regression effect. With that energy we could achieve unity rivaling that of the Ancients. Higher civilization was at stake. You would have done the same, in our circumstance."

"I would *not* have done the same!" Flint played back strongly.

"Yet you called down explosive bombing on your own head and destroyed the most valuable reservoir of science in your galaxy."

"That was to *protect* my galaxy!"

"What I do is to protect *civilization*," she played softly.

She had a note, he had to admit. Solarians had practiced destruction and genocide to further their interests—in the name of civilization!—as long as they had had the ability. He remembered how his tribe had killed the dinosaur Old Snort, taking the magnificent creature's life merely to provide bodily energy in the form of food. How did that differ, except in scale, from what Andromeda was doing? No, his kind was not morally superior, and there *was* something to be said for spreading civilization. There were many species and many Spheres, but there had been only one achievement like that of the Ancients. To realize that potential again—maybe it was worth the price of a galaxy.

He wavered, then played firmly: "Yet I am *of* my galaxy. I cannot sacrifice its interest. The Milky Way did not set out to destroy Andromeda; we only defend ourselves."

"An accident of situation," she responded with a hint of dissonance. "Had you come across that site five hundred years ago, you would have learned how to transfer energy, and inevitably raided *us*. You have no moral claim, only the innocence of the lack of opportunity."

"Agreed." Flint clapped over and tried the door, but it was firm against his push and he lacked the musical key to solve the lock. These devices were sophisticated, his host-memory told him; he could try melodic variations for the rest of his life without coming close. The phone—actually quite similar to the Earth instrument of the same purpose—was similarly keyed. He could not communicate with the outside unless Andromeda allowed him—and of course she would not.

"You *agree*?" she played after a pause.

"Yes. I personally feel civilization is not worth the price of macro-genocide. But I'm only a Stone Age man. My species obviously feels otherwise. Self-interest is our guiding force. Polaris may be morally superior, but not Sol. I don't like the truth, but I acknowledge it."

She was silent. She had led him into this trap so that she could kill him conveniently and without fuss. But she was not in her Amazon Andromedan body now. She had no cutting disks, no burning lasers. She was in a true Mintakan host, as he was, and though these bodies were of uniform sex, his masculine nature had oriented on a large, strong host, while her feminine nature had taken a petite one. She had appearance; he had power. Thus he had a physical advantage.

And if the Mintakans suspected what was happening, they would come immediately and use the overriding master-tune to open the door. They *should* catch on—for two host bodies were gone. All he had to do was stall Andromeda long enough.

"You must have been here before," he played with a counterpoint of annoyed admiration. "You are familiar with Mintakan nature and custom, and had this chamber all set up—"

"I oriented on the Mirzam transfer to Mintaka," she agreed. "I was late, because of your fiendish ploy at Spica—"

Flint burst into a fibrillation of mirth. "So now your true sentiments come out! You don't want to return to Spica!"

Her chords were intensely hostile. "I am glad I have the opportunity to destroy you tediously."

"So you were late, and Mintaka was already into transfer technology," he played liltingly. "So when this Ancient site discovery came up you intercepted Mirzam's next envoy and impersonated Mintaka on Godawful IV. But because your Spican bondage had depleted your aura, you couldn't transfer to a local body. That would have given you away anyway. Your galaxy had to undertake the hideous expense of intergalactic mattermission—"

"We shall recover that energy from the essence of your galaxy!" she twanged.

"And then you lost your body, and must die along with me."

"But my mission is accomplished," she played. "You shall not relay the secret of energy-Kirlian, so shall not achieve parity with us."

"But I *did* relay the secret of transfer orientation to the Canopian," he played. "So now our Spheres will be able to trace your transfers, even as you traced ours, and send counteragents to weed out all your spies. And we'll locate and destroy your energy-relay stations too. But first we'll study them, and get the secret of energy transfer anyway. We may not be able to do to Andromeda what you have tried to do to us, but we can now protect our galaxy from yours."

"Your schlish myriad-image ploy," she complained. "Had I been able to kill you in time—"

"And without that ill-gotten energy, your civilization will have to regress at the Fringe, just as our Spheres do," he continued. "You will be pleasantly primitive at the rim, and no threat to your neighbors."

"We shall develop other sources of supply."

"Not if we run tracers on your intergalactic transfers and warn alien Spheres of—"

She emitted a sudden blast of discordance so powerful it disrupted his own instrumentation. It was a painful experience, and he damped violently and automatically. These creatures could kill with mere sound! He lost his balance as he fought off the terrible noise, and one drum-deck brushed hers.

There was the electric tingle of one intense aura impinging on another. As always, it affected him profoundly —and more so this time, because the shock of discordance had made him vulnerable. Suddenly he didn't want to fight her any more. But he knew he had to, for the information he had could make his galaxy paramount. Not just Kirlian-energy, but something the Andromedans lacked: involuntary hosting, whereby a high-Kirlian entity could be projected to a fully functioning entity and take over that entity. It was right there in his memorized formulas. If only he could get it to his galaxy. . . .

"So you have sentient feelings," he played as his strings relaxed. "You're not the complete huntress after all."

"Huntress?" she played, her anger muted but still audible in the background melody.

"Too bad you didn't visit Sphere Sol," he played, and now his tune was of affected pity. But was it pity for her—or for himself? His Kirlian missions had cost him his fiancée and his Paleolithic innocence—and these seemed unbearably precious in retrospect. "We have a rich mythology based on the visible stars. If you will desist from trying to kill me for a while, I'll tell you about it."

"I haven't been trying to kill you. I brought no weapon. We both will die anyway. I merely render you incommunicado until your aura fades."

So that was it! If he killed her, he would still be trapped here. He would win release only if he could make her release him—and that was extremely unlikely. She was a hardened professional intergalactic agent, inured to the concept of genocide, a ruthless killer, the Queen of Energy.

Unless he could prevail upon her suppressed femininity, and make her *want* to release him. Maybe that was what she wanted, in whatever subconscious her kind possessed. Maybe their interactions in the Spheres of Canopus and Spica and the open cluster of the Hyades had developed an affinity. It *had* been fun mating with her as Impact-Undulant, and they *did* have matching Kirlian auras. . . .

"If we must die together, we might as well be social," he played sweetly. "I'll play you our legends, and you play me yours."

She made noncommittal music. Good, she was amenable.

"In our pantheon, Mintaka is one of three bright stars forming Orion's Belt," he played. "It is perhaps our most impressive constellation, that glowing Belt, with red Betelgeuse—children call it 'beetle juice'—above and white Rigel below, making the giant's shoulder and leg. Orion was a handsome giant in our old Greek mythology. His parents desperately wanted a son, so three visiting gods urinated on the hide of a heifer and buried it in the ground. Nine months later Orion, their son, emerged."

"This is your normal mode of reproduction?" she inquired with vague dissonance.

"No. It's a pun on 'Orion' and 'urine,' terms which are similar in more than one of our languages." He paused, aware that the concept of urine had no relevance to a Mintakan body, whose wastes were powdery. However, this was an Andromedan, and she seemed to comprehend. "But actually there *is* some relevance. In the human body, the urination outlet of the male is also used for inserting the seed into the body of the female, where it combines with her egg cell and grows in nine months to a separate entity. So maybe the myth actually describes the gods using that urine tube to impregnate the 'heifer' —which may be taken as Orion's mother. Possibly his father was impotent or sterile, so this was the only way to beget a son. Of course, in some of our cultures it was the custom for the husband to lend his wife to visitors, part of the hospitality of the house. So it may have been a legitimate situation, albeit somewhat delicate. Men are proud of their virility." He was waxing unusually philosophic, but why not? Maybe he could have been a philosopher in other circumstances, had he had an education extending to more than the lore of the stars.

"Disgusting," Andromeda played, and Flint wasn't certain to which aspect of his commentary she referred. "Continue."

Flint avoided any musical chuckle. She was hooked, all right—and his tale had just begun. As an extragalactic sapient about to die, she wanted to assuage her curiosity while she could. And *any* sentient, sapient or not, was fascinated by the conventions of reproduction; it was an inherent function.

"Orion had a dog called Sirius—and that is also a star in our firmament, not far from the Belt. Or so it appears from Sol. Actually Sirius is within nine light-years of Sol, while Alnitak, Alnilam, and Mintaka of the Belt are sixteen and fifteen hundred light-years distant. But to our primitives, it was Canis Major, the big dog standing by his master."

"In our sky, at home in Sphere /," Andromeda played reminiscently, "there is a great double-circle of bright stars: the two outer disks of our mightiest hunter. He was created from the collision of two supernovas—"

"Collision of novas!" Flint tootled.

"Our legends are no more ludicrous than yours! Better a birth by novas than by urinating into your female."

"Could be," Flint agreed, reminding himself that it was not his purpose to antagonize her. "You /s reproduce by means of light?"

"We lock together two lasers on the mating frequency and—but what business is it of yours?"

"I admit we two are as dissimilar physically as two species can be," Flint said. "That was some fight, in the Hyades! But we seem to have similar personalities, and the aura—"

"We are enemies!"

"You never mated in Andromeda, did you?"

"I was too busy protecting my galaxy!"

Uh-huh. "Orion married a beautiful girl named Side, who I think was very like my Honeybloom. But she was vain—"

"You are married?" Andromeda queried sharply, so that he had to damp down the sympathetic vibration of the overnote in his own strings. She employed a combination of concepts: mating, permanency, and societal authentication. There was, it seemed, no marriage in Sphere Mintaka—but the Andromedan / pattern was similar to that of Flint's own species. The slicing disk and the stabbing spear: aspects of the same urge. Could it be that she was jealous?

"I was married in my fashion. Posthumously, as it were. I, too, had my personal life preempted by the needs of my galaxy. It is a sad thing, isn't it."

As he played his comment, she accompanied him with a haunting tune of agreement. The sheer beauty of the impromptu duet startled him. When Mintakans communicated, they really did make beautiful music together! It was far superior to the human forms, both as dialogue and music. In that affinity of sound, he realized how lovely she could be when she chose. If he were not careful, he could fall into the same snare he was fashioning for her. The lure of a Kirlian aura matching his own. . . .

"Side boasted of her beauty, and was sent to hell by the jealous queen of the gods," Flint continued. As was Honeybloom, shamed, exiled by her tribe, deprived of her luster; existing in a living hell. How he missed her, now that he could never recover what had been.

"So was Starshine," Andromeda played softly. "Her

beams were the clearest, and so she was banished for life, and her star still glows near the indomitable disks of the Hero. . . ."

A strikingly similar legend—or was she making it up, playing a variation of his tune, teasing him? It hardly mattered; the theme was still new. "Then Orion fell in love with Merope, and killed all the savage beasts on her father's island kingdom," Flint continued. He was enjoying these mythological memories. Myths were very important to Stone Age man, especially myths relating to the visible stars. The constellations had been different from Outworld, but the Earth myths, easier to relate to than modern Earth, remained. "This was to find favor with her father, Oenopion, so that he would permit them to marry. When Oenopion rejected him, Orion took Merope by force."

"How is this possible?" she played. "Either party can interrupt the beam—"

"In other Spheres involuntary mating is possible, as in Spica." Where Andromeda herself had been raped. "A Solarian's urination tube can become very stiff: it can penetrate against resistance. And Merope may have been amenable; it was her father who objected."

"As one's galaxy may object, enforcing by powerful conditioning." She played so softly he barely received it. But the meaning was startling: She had been conditioned against him? She must, then, have evinced some inclination, as had Merope.

And in his own life, was Merope the Polarian Tsopi? He could not marry her, for they were of different Spheres. Anyway, her culture and nature forbade permanent liaisons. But while it lasted, it was wonderful, once cultural misunderstandings were resolved. Call Sphere Polaris Oenopion, blinding him to its secrets . . . no, there was no good analogy here. And why should there be? This was only a game. Or was it?

"Illicit beam exchange!" Andromeda played, comprehending. "Yes, that happens, despite serious opposition. It is mooted as most intense. The stigma of his prior exchange made him an unsatisfactory liaison. . . ."

"You're catching on. So Oenopion drugged Orion into a deep sleep and put out his eyes. Lenses, to you."

"He blinded the giant!" she played.

"That's in your legend too?"

"That's what you are doing to my galaxy. You are cutting off our ability to transfer into other galaxies, to investigate their sentient Spheres."

"Because your are stealing our vital energy!" Flint played back fortissimo, his harmonics jarring against her melody.

She did not respond directly. "Did you mean it, about the morality of your species being no better than ours?"

Again, he forced himself to express the truth, rather than uttering human or Milky Way patriotism. "Yes. I may have been more cynical at the outset, but my experiences in other bodies and other cultures have changed me. In Canopus I learned that to be humanoid was not to be superior; in Spica I found three sides to any question; in Polaris I appreciated circularity. I have learned that there are many validities, and like the Tarotists I find myself concluding that they *all* are proper. If I went to Galaxy Andromeda I would probably come to appreciate that reality too. I am not the same entity I was, either as an individual or a species."

"Concurrence." The tune was hardly more than a wish. Then: "Was that the end of Orion?"

"No. He learned that he could recover his sight by traveling toward the sun—"

"By seeking a new source of energy!"

"Maybe. When he could see again, he went to Crete and went hunting with Artemis or Diana—"

"What name?"

"Artemis in Greek, Diana in Roman. Same girl. Diana was a beautiful, skilled, chaste huntress who loved no male. She—"

"You are making sport of me!" Andromeda clanged, and the notes of her voice were like lasers.

"Believe me, that's really the legend. I may have reason to kill you, but never to ridicule you. But don't be concerned; *she* killed *him*."

"Oh," she played with a mixed background. Mintakan chords could convey so much meaning! "Sing me Diana."

"She was a musician who liked singing and dancing, and was skilled in all things except love. When she and Orion went hunting together, he was struck by her beauty and competence, and he touched her—"

"As you touched me in Spica!" she played angrily. "How lucky I was that it wasn't in Sol, or you would have rammed your defecation tube—"

Flint let the description pass. "That's possible," he agreed. "You're quite a female in your fashion."

"My fashion is Sphere / of Andromeda!" But in a moment she muted. "How did she kill him? With a laser?"

"Not as clean as that. She summoned a scorpion to sting him to death. That's a bug with a jointed tail containing venom, very potent. Now that scorpion is also in the sky. When it rises, Orion's constellation fades, hiding from it."

"I wonder whether there are Mintakan scorpions?" she played musingly.

"Let's go out and see."

She trilled her laughter. "You are very clever, no matter what host you bear. We remain here. We shall be blinded together."

Until the Mintakans traced the missing hosts, Flint thought. "That could be very tedious," he played. "I have aura to carry my identity at least sixty days, and probably you do too. What will we do to pass the time? Make love?"

"I suspected you would think of that," she played. "It seems to be characteristic of males all over the universe. Even here, where there are no sexes, some entities are constantly eager to make music together."

"Not physically, not by laser exchange, but by making music together? I'd really like to know how—"

"Don't be concerned. Death hastens the demise of the aura, and even transfer cannot extend it long. A living body suffers in the absence of its aura, and the aura suffers in the absence of its natural host."

"So *that's* what happened to my body when I returned from Sphere Polaris! I was so sick—"

"Yes. The body must be reanimated periodically, exercised, or it gets rusty. You did not know?"

"Our species is new to transfer."

"Then accept my information: Our Kirlian auras have faded considerably already, because the tie to the natural host is never completely severed, and death is the ultimate burden. In just a few hours we shall expire."

"A few hours!" There went his hope. In sixty Earthdays discovery was almost certain; in six hours it was prohibitively unlikely, unless the Mintakans were a lot more sophisticated about such things than the average Sphere bureaucracy. So Andromeda had won after all. He believed her; now he could feel his own aura depletion, like the loss of blood, an insidious draining of his most vital resource.

"It is ironic but perhaps fitting that the two most intense Kirlian entities in our galactic cluster should terminate quietly together," she played hauntingly.

"It must have been foreordained. When I read the Tarot in Sphere Polaris—" He paused in mid-chord. "Tarotism hasn't spread to Andromeda yet, has it?"

"Not as a cult. I made a report on it as part of my mission, as it seems to relate indirectly to the powers of the Ancients."

"Well, there's something *about* the cards, whatever their rationale. They informed me that I was crossed—that is, opposed—by the Queen of Energy, defined as the Devil, in turn crossed by the Four of Gas. They said I could not destroy her, only neutralize her. I did not know then that—"

"It might be that Diana had never encountered a male worthy of her," Andromeda played, seemingly oblivious to his tones. "Perhaps she had the most intense aura ever measured, and could not squander it on inferior entities. When she met her equal, crude and alien though he seemed at first, she felt the first stirrings of . . . of . . . ." Her melody faded out in confused dissonance.

So she had suffered the impact of their similar auras too! There had been a magic about her from the outset in Sphere Canopus, not sexual attraction but the unique Kirlian aura. Officially he had been on a mission to save his galaxy, but personally he had been questing for his natural mate. That, despite the complication of intergalactic politics, was / of Andromeda. She had strength and courage and intelligence and beauty and aura—and the last overwhelmed all the rest. If she reacted similarly to his aura, she was already largely captive to her fundamental instinct to reproduce; not her *species*, but her *aura*.

"The Hermit and the Queen of Energy," Flint played musingly. "Neither able to prevail or to trust the other, playing at potential love. What would the cards say?"

Yet her sentiments paralleled his, keyed by the music that acted as virtual telepathy. "Even though he raped her as Merope, and cost her much pride and much time, she recognized in him a force and intelligence that matched her own. Her culture forbade it, but he was her ideal mate, and the call of the aura had to find expression.

Then she became revolted at her own suppressed passion, and knew she had to kill him, though it was really that element within herself she hated. So she summoned the scorpion—or perhaps forced *him* to summon it—but she really died with him."

"You flatter my intellect without believing in it," Flint played harshly, denying his own urgings. "You are trying to seduce me, not kill me. You want the secret of involuntary transfer-hosting for your galaxy, and I alone possess it." But he was bluffing, though he knew there was truth in his words; she *had* moved him by the insidious appeal of her melody, making his strings vibrate sympathetically, and his drums and tubes follow. They were indeed ideal mates, despite grotesque distinctions of form, and now there was little reason to fight it. He, too, felt superior because of his Kirlian aura; he, too, had a fundamental urge to produce offspring with a Kirlian aura intensity that matched his own. Left to chance, a similar aura might not appear for a thousand years; this way, a new, high-Kirlian strain might be initiated immediately.

Yet of course their Mintakan host-bodies carried none of their original genes. Still, phenomenal things happened in the diverse universe, and the limits of Kirlian potential were not known. "You could have locked me in here alone and let me die while you transferred home to make your report. Why didn't you?"

"We both are dead," she played sadly. "That is irrevocable. But there will be no other chance to establish our kind. We, you and I, are Kirlians, not Andromedans or Milky Wayans. I had hoped that before we expired—"

He understood her perfectly. Yet there was also that in him that made him resist. "It may come," he played. "But only if you play me the truth. You are the professional huntress, well able to live and die without romance. What do you really want of me?" Maybe he was just trying to establish his male dominance. They both knew the stakes: the formulas in his mind. Whichever galaxy got them would win. He could not allow her to seduce him into giving that information to Galaxy Andromeda.

She played an intricate little tune of submission that was thoroughly alluring. "You have eidetic recall."

"Yes, of course. Don't you?"

"No. I have many talents, but lack that one. Otherwise

I would have instantly memorized all the equations you evoked in the Ancient field and broadcast them to our relay station."

"There was more there than you possess?" He knew there was, but he wanted her to admit it.

"Much more. The Hyades site was the best-preserved one yet discovered in the galactic cluster. In those equations are techniques millennia ahead of anything we know. Perhaps the whole answer to the energy problem is there. If we had that, there would be no need to draw from other galaxies. . . ."

"And so you want me to spell out those equations for your technicians."

"And yours too! There need be no further strife between the galaxies!"

This caught him by surprise. Not one galaxy or the other, but both, joined in one superior civilization, the ethic of energy now unifying them instead of dividing them? It was a mighty vision, and an appealing one. "Why didn't you just tell me this at the outset?"

"I knew you would not believe me—"

"Unless you softened me up first. Very calculating." And *that* was his true objection. Her intellectual and aura appeals struck him as valid, but he did not appreciate being used, manipulated, or deluded. As long as she tried to use one technique to soften him for another, she was practicing deceit, and he would not have it that way.

"There was also—" She lost her tune, and had to start over. "Orion and Diana. I used the political situation as a pretext to enable the personal one. There is so little time remaining. I don't know how to—"

"How to love?" he asked. This inversion undercut his position abruptly. If she were not playing at love for the sake of politics, but was playing at politics for the sake of a love she could not confess. . . . "And you wanted to?"

Her music stopped completely, making an awkward silence. He remembered that she had been conditioned, and he was sure her galaxy had fiendishly efficient techniques for that. But if that conditioning remained in force, he certainly could not trust her.

At last a single, faint, half-muted chord. "Yes."

Could he believe her? Conditioned or not, she was a devilishly clever and ruthless huntress. Yet the Kirlian quest might override all other considerations. They could not have interfered with her aura without destroying *her*.

"Prove it."

"I don't know how." Now her tune was pleading.

"I can show you how to love, once I figure out the Mintakan system. I've had experience." In several Spheres. But in his mind he saw Honeybloom's body laid out for the carrion-feeders, symbol of the loss of his love for her through no fault of hers; an awful vision. Honeybloom's love had been true, his flawed. "I mean, prove your sincerity about galactic cooperation."

She played the key tune, and the door opened.

"I am free to go?" Flint inquired dubiously.

"Only if I am allowed to broadcast the information to my station before your aura fades entirely and you forget the knowledge of the Ancients."

"I don't trust this."

"Then you make both broadcasts. I will give you the code for my station, betraying its location."

The bait was too tempting. Where was the trap?

"Address it to the Available Entities of the Council of Andromeda: *, —, : :, $^0{}_0$ or to the head / of my own Sphere. * is always on duty. Tell them you are providing the information to both galaxies on condition that they cease hostilities. If the Council gives concurrence, they will honor that."

"They might launch a last-ditch attack instead."

"Lock me in here, then. You can reset the door to your own tune. Do what seems best; I trust your judgment."

"All right," Flint agreed, still not crediting this seeming victory. With his host-memory guiding him, he reset the lock and closed the door. Andromeda made no protest.

He summoned a wirecar. In a moment one drew up. He got in, knowing that he never had to return.

/ of Andromeda had extended her trust to him.

He got out, returned to the privacy chamber, and sung it open. Andromeda made a little trill of query and hope.

"I forgot the equations," Flint played.

"Why lie? I gave you freedom."

"I believe you, now. I don't trust the galaxies—yours *or* mine—with this technology. There is parity as it stands. Why meddle further?"

"Maybe that is best."

"And before our auras fade—"

"We must name it 'Melody,'" she played.

He closed the door.

Epilogue

Flint the Hermit or King of Gas of Planet Outworld of Sphere Sol of Galaxy Milky Way made beautiful music with the Queen of Energy, agent of Sphere / of the Concurrence of Galaxy Andromeda. Their melodious union budded a completely normal neuter sapient sentient of Sphere Mintaka; there was no transfer of high-intensity Kirlian aura to the offspring. Melody was raised by both parent entities, who never played the tunes of distant stars they no longer remembered, but remained deeply in love until mutual expiration. Melody grew and made music and budded according to the Mintakan cycle of life, and her offspring did likewise. All were normal.

Meanwhile, the single facet of Ancient technology was conveyed by Sphere Canopus to the galactic coalition of Spheres. They methodically routed out the Andromedans among them, eliminating the threat to the Milky Way. Andromeda, deprived of its exterior sources of energy, stagnated, slowly breaking up into lesser Spheres, yet remaining at a high overall level of civilization. Sphere Sol's influence expanded in the Milky Way until it was the hub of a confederation extending from Mintaka to Sador, almost five thousand light-years in diameter.

But crowded, resource-depleted Earth could not handle this huge para-empire. The limitations of inadequate energy remained prohibitive. For a time the nexus of power shifted to Sphere Polaris but it also proved inadequate. At last, after a century-long economic and social revolution, the power lodged in the newest and brashest of the worlds: Planet Outworld.

Outworld, in the course of these six centuries, had progressed from the tribal leadership of Honeyflint in the Old Stone Age to the neo-transfer or modern Super-Spherical Age. Its population was small, its planetary and system resources great, and its dual Solarian/Polarian species vigorous. It now possessed the most modern technology combined with its primitive vitality. Representatives from many Spheres transferred to the small army of host-bodies in order to bring their problems to the attention of Imperial Outworld. Action was generally rapid and decisive, in the human manner, or circuitous and satisfying, in the Polarian manner. It became fashionable to employ Solarian or Polarian hosts for all official functions.

In the next three centuries, Sphere Etamin extended its influence well beyond the old Solarian perimeter, until at last it bordered the demesnes of Knyfh, a Sphere that had undergone similar growth. Finally, Spherical expansion was no longer feasible, and in any event the sophisticated mechanisms of transfer made this unnecessary. Growth became irregular, but always with the vital nerves of communication leading back to Outworld. It finally stabilized as a Segment of the galactic disk, ten thousand light-years from edge to edge.

There was slow progress in Kirlian transfer technology. By utilizing inhabited hosts in volutary transfer, the period a given entity could occupy a foreign host was finally extended to ten times what it was formerly. Thus only one Kirlian unit was lost in ten days of transfer. This enabled high-Kirlian administrators to undertake months-long transfer tours of duty, facilitating organized uniformity of government suggestive of that of the Ancients. The Society of Hosts protected host rights.

Then Galaxy Andromeda, chafing for a thousand years under the frustrations of parity, achieved another breakthrough. It learned how to initiate involuntary hosting. That meant high-Kirlian auras could take over alien bodies, suppressing the original personalities against their will. This was called possession; the body taken over was a hostage. In this manner Andromeda infiltrated key elements of Milky Way Segment governments and wreaked havoc. There was war between the galaxies, and the Milky Way was in serious trouble.

During this period of crisis the most intense Kirlian auras had to be marshaled for action. By an anomaly of transfer and regressive mutation that transcended ordinary genetics, the greatest aura intensity ever measured in the modern galactic cluster imbued the person of a lineal descendant of Flint and Andromeda, with no prior manifestation in the intervening line. It was 223, and the entity's name was Melody of Mintaka, and she was ten Mintakan years old, a reader of Tarot, with a mind as fiercely individual as her amazing aura.

Chaining the lady would be quite a task!

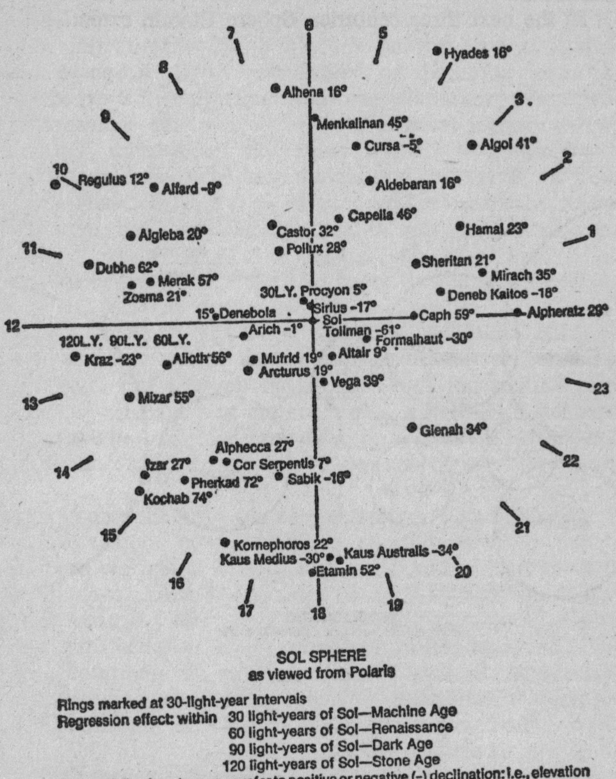

SOL SPHERE
as viewed from Polaris

Rings marked at 30-light-year intervals
Regression effect: within 30 light-years of Sol—Machine Age
60 light-years of Sol—Renaissance
90 light-years of Sol—Dark Age
120 light-years of Sol—Stone Age

Figures following star names refer to positive or negative (-) declination: i.e., elevation above or below the disk shown (example: Etamin and Kaus Australis are *not* close together, but separated by 86 degrees, or about 150 light years)

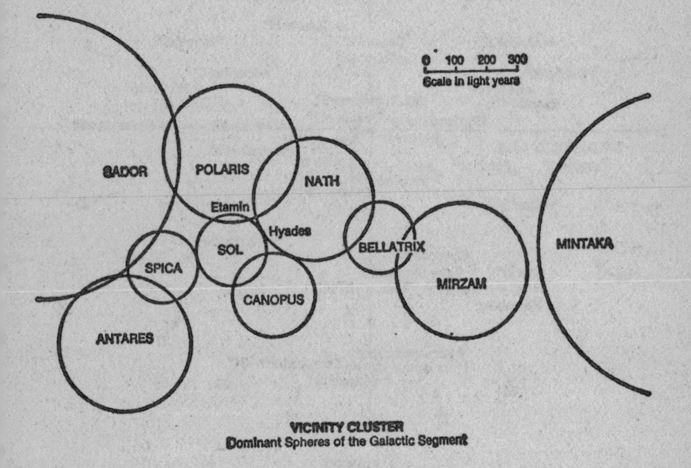

VICINITY CLUSTER
Dominant Spheres of the Galactic Segment